D1132489

a Love Surrendered

DEC 2012

Books by Julie Lessman

THE DAUGHTERS OF BOSTON

A Passion Most Pure
A Passion Redeemed
A Passion Denied

WINDS OF CHANGE

A Hope Undaunted
A Heart Revealed
A Love Surrendered

WINDS of CHANGE • BOOK 3

a Love Surrendered

A NOVEL

JULIE LESSMAN

Revell

a division of Baker Publishing Group
Grand Rapids, Michigan

© 2012 by Julie Lessman

Published by Revell
a division of Baker Publishing Group
P.O. Box 6287, Grand Rapids, MI 49516-6287
www.revellbooks.com

Printed in the United States of America

All rights reserved. No part of this publication may be reproduced, stored in a retrieval system, or transmitted in any form or by any means—for example, electronic, photocopy, recording—without the prior written permission of the publisher. The only exception is brief quotations in printed reviews.

Library of Congress Cataloging-in-Publication Data
Lessman, Julie, 1950–
    A love surrendered : a novel / Julie Lessman.
        p.   cm. — (Winds of change ; bk. 3)
    ISBN 978-0-8007-3417-6 (pbk. : alk. paper)
    1. Sisters—Fiction. 2. Nineteen thirties—Fiction. 3. Boston (Mass.)—Fiction. I. Title.
PS3612.E8189L68 2012
813′.6—dc23   2012023495

Scripture used in this book, whether quoted or paraphrased by the characters, is taken from the King James Version of the Bible.

This book is a work of fiction. Names, characters, places, and incidents are the product of the author's imagination or are used fictitiously. Any resemblance to actual events, locales, or persons, living or dead, is coincidental.

The internet addresses, email addresses, and phone numbers in this book are accurate at the time of publication. They are provided as a resource. Baker Publishing Group does not endorse them or vouch for their content or permanence.

12   13   14   15   16   17   18   7   6   5   4   3   2   1

To my beautiful daughter-in-law, Katie—
who taught me that "a son surrendered"
does not mean surrendering a mother's love,
but multiplying it beyond my wildest dreams.

The Lord is my shepherd;
I shall not want.
He maketh me to lie down in green pastures:
he leadeth me beside the still waters.
He restoreth my soul:
he leadeth me in the paths of righteousness
for his name's sake.

—Psalm 23:1–3

1

Boston, Massachusetts, May 1932

So help me, if I get caught tonight, Peggy Pankow's name is "Mud." Susannah Grace Kennedy braced herself against the cool of the salty sea air—*and* her guilt—and hurried down the dark street toward Revere Beach, almost regretting she'd let her new friend talk her into sneaking out of the house. A crescent moon rose while the waning light of dusk cast purple shadows on the boardwalk where streetlamps were just beginning to glow. People milled on the seashore, mere silhouettes backdropped by a fuscia sky glinting across restless waters. The sound of music drifted in the air along with the scent of the sea, and suddenly a tingle of excitement trumped any worry she had.

"Hey, Suzi-Q," Peggy had said after class last week, "my big sis says we can tag along to Ocean Pier on Friday night." Her brown eyes had sparkled with the dare of adventure. "Wanna go?"

Suzi-Q. Susannah winced, the little-girl nickname her family had coined, a painful reminder of just how much her life had changed in three months. Her smile was patient. "Peg,

7

it's Anna now, remember? Not Suzi-Q or Suz or Susannah or Gracie or anything else that reminds me of a past I'm trying to forget." She battled the familiar malaise that always accompanied thoughts of her once-happy home. "Besides," she said, her voice trailing to a whisper, "I'm not that girl anymore."

"Okay, okay, but I refuse to call you Anna. Too stuffy." Peg pursed her lips. "I should call you Dr Pepper Girl the way you guzzle the stuff when Aunt Eleanor's not around, but with that strawberry-blonde hair and cute freckled face, you're an Annie through and through."

"Annie" chewed on her thumbnail. "I don't know, Peg, you don't think 'Annie' sounds too young or rural?" she asked, anxious to shed her small-town roots. "After all, I'm a city girl now, looking for a new name and a new life."

"Nope, it's perfect." Peggy wriggled her brows. "And you mean *love life*, don't you?"

Annie's stomach dipped and rolled like the seagulls over Revere Beach, and she gulped down a sliver of nail. *Love life*. Not just sterile words written in her diary this time back in her hometown of Badger, Iowa, or in one of her many handwritten novels. Nope, this would be real flesh-and-blood kisses from real flesh-and-blood men. She swallowed hard. "Uh . . . maybe."

"No maybes about it, kiddo," Peggy said with a wink. "A deal is a deal. You tutored me in algebra? I tutor you in love. What kind of romance writer will you be without research? Not to mention our bet—you swore you'd get your first kiss at Revere Beach or I get to keep your favorite sweater, remember?" Peggy sighed when Annie hesitated. "For criminy sakes, Annie Lou, you're a woman who's never been kissed, and this is your chance. Besides, Ocean Pier is the perfect place to lose your heart." She elbowed Annie in the side, eyes agleam with mischief. "*Or* your reputation. What do you say, wanna go?"

Did she want to go? To Revere Beach? The Boston hot spot her older sister Maggie raved about in her letters from college? A shiver of excitement tingled as anticipation swelled. What seventeen-year-old girl wouldn't want to go to Revere Beach?

Especially after her older sister's chatter about the thrill of the Cyclone Rollercoaster, the romantic Hippodrome Carousel, or moonlight strolls on Ocean Pier with Steven O'Connor, Maggie's old flame?

Goodness, Annie had boxes of Maggie's old letters hidden away, boasting of good times at Ocean Pier with the "gang." Names like Joe Walsh and Joanie Pankow, Erica Hogan, and Ashley Roberts were emblazoned in her memory. A small-town transplant mid-senior year, Annie had felt like an outcast, but the moment she'd heard Peggy Pankow's name in roll call, she'd sought her out, elated Peggy had a sister named Joanie. Anxious to connect with anyone who'd known Maggie, Annie was thrilled when Peggy took her under her wing, transforming her drab small-town look into one more acceptable and stylish. The two became friends, not only because Peggy was crazy and fun but because she was the key to Maggie's past. A past Annie had no inclination to share with Peggy just yet. No, not when Maggie's later letters indicated a rift in the gang, convincing Annie that Erica and Joanie bore a monumental grudge against her sister.

Did she want to go to Revere Beach with Maggie's old gang? Annie sighed. More than anything in the world. After all, everybody loved Revere Beach.

Everybody but Aunt Eleanor, that is, who'd forbidden her to go. A gust of wind brought her back to the dark streets en route to the beach, flapping her bulky cardigan and chilling her to the bone. A group of men whistled as she passed, and Annie instinctively wrapped her sweater close, wishing she'd asked Peggy for a ride instead of walking to the Pier alone. But she couldn't risk leaving the house before Aunt Eleanor retired, so she'd waited in her room until dark. Because as Peggy had so artfully argued, what Aunt Eleanor didn't know wouldn't hurt her. Annie's palms began to sweat despite the cool of the night. *I just hope it doesn't hurt me . . .*

"Hey, doll, what's your hurry?" Two men strolled from the shadows of a dark alley and blocked her path, forcing a gasp to choke in her throat. One delivered a lazy smile distorted by the flicker of the tungsten lamp overhead, his white shirt rolled to reveal muscular arms. His thumbs hooked around suspenders while smoke furled from the cigarette glowing red between his teeth. "Well, looky here, Grove, this little dish is all by herself. Ya need some company, sweet thing?"

Annie faltered back, cigarette smoke and garbage from the alley making her as nauseous as the man before her. Her gaze darted down the empty street she'd taken as a short-cut, and her throat went dry. A stone's throw from the Pier, she doubted anyone would hear her cry, not with the roar of the waves, the screech of coaster rails, or music from the ballrooms along the boardwalk. Her throat convulsed as she cinched her sweater tight. "Uh . . . no, thank you, I'm meeting friends at the dance pavilion. They're waiting now."

The man called Grove sidled close to drape an arm over her shoulder. "Come on, doll, you'll have more fun with Harv and me than you will with them. What's your name, sweetheart?"

Fear crawled up her windpipe to steal her air. "P-please, no." She twisted free, but Harv jerked her back, his calloused hand smothering her cry. Eyelids flickering, she grew faint as he casually forced her toward the alley. "Come on, baby," he whispered, "you wouldn't be here by your lonesome if you weren't looking for a little fun." He attempted to grind his wet mouth against hers, and she dropped her purse, lashing her head to the side to avoid his lips. Her stomach curdled at the stench of liquor on his breath, and when she thrashed and tried to scream again, vomit rose in her throat. *God, please, no.*

Harv pinned her arms behind. "Whoo-ee, a regular she-cat, ain't she though?"

"Let her go . . ." A warning bit into the night, as deadly as the lash of a whip.

Harv spun around, muscled arm looped to Annie's waist as he squinted into the dark where a shadow emerged, not twenty feet away. Annie cried out when Harv jerked her close, his fingers gouging her side. "Yeah? Says who?"

The stranger's face was obscured by the night, but the dominance of his tone left no room for rebuttal. "Says an officer of the law, wise guy." In slow, deliberate motion, he reached into his coat jacket to open a battered leather wallet where a nickel badge glinted in the lamplight. "Let her go—*now*."

A guttural laugh iced Annie's skin when the man called Grove ambled forward and spit, fingers sliding along the back of his waistband. With a faint swish, a blade shot forth from a knife in his hand, and Harv muffled another scream from Annie's throat. "You ain't got no authority here, flatfoot, so scram."

"Got all the authority I need, dirtbag," the officer said quietly, the lightning click of his revolver faster than the hitch of Annie's breath. "Had a lousy day, scumball, so I'm just itching for a reason to vent. I suggest you drop it real slow."

Grove hesitated for several seconds before hurling the knife down, his surly look as sharp as the blade that clattered to the sidewalk.

Two-fisting the gun, the officer eased toward Harv, arms extended and aim level. "Not going to tell you again. *Let her go*."

With a muttered curse, Harv shoved her away. Annie stumbled forward, and the officer steadied her with a firm grasp before calmly steering her behind him.

His voice was as steely as the gun in his hand. "I suggest you lowlifes call it a night, 'cause if I find you anywhere near the beach again, you'll be picking on fleas in a jail cell instead of little girls in the streets."

"Didn't mean no harm, officer," Harv said quickly, his tone conciliatory even if Grove's menacing look was not. "Just thought Little Miss might need some company, that's all. Come on, Grove, Ann Street's got better action than this." The men backed away, their glares prickling Annie's skin until they disappeared down the alley.

The air rushed from her lungs, body quivering like the lights looping the boardwalk, swaying in the breeze. She peeked up at her savior, studying his broad back as he watched the men slink away. He dwarfed her with his height, maybe six foot two to her five foot one, and his hair was as dark as the umber sky. She exhaled loudly when he holstered his gun and bent to pick up the knife, feeling safe for the first time all night. "Thank you so much, Officer."

He turned, lamplight illuminating blue eyes that singed her to the spot. "What the devil are you doing walking this street alone at night?"

She blinked, shocked as much by his handsome face as his sullen look.

"What's your name?" he asked. A tic twittered in his hard-chiseled cheek, indicating he was clearly perturbed. "And how old are you?"

"A-Annie . . . and I'm seventeen . . . almost e-eighteen."

His shuttered gaze traveled the length of her, down her body and up, settling on her face with obvious disapproval. "You don't look seventeen to me," he muttered. He slacked a hip. "Does your mother know where you are?"

Her chin shot up. "My mother's dead," she snapped, the fire in her eyes challenging the nasty look in his. "And you don't look like an officer either."

She heard his heavy exhale as he tunneled blunt fingers through perfectly groomed hair, disrupting several dark strands that toppled over his forehead. The tight line of his angular jaw softened. "Look, I'm sorry, miss, but you have no business walking these streets alone at night. Do you have any idea what could have happened if I hadn't come along?"

His question unnerved her, and she clutched her arms to her waist, moisture pricking her eyes at what might have happened if not for him. She swallowed hard and nodded, dropping her gaze.

"If you were my sister, I'd cart you home right now and let your father deal with you."

Her head jerked high, temper charred once again. "Well, I'm not, so why don't you go bully somebody else?"

His eyes narrowed. "You've got a smart mouth and not a

12

lot of brains, you know that, kid? Your daddy needs to keep an eye on you."

Her chin lashed up. "Yeah? Well, he's dead too, are you happy?"

He blinked, lips parted in shock. His voice was a rasp. "You're an orphan?"

The sound of that awful word stabbed anew, and anger resurged. "Yes." She fought off the sting of tears. "Can I go now?"

"Hold on." His hand stayed her arm, his voice suddenly kind. "Where do you live?"

"With my aunt," she said quietly, chin quivering. "And my little sister."

With another heavy blast of air, he stooped to retrieve her purse and nudged it into her hands. The gentleness of his voice sparked more tears in her eyes. "Look, kid, this area's not safe after dark for any woman alone, seventeen or seventy, so promise you won't do this again."

She nodded, but her cheeks burned at the way he made her feel—seven instead of seventeen. Her gaze dropped. *Just like Aunt Eleanor.*

"So, where ya headed?"

She hooked a stray curl over her ear, careful to avoid his gaze. "To meet my friends at Ocean Pier Dance Pavilion," she whispered. Tucking her purse under her arm, she pinched her thick sweater closed before gingerly backing away. "Thank you, Officer . . ."

"Wait." His touch jolted her, forcing her eyes to span wide. A hint of a smile played on his lips as he released her. "I'm going that way, so I'll walk with you."

"No!" Heat swarmed her cheeks. *A police escort in front of my friends?* "I mean, I'm late, Officer, but thank you again." Before he could object, she sprinted the half block to the boardwalk as if she were escaping the ghost of Aunt Eleanor herself, finally darting across Atlantic Avenue onto the sandy beach. She almost tumbled over a stray piece of driftwood, but she dared not stop till she reached the cobblestone landing of the Pier. Chest huffing, she glanced back. Her eyes scanned the dusky boulevard for any sign of him among the smattering of people and autos, but it was as if he'd disappeared into thin air. A sigh shivered from her lips, tinged with more than a little guilt. She put a shaky hand to her eyes, squeezing them shut. *I should have never come. Never defied Aunt Eleanor. Never risked getting caught.*

And never grow up?

Her eyelids popped open. No! Adjusting her sweater, she sucked in sea air like sustenance, determined she *would* do this. *Needed* to do this. It was bad enough Aunt Eleanor treated her like a child, uprooting her and her sister from their tiny Iowa town after Daddy died three months ago. Nor did it help she was petite with an innocent face that made her look fifteen rather than the eighteen years she'd celebrate in two months. Goodness, she wasn't a little girl anymore, no matter what her spinster aunt thought. She was Susannah Grace Kennedy, a woman who'd spent the last two years caring for her little sister Glory after Mama died and keeping the house up for Daddy.

Daddy. She steeled her jaw and fought the prick of moisture that stung whenever she thought of the man she'd all but worshiped, followed by the anger that always rose on its heels. Anger at *his* God—the same God she'd espoused herself until three months ago. A God who'd snatched the life of her mother two years past, despite the prayers of her minister father who'd devoted his life to him. Until God allowed cancer to take him away too, robbing her and her sister of his love, his kindness, his protection . . .

"*Do you have any idea what could have happened if I hadn't come along?*"

Goose bumps prickled, reminding her how close she'd come to evil. Yes, someone protected her tonight, but she refused to give the credit to God. Where was he when her parents needed him? No, when her father died three months ago, she buried her faith along with him, intent on living without God, just like she had to live without her parents.

Thrusting her chin up, she swiped at her eyes and continued down the wood-slatted pier. She was tired of being the good girl, obedient to a fault. What good had it done? Her lips cemented into a firm line. In a few short weeks, she'd graduate high school and then off to college in the fall, the ideal time to leave her childhood behind. She pushed the hair from her eyes with shaky fingers. *And a God I no longer trust . . .*

Music and laughter carried on the ocean breeze as she darted down the crowded pier where couples snuggled and kissed, but Annie was too shaken to notice. Her stomach still roiled at the memory of Grove's hands on her body, his mouth on her cheek, and all she wanted to do was go home. But that was no longer an option. She had no choice but to wait for Peggy's sister to drive her home, well aware her body still quivered from the shock of the near attack.

"Get ahold of yourself," she whispered, sucking in sea air to calm down and forget about Harv and Grove. After all, this was her chance to grow up and experience Maggie's world, and by golly, she intended to do it despite Aunt Eleanor's objections. Unbidden, thoughts of her handsome rescuer invaded her mind and she shuddered, mortified at the prospect of being seen with an officer in tow. Heaven knows she'd be the youngest among Peggy's sister's group anyway. The last thing she needed was more scorn about her age or small-town upbringing.

With a catch of her breath, Annie slowed, jaw sagging while her eyes slowly scanned upward, thoughts of the attack all but forgotten. Mouth agape, she stood mesmerized by the towering sight before her, hand fluttering to her chest. Oh my, but it was grand! Everything Maggie had written and more.

Jutting high in the sky at the end of a pier, the famous Ocean Pier Dance Pavilion rose from the water like a glittering fairy-tale castle, terraces and towers aglow with endless strings of lights. Maggie told her the Pier had been built in 1911 and extended 1,450 feet over the water, beckoning patrons to a palatial structure housing dance marathons, a sumptuous café, and a roller-skating rink. Light glimmered across the bay, reflecting the revelry inside, and Annie's heart squeezed at the memory of a big sister she idolized and seldom saw, now living in California. Maggie had always been dazzled by lights, first the big-city glimmer of Chicago where she was born and raised until college, now the glitz and glitter of Hollywood where she soon hoped to be a star. At Radcliffe, she seldom came home for summers after they moved to Iowa because she'd despised Badger, and her letters had always been filled with the shimmer and shine of Ocean Pier.

Annie craned her neck to stare at the arched pillars overhead with a reverent sigh, more determined than ever to follow in Maggie's footsteps. Squaring her shoulders, she opened the door with a grunt, grateful the officer hadn't followed her to the Pier. Heavens, if she was going to succeed tonight with new friends, it certainly wouldn't be in the custody of some stiff-faced arm of the law. His memory suddenly prompted an odd quiver in her stomach, and Annie swallowed hard, hoping she'd never have to see him again. No matter *how* handsome he was.

Steven shook his head, watching her bolt away as if he were the one who'd attempted to accost her. Little girls. They were as bad as the big ones. She was darn lucky he'd happened along and been armed, something he usually avoided while off duty. But he'd had an uneasy feeling tonight about the beach, which tended to attract trouble on weekends, and any girl with half a brain had sense not to walk it alone. Which pretty much confirmed the kid was either brainless or had her head in the clouds.

Heaving a sigh, he made his way to the phone booth at the end of the boardwalk to report the thugs who'd bothered the young woman. His mouth crooked. Make that "little girl." One with a smart mouth who belonged home in bed on a

Friday night, not at a dance hall. He placed the call and hung up, hand fused to the receiver as he squinted at the Ocean Pier Ballroom, a blur of lights at the end of a pier he'd walked more times than he could count. His eyes trailed into a faraway stare while memories teased and taunted, endless strings of lights swaying and sparkling, like Maggie when he'd whirled her on the dance-room floor. Warm, steamy nights spent holding her, kissing her on the veranda, making plans for a future that would never come to pass. A dull ache surfaced in his chest. Chilling proof that despite the fact he'd been the one who'd ended it, Maggie Kennedy still had a hold on his heart.

He shoved his hands in his pockets and ambled toward the Pier, his mind a million miles away, not unlike the woman he'd loved. *Still loved*, if truth be told, despite being a full coast away. Almost three years had passed since he'd ended it the night he told her he loved her but couldn't see her again. It wasn't fair, he knew, but he'd blamed her for the rift with his father, a rift so violent, it had almost stolen his father away. Steven's eyes shuttered closed, the memory twisting his gut. Because of Maggie, he and his father had shouted awful things at each other, hateful words that not only threatened his father's life but buried Steven's beneath a mountain of guilt. Guilt so strong, it enabled him to finally turn Maggie away and embark on a quest to restore his father's trust. His lips thinned. *As well as my own.*

A familiar melancholy settled on his shoulders like the mist over the bay, and he opened his eyes, suddenly missing Maggie so much the air stilled in his lungs. The music of her laughter, the dare of her smile, the glimmer of tease in eyes so blue, they'd laid claim to his soul. And his body. Heat flushed his skin and he removed his coat, slinging it over his arm with a clamp of his jaw. Confirmation once again it had never been Maggie's fault at all, but his. He was the one who should've been strong, the man in control who should've placed his love for Maggie before his desires. But in the end, he'd disrespected her as much as he had his father, and the weight of shame had driven him hard away from Maggie, his past, and the idea of ever falling in love.

Peals of laughter broke into his thoughts, and the sight of two couples flying down the wood-slatted dock brought a grin to his face. He and his friends from college used to have fun like that once. His smile was wistful. And if Joe had his way, they would again. The haunting sounds of a love song drifted over the water like a fog, hazing his mind and tugging at his heart, yet another indication Joe was right. It was time to get back in the game, to move on and maybe fall in love. To raise Steven O'Connor from the dead, as Joe liked to say. Ocean Pier loomed before him in all its glory while strains of "Stardust" floated in the air, luring him with its magic as if sent by Joe himself.

Truth be told, I could use a little magic right about now, Steven thought with a grimace. He yanked on the massive door beneath the lit portico, holding it open as several pretty girls walked through. The scent of perfume tempted his senses while the music taunted his soul, convincing him once and for all his resurrection was imminent. With a deep inhale, he made his way through the crowd, surprised he was actually glad to be there. After all, he thought, hating to admit Joe was right . . . he wasn't dead yet.

"Where on earth have you been?"

Peggy latched on to Annie's arm the second she stepped into the grand foyer, and for a moment, Annie was too stunned to respond. Her mouth hung open so far, she could have trapped mosquitoes out on the Pier. The magnitude of the foyer alone stole both her words and the breath from her lungs. A vaulted ceiling seemed to rise to the sky, flanked by palatial balconies teeming with people. Ornate gold chandeliers spilled from above, lending an ethereal air to the grand and spacious room. Annie sighed, hand to her chest, quite certain there was nothing like this in Badger, or in all of Iowa for that matter, and in one reverent intake of breath, she silently blessed Aunt Eleanor for bringing them to Boston.

"Annie!" Enormous brown eyes assessed her with concern. "Are you okay?"

Annie blinked to dispel the sudden tears in her eyes. "Oh, Peg, two men tried to accost me."

"What? Where?" Peggy's eyes spanned wide, her short, auburn waves lending an almost pixie air to her heart-shaped face. She gave Annie a tight hug. "Good grief, are you okay?"

Annie nodded with a tight swallow. "It happened on that shortcut you showed me."

Peggy's jaw dropped. "For criminy sakes, Annie, I told you to take the main streets at night, not the shortcut. You could have been killed. Tell me what happened."

Annie related the awful incident, her brush with near disaster chilling her all over again. "I was looking forward to tonight, Peg, but so far, this is the worst night of my life."

Peg tucked a curl over Annie's ear. "We'll just have to make sure it ends up as the best night of your life, okay?" Her brow puckered. "Hey, you didn't wear the makeup I gave you!"

Annie blinked. "I meant to put it on before I left, but Aunt Eleanor was in such a nasty mood . . ."

Shaking her head, Peggy rifled through her purse to retrieve her lipstick. "I swear that backwoods town of yours has addled your brain." She glanced down at Annie's sensible Mary Jane flats and groaned. "And you wore flats?! What am I going to do with you? It's bad enough your aunt won't let you bob your hair, but you barely come to my chin as petite as you are, and those freckles and fresh-scrubbed face are a dead giveaway you're straight off the farm. Here." Peggy bent to apply lipstick to Annie's mouth. "Honestly, Annie, how do you plan to catch anyone's eye when you look all of twelve?"

"I'm sorry, Peg, but I was so nervous . . ."

Peggy stood up to assess. "Well, there's not much we can do about your eyes, I suppose, since I left my eye makeup at home, but at least they're that incredible shade of green. But

I did bring my powder, thank goodness. Here." She handed Annie her compact and froze. "Wait, please tell me you wore the teal dress I suggested. You know, the one you said was too tight?"

Annie quickly unbuttoned her thick, lumpy sweater and gave her friend a tentative smile before dropping a nervous glance down at her high-necked jersey dress. She tugged at her lip, uneasy with the snug fit of the stretchy material. "I did, but not only is it too small, it makes me feel like a little kid 'cause I wore it at fifteen." She glanced up, ready to rebutton the cardigan. "I don't know, Peg, I just don't feel comfortable in it."

"That's because it's too tight, you goose. Here, let me fix it." Mischief twitched on her lips as she undid Annie's top three buttons to create a flapped-collar effect that certainly confirmed Annie was no little girl. Peggy let loose with a low whistle. "Atta girl! You may look fresh as cream with that dewy skin and baby-soft hair, but once you take that hideous cardigan off, you won't be the only one uncomfortable, trust me." She exchanged Annie's sweater for the compact. "Here, sweetie-pie, powder your pretty nose and let's go. We've got hearts to break."

Ignoring the swirl of nerves in her stomach, Annie sucked in a deep breath and eyed herself in the mirror. "Okay, Peg, wish me luck. Tonight is the night I grow up."

Peggy chuckled and clamped a hand to Annie's arm, pulling her toward the ballroom door. "Trust me, kiddo, you won't need any luck with that dress."

Annie was grateful Peggy dragged her to the other side of the massive ballroom, hopefully far from the prying eyes of any stick-in-the-mud officer. It was a hive of activity that left her breathless, and even Maggie's letters hadn't prepared her for this. Pure magic, a fairy-tale ball where hundreds of couples moved and swayed in hypnotic motion across a gleaming wood floor. Lights were low, lending an intimate air, while a mirror ball glittered overhead like diamonds in the sky. Strains of the Dorsey Brothers Orchestra's "Little

White Lies" filtered throughout, and Annie nibbled on her nail, uneasy about her white lie to Aunt Eleanor about going to bed early. She sucked in a deep breath. *Well, I did, didn't I? Lay in the bed until dark?* Guilt jabbed, but she shook it off. After all, she had a right to live her own life, didn't she?

The band eased into their version of Benny Goodman's "Help Yourself to Happiness," and a shaky smile tipped Annie's mouth when she realized that was exactly what she was trying to do. She'd had enough heartbreak to last a lifetime, and it was time to help herself to some of the happiness Maggie had written home about. Steeling her resolve, she tagged behind Peggy as they inched along the dance floor. Mouth agape, she stared wide-eyed at couples whirling and swinging to the Lindy Hop as sweat and smiles gleamed on their faces. Warmth from sweaty bodies fairly shimmered off the floor like heat off asphalt during a Badger drought in July.

Peggy leaned to whisper in the ear of an older girl who was laughing and drinking with friends at a table littered with peanuts, popcorn, and bottles of Coca-Cola. Annie's pulse skittered when the girl rose and extended a hand. "Hi, Annie, I'm Peggy's sister, Joanie. Peggy says you're new to Boston and looking for fun." She tucked an arm to Annie's waist and smiled. "Well, you came to the right place, sweetie, because any friend of Peggy's is a friend of mine."

Annie smiled and gulped, hardly able to believe she was here with Maggie's old gang.

Thumping her glass on the table, Joanie turned to the group, who looked to be in their midtwenties. "Hey, guys, listen up. This is Annie, and she just moved here, so let's make her feel welcome." Joanie waved an arm. "This is most of the gang—Erica and Ashley, Joe and Stan."

"Coca-Cola, Annie?" Joanie asked, pouring pop into one of two clean glasses.

"Just for me, sis. Annie's a Dr Pepper Girl." Peggy squeezed Annie's shoulder with a grin, lowering her voice as if it were a dirty secret. "Her aunt doesn't allow soda in the house, so the kid sneaks it when she can." Peggy sighed. "Unfortunately, it's her only vice."

"We'll have to see what we can do about that," Erica said with a grin. She pushed a black curl away from her Betty Boop hairstyle and winked an eye lidded with violet shadow. "What are you doing hanging out with Peggy? She'll just get you in trouble."

Peggy laughed and sat down along with Annie, sliding Erica a smirk. "Speak for yourself, Erica, everybody knows who the bad influence is here."

Joe stood to his feet and reached across the table to shake her hand, his smile warm in a handsome face that boasted a healthy spray of freckles. His hazel eyes seemed to twinkle, a nice complement to the sandy hair neatly slicked back. "Hiya, Annie, where you from?"

Annie liked him immediately, which helped put her at ease despite her hesitation to divulge her rustic roots. She gave him a shy smile. "Badger, Iowa."

Joe let loose a low whistle. "Small town, eh?"

Annie nodded, a grin sprouting on her face. "You can spit from one end to the other."

"Well, welcome to the big city. And just so you know, I'm the 'good' influence here."

"You mean till Steven comes," Erica said with a ruby-red pout. "Where is he, anyway? I thought you said he was coming."

Joe eyed Erica with an off-center smile. "Don't get your knickers in a knot, Miss Hogan, you'll get your chance with him. Our poster boy'll be here, as promised."

Erica leaned on the table with a grin, a hint of cleavage peeking out the ruffle of her floral dress. "You better be right, Walsh, 'cause I spent a fortune on this dress, even at a thrift shop."

"Trust me, I'm just as anxious as you for Steven to get here. I work with the guy day in, day out, remember? Nobody knows better than me that all work and no play makes O'Connor a

22

dull boy. He's been nothing but nose to the grindstone since he broke up with Maggie, and I for one am tired of it." He raised his glass to Erica. "So that's where you come in."

O'Connor? Maggie's old flame? Annie began to choke, finally sneezing to clear her air.

"Bless you." Joe winked.

"Where I come in, huh?" Erica grinned. "Back in Steven's arms again, I hope." Her smile went flat. "Where I'd still be today if not for Kennedy."

"Maggie's history," Joanie said, "don't let her spoil your evening."

"Bad history," Erica said with a grunt. "Wish I could tip your flask to forget."

"Ooops—how rude!" Joanie lifted her skirt to reveal a flask in her garter belt. "Forgot to offer a touch of giggle water to Annie and Peg. How 'bout it, girls?"

The whites of Annie's eyes expanded. "Uh . . . no, thank you," she squeaked.

"Sure, why not?" Peggy said without hesitation.

"You're drinking alcohol?" Annie's whisper rose several octaves, her eyes glazed with shock as if she'd tipped the flask herself.

"Not much, you goose, just enough to feel tipsy," Peggy said while Joanie spiked her drink. "Sure you don't want some? You could use it after the scare you had, you know."

Annie shook her head, suddenly feeling way in over her head.

Joanie offered Erica a sympathetic smile. "If you ask me, Maggie was never good enough for Steven. Too independent and definitely too wild. Steven O'Connor's the old-fashioned type who needs a good girl."

Too wild? A frown pinched Annie's brow.

"Then how'd she land him in the first place is what I wanna know?" Erica said in a pout.

Joanie chuckled. "She was a pastor's kid, remember? Flirty, yes, but white as the driven snow when Steven met her." She winked. "Come on, Erica, nobody knows better than you how hard it is to say no to a guy like Steven."

"Tell me something I don't know." Issuing a heavy sigh, Erica slumped, chin in hand. "Even so, I never liked her from the get-go. Too blonde, too loud, too much of a flirt to suit me."

Joanie chuckled. "You just hated her 'cause she had Steven wrapped around her little finger."

"That's not all she had him wrapped around," Erica said with a grunt.

"You got that right," Joanie said. "Rumor is she gave him her all."

Her all? Annie blinked, refusing to think about what that meant, but feeling the heat of her blush clear up to her bangs.

"Hey, guys, knock it off. You're embarrassing Annie." Joe popped peanuts in his mouth, his tone matching the scowl on his face. "Those rumors are way off, and Maggie's one of my best friends, so leave her be. Besides, she may have had her influence, but it was Steven who called the shots. And don't forget, *he* broke it off with her." Joe eyed Erica, brows knit. "I hope you're not drinking, 'cause he'll taste it in your kiss and you won't stand a chance."

"Are you kidding?" Erica splayed a hand to her chest. "After he read me the riot act last time? Not on your life. I know what a straight arrow he is."

"Good." Joe tossed another peanut as his gaze landed on Annie. All at once, he jumped up, his smile apologetic. "Gosh, where are my manners? One Dr Pepper coming right up."

Peggy watched Joe stride to the bar, then leaned close to Annie. "Joe and Steven are such sweethearts," she said with a sigh. "Gorgeous too, not to mention dangerous."

"Dangerous?" Annie squinted at her friend. "But Joe seems so nice . . ."

Peggy's chuckle rumbled against Annie's ear. "They're federal agents, Annie, armed to the teeth with both guns and charm. But trust me, that's not what makes 'em 'dangerous.'"

Annie blinked. *Then what does?*

"Here you go, Dr Pepper Girl, one bottled addiction." Joe plopped a glass down.

"Thanks, Joe." She took a swig, excitement bubbling as much as the soda in her glass.

"My pleasure, kiddo." He returned to his seat, then suddenly jerked straight up, waving a hand in the air. "Okay, Miss Hogan, smile pretty," he muttered under his breath, "you're on." He rose to his feet. "Well, speak of the devil. Where've you been, O'Connor, you're late."

Annie stiffened, an odd mix of dread and curiosity roiling at the prospect of meeting Steven O'Connor, the man who broke Maggie's heart. Sucking in a deep breath, she exhaled before turning around, going for a nonchalant air. Unfortunately, both nonchalance and air died a quick death when blood drained from her face faster than the liquor from Joanie's flask.

"Sorry, Joe, had to call the precinct about a couple of thugs." The "officer" who'd saved her from Harv and Grove casually slipped his jacket over an empty chair, and she caught a peek of a shoulder holster before he buttoned his open vest. "They were hassling some silly kid who didn't have a brain in her head."

Her gasp forced Dr Pepper up her nose, and she started to hack. Peggy slapped her on the back. "You okay? Gosh, you act like Joanie spiked your drink."

"Hi, Steven, it's been way too long." Erica all but glowed. "We've missed you."

"Speak for yourself, Erica." Joe plucked Steven's jacket off the chair and tossed it across the table. "I see way too much of him as it is. He's all yours for the evening."

Steven laughed, deep blue eyes sparkling as he extended a hand to Stan. "Hey, buddy, long time, no see. And Ashley Roberts—don't tell me you're still dating this guy? I thought you'd wise up by now."

"Just waiting for you to come around, Steven, so just give me the word." Ashley ruffled Stan's hair with a smirk.

Chuckling, Steven turned. "So, Joanie, how've you—" He stopped, jaw dangling at the sight of Annie. "You," he whispered, the smile dissolving on his face. His hands settled loosely on his hips while the blue eyes narrowed. "*These* are your friends?"

Blood whooshed into Annie's cheeks, burning so much, she thought she would peel.

"You know Annie?" Joe hiked a brow while Annie died a thousand deaths.

Steven jerked a thumb her way. "Yeah, she's the brainless kid I was telling you about, the one I had to rescue from those two thugs." He shifted his gaze back to Annie and shook his head. "A female walking this neighborhood alone at night. That's just plain stupid."

"Hey, she isn't stupid," Peggy said. "Annie's class valedictorian."

The edge of Steven's lip curled. "Yeah, book smart, street stupid."

The heat in Annie's face went straight to her temper. "Well, at least *my* brains are in my head, *Officer*, and not in my gun."

"Whoo-ee, Steven," Stan said with a chuckle. "I think she just called you a dumb cop."

"Come on, you two," Joe said with a grin, "let's kiss and make up. And you, partner"—Joe aimed a pointed look at Steven—"need to lighten up. We're not on the clock here, you know, so let's have a good time." He shot Annie a sheepish grin. "Sorry, Annie, this guy doesn't get out all that much, but once you get to know him, he's really not so bad. Right, Erica?"

Erica's smile went to work as she leaned in to give Steven the benefit of her new dress. "I'll vouch for that." She patted the chair beside her. "Be a good boy, Steven, and come sit down."

Steven didn't budge, gaze flicking from Erica to Annie while a storm brewed in his eyes.

"Okay, then let's start over." Joe directed an arm to Annie.

"This is Peggy's friend, Annie, and she's new to Boston, straight from Badger, Iowa, which," he said with a lift of brows, "is probably why she didn't know not to walk the Pier alone at night." He grinned at Annie with a quick nod at Steven. "This is my partner at the Prohibition Bureau, Steven O'Connor, a stickler for the law who was actually a lot more fun in college when he broke it on a regular basis."

Prohibition officers? Annie gaped, stunned. Joe hadn't blinked an eye over Joanie's flask. She noted the hard line of Steven O'Connor's jaw and guessed it wouldn't be the same with him.

"So what do you say, you two. Truce?" Joe glanced from one to the other.

Despite a wobble in her legs, Annie rose and held out a shaky hand. "I'm sorry we got off on the wrong foot, Offi— uh, Steven. I hope we can be friends."

"Atta girl, Annie." Joe turned to his partner and arched a brow. "O'Connor?"

Steven stared, irritated the smart-mouthed kid he'd rescued in the street could not only set off his temper but apparently his pulse as well. He scowled. In the dark, she'd looked like a kid, barely fifteen, but here in the intimacy of the low-lit ballroom and without the baggy sweater, she appeared older, cute even, aglow with an innocence that rankled. His eyes narrowed. She didn't belong here, mixing with a crowd who would only set her on the wrong path. She was seventeen, for pity's sake, and the wide green eyes void of makeup and dewy cheeks growing rosier by the second told him loud and clear she was nothing more than a naïve Pollyanna. Chaste, innocent, everything the women around her were not, and it chafed that he found himself in the unlikely role of big brother. To protect her, to steer her away from all this, to save her from ending up hard and loose like all the women he knew.

Women like Maggie. Regret stabbed immediately, as always whenever he thought of the woman who'd stolen his heart.

But then he'd stolen her innocence in college, in the backseat of Joe's father's car, and no matter how hard he tried, nothing could erase that stain of guilt from his soul. Not breaking up with her, not giving up drinking, not even pursuing the law in an effort to vindicate his past. A past that had almost cost him the life of his father.

"Ahem . . ." Joe cleared his throat.

Steven jolted, suddenly aware he was staring. Forcing a smile, he gripped her hand. "I'm sorry too. Professional vice, I guess. When I see someone in danger, it just puts me on edge."

A soft shade of pink dusted her cheeks as her small hand slipped from his. "That's understandable. And thank you again for coming to my rescue."

She tucked a strand of reddish blonde hair over her ear, an action that seemed both sweet and sensual at the same time. The motion drew his attention to the soft curls that trailed her shoulders, a stark contrast to the fashionable bobs of the day. Further evidence of her innocence, he thought with a press of his jaw, and his protective instincts notched up. Without meaning to, his gaze traveled down, taking in generous curves previously hidden by a sweater, and when his eyes met hers once again, the flaming blush in her cheeks tugged a grin to his lips.

"Besides," he said, flicking Joe on the head, "I always get a little testy when I see a nice girl like you mixed up with trouble like this."

"Hey, need I remind you that you used to be 'trouble' too?" Joe winked at Erica. "And . . . if I have my way, you will be again." He poured Coca-Cola into a fresh glass and handed it to Steven. "Here, take the badge off, O'Connor, and let's show these ladies a good time."

"Speaking of which," Joanie said with a drawl, "how 'bout a touch of giggle water to take you back to the good ol' days?"

Steven's smile soured. "You know better than that, Joanie. College is over, and I'm in the Justice Department now, a working stiff sworn to uphold the law."

Joe grunted. "'Stiff' being the operative word. Come on, Steven, lighten up. Prohibition will be dead by the end of the year, so what's the big deal? We're not on the payroll now."

Huffing out a sigh, Steven ambled over to sit next to Erica. "Obviously." He caught Joe's pleading glance and exhaled again, realizing his best friend was probably right . . . *again*. He *was* stiff. *And dull and boring and downright miserable.* He stared at Joe's and Stan's open-necked shirts and suddenly yanked at his tie and shoved it in his coat pocket, loosening his own shirt. An ocean breeze from the window cooled the sweat on his chest, and all at once he realized how stagnant his life had become.

"You used to be the life of the party, O'Connor," Joe had said when he'd strong-armed Steven earlier in the day. "What the devil happened?"

His smile thinned as he rolled up the sleeves of his shirt. *Maggie happened.*

"Mmm, get comfortable, why don't you?" Erica said, wisping painted nails through the dark hairs on his arm. And for the first time in a while, he missed spending time with a woman.

"My thoughts exactly," he said as he tugged her to her feet and led her to the dance floor. He pulled her into his arms, and the scent of Chanel No. 5 toyed with his senses. They moved slowly, the mellow sound of "Hold Me" soothing his nerves and draining the tension from his neck. *Exactly what I have in mind*, he thought, the lyrics underscoring his resolve. He rested his head against hers, pushing aside all thoughts of Maggie.

"It's nice to be in your arms again, Steven," Erica whispered, her husky tone reminding him of the fling they'd had during one of his breakups with Maggie.

"It's nice to have you here, Erica."

She stared up, lips parted and an invitation in her eyes, and a once-familiar desire kindled deep in his gut. It'd been too long since he'd been drawn to a woman, and he found he no longer wanted to avoid it. Almost three years on the high road had made him a lonely man, one who didn't feel anything for any woman, nor wanted to. But with Erica so close, so willing, he could feel it now, and he couldn't deny it felt good, natural, to be here again. Eyes lidded, she slowly lifted on tiptoe to brush her lips against his, and upon contact, her arms swept around his neck, drawing him down. A forgotten desire flamed and he deepened the kiss. The taste of her intoxicated him, and with a silent groan, he clutched her so tightly, he felt her breathe when she molded close.

"I've missed you," she whispered, and he closed his eyes to enjoy the feel of her body against his, the clean smell of Breck shampoo in her hair, the scent of her skin.

"Now, see? This isn't so bad, is it, O'Connor?"

Steven opened his eyes to see Joe grinning at him with Annie in his arms, and for some reason, his neck stiffened all over again, dampening his good mood. *You're an idiot, O'Connor, what do you care?* He tightened his hold on Erica and deflected his feelings with a cocky grin. "Oh, it's bad, all right. Bad for my work ethic. I could get used to this."

"Mmm . . . me too." Erica laid her head on his chest.

"That's the whole plan," Joe said. "To get you back into the land of the living so you don't drag me down too."

He winked at Erica and spun Annie away, holding her closer than Steven liked. His lips compressed into a near scowl. *Leave her alone, Joe, she's just a kid.*

The dance ended and Joe took Annie back to the table, allowing Steven to breathe easier and enjoy Erica in his arms. They danced to several more songs before Steven escorted her back, feeling more relaxed than he had in a long while. "Thanks, Erica," he said, "I needed that."

"Me too, Steven." She pressed a soft kiss to his cheek. "Don't go anywhere, okay?" She gave Joanie a secret smile and inclined her head toward the ladies' room. "Want to come?"

"Sure," Joanie said with a ready grin, then followed as Erica led the way.

Steven leaned back, arm draped loosely over Erica's chair as he squinted at Joe. He nodded toward Annie's empty spot. "Where's the kid?"

Joe's gaze shifted to the dance floor. "Peggy's dancing with some guy I don't know and Annie is with . . ." He hesitated, his mouth leveling flat. "Brubaker."

Steven sat up. "Brubaker?" He leaned in, fingers gripped to the table. "And you *let* her?"

Joe sighed and downed his Coke, slumping back in his chair. "And how are we supposed to stop her, Steven? We have no control over her. Besides, it's only a dance."

"She's a kid, Walsh," Steven said sharply, his jaw hard as rock. "For pity's sake, she's still wet behind the ears without a lick of sense to know that Brubaker's a snake." His eyes scanned the crowd, seeing Peggy, but no sign of Annie. "Where is she?" he snapped.

"Why? What are you going to do? Make a scene?" Joe slanted forward. "You know you have no patience where Brubaker's concerned, so why borrow trouble?"

Steven rose. "One, because I flat-out don't like the guy, and two? Because I'm not gonna let that slime ruin another girl's reputation, especially some kid from Podunk, Iowa, who doesn't know which end is up." He jerked his jacket off the chair and put it on, then tempered his anger with a stiff smile. "Come on, Joe, isn't this what you're always harping about? For me to get back in the game?"

Joe scowled. "Yeah, but with the ladies, not your fists. You're a law official, O'Connor, not a vigilante. You're supposed to head off trouble, not start it."

"Exactly," Steven said with another quick scan of the floor. "And that's exactly what I intend to do." He slammed his chair in, shooting Joe a reassuring grin. "Don't worry, partner, you have my word I won't throw the first punch." He took a quick stab at the peanuts and tossed a handful in his mouth. "But if it comes to that?" He offered a quick salute. "You can bet I'll deliver the last."

2

Uh-oh, this is a mistake . . . Annie tensed the moment Billy steered her out to the piazza, the brisk sea air delivering as many cold chills as the man holding her hand, a bitter reminder she'd left her sweater inside. Isolated couples lingered here and there, some nuzzling at the railing while a ripe moon lent a hazy glow with a stripe of gold across Massachusetts Bay. Others chose darker nooks to engage in behavior that forced a lump to her throat, bringing heat to her cheeks that belied the cool of the night. She buffed her arms, feeling the goose bumps popping everywhere beneath her thin dress, and Billy instantly pulled her into his arms.

"I'll keep you warm, doll," he whispered, fondling her ear with his mouth. Lights from the piazza danced across the water, while shivers danced down her spine, as much from his touch as from fear of where it might lead. She squeezed her eyes shut, body stiff as his lips wandered her throat. But it didn't matter how scared she was, because the truth was, it was time.

"Book smart, street stupid." Steven O'Connor's words haunted, confirming what she already knew. When it came to life, she'd always done things by the "book," the tomboy who was smart, responsible, and mature beyond her years.

Excelling in school and faith while Maggie excelled in living life with a passion. Well, Annie was tired of waiting for her life to begin and the magic to start. The same magic that had filled every one of her sister's letters, beckoning her toward this pivotal moment when she was no longer a little girl but a woman like Maggie, experiencing things that, up to now, she'd only dreamed or written about.

Like my very first kiss.

Billy eased her to the steel railing, and she shivered again, remembering "Harv's" near kiss on the boardwalk. That was the first kiss any boy ever tried to give her, and she was quite sure it didn't count. No, it'd left her shaken and nauseous, and a true first kiss had to be magical.

Didn't it? Like a moonlit kiss on this piazza with a handsome man like Billy who actually stirred her pulse? Her mind suddenly leapfrogged to Steven O'Connor, and heat braised her skin. All at once her stomach lurched when Billy molded his body to hers, causing panic to rise in her chest. His mouth slid softly to her throat, and she forced herself to relax, determined to enjoy this milestone in her life. And then with a harsh catch of her breath, he feathered her ear with his mouth, tongue invasive. Frantic, she tried to push him away, but he only locked her tighter, his breath hot against her skin. "Oh, babe, I never met a girl like you—"

"Sure you have, Brubaker, dozens of times, at this very railing alone." Steven O'Connor strolled forward, hands loose in the pockets of his blue serge slacks and lips sculpted in a smile colder than the cast-iron statue she'd passed on the Pier.

Heat singed Annie's cheeks when a swear word hissed in her ear, and she gasped when Billy spun around. "You looking for trouble, O'Connor? Because if you are, I'll give it to ya."

Steven folded his arms, tone casual despite a tic in his jaw. "Trouble? Naw, but you are." His dangerous smile gleamed white in the dark. "Ever hear the term 'age of consent'?"

Billy didn't answer right away, but Annie saw the strain in

the clench of his fists. "What the devil are you talking about?
I ain't done nothing wrong."

"Not yet." Steven nodded at Annie. "But look at her, Brubaker,
she's jailbait and way too young for what you got in mind."

"That's her decision, fuzzball, not yours."

Annie eased away, arms clutched to her waist as Steven
arched a brow. Gaze lidded, his chiseled face was calm and
matter-of-fact as he held out a hand. "Want to stay with him,
Annie, or come with me?"

She shot into his embrace, burying her face in his shirt
while she sobbed against his chest. His arms closed around
her like a steel fortress, and when he spoke, his voice was as
biting as the sudden gust of wind whipping her back. "If I ever
see you around Annie or anybody this young again, Brubaker,
I'll toss you in the cooler so fast, you'll have frostbite."

"Yeah? On what charges, flatfoot?"

Amusement laced Steven's tone. "Oh, don't worry, you
two-bit greaseball, I'll come up with something—assault,
maybe, or even that rotgut stashed in your coat."

Annie sniffed and pulled away. The steely smile on Steven's
face appeared all the more ominous, given the shadow of
bristle on his hard-angled jaw.

"Or maybe just because you're downright ugly. Either way,
I have friends in the precinct who owe me favors, so go ahead,
Brubaker, I'm beggin' you to just give me a shot."

Billy cursed and shoved past, leaving Annie quivering in the
cold while she stared at the floor, too embarrassed to meet
Steven's eyes. She heard his noisy sigh before he took off his
jacket and draped it around her shoulders with a parental
air. "I'm taking you home, kiddo."

"But Peggy—"

He gripped her arm, pulling her up short, his glare making
her squirm. "I don't care about Peggy. She can handle this,
you can't. You're too young."

"I'm as old as she is," she said, a pout in her tone as he
dragged her inside. "Or will be."

34

He held the door, palm hard against the small of her back, steering her in. "Peggy's been around, you haven't. In a place like this, you stand out like a sore thumb, begging for trouble."

She wheeled on him with fire in her eyes. "I am *not* stupid, you know, nor some dumb cluck who's gonna let every Tom, Dick, and Harry take advantage."

He angled a brow. "No . . . just every Harv, Grove, and Billy."

She blinked, cheeks burning at the truth of his statement. She looked away, tone angry despite tears pricking her eyes. "I don't care, Steven, you treat me like I'm a kid and I'm not."

He chucked a finger to her chin, his tone suddenly soft. "No, you're not. You're a young woman too special for a place like this, Annie, mixing with the likes of Joe, Peggy, and Erica."

"And you?" she said with a hike of her chin.

He smiled. "Yeah . . . especially me." He folded his arms. "So . . . you gonna let me walk you home, or are you going to stay and get in more trouble?"

She heaved a heavy sigh, suddenly wanting nothing more than to be home safe in her bed. She crossed her arms to her waist and peered up with a jut of her jaw. "I'll go," she said with a threat in her tone, "but I'd stay if I wanted to."

He grinned, gently pressing her shoulder to the wall. "I'm sure you would. Stay here. I'll get your sweater and purse and tell the others."

"Wait!" She jerked forward, hand to his arm. "You're not going to tell 'em anything to make me look like some, some . . . ," she gulped, cheeks warm, "little baby, are you?"

A boyish smile curved on his mouth as he tweaked a lock of her hair. "No, 'baby doll,' " he said, a hint of laughter twinkling in his eyes. "I'll just tell them you're sick to your stomach."

"But I'm not," she said, no longer comfortable with telling any more lies.

With a gentle tap of her nose, he gave her a look that quivered her belly. "Oh yes you are, kiddo." He turned to weave his way through the crowd, but not before delivering a final glance over his shoulder. "'Cause if kissing Brubaker didn't make you want to throw up your supper, you either have a cast-iron stomach . . ." his smile took a slant, "or one monumental tolerance for pain."

⁓

A grin tugged as Steven made his way through the crowd to where Annie stood welded to the wall, hugging his jacket like a shield to ward off unwelcome attention. It all but swallowed her whole as her anxious eyes scanned the throng of people, reducing her to the little girl he'd rescued in the street. His grin broke free and he shook his head. *A sore thumb, no doubt about it*, he thought with a sigh. *Snow White in a sea of scarlet women . . .*

A man approached her, and every muscle in Steven's body tensed as if it were his little sister plastered against that wall. He watched as she shook her head before dropping her gaze to the floor, and the knot in his stomach slowly unraveled. *Good girl.*

Her pinched look relaxed when she spotted him, and instantly a soft wash of pink stole into her cheeks. He exhaled slowly, certain he was doing the right thing by taking her home.

"Here." He replaced his coat with her bulky sweater. "Button up, 'cause sea air gets cold." Waiting, he finally returned her purse and put his own jacket on, then hooked her elbow. "Where do you live?" he asked, his tone as impersonal as if he were processing paperwork at the office.

Where do I live? Air clotted in Annie's throat at the revelation he'd be walking her home to a house he might recognize if Maggie had taken him there. She absently gnawed on her lip. *Probably not, though.* Maggie lived in the Radcliffe dorm and couldn't abide Aunt Eleanor either, even though her aunt's money afforded an education few women enjoyed. Annie drew in a bolstering breath, realizing she'd have to take her chances. And if Steven O'Connor and his friends found out she was Maggie's sister? A knot dipped in her throat. Well, then so be it. She certainly knew she'd have to tell them eventually, but not just yet, at least not till she had a chance to try her wings and experience what Maggie had.

She sucked in a deep draw of air. Besides, from the rift mentioned in Maggie's letters between her, Erica, and Joanie and their catty comments tonight, Annie was pretty sure neither of them would want anything to do with her, nor would Steven, most likely. She peeked up, noting dark stubble on his clean-shaven jaw as he towed her down the moonlit piazza to the ramp of the Pier and suddenly decided she wanted more time in Maggie's world. After all, it wasn't as if she were lying, actually . . . She gulped. Just delaying the truth a wee bit.

With another deep breath, she finally mustered the courage to tell him her address. "Beacon Hill," she muttered, out of breath from trying to keep up.

The sculpted profile turned, a ridge forming between dark brows. "Whereabouts?" His curious gaze flitted down her misshapen, bulky cardigan in apparent sympathy, as if he knew it were a faded hand-me-down from her mother.

Heat burnished her cheeks. "Louisburg Square."

Steven whistled while he studied her with a half smile. "A little rich girl, huh?"

"Not me, my aunt," she said with a bite in her tone.

"You don't like her?" He eyed her with a squint.

She huffed out a weary sigh, guilt creeping in over the strained relationship with her mother's sister. "Not really, but we just moved in three months ago, so maybe it'll change." She pulled on the sleeves of her sweater to tuck her fingers inside, wishing she'd worn her coat and gloves as Aunt Eleanor always nagged her to do. "Although I have my doubts."

"Why?" He clasped her arm to help her across the dark beach.

Pulse racing, she forced herself to concentrate. His firm hold made her forget all about the cold, and she stumbled over a lump in the sand, causing his grip to tighten. "Well, Aunt Eleanor never married, you see, so she knows nothing about being a parent or a guardian. Despite the fact I'll be eighteen in two months and I took care of Daddy and my little sister after Mama died, she treats me like a child." They reached the boulevard, and he looked both ways, carefully steering her across. On the other side, he released her arm, and immediately the fog cleared from her mind, allowing her to focus on her aunt. "When it comes to my life, she's as rigid as the wood in this boardwalk. Things like ridiculous curfews, forcing me to go to catechism class, and refusing to let me bob my hair."

He shot her a sideways grin. "Sounds like a smart woman to me."

She peered up, head cocked. "Spoken like a true tight-lipped arm of the law, Agent O'Connor, nose to the grindstone as Joe so aptly pointed out."

A boisterous group of men and women spilled out of a noisy dance hall, and Annie's heart swooped when Steven shored up the small of her back, guiding her past. He glanced over, his angled smile matching hers. "A tight-lipped arm of the law with his nose to the grindstone who saved your pretty hide tonight, I might add—*twice*."

She exhaled wispy air. "So you keep reminding me." She peered up, eyes in a squint. "How old are you anyway?"

He grinned. "Old enough to agree with your aunt. Twenty-five tomorrow, as a matter of fact."

She beamed. "Well, happy birthday," she said with a bright smile that quickly sloped off-center. "But that's hardly old."

"Yeah?" He crooked a brow. "Old enough to keep you out of trouble, kiddo."

They turned at the corner, leaving the bright lights of the boardwalk for the shadowed lamplight of Revere Street, and suddenly the memory of Harv and Grove made her shiver.

"Cold?" He immediately took off his coat again and draped it over her shoulders, buffing her arm with his palm as they walked, producing a shiver of another kind.

"A little," she whispered, suppressing a gulp as she wrapped his coat tight, the scent of Bay Rum taking her captive. "So . . . I suppose Erica's none too pleased I stole you away?"

He chuckled. "Nope, but she'll be there when I get back."

Annie frowned. "Is she . . . your girlfriend?"

His laugh had a definite edge. "Nope. Don't have one."

"Why?" she asked, shock halting her in her steps.

He assessed her out of the corner of his eye with a ghost of a smile, prodding her along with a hand to her back. "Because women are nothing but trouble. You should be proof of that."

"But you kissed her!" she blurted, the words warming her cheeks as her heels ground in.

He faced her, hands latched to her shoulders like a big brother. "That's right, because news flash, kiddo, most men like to kiss women. It feels good and a lot of guys will say or do anything to get as much as they can, *which* . . . ," he said with a stern hike of his brow, "is why you don't belong in a place like that, at least not till you get a little older."

She bristled and folded her arms. "Maybe I want to be kissed. Ever think of that?"

Heaving a cumbersome sigh, he started walking, leaving her no choice but to follow.

"Are you one of those guys?" she asked, running to keep up.

"What guys?"

"You know, the ones who'll say or do anything to get as much as they can?"

He exhaled heavier this time. "Used to be. Which is why I know what I'm talking about."

She skidded to a stop, heart racing. "With Maggie?"

He stilled, jaw tight as he seared her with a look. "Who told you about Maggie?"

She swallowed. "Joe mentioned her."

A scowl tainted his face, making him appear harsh in the lamplight. "Well, Joe should keep his mouth shut. It's none of his business and it's none of yours." He kept walking.

"Did you . . . love her?" she whispered, heart thudding.

Her words froze him on the sidewalk, broad back stiff for several seconds till he finally turned. He folded his arms with a casual air, but moonlight revealed a twitch in the hard line of his jaw. "I repeat, it's none of your business, so either change the subject or you'll walk home alone."

"No, I won't." She jutted her chin and passed him up, shooting a smirk over her shoulder. "Nose to the grindstone, remember? Heaven forbid Agent O'Connor shirk his responsibility."

A smile nudged at his lips. "Yeah, well, you're not my responsibility. I'm just a nice guy who'd do the same for anybody's kid sister." Headlights careened toward them at a fast clip, and in the catch of her breath, he yanked her from the curb. "You trying to get yourself killed? For somebody who claims to be smart, you sure don't think a lot."

Annoyed, she jerked free and darted ahead. "Yeah? Well, I'm not your little sister or anybody else's, so you can shove the big-brother act in your coat along with your pistol."

Steven grinned, thinking how cute she looked, stomping away in a huff with a pretty pout on her lips. Head high she barreled ahead, wrapped in his jacket like a cocoon, and he shook his head. Beneath the lamplight, a hint of copper glinted in lustrous blonde hair that bounced on her shoulders. His eyes trailed to shapely legs, and heat swarmed, a painful reminder of how quickly innocence could be lost. He adjusted his thinking and returned to "big-brother" mode, choosing silence rather than offending her further. He caught up at the streetlight before the turn into Louisburg Square, where she stared straight ahead, refusing to acknowledge him.

He grinned. "So what d'ya do when you're not spending time with people you shouldn't, Annie . . . ?"

"I'll be a freshman at Radcliffe," she said sharply, obviously ignoring his request for a last name. "Where, oddly enough, they haven't yet realized I'm just a 'kid.'"

Radcliffe? He frowned. "That's a great school. What field of study?"

She never broke stride when the light turned, just charged across with back squared. "Education," she said, tone clipped. "'Cause when I *do* grow up, I hope to teach little kids like me."

He halted her with a gentle grip on the other side, an apology in his eyes. "Annie," he whispered, drawing her gaze to his. "I think you misunderstand me. It's not that I think your age makes you young . . ." His eyes softened at the look of hurt in hers. "It's your innocence. You're different than most girls I know—sweet, naïve, pure. I just wanna see you stay that way, that's all. But you won't if you spend time with people like Peggy and her sister."

Moisture glazed her eyes. "Nobody stays innocent forever, Steven. Little girls grow up into women, and women fall in love."

He cupped a hand to her cheek. "Yeah, they do, kid, but the smart ones guard their innocence, because someday, it'll be a priceless gift to the man they marry." He exhaled and slipped his hands in his pockets. "You have something special, Annie. Don't throw it away like Peggy or Joanie or Erica, okay?" He nodded at Louisburg Square. "Which one?"

"The second house on the right," she whispered.

He ushered her through the iron gate and up the steps of a Georgian brownstone where graceful arches hovered over endless rows of windows, suddenly grateful the kid had an aunt who could take care of her. "Do you understand what I'm saying, Annie?"

Yes, I understand . . . But the only thing she *really* cared about at the moment was that Steven O'Connor was a man whose touch tingled her skin and quivered her stomach, something she'd never felt before. Pressing a shaky hand to her throat, her breathing shallowed when a strange warmth coated her insides like heated honey. *Heaven help me, is this how he made Maggie feel?*

"Good." He ushered her to the front door and turned the knob, only to find it locked. He glanced at his watch, then up at the dark windows. "Ten o'clock. I guess your aunt's in bed. Do you have a key?"

Cheeks burning, she rifled through her purse. "Uh, I may have left it in my room." She looked up, heart stuttering when her gaze flicked to his lips. Peggy's words taunted. *"For criminy sakes, Annie Lou, you're a woman who's never been kissed, and this is your chance."*

She sucked in a wobbly breath, well aware this was not only a chance to remedy that *and* win a bet but the moment she'd waited a lifetime for—a first kiss that would matter. Guilt squeezed. *But . . . with Maggie's old boyfriend?* She nibbled at her lip, wondering what her sister would say if she knew. *But it's just an innocent bet*, Annie argued, *nothing more than a kiss on a dare*. Stomach trembling, she lifted her eyes to his, adamant that Steven O'Connor was just a means to an end, not anyone she ever intended to see again. Right?

"Uh, the back door is probably open," she whispered, throat dry as dust. "So, I'll just say goodbye here." She took a halting step forward, heart hammering at what she intended to do.

He slacked a hip and stepped away, thick, dark brows dipping low with a fold of his arms. "Wait a minute. You didn't sneak out, did you?" His words were sharp with suspicion.

Heat flooded . . . but not the kind she'd hoped for. "W-what?"

He vented with a noisy breath. "Man alive, I can't believe you snuck out." Gripping her elbow, he dragged her down the porch and around the house. "How long have you been friends with Peggy anyway?" he snapped, tugging her up the steps of the back porch. He rattled the knob and shook his head. "The back door is probably open, huh?" He stepped away to survey the house, eyeing a sturdy rose trellis that climbed to just below the second-story windows. His mouth went slack. "You climbed down *that?*"

She nodded with a bite of her lip, peeking up at the sag of his jaw.

Exhaling loudly, he braced her shoulders with a plea in

his tone, his hands burning through his suit coat. "Annie, *please*. You're too special. Don't stoop to things like this."

Tears welled. *Special?* Maybe once, but not anymore. Not with Daddy gone.

Ducking his head, he tucked a finger to her chin. "Promise you'll stop this lying, sneaking out, acting loose like the others." His expression intensified as he cupped her face. "I don't see girls like you very often, kid, and I'd hate to see them ruin you too. Promise you'll stay as special as you are, at least till the right guy puts a wedding band on your finger."

She nodded, the lump in her throat coupled with tears in her eyes. Her heart suddenly ached, wishing that somehow, someday, that man might be somebody like him.

He led her over to the brick wall next to the trellis and glanced up. "I don't guess you need any help," he said, lips in a dry bent.

"No," she whispered, suddenly desperate to prove she was no longer a little girl but a woman with feelings. To convince herself and Steven O'Connor that she was not some naïve, backwoods kid adrift in the big city but a passionate woman poised to begin the story of her heart. A story in which the man before her might very well be the first chapter.

Her back to the brick wall, Annie tucked a strand of hair behind her ear while goose bumps skittered her arms. She drew in an unsteady breath and rubbed sweaty palms down the sides of his suit jacket now hanging limp on her frame, then extended a shaky hand. The tips of her fingers peeked out from the sleeve of his coat. "Thank you for walking me home."

He delivered that deadly smile that'd tumbled her stomach all night, eyes twinkling as he gave her palm a light squeeze. "You're welcome, kid, it was my pleasure." He tapped a gentle finger to her nose. "Be good, you hear?"

Oh, I hope so! She eased forward with her heart in her throat.

He held out his hand, eyeing his suit coat. "Uh, aren't you forgetting something?"

"Yes," she whispered, and with a jerky nod, she slipped trembling hands to his waist. Before he could blink, she lifted on tiptoe to kiss him full on the mouth, her awkward attempt clearly taking him by surprise.

Time stood still and so did he, stone cold for several seconds while her lips tasted his, and then in a harsh catch of her breath, he pressed her to the wall so abruptly, the shock forced all air from her lungs. He kissed her hard, the dominance of his mouth unleashing a throb of heat that wrenched a soft moan from her throat. Her purse dropped to the ground when he jerked her close, the hard, cold steel of his gun cutting into her side. His lips were urgent and rough, heating her body till she was near limp in his arms. "I never met a girl like you," he whispered, Brubaker's words hot and hoarse as he nipped at her ear. His hands slipped inside the suit coat to explore with a brush of her hips, a slide of her waist, and she jerked free as her heart seized in her chest.

"No!" Her rib cage heaved when she pushed him away. Cringing against the wall, her voice was a painful stutter as tears stung her eyes. "I'm n-not that k-kind of girl."

He jerked her chin up with a hard grip, the fire in his gaze smoldering while a dangerous tic pulsed in his jaw. "Then don't act like it," he hissed, his tone as cold and blunt as the brick gouging her back. Without another word, he strode down the porch steps and disappeared around the corner, apparently too angry to remember she still wore his coat.

Another heave shuddered from her throat and she slumped to the wall. Hand to her mouth, she squeezed her eyes shut, tears of shame and hurt welling beneath her lids. *He's just like Brubaker*, she thought, and instantly knew it was a lie. Just like the lie she'd told Aunt Eleanor about going to bed early or the promise she'd made Steven to stop acting "loose." He was as far from Brubaker as she was from being the girl he believed her to be.

"You have something special, Annie. Don't throw it away . . ." But she had. Offering something he'd neither asked for nor wanted, winning his wrath instead of his heart.

"You're different than most girls I know . . ."

Chest quivering, she bent to pick up her purse, her remorse as thick as the shame in her throat. *Apparently not*, she thought, heart sick with regret.

At least . . . not anymore.

<hr />

Steven heaved the iron gate open with a grunt, letting it slam behind with a loud clang. "Women," he muttered, storming toward Pinckney Street with his pulse throbbing in his throat. Or little girls who *think* they're women. Ignoring a red light, he sprinted across, wishing he'd never gotten involved with the kid from Podunk. Nothing riled him more than innocence gone awry, and from the stunt Little Miss Annie Whatever-Her-Name-Was just pulled, it appeared she was well on her way. His jaw settled into a tight line. *Stupid, naïve little kid—kissing a total stranger!* Didn't she understand most guys had one thing on their minds? That her innocence was at risk every time she even flirted with the wrong one? Men who would tell her she was special, then push until she was just like everyone else. *Men like I used to be*, he thought with a harsh vent of air. His old life was certainly proof of that, wasn't it?

Not to mention the fire throbbing in his veins over kissing a kid. *A kid!* Not even eighteen and so wet behind the ears, his suit coat was probably drenched. He froze midway through an intersection, almost oblivious to the honk of a car headed his way. *My coat!* A rare swear word hissed from his lips. The driver laid on the horn, and he sprinted from the car's path with a loud groan. It was bad enough his blood was still hot over an angry kiss meant *only* to teach a lesson, but now he had to see her again too, something he had no desire to do.

Correction. He had desire . . . just not the right kind.

He groaned again and glanced back at Louisburg Square. Well, it was too late to go back now, and he was almost grateful. His body still hummed from a kiss that had taken him by surprise. Not only the sweet, gentle one she'd given him, but the rough one he'd given her, hoping to scare her half to death. Only it had scared him instead. Talking to her, touching her, holding her had felt way better than it should. She was too young and vulnerable, for pity's sake, too susceptible to someone who could steal her innocence away.

Someone like me.

He scooped up a pebble and hurled it, muttering words that sizzled the air. Ramming his hands in his pockets, he continued on to Revere Beach, determined to stick with his own kind—women like Erica and Joanie with nothing to lose, out for fun and no strings attached. Women who couldn't tempt him with the wide-eyed innocence that seemed to be a weakness for him—a weakness he had *no* desire to revisit.

He rounded the corner and cast a wary eye at the Ocean Pier Dance Pavilion as it glittered and glowed on the moon-rippled bay. Avoiding women the last three years had netted him nothing but bitterness and boredom, but girls like Annie were not even an option. He didn't trust himself with them any more than he did with women like Maggie, and from what Steven could see, there were precious few in between. No, he'd do what Joe wanted him to do—laugh, dance, and have a good time—but nothing more. His conscience wouldn't allow it. Nor would the deep faith of his family, a faith that hounded him daily to atone for his past. Jaw grinding, he made his way down the wooden pier, hypnotic music and memories enticing him on. Thoughts of both Maggie and Annie invaded his mind, and he blasted out a sigh. Never again would he give his heart or his body to a woman he didn't respect. And heaven help him, he had no stomach for ruining the ones he did.

⌒⌒⌒

Still half asleep, Annie languidly stretched in her canopied bed, reveling in the sumptuous feather bed with a sleepy smile. *Oh, what a night!* She sank under the covers with a glorious sigh.

The man! The kisses! The warm, gushy feeling!

And the guilt?

Her eyes popped open to her luxurious bedroom with its lemon-polished Victorian furniture and floral-papered walls in lavender and mint green and instantly gnawed on her lip. Sunlight peeked through lacy bedroom sheers, its hazy streams of light only illuminating the accusation in her mind. "But I didn't do anything wrong," she explained to Mr. Grump, their pet basset hound Aunt Eleanor reluctantly allowed. He watched through droopy-eyed slits at the end of her bed, chin on the white eyelet bedspread. Mr. G. yawned, the effect almost a growl, then rolled over, obviously unconvinced by her ardent defense. She frowned and pulled the coverlet to her chin. "It was just an innocent kiss, Grump, and nothing more," she whispered.

Only she knew better.

The angry spark in Steven O'Connor's eyes told her loud and clear it was anything but innocent. Naïve and stupid, maybe, but never innocent. She groaned and slumped under the covers, sick over the kind of woman he must think her today. Fast and forward and loose, everything of which he didn't approve. And everything he seemed to disdain.

Shame settled thick in her throat as she reached for his folded coat on the pillow next to her own. She rolled on her side, his jacket bunched to her chest. Closing her eyes, she breathed in his heady scent, and even now, the spicy taunt of his aftershave prompted a surge of warmth that tingled her body. "What am I going to do?" she whispered. "I never knew it could feel like this."

But Maggie knew.

More guilt jabbed, as rigid and cold as if Steven's gun still impaled her ribs. Maggie had probably felt like this and more, so in love with Steven O'Connor that his name filled every letter she wrote. Annie idly brushed her fingers to her lips, remembering the dizzy sensation of his mouth against hers—the same mouth that had kissed Maggie's.

"Rumor is she gave him her all."

Moisture stung, an odd mix of remorse, allegiance, and jealousy that she had dared to kiss the man her sister loved.

Had loved. Annie gave a quick sniff. Wasn't it obvious the way Maggie moved to California after graduation, as far from Steven O'Connor as she could possibly get? Mama had begged her to come home, but Maggie had Hollywood dreams of becoming a star. And yet, from her sister's letters, Annie knew how tortured she was after her breakup with Steven. He'd changed after the near death of his father, she'd written, and wasn't the same man she had loved.

Or so she said.

Annie pushed the blankets off, unwilling to believe her sister was still in love with the man who wreaked havoc with Annie's pulse. *The man I have to see again*, she thought with a quivering sigh. It was almost three years since Steven broke up with her sister, and Maggie's letters never mentioned him anymore, at least not since she'd fallen in love with Gregory, a promising film director. Annie sat up, drawing in a calming breath. No, she had no reason to feel guilty where Maggie was concerned. Her sister was happy now, or so it appeared from every letter she wrote. Gregory proposed and Maggie was deliriously engaged. A smile tipped Annie's lips at the memory of Maggie's visit at Easter. The twinkle in her sister's blue eyes and sassy glint of platinum hair bespoke a woman in charge of her life and happily so. Which meant, Annie thought with a hug of Steven's coat, Steven O'Connor was fair game! Her smile faded a hair.

Wasn't he?

Shaking off the uneasy feeling, Annie slipped his jacket on and wrapped it close, stomach swooping at Steven's scent.

"You're up!" The door of her bedroom blasted open, and a tiny, towheaded blonde flew in, nightgown flaring and bare feet slapping the glossy wooden floor. Mr. Grump bounced in the air when she vaulted on the bed with giggles and shrieks guaranteed to awaken the dead.

The little stinker tumbled over her to burrow into her sides, and Annie laughed. "Shhh . . . you're going to wake up the queen."

"Aunt Eleanor's a queen?" The five-year-old paused, blue eyes as round as her rosebud mouth. Her battered rag doll, Queen of Sheba, hung limp in her hands.

Annie chuckled and looped an arm around her sister's waist, tickling as she shimmied her close. "No, but she sure acts like it, doesn't she? Ordering poor Frailey around?"

"And us," Glory said with a sparkle in her eyes.

"Mmm . . . especially us," Annie confirmed, ruffling her sister's hair.

"Why you wearing Frailey's coat?" Glory squinted. "Did you steal it?"

"Gloria Kennedy, stealing is a sin and you know it." Annie quickly removed the coat and placed it on her nightstand. "Besides," she said, cheeks hot, "it's not Frailey's, it's a friend's."

"Who?" Glory clapped to coax Mr. Grump to join in on the fray. Apparently content where he was, the basset peered through narrow eyes as if she were feline instead of female.

"Just a friend I met when I was out with Peggy, that's all, sweetie pie."

Glory pulled away with a grunt to plop beside Mr. Grump, promptly straddling the Queen of Sheba spread-eagle on his back. Lying on her stomach, she crossed stubby legs in the air, ignoring a low growl when she tried to tie Grump's ears in a knot. "But why were you snuggling with it in bed?" she asked, her tone matter-of-fact. Face scrunched, she glanced over her shoulder, a riot of white-blonde Shirley Temple curls springing from her head. "Is it like my blankee that smells good and keeps you really warm?"

Heat whooshed into Annie's cheeks. "No, silly," she said, painfully aware it was the man, not the coat, that'd been keeping her warm. "And leave poor Mr. Grump alone, would you, please? How would you like it if somebody played with your ears?"

"I'd like it just fine," Glory said with a pert lift of her chin, as if she'd given it serious thought. "Wouldn't you?"

Annie blinked, thoughts of Steven nuzzling her earlobe instantly scalding her face.

"Snivelin' snot, Annie, you gonna throw up?" Glory quickly scrambled to the other side of the bed, the bunch of tiny brows indicating concern.

"Now where on earth did you learn an expression like that, young lady?" Annie reeled the little girl in with a tickle. "That's an awful thought!"

Glory giggled and squirmed, rocking the bed so much Mr. Grump took his business elsewhere. "No, it isn't, it's swell. Johnny says it all the time."

Annie leaned in and gave Glory the eye. "And who is Johnny, may I ask, besides someone with a questionable vocabulary?"

"He's my new friend," Glory announced with no little pride, plunking down on Annie's pillow. "Did you know he can blow bubbles of milk through his nose?"

Annie arched a brow. "Mmm, very impressive . . . I think."

"He's my boyfriend," she clarified, hands tucked behind her neck. "I kissed him."

"Gloria Celeste Kennedy, proper young ladies do not go around kissing boys!" Her words barely left her tongue before their impact hit, sending another swell of heat to her cheeks.

"Why not?" Glory asked, the picture of innocence. She cocked her head, delicate white-blonde brows crimped in question. "It's fun."

"Because only hussies kiss boys," Annie explained with the patience of a big sister, ignoring the fire in her cheeks.

"Who says so, the Queen?" Glory squinted at her sister and emitted a grunt way too big for a little girl. "Because Johnny says she's nothing but an old maid." Her tone was matter-of-fact, the firm jut of a pink lip indicative of what she thought of Aunt Eleanor's opinion.

Annie gasped and clamped a hand to Glory's mouth. "Hush," she said with a peek at the door, "you want her to hear? How do you even know what an old maid is, you little stinker?"

"Johnny told me. He says it's a lady nobody wants and never been kissed." Her tone took a turn toward sweet. "Like you!" she squealed, darting away with a high-pitched giggle.

"Why, you little scamp!" Annie dove across the bed to scoop her up in a tickle fight, bedsprings squealing in a blur of nightgowns and giggles.

"For the love of all that is decent, what is the meaning of this?"

Girls and bedsprings froze, the sisters' labored breathing the only sound to be heard.

Aunt Eleanor strode into the room like disgruntled royalty, back ramrod straight and ash blonde curls swept high on her head like a crown. Her belted charcoal Elsa Schiaparelli dress revealed a tall, slender figure that would have turned heads had she not given off all the appeal of an ice sculpture. Finely chiseled features seemed severe with the frown she wore, further hardened by the absence of soft curls or bangs around an oval face. But at the age of thirty-seven, her ivory skin was flawless and void of lines most likely because she seldom smiled, imparting the unmistakable air of delicate heirloom china. And like bone china, Annie mused, her face would probably shatter should laughter ever cross her lips.

There were times when Annie could see glimmers of her mother in Aunt Eleanor's face, in almond-shaped eyes that fluctuated between hazel and green, and high cheekbones that framed a classically straight nose. Her lips were full like Annie's mother's, but where Aurora Kennedy's had been lush and inviting with a ready smile, Aunt Eleanor's were tight and pinched, making her cold and stiff by comparison. Despite the constant disapproval that emanated from her aunt, Annie had to admit she was a beautiful spinster . . . that is, if one didn't mind frostbite.

Aunt Eleanor glanced at her diamond Rolex and folded her arms with a purse of her lips. "I suggest you stop acting like street hoodlums and get dressed." She marched to the window to fling the curtains aside and throw up the sash. Spring drifted in with the heavenly scent of lilacs and mulch, wonderful smells that collided with the scowl on her aunt's face.

Suddenly remembering Steven's coat, Annie lunged for the nightstand, snatching it up. Her aunt turned just as Annie stuffed it under the covers, her patrician nose in the air as if she smelled garbage rather than spring. "Susannah Grace, I distinctly told you to pin-curl your hair, did I not? Have you forgotten we're expected at the Bentleys' for brunch?"

"No, ma'am," Annie muttered, wondering how her aunt managed to make her feel younger than her five-year-old sister. She pushed her shoulder-length hair from her eyes. "I can have it washed, curled, and dried in two hours, I promise."

Arching a penciled brow, her aunt folded her arms once again. "Which would be lovely, dear, if we weren't expected in an hour."

Annie gulped.

Aunt Eleanor waved a manicured hand on the way to the door as if to dismiss any notion Annie might have to respond. "There's no time to wash your hair. Just wear the new dress I bought from Filene's, is that clear?" She turned and beckoned Glory with a finger. "Gloria, come. Mrs. Pierce will get you dressed. And, Susannah, you will remember to powder your nose and wear lipstick, won't you? The Bentleys' son Erwin is home from college."

"Yes, ma'am." Annie stifled a groan. *Great*. The twerp with a lazy eye who picks his teeth!

"Come, Gloria." Her aunt sailed through the door while Glory mimicked behind with hands on miniature hips and a wiggle in her walk, her pert, little nose high in the air.

Annie suppressed a giggle and stretched, stopping mid-yawn when Glory dashed back to snatch her doll from the floor. Choking out a sob, she launched into Annie's arms.

"She's not a queen, she's a witch," the little girl said with a wobble in her voice. "I miss Mama."

Heart wrenching, Annie scooped her sister up and squeezed, smothering her with kisses until giggles rolled from her rose-bud lips. "I miss her too, dumpling," Annie whispered, "and Daddy and Maggie. But at least we have each other, right?"

Glory sniffed and nodded, and Annie tenderly wiped the tears from her face. She kissed her nose. "Hey, how 'bout a secret sleepover in my room tonight. Would you like that?"

Dimples emerged on Glory's blotchy face. "And the Queen of Sheba too?"

"Sure, and even Mr. Grump, if he's not too cranky."

Glory giggled. "Just like Aunt Eleanor—a nasty grouch."

Mr. Grump's namesake bellowed from the hallway. "Gloria Celeste—one . . . two . . ."

"Uh-oh, you better scoot or Aunt Eleanor will make Mr. Grump look like Mr. Sunshine." Setting her back on her feet, Annie propelled her sister from the room with a pop on the bottom.

"Love you, Annie." Glory streaked out the door in a whoosh of blonde curls.

"Love you too, sweetie," Annie said, following behind to close her bedroom door. With a heavy sigh, she returned to her bed and retrieved Steven's now-crumpled coat, tentatively slipping it back on her shoulders. Wrapping it around her body, she modeled it before the mirror, wishing it were his arms instead. She closed her eyes to envision his kiss, and his scent merged with her memories, prompting a delicious heat to shimmer her skin.

A lady nobody wants and never been kissed.

Johnny's definition of an old maid flashed through her mind, and she let the coat tumble off her shoulders. The bad news was Steven O'Connor didn't want her. *The good news?* Her stomach quivered at the memory of his kiss, quirking her lips. *At least I'm not an old maid.*

3

*W*ell, if it isn't the birthday boy! So . . . did Eliot give you a present?" With a wiggle of perfectly penciled brows, Steven's older sister Charity threaded a needle in their mother's kitchen, a shaft of sunlight glinting off golden waves of her shoulder-length bob. The ping of horseshoes drifted in through the open window where the men of the family congregated in the backyard, along with the shouts and laughter of cousins playing Red Rover.

Steven paused, one hand flat to the swinging door while the other loosened his tie. His four sisters and sister-in-law congregated in a sewing fest around a large oak table scuffed with many a memory—his mother's effort to supplement income during hard economic times. Six potpies cooled on the stove for his special dinner, a simple and inexpensive way to feed the hordes of cousins and brothers-in-law for his twenty-fifth birthday. Pushing a silver-blonde strand from her face, Marcy O'Connor hoisted several 9" × 12" pans of devil's food cake—his favorite—onto the counter, and the smell instantly made his mouth water.

"Wow, smells great." He strolled over to plant a kiss on his mother's cheek before heading to the icebox for a glass of milk, tweaking Charity's hair on the way. It was days like this, coming home to a favorite meal and the warmth of family, that he was grateful he hadn't moved into a flat with Joe like they'd planned after college. Not that he didn't itch to be on his own, especially now that he and Joe could afford it. But with his older brother Sean getting married last year and moving out, Steven felt an obligation to stay and contribute rent. His parents needed the income, and after the role he'd played in his father's near heart attack at the onset of the depression, the truth was that Steven needed the redemption just as much.

Clunking the milk bottle on the counter, he reached for a glass from the cabinet and shot a smirk over his shoulder. "Did Eliot send me a present? Sure, a fruit basket from Chicago, signed 'Fondly, Eliot Ness.'" He crossed two fingers. "We're like this, you know."

"Oh, how I wish you were," Charity said with a sigh. "That is one gorgeous lawman, and I for one would love to shake his hand. Besides," she said with a crook of a smile, "if Mr. Ness can keep Al Capone in line, just imagine what he could do for Henry."

Marcy O'Connor chuckled while placing dishtowels over the cakes. "Charity Dennehy, don't you dare compare my grandson to that mobster."

"Why not?" Charity squinted at the hem of a skirt. "The boy shoots his mouth off as much as Capone shoots his gun."

"Actually, sis," Steven said with a patient smile, "Capone always had thugs at his beck and call, ready to do his dirty work at the snap of a finger." He winked and butted against the counter with glass in hand. "You know, kind of like you with Mitch?"

Charity's smirk went flat. "Humph . . . in my dreams."

"Or Mitch's nightmares." Steven's oldest sister, Faith, chuckled, sending a sympathetic smile in her brother's direction. She tucked an auburn curl over her ear. "Sorry you had to work, Steven. On a Saturday and your birthday no less. Another special assignment?"

Steven upended his milk and set his glass down. "Yeah, a tip on a fisherman that netted a haul of whiskey from Canada. Our patrol boats have been on to him for a while, but we couldn't catch him with the goods till today." He folded his arms, lips clamped tight. "But you catch one, and there's still a thousand more lined up on Rum Row, waiting to take his place. And why not when they can make more money running booze in a day than a year fishing on their boats?"

"Well, it'll be a moot point before long anyway," Steven's youngest sister, Katie, said, threading the needle in her hand with the same focus and precision she devoted to attending law school during the week. "Prohibition will be history soon. It's only a matter of time before the eighteenth amendment is repealed."

Steven peered up, his sister's words triggering a hot spot. He jabbed a thumb against his chest. "Yeah, well, until then, it's still the law, sis, and *my* job to enforce it." He worked hard to soften the edge of his tone, but his words were tinged with a temper he seldom displayed. "And the mom-and-pops and regular joes who smuggle moonshine, bathtub gin, and home brew across state lines?" He huffed. "I say string 'em all up—bootleggers, rumrunners, speakeasies, and more."

The echo of his anger was deafening in the silence of the room where his sisters and mother stared with concern in their eyes. He pinched the bridge of his nose with a noisy sigh. "Sorry to snap at you, Katie, but it's not just blatant disregard for the law that makes me so crazy," he said quietly, "it's what happens when the law is repealed. Suddenly it's carte blanche for some men to drink themselves into oblivion again, ruining their family's lives."

His gaze flicked to the faint scars on his sister-in-law Emma's face from a former drunken husband, a chilling reminder of what alcohol could do to a man. Like Joe's dad staggering in from the tavern when Steven would spend the night, slamming Joe's mom so hard, Steven would shiver in Joe's room along with the pictures on the wall. Not to mention his own

56

guilt during college when alcohol not only took a friend's life but weakened Steven's resistance to Maggie, fueling his father's ire.

He plowed a blunt hand through dark hair as wilted as his mood. "I know I can't stop the inevitable any more than the repeal of Prohibition can, but when you have 100,000 speakeasies in New York alone, twice the legal bars before Prohibition, and so-called reputable doctors writing as many scrips for medicinal whiskey as medicine, it just makes you wonder if there are any decent people out there with respect for the law."

Marcy rose to tuck an arm to his waist. "You know there are, Steven," she said quietly, "including each of us here. It's your birthday—try to forget the job and have some fun."

"Mother's right." A slow grin curled on Faith's lips. "The love of my life has been a tad cocky since winning at horseshoes today, so maybe you can vent and have fun at the same time."

Steven's face eased into a welcomed grin. "Collin? Cocky? Well, we can't have that, can we?" He shot his pregnant sister Lizzie a crooked smile. "What, is Brady and everybody else playing with their hands tied behind their backs?"

Lizzie's near-violet eyes sparkled as she stitched a shirt, a neat little mound protruding beneath her lavender maternity shift. "Nope, but Brady swears Collin has some strange magnetic quality since horseshoes seems to be the only game he can win."

"Luke thinks so too," Katie said, lips in a swerve. "He goes nuts when Collin beats him."

"Magnetic quality, huh?" Snapping a piece of thread with her teeth, Charity slid Faith a look of envy. "I'm sure Faith can attest to that. Lately she and Collin seem joined at the hip."

A pretty blush colored Faith's cheeks as she returned to her seat, green eyes twinkling. "What can I say? Collin's always more affectionate when he's hankering for a boy."

Charity's lips crooked up. "Oh, honey, I can cure him of

that. One week with Henry is all it would take." She shook her head. "Fathering three girls has deluded the man's mind."

Marcy chuckled. "Goodness, Charity, having daughters is no guarantee of easy, compliant children. You and Katie are certainly proof of that."

"Mother!" Katie stared, mouth parted in an incredulous smile.

"Face it, Katie Rose, Mother's right and you know it." Charity exhaled loudly. "You and I were the terrors while the rest of them were all little angels." A faint shiver traveled her body. "Only heaven knows the payback coming our way. Why, you and I could both have another Henry or worse yet . . ." Her blue eyes twinkled. "A bullhead like his father."

"Bite your tongue," Katie said. "I already have Luke McGee, remember? Surely butting heads with that man is payback enough."

Steven shook his head, a tease edging his lips. "I don't think so, Katie Rose. With all the grief you gave me growing up, and Mom and Pop too, I'd say your payback is just beginning."

"Ha!" Katie spiked a brow. "Don't think you'll get off scot-free, Agent O'Connor. I remember a few years of payback yourself before you put on that badge." Her tone took a turn toward smug. "I'm guessing there could be a Henry or two in your future as well."

Refilling his glass, Steven plucked oatmeal cookies from the cookie jar, tossing a grin over his shoulder. "Not real likely, sis," he said with a wink, "given it takes two to tango."

"Oh, that reminds me!" Charity sat straight up with a gleam of hope in her eyes. "Emma and I just hired a new salesgirl at the store that I think would be just perf—"

"Oh no you don't . . . ," Steven said with a hand in the air, cheeks bulging with cookie. He swallowed hard and swiped crumbs from his lips. "Since Emma coerced Sean to give up the title, I'm the confirmed bachelor in this family, so save your matchmaking for somebody else."

"Coerced?" His sister-in-law looked up. A soft strand of

chestnut bangs swooped over her face, unable to hide the sparkle in her gray eyes. "I'm afraid there's not much coercion when it comes to love, Steven O'Connor, as I suspect you'll soon find out."

"Ignore him, Emma." Charity rose and patted Steven's cheek. "He'll get his comeuppance just like Sean got his when he married you."

Emma's smile tipped up. "One always appreciates the support of their best friend."

Charity blinked. "Oh, you know what I mean, silly, in a good way." She turned back to pinch Steven's cheek. "Steven needs to learn marriage is bliss when a man has someone to look after him like you do for Sean." She dusted more crumbs off his shirt.

Steven grinned, cookies in hand. "I have Mother for that, not to mention a bossy sister."

"Leave Faith out of this and give me that." Charity snatched a cookie back with a lift of her chin. "One's enough—you'll spoil your dinner."

"Wanna bet?" Steven filched two more before making a beeline for the door.

"Henry! Drop the mud pie or I'll sic your mother on you." A gruff male voice floated in from the backyard as Charity's husband, Mitch, corrected their son, edging Steven's smile into a grin. Pushing the screen door wide, he bit into his cookie with a nod at the backyard. "If I were you, I'd save my energy for more important things, sis." He gave his sister a wink before heading out. "'Cause something tells me you're gonna need it."

"Steven may be right, darling." Marcy laughed, squeezing Charity's shoulder on her way to make icing for the cake. "Best to focus on the things over which you have control."

"Oh, pooh," Charity said, "why on earth are Irish men so bloomin' stubborn?" She plopped back in her chair, her brother's bachelorhood obviously spoiling her good mood.

"Oh, I don't know," Faith said, voice laced with tease. "Self-preservation?"

Charity grunted. "I'd say it's the other way around." She picked up her sewing, gouging the needle into a pair of men's slacks with a little too much force. "Is it so wrong to want to see my brother happy? He's twenty-five, for pity's sake."

"No, darling, it's not," Marcy said over her shoulder, pulling butter from the icebox. "But take a deep breath. Your brother has plenty of time to settle down." She noted Lizzie's damp face and retrieved the cold tea as well. "Lizzie, how 'bout a cool drink?"

"Oh, that sounds heavenly, Mother, thank you." Lizzie fanned herself with a magazine, the blush of pregnancy heating her cheeks. "Remind me not to be pregnant in the summer."

"Oh, I don't think it's so bad, Lizzie," Faith said with a secret smile.

Marcy turned at the counter, pitcher in hand. "My memory isn't all it should be, Faith, I know, but I don't recall you being pregnant through a summer, were you?"

"Nope." She focused on a stitch, avoiding everyone's eyes, her smile still in place.

Ever the analytical law student, Katie leaned in, eyes narrowing. "Then how exactly would you know if you've never been through it?" she asked. One blonde brow jagged high while the seeds of a smile sprouted on her face. "Unless, of course," she said with all the drama of a skilled prosecutor, "there's something you haven't told us?"

Marcy whirled to face Faith, almost spilling the glass of tea in her hand. "Sweet chorus of angels," she said in a rush, "you're not pregnant, are you?"

Faith squinted to thread her needle, the tip of her tongue tucked at the edge of her mouth before her gaze finally rose. "Well, let's put it this way, Mother. That persistent husband of mine, whose athletic abilities have been openly maligned today?" She tilted her head, mischief in her smile. "Has finally hit the ball out of the park."

"Oh, Faith!" Marcy set the glass down to give her daughter a squeeze. "I am so thrilled!"

Charity chuckled. "Uh-oh . . . you just may get a sweet, little Henry of your own, sis, so congratulations." Her smile slanted. "I think."

"How far along are you?" Emma asked, her excitement mirroring Marcy's.

"Ten weeks," Faith said, caressing her stomach. "But I've been so queasy in the mornings, I have to force myself to eat, which is the exact opposite of the girls, so I'm hoping I can give Collin his boy at long last."

"Oh my goodness," Lizzie said, her face aglow from more than the heat. "Five years of trying for a boy, and this could be it! I bet you had to peel Collin off the ceiling."

Faith's smile faded with a nibble of her lip. "Well, I haven't exactly told him yet . . ."

"Good heavens, Faith," Marcy said, "the man has lived for this moment. Why not?"

"Well . . ." Faith hesitated, inhaling sharply through a clenched smile. "Mostly because we've had so many false alarms I didn't want to risk crushing him again." She blew out a weary breath, smile tentative. "So this time, I decided to make good and sure."

"Why don't you just go to the doctor?" Katie said in a matter-of-fact tone. "There's a new blood test where they inject your urine into a rabbit, and if it dies, bingo—you're pregnant."

"No!" Marcy whispered, her stomach queasy at the mere thought. "The rabbit dies?"

"Goodness," Charity said, "and I thought homework with Henry was a sacrifice."

Katie grinned. "Yes, Mother, the rabbit dies, but it's for a good cause, I promise."

"Actually, Katie, as tempting as that may be . . ." Faith paused, casting a nervous look around the table while a touch of guilt threaded her tone. "I actually *do* have another reason for my silence right now. Remember how I had to beg Collin to let me teach the catechism class for Sister Bernice? Well, before he finally agreed, I prayed, pleaded, and plotted, using everything I could to get the man to say yes, but nothing worked."

Charity sat straight up. "Nothing? Tears, tantrums, a new negligee? *Nothing?*"

"Nothing." Faith's smile went flat. "Claims his children would suffer if their mother was, and I quote, 'out flitting one night a week.'"

Charity grunted in the grand fashion of her husband. "His children, my bucket. He's the one who would suffer because you wouldn't be under his thumb one measly evening a week."

"So I decided to fight fire with fire." Faith hiked her chin. "I've been praying nonstop about it for the last year." A hint of a smile tugged at her lips. "And it worked."

Charity leaned in, her interest obviously piqued. "You mean the mule actually said yes? Spoke it out loud just like that donkey in the Bible?"

Faith grinned. "Uh-huh." Her smile wilted. "But now you understand why I want to wait to tell him about the baby, at least until I start teaching, which is in two weeks." She drew in a full breath, releasing it again in a wavering sigh. "If Collin knew I was pregnant right now, I just know he'd refuse to let me teach, and honestly, you guys, I think I would just die if I couldn't do this." She glanced around the table with a nip of her smile. "Do you think I'm awful?"

Charity frowned. "Yes, I do—awfully brilliant."

"Me too," Katie said with a gleam in her eye.

Marcy shook her head, a smile in place. "You girls . . ."

"Anyway," Faith said, "I just couldn't *not* tell you guys, so mum's the word, okay?"

Crack! The screen door slammed to the wall, vibrating Marcy's kitchen. Her foster daughter Gabe skidded to a stop in front of Charity, freckled face flushed and a glass of lemonade in her hands. Small for her age, the O'Connors' resident tomboy could pass for eight instead of almost eleven, rich brown curls trailing overalls bearing telltale signs of mud pies gone awry. "Hey, Charity, Henry spit in my drink. Will you punish him, please? Mitch says you're good at that."

"Mmm . . . not as good as Henry." Charity took Gabe's glass and peered in with a wrinkle of her nose. Rising, she placed the defiled glass on the table and calmly poured another, handing it to Gabe with a quirk of her lips. "Here you go, honey. In the meantime, tell Henry we do not spit in our drinks. If he does it again, he'll be 'spit'-shining dirty dinner dishes for a month instead of the week he now has for drooling in yours."

"Yes, ma'am!" Gabe stole Marcy's heart with a pixie grin before flying out the door.

Charity glanced at Marcy with a nod in Gabe's direction. "You haven't mentioned adoption lately, Mother—are we any closer with Gabe?" She resumed her sewing with a twist of a smile. "Because frankly, with Henry, I think we could use her in the family."

Just the mention of adoption caused Marcy's stomach to churn, and her tongue made a quick pass over her lips. She peered out the screen door at her husband playing horseshoes with his sons and sons-in-law and took a quick sip of her tea, mouth suddenly parched.

Faith touched her arm. "You still haven't asked him, have you?"

Marcy shook her head, the tea settling in her stomach like sludge.

"Why not?" Lizzie asked, her concern mirroring Faith's. "We all love Gabe like a sister and we want her in this family as much as you do. Why put it off?"

A chill shivered through Marcy, and she absently buffed her arms. "I suppose I'm afraid," she whispered. "Afraid he'll say no."

"Father loves you and he loves Gabe," Faith said softly. "He'll do what's right—he always does—and it's right to adopt Gabe." She squeezed Marcy's hand. "You need to ask him."

Marcy drew in a deep breath, taking solace from her daughter's words. "I know you're right, and I did try to bring it up last year as you know, but he was more than resistant to the idea, so I've been biding my time." She forced a smile. "But as we all know, Gabe's not the easiest of children to raise, as your father has pointed out on many an occasion, so I keep waiting for the right time to broach it again." Her lip cocked in a rare show of sarcasm. "Like when the child has actually behaved for a full twenty-four-hour period, which, unfortunately, is about as rare as Henry."

Charity sighed and commiserated with a smile. "We definitely have our work cut out for us with those two, don't we, Mother? And I'm twenty years younger than you—I don't know how you do it. Although heaven knows, you don't look it. I laughed when Bruce McKenzie mistook me for you last week. Sweet saints, I hope and pray I look like you when I'm your age."

"Goodness, Charity, Bruce McKenzie is blind as a bat and everyone knows it." Marcy offered a dry smile, heart going out to the widower neighbor who always darted over to talk whenever Marcy wandered out front. "The poor man is just lonely."

"Lonely, yes, but also taken with you, Mother," Faith said, admiration brimming in her tone. "Which just proves Charity's point. Why, in Sean and Emma's wedding pictures, you could pass for our sister instead of our mother. Personally, I think the man is a little smitten."

"Who's smitten?" The screen door squealed open, ushering in the love of Marcy's life. Patrick winked at his daughters. "Besides me, that is. And more importantly," he said with a mock scowl, "will I get dinner before him?"

Marcy glanced up, a smile creasing her lips at the sight of her husband. Editor for the *Boston Herald*, Patrick's usually meticulous shirt was now void of a tie and open at the collar, revealing a peek of dark and silver hair on a chest just starting to tan. Sleeves rolled halfway up indicated muscled arms that could have easily belonged to a man younger than fifty-four, evidence of an exercise program ordered by his doctor after a heart-attack scare almost three years ago. Despite wisps of silver at his temples and threaded through curly dark hair, Patrick O'Connor still fluttered her pulse. Possibly more so now, with their children grown and almost gone. After thirty-six years of marriage, Marcy hadn't believed she could love Patrick any more than she did, but every day their bond grew deeper and stronger, a gift from God that never failed to bring awe to her soul. Or a swirl to her stomach, apparently, given the warmth braising her cheeks now that her "change of life" had changed his—a man able to make love to his wife without the worry of more children. Her chest expanded with a sigh that withered on her lips. Except, that is, for one freckled sprite of an orphan who had yet to steal his heart.

Casting a glance at the clock on the wall, Marcy silently beseeched the Lord on Gabe's behalf before imparting a patient smile. "Patrick O'Connor, you know we never eat before five. I have cakes to ice and a salad to finish, so I suggest you focus on horseshoes rather than dinner."

His low chuckle caught her by surprise when he slipped sturdy arms to her waist and nuzzled her neck. "If you don't mind, darlin', I'd rather focus on something else," he whispered.

"Patrick, stop . . . ," she said softly, face on fire. She squirmed from his hold while her daughters chatted away, apparently oblivious to their overaffectionate father.

"What?" he asked, gray eyes wide in mock innocence. He snatched several oatmeal cookies before giving her a shuttered smile. "I was talking about the cookies, Marceline, what did you think I meant?"

More heat flooded as she slapped him away. "Oh, go toss horseshoes. We'll be eating at five and not a moment before." She glanced at his cookies. "That is, *if* you're still hungry."

He strolled to the door. "I wouldn't worry about that, darlin'," he said with a wink. "I'm the only one who's beat Collin at horseshoes so far, and winning always whets my appetite."

The screen door rattled closed and Faith rose from the table, chuckling as she washed her hands. "Collin losing doesn't bode well for me," she said, reaching for a knife from the drawer, "but it sure has put Father in a good mood. Maybe tonight's the night to broach the subject of adoption. He and Gabe are getting along better these days, aren't they?"

"Not that I can see," Charity said, staring out the window. "Father just yelled at Gabe for putting a mud pie down Henry's back." She heaved a weighty sigh. "Fair payback, I suppose, for the time he put worms down his sister's, but I'll have a terror of a time cleaning that shirt."

"Oh dear, no . . ." Marcy plopped in her chair and patted her damp brow with her apron. "For the life of me, I don't know why Gabe persists in bullying little boys and aggravating your father. When she's alone with me, she's a perfect angel and nearly as sweet as the other girls, but with him or Henry or the boys at school?" A shiver coursed the back of her neck. "She's like a different child."

She sighed, a tender smile chasing the heaviness from her soul. "Do you know what she did just last week?" Marcy blinked to ward off a prick of tears. "When Luke first brought her to stay, she begged to visit her little friends at the Boston Society for the Care of Girls, so now it's a monthly routine. Well, last week, she insisted on making cookies all by herself, frosting each one with the girls' initials." Moisture welled, despite Marcy's best efforts. "Whenever we visit, she's like a champion for those poor little things for goodness' sake— encouraging them, loving on them, defending them from other girls who bully. I tell you, the child virtually glows, and of course they all but worship her."

Katie handed her a Kleenex from her purse, and Marcy gave her a wobbly smile. "All except your father, of course, who says she acts more like a street hellion than part of this family." She blew her nose. "But losing her parents like she did, I suppose some of her behavior is understandable. Even so, I'd give anything to know why she acts the way that she does."

Katie leaned forward, the sheen in her eyes matching that of her mother's. "Because that's how she feels inside," she whispered.

Marcy glanced up, lips parted in surprise. "What? How do you know?"

Sucking in a deep breath, Katie scanned the faces around the table. Her gaze returned to her mother and she paused. "Because Luke told me what happened before her parents died."

The air seized in Marcy's lungs. "Good heavens, Katie," she whispered, "what could possibly be worse than the death of one's parents?"

Katie clutched her mother's hands and leaned close, her eyes awash with tears. "Abandonment," she said quietly, the very word sodden with grief. "Luke made me promise not to say, Mother, but it's breaking my heart because you need to know." She engaged the familiar jut of her jaw. "*No*, you have a *right* to know the heartbreak that little girl carries."

"Oh, please, no . . ." Marcy's eyes fluttered closed, no power over the wetness welling beneath her lids. Deep down inside she'd known God had called her to rescue that child, to nurture her, to bring the balm of love to an orphan's heart and the wounds that she bore through the loss of family. To restore what the locust had eaten with hope and healing, laughter and joy. *And love.* Marcy pressed a quivering palm to her lips to silence a heave. *Oh, Lord, so very much love!*

Katie's voice continued, soothing and low. "Luke didn't know either, Mother, not until last month when he ran into the social worker in charge of Gabe's case. Somehow Gabe's files were misfiled or lost, so he never knew Gabe's parents abandoned her at the age of five." Releasing Marcy's hands,

Katie eased back in her chair. Her gaze flicked to the screen door and back, as if to make sure Gabe was nowhere in sight, then met those of her mother and sisters. "Luke was afraid it'd be too painful to hear, now that Gabe is one of our own." She heaved a weighty sigh. "And frankly, he was worried about Father," Katie said quietly. "Luke knows Gabe's been a burden to him and he's afraid if Father knew the emotional trauma of her past . . ." Katie paused, her voice fading to low. "It'll be reason enough to think she could never change . . ." A muscle hitched in her throat. "And maybe reason to send her away."

"For the love of decency, how can parents abandon a child?" Marcy felt faint.

Katie pierced her with a pained look in her eyes. "I don't know, Mother, but they did." Her tone hardened. "Apparently they were alcoholics and raising their own child was too much trouble. Once, they apparently ditched her at the city dump like so much trash, leaving her to fend for herself, but a neighbor found out and reported them." Cheeks glazed with tears, Katie continued. "A year after Gabe went to live at the BSCG, they died in a fire, and never once did they try to see her or get her back before that." Dabbing her face with a tissue, Katie shuddered, her eyes as glazed as Marcy's mind. "Remember how Gabe never cried the first two years she was here, even when she cut her knee and needed stitches?"

Marcy nodded slowly, fear slithering in her stomach.

"The social worker told Luke that Gabe's father was a nervous drunk who didn't like a baby to cry, so he beat Gabe, which is why Luke thinks she's so hostile to males today."

Marcy could only stare while tears coursed her cheeks, her skin and her blood ice cold.

"Not only that, but the social worker said Gabe was nothing but skin and bones and bruises when the police found her, which could be why her growth is so stunted today."

Marcy's eyes twitched closed and with a broken sob, she

put her head in her hands, her body quivering with heaves. Katie squeezed her in a tight hug while Faith and Lizzie hovered, stroking Marcy's head and shoulders with a daughter's loving touch. Grief swelled in her chest until it spilled from her eyes. If she'd had any guilt before for using her wiles in coaxing Patrick to consider adoption, it was all gone now, forever obliterated by abuse so heinous, Marcy had no choice but to forge ahead with her plan to adopt Gabe. To make a difference in the girl's life, to receive her into a family who could heal her wounds like God had called them to do . . .

And whoso shall receive one such little child in my name receiveth me . . .

"Mother, we need to pray." Faith glanced at the clock on the wall. "I think I hear the collective growl of stomachs outside," she whispered, her tone edged with the faintest glimmer of humor in an obvious attempt to help lighten the mood.

Katie squeezed her mother's hand with a sniff. "While we're at it, Luke and I could use some prayer too." She slid them a shaky smile, apparently following Faith's example to steer the conversation away from the abuse inflicted on Gabe.

"You?" Charity grinned, the shimmer of wetness in her own eyes belying the smile on her face. "Oh no, what have you done to that poor boy now, Katie Rose?"

True to her name, a hint of rose crept into Katie's cheeks. "Trust me, something the 'boy' is not going to like one iota." She peeked up, brows tented. "Jack offered to tutor me, and I . . . accepted."

"*Jack?*" Faith slid back into her seat, eyes wide. "As in your old fiancé Jack? Why on earth would you do that, Katie? Are you crazy?"

Marcy blinked and swiped at her face with the Kleenex. "Oh, Katie, no . . ."

Katie's chin jutted high, her pride obviously engaged. "Well, I can't ask Luke because he's always bogged down at the BCAS, especially now with an upcoming board meeting, so what am I supposed to do? Jack's a whiz at Harvard Law and I need help. So when I ran into him at the Harvard Library and he offered to tutor me, well, it was like an answer to prayer. I'm miserable at contract law and can't afford to fail, so what could I say?"

Charity gaped. "Uh, *no*, maybe? Instead you let your former fiancé—whom your husband despises, I might add—tutor you?" Charity stared at her sister as if she had just spit in *her* lemonade. "Saints almighty, even I wouldn't do something that stupid."

Emma bit her lip and gave her best friend an affectionate pat. "Oh, sure you would."

Charity's eyes narrowed before her lips curled into a one-sided smile. "Okay, maybe I would, but that doesn't change the fact that Luke will be furious."

Faith cast a nervous glance at the clock on the wall. "Which is why we need to pray about this pronto, Katie, along with Gabe's situation and Mother talking adoption with Father." She extended her hands, sobriety in her gaze despite the hint of a smile on her lips. "Before the plague of locusts descends from outside, demanding potpie."

"I agree." The knots in Marcy's stomach slowly unraveled as she released all the angst in her chest in one heavy exhale. Joining hands, she sucked in a deep swallow of air and gave each of her girls a most grateful look. "And speaking of pie," she whispered, elevating her chin to the point of resolve, "I'll tell you one thing right now. If Gabriella Dawn turns out to be half the daughter as all of you, Patrick O'Connor will be eating pie for a long time to come." The shaky semblance of a smile surfaced on her lips. "And I'm talking the 'humble' variety," she said with a tilt of her mouth, "not coconut cream."

Stomach queasy, Annie eased the window sash up and shot a nervous glance at her bed, blankets bunched under her covers in a lifeless lump. Out of sheer habit, she uttered a silent prayer that no one would discover she was gone, then doubted God would listen since she was defying her aunt to sneak out to "the devil's playground" for the second Friday in a row.

Her breathing suspended as she slipped one foot out the window and then the other, purse looped around her neck and Steven's coat tied securely to her waist while her high heels peeked from his pockets. The scent of Aunt Eleanor's climbing roses tickled her nose as she lodged her Keds into the trellis slots, careful to avoid the thorns hidden on the rambler's sturdy canes beneath glossy green leaves. She chewed at her lip. Heaven knows she didn't want to go against her aunt's wishes, but she had to return Steven's coat, right?

Ouch! She gasped at the prick of a hidden thorn, certain it was punishment for lying to herself as well as to Aunt Eleanor. Because the truth was, she *wanted* to see Steven O'Connor again, pure and simple, and the guilt over disobeying her aunt was clear indication her motives were neither "pure" *nor* "simple." The kiss she now suspected he'd given to scare her away from flirtatious ways had only deepened her resolve to catch his eye, invading her thoughts and dreams on a daily basis. Her Keds hit the ground with a soft thud, and immediately she sucked on her bleeding finger, a small price to see Steven O'Connor again.

"Do you think *he'll* be there?" Annie had asked days prior when Peggy invited her to join her sister's group the next weekend at the Pier.

Her friend's mischievous smile had bolstered her hope. "After the kiss you said he gave you?" She winked. "I'm betting he'll be looking for more than his coat!"

Heat broiled Annie's cheeks, but she couldn't deny, deep down, she hoped Peg was right. The night was warm, but Annie slipped Steven's jacket over her shoulders nonetheless, tiptoeing around the house before breaking into a breathless run to meet Peggy at the corner.

"That coat swallows you whole," Peggy called with a chuckle when Annie sprinted up. "Just like Steven will if you did what I told you." Folding her arms, she assessed Annie in the glow of the streetlamp overhead. "Let's see—eyeliner, shadow, lipstick." She lifted Steven's lapels to open his coat wide. "Mmm . . . very nice, especially that sweater we found at Filene's guaranteed to bug the eyes out of any man's head."

Skitters in her belly, Annie fingered the soft baby-blue pullover Peggy insisted she buy one size too small. Completely self-conscious, she tugged the V neckline up to hide the cleft of her breasts. "Are you sure it's not—" she drew in a shaky breath, rib cage as tight as her sweater—"you know, suggestive?"

Peggy's laughter fairly echoed down the busy street where Friday-night traffic milled, even at the late hour of ten o'clock. "Oh, it's suggestive, all right. It suggests loud and clear you aren't that small-town little girl Steven O'Connor thinks you are." She fluffed the bottom of Annie's strawberry-blonde hair with the palm of her hand. "And even though your aunt won't let you bob your hair, pin-curling it to get those soft, loose waves to your shoulders looks very Greta Garbo-ish in the movie *As You Desire Me*. Especially with your part on the side." She pulled a wave of Annie's hair over one eye. "There, perfect! Very 'come hither.'"

Annie peeked up at the half curtain of bangs, stomach in a tizzy. "Not too 'come hither,' I hope. Steven doesn't like fast girls."

Peggy hooked her arm through Annie's and led her down the street, a throaty giggle on her lips. "The trick with a man like Steven O'Connor," she said with an air of authority, "is to look 'fast' enough to catch his eye, but proper enough to keep him interested. Apparently he's an old-fashioned guy. Tends to fall for the vamps, but then dumps 'em if they're too fast, or at least that's what Joanie said happened with his old girlfriend."

Maggie? Fast? The notion stung every time Annie heard it, and she suspected and hoped it was Erica and Joanie's jealousy talking and not the truth. Even so, she was going to have to confide in Peggy that she was Maggie's sister. Tonight, before they met with the gang. A knot shifted in her throat. "Did you know her? Maggie, I mean?" she whispered.

"Naw," Peggy said, glancing both ways at the next intersection before dragging Annie across. "But Erica and Joanie did. They were all part of the same crowd from college."

"It could be a rumor, you know," Annie said quietly, determined to stick up for her sister. "Erica seems to dislike her a lot, so maybe she spread nasty things about her."

"Yeah, maybe. Joanie says Erica's always been crazy for Steven, so I wouldn't be surprised." She nodded toward the beach, where the welcoming sounds of music could be heard several blocks away. "Hear that? Joanie says it'll be crowded because Paul Whiteman is playing." Her excited chatter continued all the way to the Pier before she halted in front of the dock to pluck Annie's heels out of Steven's pockets. She handed them to her friend with a gleam in her eye. "Coat off and heels on, Annie Lou, you've got a man to catch."

Pulse pumping, Annie kicked off her Keds, which Peggy quickly stashed under the pier. She slipped into two-inch heels that boosted her confidence as well as her height, then reluctantly slid Steven's coat from her shoulders, immediately missing its warmth. Peggy chuckled at wolf whistles from a group of guys passing by, but Annie didn't dare look, certain her cheeks were aflame. With a roiling in her stomach that rivaled the churn of the bay, she folded Steven's jacket over her arm and blinked at Peggy, nerves as shaky as her two-inch heels on the cobblestones beneath her.

"So . . . how do I look?" she asked with a crack in her voice.

Peggy laughed and tugged Annie's sweater a smidge south before delivering a sassy wink. "Like a woman who's going to steal Steven O'Connor's heart—and every other guy's if they're not careful. Let's go."

"Uh, Peg?" Annie stalled, wobbling in place. "I have something I need to tell you."

"Yeah?" Peggy turned.

73

"Steven's old girlfriend?" A lump shifted in her throat as she absently pulled the sweater back up. "She's my sister."

Peggy blinked before her eyes flared wide. "Holy smoke, Annie, are you kidding?"

She shook her head, sneaking a peek at Peggy with tented brows. "So, I kind of don't want anyone to know my name is Kennedy just yet, you know? *Especially* Steven." A sigh withered on her lips. "But I'm not real sure how to do that because I don't want to lie."

Peggy looped her arm through Annie's with a wink. "Leave it to me, kiddo," she said with a grin. "But, wow, if this shocks me, just think what it's going to do to Steven."

"Yeah, I know." Annie gave her a weak smile. "But for now it's our secret, okay?"

"You bet," Peggy said with a chuckle. "Heaven knows I'm a sucker for surprises." She towed Annie down the ramp, and the moment they stepped in the ballroom, the magic was back, causing Annie's stomach to whirl as much as the couples on the floor. She followed behind Peggy, inching through a crowd that shimmered with excitement like the mirror ball overhead.

"You made it," Joanie said when they reached the table. "I thought you weren't coming."

"Sorry, Annie's aunt doesn't approve," Peggy explained, pulling chairs out for them both, "so she has to wait till she's asleep to sneak out."

"Well, I sure approve," Joanie said with a quick scan of Annie's outfit. She spotted Steven's coat draped over Annie's arm. "Hey, what's that?"

"Oh, Steven lent Annie his coat to keep warm while he walked her home last week," Peggy said effortlessly, sliding into a chair next to Erica while Annie followed suit.

"Gotta hand it to you, Peg, the kid looks like a new woman, don't you think, guys?" Joanie glanced over at Joe, Stan, and two other men who were staring so blatantly, more heat swarmed Annie's cheeks.

Joe winked, his ready smile putting her at ease. "You bet—

you look gorgeous, Annie. How 'bout a Dr Pepper? And, Peg, Coca-Cola?"

"Thanks, Joe, I'd love one," Annie said.

"Oooo, me too, Agent Walsh." Peggy gave him a playful bat of her eyes.

"Got it. Coca-Cola for Miss Pankow and Dr Pepper for Miss . . ." He grinned. "Say, Annie, I don't believe we know your last name."

"Annie hails from the Martins of Beacon Hill, don't you know," Peggy said smoothly, her snooty tease sidestepping the Kennedy name without a twitch of an eye. "She lives with her aunt, Eleanor Martin."

Annie gulped, uneasy with deception, but grateful she'd confided in Peggy. *So, not a lie exactly* . . . Her palms began to sweat. *More like an assumption that I'll correct soon enough.*

"Well, then, Miss Martin," Joe said with broad smile, "one addiction coming right up."

He disappeared and Joanie introduced the other two men as Allan and Mark, friends of Joe's. Annie smiled shyly, then nodded at Ashley and Erica.

"You certainly clean up well," Erica said with grudging respect. "Nice job, Peg."

"Thanks," Peggy said with pride, "but it wasn't hard with those cheekbones and body." She glanced around. "So . . . where's Steven?" she asked in an innocent tone.

Heat suffused Annie's cheeks at the mere mention of his name.

Erica's coffee-colored eyes narrowed to feline mode. "Out there," she said, her voice and gaze noticeably sharp, "with some bimbo."

Annie fingered Steven's coat, refusing to glance in the direction Erica had indicated.

"Come on, Erica, the man's been out of commission for a long time now," Allan said with a chuckle. "Let him have a little fun, will you?"

Her lips slanted into a tease as she took a slow sip of her drink. "Believe me, I'm trying."

Allan stood and extended his hand with a grin. "Care to make the man jealous?"

"Thought you'd never ask," she drawled, standing up to smooth a silk dress that hugged generous curves before it flared midcalf. Fingers linked, they disappeared into the crowd.

Stan ushered Ashley to the floor and Joanie left with somebody Annie didn't know. Mark smiled at Peggy. "You game, Peg?"

"Sure thing!" Peggy bounced up as Joe returned. "Hey, Joe, Annie needs a partner."

Joe set the drinks down. "Sure. What d'ya say, Annie? I promise to stay off your toes."

She laughed, thinking if she ever had a brother, he'd probably look like Joe with his freckles and country-boy good looks. "I seem to remember you being pretty light on your feet, Agent Walsh," she said, laying Steven's coat down on the seat of her chair.

On the floor, Joe took her in his arms with a whirl, his soft crooning to the lyrics making her smile. She released a heady sigh, finding it easy to relax in his hold. "Well, it seems you not only dance well, but you sing well too."

His chuckle rumbled deep in his chest. "I suppose I do have one or two attributes—dancing, singing . . ." He spun her lightly, a glimmer of tease in hazel eyes. "Loyalty to my best friend." He paused, studying her with a knowing squint and a ghost of a smile. "So . . . why don't you tell me, Miss Annie Martin," he said softly, "just what exactly did you do to my partner?"

She tripped and he laughed, sweeping her close with an iron grip, cheek pressed to his chest. "W-what do you mean?" she asked, thinking the fire in her face just might scorch his shirt.

"I mean," he said, voice as easy and fluid as his dancing, "seldom have I seen Steven so off his game, so preoccupied, so, well . . . downright surly . . . than after walking you home."

Her heart skipped a beat. "What makes you think it has anything to do with me?"

He laughed again, twirling her in a spin. "Oh, I don't know. Maybe the crowbar I needed to pry him away from work tonight when he thought you'd be here?"

"He said that?" The song ended and she blinked, unable to keep the hurt from her voice.

He tucked a finger to her chin with a gentle smile. "Not in so many words, but Steven's been my best friend since I was five, Annie. I know him better than I know myself. Paul Whiteman's one of his favorites, so when he hemmed and hawed about tonight, I had a feeling it had something to do with you and the funk he was in after walking you home."

Her chin inched up. "Yeah? Well, it's a free country, and I had to return his coat."

Another song began and Joe tugged her back. "Yeah, I know." In a graceful move to the music, he tucked his head against hers. "He asked me to pick it up from you tonight."

His words stabbed. "So why is he here, then?" she asked, her ire keeping up with her hurt.

She sensed his grin over her shoulder. "Because I did what any loyal friend would do when his best buddy is dying on the vine. I lied. Told him you and Peggy wouldn't be here."

"Well, he'll just have to get used to it, then, now won't he?" Her words came out clipped.

He chuckled. "Steven has trouble getting used to anything out of the norm, I'm afraid . . ." He paused, his next words stealing her wind. "Especially the idea of falling for a kid like you."

She jerked back, mouth so dry her voice was a croak. "W-what?"

A grin eased across his lips. "I think he likes you, Annie, a lot. Don't know what you did to the man when he walked you home, but the guy who came back here was in a royal snit. He's been a bear all week at work and then refuses to come see his favorite band until I tell him you won't be here." He pulled her into a spin that made her dizzy, both in her head and her heart, then gave her a slow wink. "So you figure it out, kid."

Her mind whirled along with her feet as he spun her on the floor, a heady giggle bubbling in her chest. A ball of jitters rolled in her throat as she stared. "But, how do we know for sure?"

The music ended, but Joe didn't release her. "We test our theory."

"How?" she asked, her breathing as ragged as her pulse.

He leaned close. "Well, he was in a great mood when we got here. How's he look now?"

Her gaze flitted over Joe's shoulder to where Steven sat with a scowl on his handsome face, and joy fizzed inside like a warm Dr Pepper. A giggle broke free as she nestled her head beneath Joe's. "Like he did with Brubaker last week."

"Thought so," Joe said, his laughter low as he swept the back of her sweater. "I can feel holes burning in the back of my head." He squeezed her shoulders and pulled away. "So, Annie Martin, you willing to smoke him out, get him to admit his true feelings?"

She couldn't help it. She launched into Joe's arms and gave him a ferocious hug. "Oh, Joe, yes, yes, a hundred times yes! I'm crazy for the guy, so I'll do anything." She hesitated, her smile fading as she squinted up with curious eyes. "But why are you doing this?" she whispered.

He gave her nose a gentle tap. "Because I love Steven like a brother, and I'd give my right arm to see him happy again." He cocked his head, his expression as reflective as hers. "And something inside tells me you'd be good for him, Annie Martin."

Blood flooded her cheeks. *Kennedy*, she thought with a shift of her throat, wondering if Joe would feel the same if he knew.

"Come on, kid." He looped an arm to her waist. "Let's go poke a stick at the grizzly."

4

I'm gonna kill him. Steven jerked his tie off, fumbling with the top two buttons of his white dress shirt as he seared his best friend with a look as deadly as the gun strapped beneath his vest. Grinding his jaw, he rolled the sleeves of his shirt with a vengeance. What the devil did Joe think he was doing? She was just a kid.

His anger surged. *Yeah, right.* Only the "kid" was nowhere in sight, obviously lost inside a body that spiked Steven's temperature more than the fury scorching his neck. He tried not to stare, but his gaze had a mind of its own, traveling from strawberry-blonde curls skimming her shoulders, down a turquoise sweater that molded to every curve. His eyes traced the slender lines of a pencil skirt leading to beautiful legs that tripled his pulse. Jaw tight, he scanned up to a face flushed with embarrassment, judging from fingers that nervously tugged at the V of her sweater. She avoided his gaze, and her lowered lids revealed the longest lashes he'd ever seen, making her appear demure and deadly at the same time. Older yet somehow still innocent, invoking a deep-seated urge to rip the tonsils from his best friend's throat.

"Look who's here, O'Connor," Joe said with an easy smile

and a hand to the kid's waist. "Your damsel in distress. Only tonight it's my turn to look out for her."

"Hi, Steven," she whispered, her breathless voice only irritating him further. She bent to retrieve his stolen jacket from her chair, hand splayed to her neckline in a futile attempt to cover a cleft in her breasts. She held his coat out with a repentant smile. "I forgot to give this back last week. Hope it wasn't an inconvenience."

An inconvenience? Yeah, but not the coat. He snatched it from her a little too abruptly, forcing his lips into a tight smile. "No problem," he said, fisting it in his hands. His face suddenly wrinkled as he paused to sniff the jacket. "What the devil did you do, sleep in it?"

"You should be so lucky," Peggy said with a grin.

A healthy shade of rose stained the kid's cheeks as she chewed on a pink lower lip. "Sorry," she muttered self-consciously. "It's called Tabu."

How appropriate. His lips twisted as he slung the coat over his chair. "Yeah, well, thanks. I'm sure I'll be a hit at the office."

"Watch your manners, O'Connor, will ya?" Joe sat and took a drink of his Coca-Cola, eyeing Steven over the rim. "What's eating you, anyway? You were in a great mood when we got here tonight. Now you look like you just picked a fight with Brubaker."

Close. He singed Joe with a look and a curt nod toward the veranda. "Got a minute?"

The band started and a lazy grin curled on Joe's lips. "Yeah, right after I dance with Annie again." He winked at the kid. "What d'ya say, beautiful?"

She shot up faster than a Roman candle at a Revere Beach Fourth of July. "You bet," she said with a high-voltage smile that would have melted Steven's wiring if fury hadn't fried it first. He glared when she closed her eyes to sway. " 'Three Little Words' is one of my favorite songs."

Steven's fist clenched along with his teeth. *I'll give you "three little words,"* he thought with a scowl. *Leave. Her. Alone.*

"Great." Joe strolled over to push the kid's chair in, then grabbed her hand with a grin over his shoulder. "Hold that thought, will you, O'Connor? We'll be right back."

Steven clamped Joe's arm. "How about I hold my temper instead, and we talk now?"

Joe grinned. "Sorry, Annie, best not to cross him when he gets like this. Rain check?"

"Sure," she said, and Steven bristled when she lifted on tiptoe to kiss Joe on the cheek. He prodded his partner toward the veranda with no little force.

Barely outside the door, Joe spun around and pushed back. "What the heck is wrong with you? You're acting like a moron."

Steven shoved him hard and several couples scattered away from the railing where sparks of moonlight glittered on the water, not unlike the anger in Joe's eyes. "Yeah, well, at least I'm not acting like Brubaker, trying to take advantage of a kid."

Joe propped arms low on his hips. "She's almost eighteen, Steven. Besides . . ." He hesitated before giving a sly wink. "One look will tell ya she's no kid, if you know what I mean."

Steven rammed him so fast, Joe never saw it coming. He staggered back and hit the ground, lunging up with eyes blazing. "I knew it! You have a thing for her, don't you?"

Joe's words slammed like a fist, and Steven felt the blow clear to his gut. He stood there heaving, hands clammy and mind numb that he'd just struck his best friend. He shook his head, as if to clear the fog in his brain. "Look, Joe, I'm sorry. I don't know what happened."

"Well, I do." Joe flexed his fingers, eyes as thin as his patience. "You like the kid, O'Connor, why don't you just admit it?" A smirk lined his lips just like in the fifth grade when Steven had a crush on Marella Smith. "I knew if I made a play for her, you'd tip your hand."

"What are you talking about?" Steven groused. "I just don't like to see anybody take advantage of a nice kid, that's all."

"Is it?" Joe exhaled loudly and folded his arms. "Okay, you're right, she is a nice kid . . . and smart and sweet and incredibly pretty, which is exactly why you need to take a second look."

Steven's mouth fell open. "What?"

"You heard me. I think she'd be good for you."

He grunted, fanning fingers through his hair. "Yeah, no doubt about that, but it's not me I'm worried about, Walsh, it's her."

Joe huffed out a sigh and cocked his head to study his best friend. "She's not Maggie, Steven," he said quietly, "she's a nice kid who I have a feeling will keep you in line."

"And if she doesn't?" Steven peered up, the shame of his past making him nauseous. "I can't go there again, Joe. Better to stick with my own kind of women like Erica, who I can have fun with, dance with, even kiss on occasion without anything more."

"You were in love with Maggie," Joe said quietly. "You can't blame yourself for that."

"Yeah, I can, because it was wrong no matter how you paint it. What I felt for Maggie may have started out as love, but lust cheapened it, made it something ugly and dirty." He jabbed a thumb to his chest. "I made it ugly and dirty, and I'm done. Innocent girls like Annie only bring out the worst in me . . ." He heaved a weighty sigh, slowly slipping his hands into his pockets. "Like Maggie used to be," he whispered.

"So you spend time with women like Erica, where marriage isn't even an option?"

"Yeah, because I'm not looking to get married." A bay-scented breeze cooled Steven's face, chilling his body despite the warmth of the night. Couldn't Joe see it? That he wasn't cut out for marriage? His relationship with Maggie had made that abundantly clear. A love-hate relationship that almost destroyed everything good in his life—his family, his faith, his own self-respect. Not just as a son or an O'Connor, but as a man. He thought he loved Maggie to the depth of his being, but the more they explored that love, the deeper his guilt. Guilt over loving her so much that he craved her love, and then guilt over hating her when she gave it. A guilt that became a two-edged sword, severing his ties with everything he held dear while disgust and desire warred for his soul. If that was love . . . marriage . . . then he wanted nothing to do with it.

"How long you gonna punish yourself for what happened with Maggie?" Joe said quietly.

Steven exhaled and pinched the bridge of his nose. "Till this awful feeling goes away whenever I think of her." Regret constricted his throat. "Of what we did."

"It was a lousy mistake, Steven . . . and Maggie miscarried before anyone ever knew."

Guilt lapped at his soul like the black, murky waters lapped against the dock, drowning his peace. "I *knew*, Joe," he whispered, "and that's all that matters." He shook his head. "You'd think after the grief and worry I put her through, I'd never risk it again. But I did, over and over." His laugh was harsh. "A man in love, but too weak to say no . . . until it almost killed my father."

Joe slapped him on the back. "Come on, Steven, lighten up. You haven't done anything the rest of us haven't. It just got a little messier with you and Maggie, that's all. And it's over now, part of your past. Don't make it part of your future too."

"Trust me, I have no intention of making it part of my future, not with the kid or anyone else."

Joe's lip curled as his tone took a turn toward dry. "Or mine, I hope. I hate it when you're in the dumps, O'Connor, because you drag me there too."

Steven smiled. "So, this is about you, then?"

"Absolutely. I just want you happy, because when you have fun, I have fun."

Steven's smile faded as his eyes locked with Joe's. "Yeah, but not with the kid, okay?"

Joe studied him through lidded eyes. "Can't protect her from every guy out there."

The corner of Steven's lip quirked up. "No, but at least I can protect her from me." He hooked Joe's shoulder in a show of affection. "And you, of course, buddy boy. Then maybe between the two of us, we can ward off the rest of the bums."

"Kind of like good-looking big brothers, huh?" Joe's grin eased into wicked. "I'm not worried about me, O'Connor, because I know I can do it, but you?" He shook his head. "When we came back to the table, I thought I was going to have to wipe the drool from your mouth."

Steven laughed, easing the tension in his shoulders. "Yeah? Well, I already told ya my college days are over. From now on it's the straight and narrow. I'll keep my chin dry and the kid safe, just like I'd do for my own baby sister."

"I don't know," Joe said, shaking his head. "She's got it bad for you, Steven. What the heck did you do to her on that walk home anyway?"

Steven ambled to the door, hoping to deflect his discomfort with a show of bravado. "Not a blasted thing, Walsh, just pure, unadulterated charm." He grinned. "Just like all the others."

"Uh-huh." Joe gave him a narrow look. "Problem is, she's not like all the others."

Steven held the door with a tight smile. "Yeah, and if I have my way, she never will be."

※

"Something's not right," Annie whispered to Peggy when Steven steered Erica onto the floor.

She peeked at Joe across the way. He hadn't made eye contact since he and Steven returned an hour ago, and she was pretty sure he'd switched camps. In fact, both men acted as if she wasn't even there, dancing and flirting with other women or cutting up with the other guys.

"What d'ya mean?" Peggy slipped into her seat. A welcome breeze, thick with the loamy scent of the mossy dock, drifted in from a window overlooking the bay, fluttering her curls.

Annie yanked the V of her neckline up for the umpteenth time, then slipped her heels off to rub her sore feet. "I mean an hour ago, Steven was fit to be tied and Joe intent on proving him jealous. Suddenly they're back, thick as thieves, and neither one has said boo to me."

Peggy slapped a limp strand of hair from her eyes. "Well, that's just plain rude. If those two are going to play games, then we can too."

"Uh, I think we already are," Annie said with a long face. She tugged her neckline up again and snatched a flyer from the table to fan her face, ready to melt. "And from where I'm sitting, it seems like Steven isn't interested, which means I debased myself for nothing."

A throaty laugh rolled from Peggy's lips as she took a sip of her pop. "Trust me, Annie Lou, the way Steven O'Connor ogled you, I doubt it was for nothing. I'm guessing from all his big-brother lectures last week, he thinks you're too young, which is why he's keeping his distance." She winked. "Otherwise, I'll bet there wouldn't be any distance or space at all."

Heat steamed Annie's cheeks. She shot a glance over her shoulder and spotted Steven through the crowd, Erica plastered against him so tight, they may as well have been one person. Her heart sank. "Maybe he's right, maybe I am too young. He's seven years older than me and used to women with a lot more experience. Maybe I don't have what it takes."

"Oh, you got what it takes, all right. We're just not using the right bait."

"What do you mean 'the right bait'?" she said, pulse tripping along with her stomach.

"I mean you rattled Steven's cage when he thought Joe was interested, right? Well, since Joe obviously bailed on you, we just have to rattle it again." Peggy pursed her lips, conspiracy bright in her eyes. "You know, with somebody Agent O'Connor can't abide?"

Annie blinked and then gasped. "Oh no you don't, not Brubaker!"

"Why not?" Peggy asked, a bit indignant. "You want to light a fire under Steven or not?"

Butterflies did the Lindy Hop in her stomach with more swoops and swirls than Steven and Erica in the band's last song. Annie closed her eyes, wishing she didn't have to resort to tricks and ploys. She peeked up. "Okay, but not Brubaker. How 'bout one of the others I danced with?"

Peggy hiked a dark russet brow. "Have you seen any smoke coming out of Agent O'Connor's ears tonight, other than when you danced with Joe?"

A depleted sigh huffed from Annie's lips. "No."

"Then you best leave the finagling to me," Peggy said with a wry smile. "Because you may be class valedictorian, but honestly, Annie, when it comes to romance, you're just—"

"I know, I know—book smart, street stupid." Annie's chin slumped in her hand just as Joe escorted his dance partner back to her table. Swiping a quick swig of his pop, he gave Annie a wink, then turned to laugh and chat with the guys. Annie sat straight up. "Wait, why don't I just come out and ask Joe?" She slapped herself in the head. "Goodness, I am street stupid."

"Sure . . . if you think you can get him to talk to you," Peggy said with a grunt.

"Well, maybe I'll just . . . just . . . I don't know, ask him to dance." An involuntary shiver rippled her sweater. "All I know is, Brubaker gives me the creeps."

Peggy checked her lipstick in her hand mirror, then glanced up. "Wait, there was this one guy Joanie mentioned once." The whites of her eyes expanded. "Hey, that's it! Dale Brannock! Joanie had a crush on him, but then all the girls did. He's a bigger sheik than Steven, if you can imagine, and the guys hate him." She wriggled her brows. "*Especially* Steven."

"Why?" Annie asked, curious.

"Who knows? Maybe it had something to do with Maggie, but the guy is as gorgeous as Valentino and just as dangerous, from what I hear, so I'll just ask Joanie—"

"No!" Annie nabbed her friend. "Joanie can't know I like Steven. She'll tell Erica."

"Don't get your garter in a glitch, Annie, I'll be discreet."

"Oh yeah, about as discreet as this shrunken sweater you forced me to wear." Annie's whisper was harsh, her patience shrinking along with the pullover.

Peggy hiked her chin. "Well, if you don't want my help . . ."

"I do, Peg," Annie pleaded, "I just don't want anyone else to know, okay? Please?"

"Mum's the word," Peggy said with an imaginary lock of her lips. She looked up when Joanie returned from a dance. "Hey, sis, did ya happen to notice if Dale Brannock is here tonight?"

Joanie slid into her chair, the edge of her lip zagging up. "Notice Dale? You kidding? Any girl who doesn't is either cold or dead. Yeah, why?"

"Oh, nothing, I was just telling Annie what a sheik he is, and she wanted to see him."

Joanie leaned in, a look of longing in brown eyes framed by russet brows. "Oh, honey, trust me. The man makes Valentino look downright homely." She sighed and nodded toward the bar. "Yeah, I saw him surrounded by his fan club over there." She scoped out the dance floor. "I see Erica's making headway with Steven. Good for her. That must be their sixth dance."

"And her last if we have any say," Peggy muttered in Annie's ear.

Joanie jumped back up, purse in hand. "Hey, Peg, if Erica's looking for me, tell her I went to powder my nose." Her brows did a dance. "*And* catch a glimpse of Dale Brannock."

The instant Joanie disappeared, Peggy tugged Annie up and pushed her toward Joe. "You're on, Annie Lou. Get the scoop from Joe while I hunt down Dale Brannock."

Annie spun around, eyes wide. "What? What are you going to do?"

"Never you mind. Your job is to get Joe on the dance floor, pronto, over there, close to Steven and Erica." With a sultry pat of her hair, Peg winked and darted off.

Legs as wobbly as her confidence, Annie headed for Joe, gaze welded to his back while he, Mark, and Allan chatted with the girls at the next table. The milk gravy she'd had for dinner lumped in her stomach when she tapped on his shoulder. "Joe?"

He looked back, eyes flaring for a brief moment before a guarded smile eased across his lips. "Annie, why aren't you dancing? All those guys wear you out?"

"No," she whispered, cheeks burning at the prospect of asking a man to dance. She swallowed her pride and peeked up beneath sooty lashes. "Actually, Joe, I was hoping . . . that is, I was wondering . . ." She gulped and sucked in more air. "Would you dance with me, please?"

He paused, gaze softening before he reached to give her hand a squeeze. "Sure, kid, come on." He led her to the floor, but when he stopped at the edge, she pulled him farther into the crowd until they were only feet away from where Steven and Erica danced cheek to cheek. Holding her at a respectable distance, Joe studied her through patient eyes, a sympathetic smile shadowing his lips. "So, what's on your mind, Annie?"

Her hands were sweating, but when she glanced up, the kindness in his face slowed her heart to a steady beat. She smiled. "Thanks for making this easy, Joe."

"Sure, kid." He pulled her close in a soft spin. "But I think it's only fair to tell you I was only half right about Steven—he does care about you, but not the way you hoped." He drew back, eyes connecting with hers. "He sees you as a little sister, Annie, and nothing more."

Heat broiled her cheeks and she jutted her chin. "That's not how he looks at me, Joe, and you and I both know it."

His weary sigh breezed against her face as he tucked her

close for another slow whirl. "He's a guy, Annie. We all look at pretty women that way. Besides, it doesn't matter how Steven looks at you, he has no intention of getting involved, period."

She jerked away. "But you were all for it before, you said I'd be good for him."

"And I still believe that, but it's Steven's decision, not mine." Joe exhaled and squeezed her hand. "He's my best friend, and I have to respect his wishes."

"He's an idiot," she said, fighting the sting of tears.

Joe nudged her chin up, eyes soft with concern. "Yes, occasionally he is, Annie, but he's also entitled to choose with whom he spends his time."

"As am I," she bit back, her chin taut against his finger.

With another weary sigh, he dropped his hand and swept it to her waist, drawing her close to the beat of the music as the song came to an end. "Yeah, you are, kiddo, but keep in mind, we're only looking out for your best interest."

"Well, don't, because I don't need—"

"Excuse me, but I don't believe we've met."

Startled, Annie looked up, vaguely aware that Joe's grip had tightened. A tall, attractive man with dark hair and blue eyes gave her a smile that fused the words to her tongue. His open pinstripe shirt revealed a hint of dark hair beneath a white undershirt, while rolled shirtsleeves displayed hard-sculpted arms on one of the most handsome men she'd ever seen.

"She's dancing with me, Brannock," Joe said none too kindly.

The man arched a brow with a confidence that stilled the breath in Annie's lungs. "I believe that's up to the lady," he said with an easy smile, his gaze all but buckling her knees.

"Yeah, it is," Joe said in a near snarl. "Tell him to scram, Annie, will ya?"

Oh, goodness, as if she could! Jaw distended, Annie stood bolted to the ballroom floor, as stiff as the pillars that circled the room. "Uh . . . uh . . ."

"The name is Dale Brannock," the man said in a husky

drawl. His gaze trailed down and up with a boyish smile. "Come on, Annie, tell this dope to take a powder and dance with me."

"Beat it, Brannock." Joe hooked Annie away, obviously hoping to steer her to the table.

"Wait!" Annie dug her heels in, suddenly aware the encounter was drawing attention from Steven and Erica a few couples away. The band started playing "Ain't Misbehavin'," and she placed her hand in Dale's with a shaky smile. "Love to," she breathed, then patted Joe's arm. "Thanks for the dance, Joe. I appreciate you setting me straight."

"Annie, wait . . ."

His voice trailed off as Dale swept her away, holding her so close, she felt like Erica.

"So . . . ," Dale said, assessing her through probing blue eyes, "I understand you need to make a certain guy jealous."

Annie looked up, his frank stare pinking her cheeks. "I . . . well, yes, and I can't thank you enough, Mr. Brannock, for doing us this favor and helping me out."

He grinned, and it was a toss-up as to which stumbled more . . . her heart or her feet. "Oh, I'm s-so s-sorry," she stuttered after her toes intruded on his.

His response was another smile that would have stolen her breath . . . had she been breathing. "Dale," he corrected. "So, who's the lucky guy, and please tell me it's not Walsh."

She laughed, his tone easing her nerves. "No, not Walsh. Worse, I'm afraid. His partner."

"O'Connor?" A low chuckle rumbled from Dale's chest. "Then you tagged the right guy. O'Connor and I have butted heads before, which explains the daggers in his eyes right now."

"Really?" Annie attempted to turn around, but Dale braced her neck, prodding her close.

"Don't give him the satisfaction, Annie. Let him stew." He leaned in to nuzzle her ear. "This should put a little heat under his collar," he whispered, the warmth of his mouth all but melting her makeup. "So what do you see in a lug like O'Connor, anyway?"

Annie closed her eyes, Dale's touch muddling her mind. "I honestly don't know," she said, wondering what it'd be like to have Steven dancing with her like this. She released a breathy sigh. "He kissed me once, so I guess he got under my skin."

"Is that all it takes?" he whispered, the sway of the music and the huskiness of his tone making her dizzy. "Because if so, what do you say we get under his?" With an easy smile, his gaze dropped to her lips before looking back up, a bold question burning in his eyes.

Annie swallowed hard, the pounding of her pulse louder than the music. She gave him a slow nod, and he eased in to gently graze his mouth over hers.

"Mind if I cut in?"

With a sharp jolt, Annie jerked in Dale's arms, blinking up at Steven as if he'd doused her with cold water. No, make that *ice* water. She pushed hair from her eyes. "What?"

The tic in his hard-chiseled face could have kept time with the music. "I *said*, do you mind if I cut in?"

"Go find your own girl, O'Connor, this one's mine," Dale said with a possessive hold.

Steven ignored him, eyes fused to Annie's. "Please? I need to talk to you."

She stared, heart thudding at the heat in his eyes.

He extended a hand, jaw hard and tone soft. "It's important," he whispered.

Her breathing shallowed as she tore her gaze from his to Dale's. "Sorry, do you mind?"

"Yeah, I do," he said, glaring at Steven. "But we can finish this later." Shooting Steven a snide look, he turned and strolled away, leaving Annie to face the wrath of Steven O'Connor.

And oh, what a wrath it was! Heat fairly shimmered from his look—the same heat that ignited her skin the moment his hand touched hers. With a solid grip that fixed her body firmly to his, Steven took control, his silence as smoldering as the look in his eyes. With a slight tremble, Annie's eyelids fluttered closed while a warm shiver licked through her at the possessive feel of his arms. Head against his chest, she heard his heartbeat, steady and strong, while the tease of Bay Rum wreaked havoc with her senses.

"Annie . . ." His voice lost some of its edge, as did his body, which transitioned from a wall of cold granite to warm muscle and flesh, strong and protective. "Why are you doing this?"

"Doing what?" she whispered, too comfortable to move.

He held her at arm's length, eyes trailing down and then up. Anger glinted in their dark-blue depths. "You know exactly what I'm talking about. The sweater, the makeup, the hair."

"What's wrong with my hair?" Her tone sparked. "Or my sweater, for that matter?"

He cocked a brow, gaze raking her before pinning her with a glare. "Nothing, kid, if you're looking to be a floozy." His smile was hard. "But then, maybe that's your plan."

Her breath caught on a gasp and she jerked free. "How dare you presume to tell me how I may dress or whom I may dance with. It's none of your business!"

She spun around to return to the table, but he wrenched her back, an arm of steel bolting her to his waist. "Why are you doing this?" he breathed, hovering so close she could almost feel the dark bristle of his jaw. "This isn't you, Annie, so tell me, please, why are you doing this?"

The plea in his tone siphoned all anger away. "You know why," she whispered, lowering her gaze. Her body began to quiver, both from her receding anger and the touch of his body.

"Annie . . ." He cupped her face, and her heart turned over at the tenderness in his eyes. "I like you a lot, kid, I do, but I'm afraid that's as far as it goes." The pad of his thumb caressed the side of her jaw, and she found herself leaning in to his touch. "You're a sweet kid, Annie, and sure, in a few years, I might be attracted to you that way . . ." His hand glided from her face down to the back of her neck, giving it a playful squeeze. "But . . ." He braced her arms, forcing her to look into eyes that were naked with honesty and a hint of something else. *Shame?* "Not now, kid. I can't get involved with you because you're too young, too innocent." He exhaled. "Remember those guys I warned you about, the ones who'll do or say anything to get as much as they can?"

She nodded.

"Well, I'm one of 'em, kid, and so is Joe for that matter and trust me, guys like Brubaker and Brannock make us look like amateurs. The truth is, I kissed you that time to try and scare some sense into you, to show you what could happen if you let your guard down around guys like us. So I want you to promise me, Annie, that you'll stop this . . . this . . . ," he waved a hand at her sweater, a lump shifting in his throat, "thing. Go home and wash your face and be the sweet kid I know that you are, one who doesn't give me or guys like Brubaker the time of day. And I wish you'd stay away from older girls like Joanie and Erica, and this place for that matter." Intensity darkened his eyes. "Because I promise you, if you do, Annie, you *will* thank me someday."

She fought the waver of her chin, heart aching to be the woman he not only protected but loved. "B-but I want you," she whispered, blinking to ward off tears that threatened to rise.

His lips lifted into a faint smile as he leaned in to press a soft kiss to her brow. "I know you do, kid, but I want you to be happy, and I can't give you that." He looped an errant strand of hair over her ear. "But I can be a big brother, at least when you're here, so promise you won't get involved with guys like me or Brannock or Brubaker, okay?"

She lowered her gaze, unwilling for him to see the hurt in her face. *No, it's not okay.*

"Annie?"

With another stroke of his thumb, her eyes opened to the painful realization that no matter how hard she tried to win Steven O'Connor's love, he had no intention of giving it.

Ducking to get her attention, he grazed the tip of her chin with his thumb. "I've told you before, kid, you're something special. Sweet and innocent, you know? With a gentle passion that almost seems pure. Promise you'll never change," he whispered.

She gave him a lifeless nod, and he pulled her near to plant a kiss in her hair. "Good girl." He hooked her close with an arm to her shoulder while he ushered her from the floor.

Good girl. Her eyelids wavered closed with a heave. *Just not good enough.* Before she could escape, a tear leaked out, compelling her to dart for the bathroom so he wouldn't see her cry.

Promise you'll never change.

Too late. She shoved the restroom door open, the truth as plain as the tears on her face.

She already had.

⌒

"Ouch!" Annie blinked, her eyes smarting at the sight of blood pooling where a rose thorn had pricked her finger. She glanced up at the trellis she needed to climb to sneak back in and fought the urge to break down and cry right there on Aunt Eleanor's lawn in the moonlight. Lip quivering, she promptly sucked on her finger, deciding this was the perfect ending to a horrendous evening spent weeping in the ladies' room of Ocean Pier.

"I've told you before, kid, you're something special."

No . . . she wasn't. Not really.

At least not to Steven O'Connor, nor to Aunt Eleanor, and certainly not to God. Maybe to Glory and even Maggie in a long-distance sort of way, but the person who'd made her feel more special than anyone alive was no longer around, no longer able to fill that void in her heart.

Oh, Daddy, I miss you so much. Against her will, a heave wracked in her chest and she put her head in her hands, a sharp stab of loneliness gouging deeper than any thorn.

"Did I ever tell you how you got your name?" he'd asked one rainy afternoon when she'd snuggled close in his sick-bed, water slithering the windowpane while tears slithered her cheeks.

"Yes," she whispered, clutching his hand tightly as if the cancer were about to steal him away. "But I like it when you do." She heard Glory's chatter from the kitchen. The smell of Mrs. Baxter's pot roast drifted into her father's darkened room, mingling with that of antiseptic and the grape juice their kind neighbor swore would fight her father's cancer.

A hoarse chuckle scratched through his dry lips and Annie instantly reached for his water, carefully tipping the glass to his lips. After a few sips he smiled, and she smiled back, though her heart wrenched at sunken eyes that even yet glowed with love. His fingers shook as he caressed her face. "I can't believe we almost lost you," he said softly, parched lips tilted equally in affection and a father's pride that never failed to warm her soul. *Except lately . . .* Her nose stung with the threat of tears and she quickly lay down, burrowing close while he gently stroked her back. Her eyelids fluttered closed as she clutched his old, striped pajamas, faded blue-and-white material that stirred thoughts of Christmas morning with cookies and cocoa and cuddling in his lap. *Oh, Daddy, please don't leave . . .*

"Well, I wanted to call you Grace after the aunt who taught me about faith in God," he continued, the strong medicinal scent of his Lifebuoy soap filling her senses with wonderful memories, "but your mama read about this woman named Susannah one day in that Catholic Bible of hers and flat-out insisted that was your name. Claimed Susannah was a beautiful and God-fearing woman with pious parents who raised her up to serve the Lord, just like we planned to do." He chuckled, the sound wispy and thin. " 'Fine,' I say, 'Susannah it is, but then her middle name will be Grace, by thunder, and that's the way it'll be.' " His weak laugh vibrated in her ear, and a ghost of a smile edged her lips. Dear, sweet Daddy.

Stern words forever toppled by a soft heart. "And a mighty good thing, too, 'cause if ever a child needed the grace of God when she came into this world, Gracie, it was you."

He shivered, and it traveled through her body like an electric current. She felt his hand tighten on her back, his touch protective as always when he told her the story of her birth. "They tell me you stopped breathing, something called apnea or some such thing, and as God is my witness, Gracie, I knew it. Knew something was wrong even though I was out there in that cold, sterile waiting room. Could feel it, sense it, like the very air had left my own lungs." His fingers shook as they skimmed into her hair, stroking her, loving her—something that came as natural to her father as breathing. A reverence seeped into his voice that thickened his words, causing a sense of awe to settle on the cozy, little room. " 'Pray . . . ,' the directive came," he said quietly, and the low cadence of his husky tone merged with the rhythm of the rain, creating the same hypnotic pull as when he preached from the pulpit. "And so help me, Annie, I collapsed to my knees then and there as if the very hand of God had pushed me, tears and prayers streaming, one faster than the other."

He'd shifted then, fingers cold as they tweaked the back of her neck. She lifted to smile into his eyes with a gaze as watery as his, and her heart cramped at his skeletal frame. "Don't ever forget, Gracie," he whispered, eyes burning in a pale face, "more than any young woman I know, you're God's girl, make no mistake. He breathed life back into you that day because he has a job for you to do, hearts to win for him. I know that as surely as I know that I love you."

He grazed her jaw with quivering fingers, their cool touch a chilling reminder of the sickness that ravaged his body. "I love all my girls, you know that, but it's no secret Maggie and I butted heads for years before she left, damaging the closeness I'd hoped to have. And Glory is a joy to my soul, make no mistake. But you, daughter, are appropriately named, a true touch of the grace of God in my life—strengthening me, encouraging me, sharing my deep faith in a God we both hold so dear. Never forget, Gracie, that as deep as my love is for you, he loves you far more, with a love everlasting . . . because you're the apple of his eye."

"No, Daddy," she hissed, her voice rising harsh to escape into the gloom of her aunt's backyard, "because one *protects* the apple of his eye." Lips compressed, she tackled the trellis once again, ignoring the sting of thorns. Slipping over the windowsill, she kicked off her Keds and tossed the heels tucked under her arm onto the floor. She stripped off her clothes and dropped them without regard, a heave shuddering her chest as she collapsed on her bed. With renewed weeping, she wished she could talk to Daddy just one more time. Hear that slow, husky drawl that always carried a smile. To be comforted by his sage advice and feel his love in the sweet crush of his embrace. The raw pain of missing him rose in sobs that echoed off the walls of her room, but she didn't care. Nothing mattered if she didn't have Daddy . . .

"Susannah?"

Annie jolted up at the sound of her aunt's knock. "Y-yes?"

"May I come in, please?" her aunt asked, voice hesitant and groggy with sleep.

Tears chilled on her cheeks as her gaze darted to the discarded clothing and shoes, grateful they were hidden from view. Blankets to her neck, she swallowed hard. "Y-yes."

The door squeaked open and Aunt Eleanor stepped in, golden hair streaming against a satin robe. "Why are you crying?" she said quietly, a faceless silhouette in the darkest of rooms.

Annie fought the heaves that rose in her throat. "I . . . I miss my f-father." The words unleashed a flood tide of grief so piercing, she crumpled to her pillow in a rending of sobs.

A whimper caught in her throat at her aunt's awkward pat. "I . . . don't know what to say, Susannah," she said softly, tone commiserating even if she could not. "But I know what to do."

She left and Annie sat up, eyes fixed on the door till her aunt returned. Satin robe swaying about her feet, she moved forward and silently placed a letter on Annie's pillow.

"What's this?" Annie whispered, eyes straining to read in the dark. Fingers shaking, she angled it to the moonlight, heart leaping at the graceful script she recognized all too well. *Gracie.*

"He wanted me to give it to you on your birthday," Aunt Eleanor said, "so you'd feel like he was here, but that's more than a month away, Susannah, and I think you may need it more now."

She blinked, the bold penmanship she'd seen on reams of handwritten sermons dissolving in a fresh wash of tears. Hand trembling, she stroked the letter to her cheek, craving his scent, longing for his touch, and suddenly realized her tears might dampen it. A gasp popped from her mouth as she jerked it away, staring at the ink that now swam in a blur. A vise crushed within. *No! My name stolen away . . . just like my daddy.*

Aunt Eleanor cleared her throat. "I'll leave you alone, Susannah," she said, her whisper hoarse and unsure. And without another word, she turned and left, the door clicking behind her.

Swiping her eyes, Annie lunged for the lamp on the nightstand, and light flooded the room. Her hands shook when she carefully broke the liturgical wax seal, heart thumping at the touch of a single onionskin sheet. Hungry for his scent, she put it to her nose. *Oh, Daddy . . .*

My dearest Gracie,

The day of your birth was one of the happiest days of my life, but only a dim foreshadow of the endless joy you would bring me as a daughter. God chose to call me home, yes, but know that

98

your mother and I celebrate this day with you from above, with a Savior as alive and real as our love for each other. He gave his all, daughter, a love surrendered so completely that we are transformed from the dark into his glorious light. The Light of the World, who in our absence will be a lamp unto your feet and a warmth to your soul, until that glorious day when we can hold you again on streets of gold. And so, as the Father surrendered his Son for us, so I surrender my daughters to him, knowing full well his hands are far more capable than my own to keep you and guide you and fill you with his joy.

My one request no matter the trials in your life, Gracie, is to hold fast to our God and never let go. For always remember where he is, we are, longing for the day we will see you again. Please love your sisters, your aunt, and serve God with all of your heart while we love and celebrate you from afar—one of the greatest gifts ever received from the hand of God.

Your loving father,
Jeremiah Kennedy

Caressing the parchment, Annie closed her eyes, face slick with new tears wrung from a prodigal heart. All at once, something warm flooded within her spirit like a rush of adrenaline, and repentance spilled from her lips like tears from her eyes. "Oh, Lord, forgive me, please . . ."

There is joy . . . over one sinner that repenteth.

Slipping to her knees, she began to weep for a long, long while, only these were tears of joy over a soul set free. She thought of Mama and Daddy, and for the first time, she sensed her anger was gone, replaced by a grief untainted by sin. "Lord, I've lost my parents," she sobbed.

I will never leave thee, nor forsake thee.

In a catch of her breath, a fountain of joy flooded within, flowing faster and harder than any tears from her eyes. "Oh,

God, I've missed you so, and I need you . . ." Somewhere far away, an owl hooted just as Aunt Eleanor's clock in the parlor chimed two, and Annie silently rose, her heart longing for God like she'd longed for her daddy. The same sense of a caress she'd felt earlier drifted over her like the gentle breeze that now ruffled the sheers at the window, and padding to the bureau, she unearthed her Bible buried deep in the lowest drawer.

Bible clasped to her chest, Annie carried the holy book to her bed and placed Daddy's letter on top. Smoothing the cool parchment over the worn leather cover, she closed her eyes, grazing the onionskin one more time before laying it aside. Fingers burning, she opened the Word of God, Daddy's legacy of love to her and his family.

Hold fast to our God and never let go.

A smile as soft as a kiss from heaven lifted the edge of her lips, and the tears that fell were as warm as the peace in her heart.

"Don't worry, Daddy," she whispered, "I won't."

5

"*T*his is stupid."

Marcy glanced up from the costume she was stitching for Abby to offer a sympathetic smile to Gabriella Dawn, the foster child she longed to call her own. Her heart squeezed. *If only my husband will comply.* Her tongue glided across her teeth as always when she was nervous, and her hand automatically smoothed the pocket of her belted housedress where a paper lay folded and tucked away. A paper to begin the adoption process so Gabe could be enrolled as an O'Connor for the school year in the fall. Acid churned in Marcy's stomach. *But only if signed tonight.*

The remnants of dusk filtered through the weathered screen door of her cheery kitchen where she, Charity, Lizzie, and Emma finished sewing the costumes for the cousins' dance recital. A hint of apples and cinnamon lingered in the air from the pie she'd made for supper, and lacy sheers fluttered with a spring breeze heavy with the scent of lilac blooms. Shrieks and giggles drifted in from the backyard where Lizzie's two children and Charity's twins played a game of King of the Hill that was obviously more important to Gabe than any "stupid" recital.

Lips in a pout, her foster tomboy seemed too petite for

ten going on eleven, skinny arms tightly crossed over a rose chiffon tutu that nearly matched the uncomfortable blush on her cheeks. Chestnut curls knotted from play spilled over tiny shoulders that appeared to carry the weight of the world rather than satin bows carefully pinned in place. The little girl's freckles bunched in a frown, tugging at Marcy's heart as she thought of the hundreds of orphans at the BSCG who might never have a family of their own. Marcy sighed. Not the least of which was the sprite before her who'd stolen her heart.

"And not just stupid," Gabe continued, jaw thrust as if to emphasize her point, "but it's not fair either." Deep brown eyes the exact shade of her hair narrowed as she glared out into the backyard. "Henry doesn't have to dance in any stupid recital."

Charity tugged on the pink netting gathered at Gabe's waist. "Pink's not my son's color," she said dryly. Her lips twisted. "Unless it's covered with dirt."

"Why did I have to be a girl?" Gabe moaned, head flung back and brows crimped in pain.

"To keep little boys like Henry in line," Charity said with a pin tucked in her mouth. She stepped back to eye Gabe's costume. "Heaven knows I can't do it all by myself."

"But you're such a pretty girl, Gabe," Emma said with a gentle smile, glancing up at her husband and Steven when they entered the room. "Sean, doesn't Gabe look pretty?"

Sean ambled over to the icebox to pour some milk for Steven and him, bestowing a quick kiss on Emma en route while his brother made a beeline for the pie. "Like a princess."

"I don't want to be a princess." Gabe scowled, delivering another nasty look to where Henry stood on the picnic table, wooden sword thrust high in his hand. "I wanna be king."

Marcy bit back a smile, her heart going out to the little ragamuffin as always when the tomboy in her surfaced and battled for control. She thought of the abuse Gabe had been through before finding refuge at the BSCG, and Marcy's smile faded with a quick sting of tears. Gabe's suspicion and belligerence toward males was certainly understandable with a monster of an alcoholic father, and for the hundredth time, the very thought clotted the air in Marcy's throat. Pushing the painful reality aside, she glanced over at Steven, who was cutting pie for Sean and himself. Worry for Gabe fresh in her mind, an edge crept into her tone. "Please leave some for your father, Steven," she warned, stomach tightening at the prospect of no pie for Patrick.

Steven squinted at the clock, which registered after eight. "Pop's running late, isn't he?"

"I suppose he and Mitch are busy, given the turmoil in Germany right now?" Emma asked, her voice as grave as the threat brewing in Europe.

"I'm afraid so," Marcy said in a somber tone that matched her daughter-in-law's. "With last year's downsizing of staff, several editors out sick, and one of Patrick's best editors retiring, it's a skeleton crew. Unfortunately, as editor and assistant editor, Patrick and Mitch bear the brunt." Marcy heaved a weary sigh. "Although Hitler owns a good part of the blame."

Charity grunted. "It's been awful, hasn't it, Mother, all these extra hours?" She adjusted the pins on Gabe's shoulder straps, cocking her head to assess. "Mitch is a grouch with an eight-hour day, much less working half the night. He may as well live at the *Herald* for all I see him. Which," she said with a droll smile, "might be an improvement, given the grump he's been." She squeezed Gabe's waist. "All right, Your Majesty, take it off and be careful of the—"

A blur of pink netting disappeared with a whoosh of the swinging door, prompting a slant of Charity's lips. "I'd be one happy woman if Henry moved that fast when I issued an order."

Steven chuckled as he retrieved two forks from the drawer. "I thought you were already a happy woman, sis. 'Marriage is bliss,' remember?"

Charity's almond-shaped eyes thinned considerably. "You might want to refrain from snide remarks, Steven, because you'll be eating those words someday, just like Sean. Which, I might add, would *also* make me a happy woman."

"Don't hold your breath," Steven said, lips tilted in a boyish smile. "I think your chances for happiness fare a little better with Henry hustling when you call."

Sean followed Steven to the door, milk glasses in hand and a crooked grin on his face. "What do you mean? Henry hustles," he said with a low chuckle, "just in the opposite direction."

"Very funny, you two." Charity aimed a finger at Sean. "And you best be careful or I'll pray Emma gives you a houseful of Henrys," she said with a smirk, pinking Emma's cheeks.

"Sounds good to me." Hand to the swinging door, Sean winked at his wife on his way to the parlor. "More than happy to do my part. The more Henrys and Hopes, the better."

Emma took a quick drink, her face near as burnished as the tea in her cup.

Charity's chuckle halted midflow as the door squeaked closed. Ducking her head, she peered into Emma's face. "Goodness, Emma, your face is redder than Henry's when I slobber him with kisses. Married a half year and you're still a blushing bride? Or are you just afraid I'll make good on my threat to pray for a houseful of Henrys?"

Cheeks aflame, Emma rose, avoiding Charity's gaze on her way to the stove. "Of course not," she said quickly, focusing on filling the kettle. "More tea, anyone?"

"Oh, me, me!" Charity jumped to her feet. "I'll help."

"Sounds wonderful, Emma, thank you." Marcy studied her daughter-in-law. "Are you . . . feeling all right, dear? You look flushed."

"I probably just scared the wits out of her, Mother," Charity said with a chuckle, bumping her hip against Emma's in an affectionate tease. She tugged cups and saucers from the cabinet. "Right, Mrs. O'Connor? Worried you'll end up with a houseful of Henrys?"

Emma stilled, her pause hanging thick in the air. A frail sob shattered the silence.

"Emma?" Cups and saucers clanked to the counter as Charity turned to grip her.

"No . . ." Emma's hand quivered to her mouth. "I'm not

104

worried about a houseful of Henrys," she whispered on a heave, "just worried I won't have any."

"What do you mean?" Urgency diminished all tease in Charity's tone.

Emma looked up, tragedy etched in her face. "I m-mean I've m-miscarried twice since Sean and I married."

Abby's tutu slipped from Marcy's fingers. "Oh, Emma, no . . ." She hurried to her daughter-in-law's side, arm to her waist. "Why didn't you tell us?"

"Because I was afraid," Emma said, eyes swimming with pain. "Afraid voicing it would make it all the more real, all the more true." Swiping at a tear, she took the handkerchief Marcy pressed in her hand, then sagged into Marcy's embrace while Charity and Lizzie hovered. "Afraid it's punishment for my past."

"That's ridiculous," Charity said, shoring Emma up on the other side. "You have nothing you need punishment for. And if you did, Rory Malloy was certainly punishment enough."

Marcy cupped Emma's face, heart swelling with love for this wounded soul God brought into their family. "A miscarriage doesn't mean you can't have children, Emma," she said softly. "Look at me."

Lizzie blinked while Charity gaped. "What?" Charity's jaw went slack.

"When, Mother?" Lizzie searched her mother's face, hand fanning her pregnant stomach.

Marcy pressed a palm to Charity's cheek and then to Lizzie's. "Once between Charity and you, Lizzie," she said quietly, "and then once again between you and Steven."

"I never knew," Lizzie whispered. "Why didn't you tell us?"

Marcy exhaled, the very memory depleting her strength. "Because there seemed no need, no reason to burden anyone else with the pain I carried in my heart, not even Patrick at first. So I kept it to myself." Her gaze returned to Emma, heart tugging at the sorrow in her eyes. "Much as I imagine Emma has with Sean. Am I correct?"

Emma nodded, eyes fixed on the floor. "I . . . couldn't bring myself to tell him, Marcy, nor anyone . . . until now. Sean is so hopeful for a family, so excited about having sons and daughters of his own, that I . . . I couldn't break his heart like that." Her gaze lifted to reveal eyes raw with regret. "If ever a man was meant to have children of his own, it's your son."

"A miscarriage, even two, is no indication you won't carry to term, Emma," Marcy said quietly, stroking her daughter-in-law's face.

Emma's chest quivered with a shuddering heave. "No, Marcy, but four miscarriages are."

"What?" She grasped Emma's arms, drawing her gaze. "What do you mean?"

The shiver of Emma's body sent a cold tremor clear up Marcy's arms. "I mean I miscarried twice before . . . when I was with Rory."

"But that was Rory's fault," Charity said, her voice as harsh as the meaning of Emma's words. "That lowlife kicked you and beat you till you lost those babies."

"Yes," Emma said, hand trembling across her abdomen, "but I miscarried two times after that, Charity, that Rory knew nothing about."

"No . . ." Lizzie's denial was little more than a gasp.

Eyes wide and wet, Charity swallowed her best friend in a fierce hug. "Oh, Emma, my heart grieves for you and those babies you lost."

Emotion swelled in Marcy's throat, blocking all air. *Lord, no, six babies!* Emma's pain seared Marcy's very soul. *An entire family.* Her eyes fluttered closed. *Like mine.*

"You have no idea how good it feels not to carry this alone anymore." Emma squeezed Charity, then blotted the tears on her face before giving Lizzie and Marcy a tremulous smile. "I'm going to be fine, you know. Sean and I have a wonderful marriage and we'll continue to try." Her chin rose. "But if we can't, God is faithful. He'll bring us a family of our own."

"What do you mean?" Charity asked. "Adoption?"

Hope glimmered in Emma's gray eyes like molten silver. "Yes, adoption," she breathed. She turned to Marcy, clutching her hand. "So, you see, Marcy, you and I have a common prayer that our husbands will allow us to open our homes and our hearts to the children that God sends us. Be they from our wombs . . . ," the softest of smiles curved Emma's mouth, "or from the BSCG."

"Oh, Emma . . ." Marcy swept her daughter-in-law into a fond embrace. "You are such a joy, and we will storm heaven for God to bless you and Sean with children of your own." She pulled away to study Emma's face. "But in the meantime, when do you plan to tell Sean? You know, about the miscarriages . . . and your thoughts of adoption?"

The teapot whistled, and Charity distributed cups and saucers to the table while Lizzie provided cream and sugar. Emma's smile faded somewhat. "Soon, I hope," she said, steeping the tea, "but it won't be easy." She peeked up, cheeks pink from more than the steam from the tea. "Your son is a very competitive man, given all the sports he plays and the teams he's coached."

"So?" Charity said, nose in a scrunch. "What's that got to do with anything?"

Emma poured the tea, eyes focused on the task at hand. "Well . . . it would seem a competition has been waged." She glanced up with a nervous grate of her lip. "Between Collin, Luke, and Sean . . . as to who will sire the next boy."

Charity gaped. "A competition? Oh, I'll just bet that was Collin's idea, wasn't it?" Her lips swerved into a dry smile. "Now, there's a man who deserves a Henry if ever there was."

Emma smiled. "I think it was. But we all know with three girls, the man's pined for a son for a very long time." She released a wispy sigh. "So, I know I need to tell Sean soon, but I just kept hoping against hope that it wouldn't be necessary."

"I know what you mean," Marcy said with a twist of her lips. "I keep hoping against hope that Gabe'll be good long enough for me to broach adoption to Patrick, but so far it hasn't happened." She released a weary sigh. "And now I'm out of time."

Emma paused, concern clouding her eyes. "Why do you say that, Marcy?"

Marcy's gaze flicked to the calendar on the pantry door. "Well, tomorrow's the deadline, you see, when the paperwork has to be in . . ."

Charity jolted in her chair, fumbling her teacup. "Sweet saints, Mother . . ." Her voice rose several octaves. "You mean for the adoption?"

Lizzie caught her breath, hand to her chest. "Oh, Mother, finally!" Her breathless tone matched the soft glow in her cheeks. "So you're going to ask him tonight?"

A lump shifted in Marcy's throat. "I'm afraid so, which is why the timing is not the best, what with your father so preoccupied lately and working one grueling day after another." She sipped her tea, vaguely aware her rib cage felt two sizes too small. "The papers need to be signed and submitted tomorrow so I can enroll Gabe for the new school year—" moisture pricked in her eyes as she chewed at her lip—"as Gabriella Dawn O'Connor." Blinking to ward off the tears, she straightened her shoulders with maternal resolve. "With all her problems at school, the child needs a fresh start, as an O'Connor, not an orphan simply fostered by a family. And I intend to see she gets it, Patrick's bullheaded notions or no."

Lizzie's hand lighted on Marcy's arm. "Please, Mother, don't worry. We've been praying about this for a long time now, and hopefully tonight is the night."

"I pray so," Marcy whispered. Her gaze trailed into a stare.

"I think it's wonderful what you're trying to do," Emma said quietly. "With all the little ones in orphanages today with no families of their own, sometimes I wonder if adoption isn't the most noble path to parenthood."

Thwack. Swish. Bang. The swinging kitchen door ricocheted off the kitchen wall, rattling its hinges when Gabe darted through. Not missing a beat, she hurled the pink tutu into Charity's lap before streaking into the backyard as if lit by a fuse. With a loud clang, the screen door slammed behind her, its jarring effect bringing a wry smile to Charity's lips. "If not the bravest."

Marcy's smile was tentative. "Yes, the child's a handful, no question, but I truly believe if Patrick would give her a chance, open his heart to her, give her his name, Gabe would straighten out and make the man proud." She sighed. "All I need is one good mood, be it a favorite pie, a win at chess, or one solitary day where Gabe stays out of trouble, and Gabriella Dawn would be on her way to becoming an O'Connor before the ink could dry."

"Sean will certainly do his part to allow a win at chess," Emma said, eyes twinkling.

"Allow?" Charity said with a full hike of a brow. "Emma, without Collin here, Sean is Mother's only hope for a soul-soothing win. Unless she can bribe Steven to throw a game."

"Which I have been known to do, I'm ashamed to say," Marcy said, gaze darting to the clock once again. "But, no, I'm afraid Sean and Collin are my salvation when it comes to softening your father up for an agreeable mood."

"Speaking of Collin," Lizzie said, "where is Faith tonight? I knew Katie had a law seminar, but I thought Faith'd be here, since Brady and Collin have inventory."

"Faith is meeting Sister Bernice tonight about the catechism class she hopes to—"

"Marceline!" Patrick's unnaturally icy tone boomed from the foyer, freezing Marcy's heart into an avalanche that slid from her chest into her stomach.

"Saint's preserve us," she rasped, all blood draining from her face. "The man's in a foul mood once in a blue moon, and tonight has to be it." Making the sign of the cross, she shot to her feet. "Charity, warm the rolls in the oven, and Lizzie, pour his tea with lots of ice, please."

"What can I do?" Emma whispered as Marcy hurried to the door.

"Marceline??!!"

Drawing a deep breath, Marcy mouthed one word over her shoulder. *"Pray!"*

Moments later the swinging door flew open with a crack to the wall. "I blame this on your coddling," Patrick shouted, his handsome face mottled with red beneath a shadow of beard that indicated a particularly long day. "Well, I've had enough."

"Patrick, please," Marcy begged, "the child will hear you . . ."

Shrugging her hand off, he stormed to the back door, jerking his tie loose and shedding his coat. He hurled both onto the counter and began rolling his sleeves, not even sparing Emma or his daughters a glance as he glared into the backyard. He slammed a hand to the screen door, wheeling it open. "Gabriella? In the house *now*!"

"Patrick, you're tired and hungry," Marcy reasoned, the plea in her tone as frail as his patience. "Please, can't this wait till after you eat?"

He turned, gray eyes glittering like black onyx. "No, Marceline, it can't. I've obviously waited too long as it is when a child under my care borders on expulsion from school." A nerve flickered in his temple. "I suspect a three months' absence of her beloved Dubble Bubble will be the only thing she'll understand."

"Patrick, no, please, her Dubble Bubble means everything to her. A week maybe, but not three months." Marcy worried her lip, stomach roiling.

"Y-yes, sir?" A greatly subdued Gabe stood at the screen door, eyes downcast and a sea of freckles dark against pale skin.

Face tight with tension, Patrick let the screen door slam with a loud bang that made the little girl wince. "I understand from Sister Mary Veronica that the youngest Kincaid boy has broken his jaw. You wouldn't happen to know anything about that, would you?"

Dark curls quivered on Gabe's shoulders as she shook her head, her short, jerky motion betraying her guilt.

110

"Well, suppose I enlighten you," Patrick said, the gray eyes mere slits of charcoal, "and tell you all about my visit with Sister Mary Veronica tonight—"

"She hates me," Gabe shouted with a sudden pool of tears, "and she lies."

"Something you have in common, apparently," Patrick said with a clamp of his lips. "Did you break Victor Kincaid's jaw?"

"No—"

"Don't lie to me, Gabe," Patrick said, latching on to her arm, "I want the truth!"

Marcy took a step forward, hand to her throat. "Patrick, please . . ."

"Did you?" he shouted, lifting her chin with a firm finger.

"No, honest—"

"Then-let-me-rephrase-that," he said, articulating each word while he leaned close, face flushed. "Did-you-swing-the-bat-that-broke-Victor-Kincaid's-jaw?"

Marcy gasped. "Gabe, no . . ."

"It was an accident," she whimpered, squirming away from his touch.

Patrick folded thick arms across his chest, lip curling in a dubious smile as hard as his tone. "Yes, I'm quite sure it was, just like the tar on Sister Mary Veronica's chair, the goldfish in the water fountain, and my personal favorite, a snake in the confessional."

"But he spit at me," she pleaded, "and I was just trying to scare him, I promise."

He loomed over her—judge, jury, and executioner of Marcy's one hope and dream—chest heaving with vindication. "Well, good job, Gabriella Dawn Smith," he said with a touch of drama, "you not only scared Victor Kincaid, his family, your classmates, *and* Sister Veronica, you scared the tar out of me. Obviously I'm an inept foster parent raising a hooligan better suited to a detention facility than a family. Consequently, I hope to put the fear of God into *you* with a detention that will convince you I mean business." Casting a steely look in Marcy's direction, Patrick fished his handkerchief from his pocket to swab at the sudden gleam of sweat on his face. "Marceline, you will confiscate Gabe's stash of Dubble Bubble immediately."

Gabe's eyes spanned wide. "B-but f-for how long?" she rasped, her little lip quivering along with Marcy's.

"Three months, young lady—no Dubble Bubble. And your stash?" He hiked a brow, his gaze as cold as the pit at the bottom of Marcy's stomach. "To be distributed—*when* he can chew—to Victor Kincaid."

"Nooooooooo . . ." Gabe's shrieks split the air as she bolted for the door.

But Patrick was ready for her, halting her dead in her tracks with a cinch of her overalls. "Oh no you don't," he said, dragging her to the table. "You will sit right here in this kitchen until your Dubble Bubble is safely hidden."

She tried to dart away, and Patrick looped strong arms to her waist, chest heaving as he lugged her back to the table. Flopping like that goldfish in the school fountain, she flailed and kicked until the toes of her Keds made contact with Patrick's shin.

A garbled groan escaped her husband's throat before he doubled over, allowing Gabe to shoot from his grasp. The little girl spun on her heels. "I hate you!" she screamed, her face near purple as Patrick's.

Marcy caught her breath, too stricken to move, vaguely aware of Steven and Sean's presence behind her. The younger cousins stood wide-eyed at the screen door until Emma ushered them away while Charity and Lizzie just stared, zombies rooted to the floor.

In a split-second reaction, Patrick lunged, and Gabe grunted at the door when he hooked her waist again, his breathing heavy from exertion. "Not as much as you will, young lady, when you can't have Dubble Bubble for a solid year. You're going to bed right now."

"Nooooooo!" Gabe bucked like a wildcat thrashing in his arms.

"Patrick, please," Marcy pleaded, heart racing as she hovered near with a wring of her hands. "Can't you just send her to her room after dinner for a few days? Along with no Dubble Bubble for three months? A year's so long, and you know how she loves it . . ."

Face somber, Steven pressed a palm to the swinging door to open it for his father while Sean stepped quietly aside, lips grim and gaze glued to the floor.

"Oh, she'll go to her room after dinner, all right, Marceline," Patrick huffed, his breathing ragged and rough. "For a solid two weeks."

The little girl twisted and dug her teeth into Patrick's hand, and with a loud howl, he let her slip from his arms.

She attempted to escape through the door, but Steven restrained her in a death-grip hold.

Jaw slack, Patrick held out his hand, panting hard as he stared at blood pooling beneath the skin of a perfectly shaped bite. There was blood in his eyes as well when his gaze slowly rose. He took a step forward, his voice no more than a choked breath. "You will pay for this, Gabriella Dawn, you mark my words. I will—" He stopped. The air seized in Marcy's throat when he winced, hand clutching his chest.

"Patrick?" She touched his arm, hysteria rising in her voice. "Patrick, what's wrong?" *Please, God, no, not again . . .*

He staggered back, his breathing shallow and rough.

"Pop!" In one violent surge of Marcy's pulse, Steven was at his father's side. Face ashen, he braced him while everyone else stood frozen in shock. "Sean, give me a hand . . ."

"You're pinching me," Gabe said, fidgeting when Charity clamped her arm like a vice.

"Hush, young lady, or I'll show you what a pinch is all about," Charity whispered.

Gabe's eyes widened, and her voice held a tremor. "Is he gonna die?"

"No, honey." Charity scooped her close, her soothing tone belying the strain in her face.

"Lizzie," Marcy shouted, "get his nitroglycerin pills! I have extras in the foyer bathroom. In the medicine chest—now, please!"

Lizzie shot from the room while Steven latched a firm hand to his father's waist. "Where to, Pop?" he said, the strong calm of his voice a stark contrast to the panic in his brother's face.

"To the parlor on the couch!" Marcy rushed to hold the door while Sean and Steven all but lifted Patrick from the room.

"No . . ." Patrick's voice was as limp as his body. "To . . . my bed."

"You're too weak to climb the stairs!" she shouted. "Take him to the parlor."

Seizing to a stop, Patrick raised sunken eyes, a hint of Irish burning hot in their depths. "As long . . . as I have a . . . breath, Marceline, I will . . . run my own life—is that clear?"

Marcy smothered a sob and nodded before taking an almost-empty medicine vial from Lizzie's palm. Hands shaking, she placed one of the pills under Patrick's tongue before she allowed Steven and Sean to assist him from the room and up the stairs. Her voice was hoarse when she glanced over her shoulder, tears streaming her face. "Charity, put Gabe to bed, please, while I tend to your father, and Lizzie, if you and Emma would be kind enough to put the food away, I'd be most grateful." A short, pitiful heave broke from her throat. "And pray," she whispered, her voice cracking along with her heart. "Please . . ." She turned away.

"Wait!" With a wrenching sob, Gabe rushed forward, eyes squeezed shut and skinny arms clutching Marcy's waist. "I'm so sorry, Mrs. O'Connor, will you forgive me? Please? And can you tell him I'm sorry, that I didn't mean—" A violent heave swallowed her words.

Marcy bent to embrace her, vision blurred and heart swelling with love for this child she loved like her own. "Oh, darling, of course I forgive you! And Mr. O'Connor will too, you'll see." She pried Gabe's arms away to cup her sodden face. "Now, you pray for that ol' grump of a man upstairs," she said. "All right?"

Gabe sniffed and nodded.

"Good girl," Marcy whispered with a kiss to her hair. "And I'll just bet if you're real good, Charity'll tell you a time or two when her father lost his temper with her, okay?" She glanced at her daughters. "Thank you, both," she said softly before hurrying to head up the stairs.

His eyes were closed when she entered their room, his once-strong body splayed on top of the covers in bare feet and rumpled clothes, quiet and still. Steven and Sean stood at either side, worry etched deep in their brows. *Oh, Lord, put angels around him,* Marcy silently prayed, *because we all love him so.* She moved to where Sean stood and slipped an arm to his waist. "You need to take Emma home," she whispered. "Steven will be here if I need him."

"I'm not going anywhere."

She pulled away to clutch his hand, her heart wrenching at the fear in his eyes. "Go," she whispered. "He just needs to rest and let the nitroglycerin take effect. This has happened before, Sean, after he was in the hospital, remember? Dr. Williamson said it might from time to time, although your father's been incident-free since then." Her heart skipped a beat when her gaze drifted to her husband, who lay deathly still, his breathing slow but steady. Drawing in a deep breath, she steeled her tone to convince herself as well as her son. "Please, take Emma home. She seems tired tonight, Sean, and Steven can handle anything I need."

"He's not leaving till I finish annihilating him in chess," Steven said, a hint of jest in his tone, and Marcy knew he was aware how badly Sean wanted to stay. "Come on, you can check on him before I send you home with your tail between your legs."

Sean glanced up, a shadow of a smile despite the pallor of his skin. "You're on. I have enough angst in my gut right now to bury you in your pride, tail and all." He squeezed Patrick's hand with a sudden sheen of tears. "Get some rest, Pop, and I'll take care of this upstart for you."

Patrick's eyelids edged up, heavy, as if roused from a deep sleep. A ghost of a smile flickered the corners of his mouth. "Well, then . . . I best get well . . . because that I'd like to see."

A grin split Sean's face despite the glaze of moisture in his eyes. "Yes, sir." He hooked Marcy in a hug before following Steven out. He turned, hand on the knob. "Want it closed?"

"Please." The tightness in her chest eased when she heard the gentle click of the lock. Kicking her shoes off, she crawled in beside her husband and shimmied over to him, resting her head on his chest while her arm looped his waist. She worked hard to allay his fears and hers with a light tone. "Are you trying to put the fear of God in me, Patrick O'Connor?" she whispered, a hint of his pipe tobacco soothing her senses with its maple and vanilla scent.

She could almost feel his smile. "No, darlin', just in a wayward child."

"Well, I'd say you accomplished that and then some. Gabe was downstairs sobbing like a baby." Marcy paused, the beat of his heart burning in her ears while a piece of paper burned in her pocket. "She wanted me to tell you she was sorry."

Her cheek rose and fell with the expanse of his chest in a weary sigh. "As am I, darlin', for losing my temper. I was wrong." He slowly slipped his arm around her shoulders, giving her a gentle pat. His words carried a touch of levity despite the fatigue in his voice. "About the temper, Marceline, not the discipline. The child needs a firmer hand than we've given her."

No, the child needs your name to know she truly belongs.

"Tonight was a scare for me, Marcy," he continued, words barely audible, but their message loud and clear, stirring her fears once again.

Oh, Lord, our youth has slipped away . . .

"Heart racing, pressure in my jaw, neck, and shoulders, and throat burning like the devil." His fingers calmly kneaded her arm, belying the turmoil waged against them tonight. "It was like I couldn't catch my breath, had no energy, nauseous. When Sister Mary Veronica told me what that girl did . . ." Marcy felt the thick shift of his throat as he swallowed, causing her to do the same. "I . . . felt defeated, betrayed, an old man bested by a child and a failure as a parent."

His last word spoken ignited a spark of hope, and she lifted her head. "But that's just it, Patrick, Gabe is not our child and we are *not* her parents. But if we were—" The dark shadows beneath his eyes halted her midsentence, tears pooling at the prospect of ever losing this man. She cupped his bristled jaw, a tremor invading her words. "Oh, Patrick, I'd be lost without you."

He drew her back, his hoarse chuckle feathering her hair. "Well, for the moment I'm still alive and kicking, Mrs. O'Connor, so don't bury me just yet."

What-ifs pummeled her mind and her eyes squeezed shut while she clutched him with all of her might. "God help me, Patrick, but I love you more than anything in this world."

" 'God help you' is right, Mrs. O'Connor, because if I had energy for anything other than sleep tonight, I'd be looking for proof." He shifted, attempting to remove his trousers. "Get my pajamas, will you, darlin', I'll be wanting to sleep."

She jumped up to retrieve his pajamas and helped put them on before tugging the covers back so he could slip under the sheet. He grunted as he tossed the top coverlet away, and that mere effort seemed to totally exhaust him. He dropped back on the pillow and closed his eyes. "Thank you, darlin'," he whispered.

"Can I do anything else, Patrick? Get you a glass of water, bring up the fan, anything?"

An almost imperceptible smile curved the edges of his mouth, although his eyes remained closed. "Stay with me awhile?" he whispered, voice fading to slumber. "I like having you near."

Her heart leapt in her chest as the pressure of tears stung in her nose. *Oh, Patrick . . .* Battling her grief, she climbed in beside him, her fear evident in the tight clutch of her hands.

"Marceline," he said quietly, "I don't want you to worry. I just forgot."

She paused, her breathing shallow. "What do you mean you forgot? Forgot what?"

"My pills," he muttered, his voice groggy. "Forgot to refill the prescription."

She shot up, eyes wide in the dark. "Your angina medicine? You haven't been taking it?" Her voice rose to a near shriek. "Sweet mother of Job, for how long?"

His eyelids lifted halfway, a drowsy apology in his gaze. "Two weeks," he whispered. "Meant to refill, but so busy at work . . ."

Her anger whooshed out as relief took over. *Oh, Lord, he's not getting worse! There was a reason for the attack.*

Patrick's gentle snore broke her reverie, peace settling as lightly as the thin sheet across his body. Lying with him awhile, she finally glanced at the clock on his nightstand, noting an hour had passed since the fateful confrontation with Gabe. She leaned to give him a gentle kiss. "I'll be back soon, my love," she whispered. Tiptoeing to the door, she expended all air when it closed behind her. A quick scan of the darkened hall meant Gabe was probably dreaming away and Marcy sighed, relief giving way to a heavy heart. Worry over Patrick's angina may have lightened, but not over his rift with Gabe.

The soft murmur of her sons and a single light in the parlor indicated Charity and Lizzie had most likely gone home, and Marcy braced the railing, head bowed. With a quivering release of air, she fingered the paper in her pocket, its feel cool to the touch. *Like Patrick's affections for Gabe.* The very thought slumped her shoulders, and she put a hand to her eyes. Without Patrick's signature, Gabe would not be enrolled as an O'Connor, and Marcy fought the sobs rising in her throat until one finally slipped through. Only . . . it didn't belong to her, she realized, and goose bumps prickled her flesh. Her gaze darted down the hall to Gabe's closed door, and the breath seized in her lungs as she strained hard to listen.

A whimper. A muffled sob. A heart breaking as thoroughly as hers. With a ragged gasp of air, Marcy flew down the hall and opened Gabe's door, stomach cramping at the tiny lump that quivered in the bed. "Oh, Gabe," she whispered, rushing to bundle the little girl in her arms. "Honey, everything's going to be okay . . ."

"N-no, it's n-not," she sobbed, her blotchy face slick with mucous and tears, painful confirmation she'd been weeping a long time. "H-he h-hates m-me."

Marcy's throat ached. "No, darling, he doesn't, I promise. He loves you. We all do!"

She shook her head violently, her frail chest quivering with every heave. "You d-do, but not h-him. H-he d-doesn't w-want m-me . . ."

Pain lanced Marcy's heart. "Of course he does," she soothed, resting her head against Gabe's, rubbing her back, kissing her hair. "He was just angry, darling, over what you did to the Kincaid boy." She pulled away to gently tuck a strand of hair over Gabe's delicate ear. "Why did you do that, Gabe?" she whispered, locking eyes with this daughter she so longed to claim.

Gabe sniffed and swiped at her eyes. "Because he spit at me and called me a street rat." Her whisper was harsh as she listed into a lifeless stare. "Said I'd always be a street rat nobody really wants. An orphan with no family of my own, no matter who I live with."

"That's not true," Marcy cried, gripping Gabe's shoulders. "You're part of our family, Gabe, and I couldn't love you more if you were my own flesh and blood."

The staunch little chin quivered as water brimmed in her eyes. "I love you too, Mrs. O'Connor," she whispered. The scent of Dubble Bubble rose in Marcy's nostrils as Gabe's tiny hand patted her cheek, eyes as lost and sad as if she still wandered the streets. "But I'm not family, ma'am. I ain't nothing more than a lucky foster kid you just happened to take in, and the truth is, sometimes it hurts so much that I . . . ," a nerve flickered in her cheek, "do things I shouldn't." Her skinny chest expanded as she lifted her chin, resolve burning deep in those waterlogged eyes. "But you have my word I'll try. Try real hard to be the foster kid you want me to be." Without warning, she lunged into Marcy's arms. "Because I love you, Mrs. O'Connor," she cried, "and if I ever had a mom, I'd want her to be just like you."

Oh, Gabe . . . Marcy's heart melted as she squeezed the little girl hard, her throat so thick with emotion, she could barely respond. "And I love *you*, darling," she whispered, planting a kiss on Gabe's little, matted head. "As a daughter I'd be so proud to have." She tugged a handkerchief from her pocket to wipe the tears from Gabe's face and then held it to her nose so she could blow. Tucking her into bed once again, she prayed with her, then pushed the curls from her brow to bestow a final kiss before leaving the room. "Sleep well, darling," she said softly, quietly closing the door. With a silent heave, she put her hands to her face, a horrendous pain wrenching inside. *Oh, Lord, it isn't fair! The child needs a family of her own—our family!*

Her hands shook as she entered the bathroom and turned on the light, mind racing for a solution. Reaching into her pocket, she withdrew the folded adoption application and smoothed it out on the vanity, the contents of her dream blurring before her eyes. *This* was the paper that could begin the entire process, only the first of many to make Gabe one of their own, to give her a family she truly belonged to. She closed her eyes, and the memory of Gabe's broken sobs shredded her heart once again, convincing her she had no choice. She needed to begin the process . . . one in which Patrick would have the final say, most assuredly, via his signature on the final document. But . . . *not* if she didn't set the wheels in motion first.

Uttering a fragile prayer, Marcy begged God's forgiveness and picked up the pen. And with hands trembling as much as her conscience, she did the only thing her heart would allow her to do.

She signed her husband's name.

6

"Annie, wait!"

She turned, one foot in the backseat of Aunt Eleanor's Packard in front of St. Stephen's as her catechism teacher scurried down the church steps. Stepping back out of the car, Annie blinked and smiled while Aunt Eleanor glanced over her shoulder and Glory peeked out the window. The earthy scent of spring mulch merged with the smell of fresh asphalt and auto exhaust as a dusk-colored sky slowly faded from deep shades of purple to the dark of night.

Mrs. McGuire hurried up to the car with Annie's leather purse tightly in hand. "You forgot this," she said, a bit out of breath.

Annie gave her a sheepish smile. "Goodness, I can't believe I left my purse behind. I'm sorry to inconvenience you like that, Mrs. McGuire, having to chase me down."

"It's no problem, Annie," she said, handing the purse over, "and please call me Faith." A twinkle lit green eyes that held a kindness Annie warmed to, a nice complement to rich, auburn curls that waved to her shoulders. "This is my first time teaching Adult Catechism class, you know, so I'm not quite comfortable with all the formality yet."

121

"Good heavens, *Susannah*," Aunt Eleanor said, emphasizing her preference of Annie's given name over her new nickname, "I do believe you'd forget your head if it weren't attached." Aunt Eleanor held a gloved hand out to Faith, lips edging into a tight smile. "Good evening, Mrs. McGuire. I'm Susannah's aunt, Miss Eleanor Martin, and I apologize for my niece. She tends to be a bit scatterbrained at times, but I assure you she's an excellent student."

"Oh, I have no doubt, Miss Martin," Faith said, shaking Aunt Eleanor's hand with enthusiasm. Her smile was apologetic. "I suspect I may be the blame for Annie leaving the purse behind, however. Annie had a few questions after class, you see, and we were just chatting away. When she realized the time, she bolted out the door, book and homework in hand, afraid she'd kept you waiting." Faith's smile was warm. "Well, I better let you go, but if you come early next week, Annie, I'll be happy to answer any additional questions—"

"Ellie!"

Aunt Eleanor's body went as stiff as her smile. A hint of rose bloomed in her cheeks when a gentleman sprinted toward the car from the rectory with a briefcase in hand.

"It's very nice to have met you, Mrs. McGuire," Aunt Eleanor sputtered, obviously shaken as she attempted to hurry Annie into the Packard. "Come, Susannah, we need to leave."

"Ellie, wait, please—I need to talk to you." The man huffed up to the car, dark hair disheveled from the run and cheeks apparently ruddy from the effort. Well over six feet tall, he was possibly a year or two older than Aunt Eleanor, maybe thirty-eight or thirty-nine, with a touch of silver at the temples. His handsome face was as strained as Aunt Eleanor's when she faced him, his well-defined jaw tight with tension. Nodding at Annie and Faith, he fixed probing eyes on Annie's pale aunt. "Ellie, you were supposed to look over the paperwork for the St. Stephen's family shelter. Did you forget?"

Chin high, Aunt Eleanor took a step back. "My apologies, Mr. Callahan, but my niece started catechism classes tonight, and I'm afraid it slipped my mind. Perhaps another time?"

His broad chest expanded and released with a quiet exhale before he spoke, his voice gentler now and the furrows diminishing in his brow. "Ellie, we've been on a first-name basis since we were seventeen. Don't you think it's time we dispense with formalities?"

The blush deepened, bleeding into Aunt Eleanor's cheeks while her gaze flicked to Faith. "If you'll excuse me, please, this will only take a moment." Her cool look shifted back to Mr. Callahan. "Perhaps it's best if we discuss our business in private." Before Faith could respond, Aunt Eleanor calmly moved to the base of the church steps while Mr. Callahan followed, their conversation lost in the chug and whoosh of passing traffic.

"Who's that man?" Glory's rosebud mouth expanded into a tiny yawn.

"I don't know, sweetheart," Annie said, brow crimped at the exchange between her aunt and the gentleman that seemed anything but friendly, given Aunt Eleanor's rigid stance.

"Mr. James Callahan, miss," Frailey supplied, posture erect as he waited by the side of the door, gaze straight ahead "Chairman for the St. Stephen expansion committee."

"Thank you, Frailey," Annie said, giving the butler a pat on his crisp uniform suit coat. Smiling at Faith, she inclined her head toward the man who'd worked for Aunt Eleanor's family most of his life. "Frailey's Aunt Eleanor's butler and, I might add, Pinochle champ of his guild."

Faith flashed a wide smile. "Why, hello, Frailey. Pinochle, huh? I'd like to see what you can do with my brother-in-law Luke McGee, in challenging his annoying luck in cards." She gave him a wink. "He tends to get a little cocky in the family games, if you know what I mean."

Annie's jaw dropped when Frailey revealed more teeth than she'd seen in almost four months living with Aunt Eleanor, except for the occasional grins Glory managed to coax. "The pleasure is mine, miss," he said in precise speech that hinted of British roots. He bowed slightly, silver hair shimmering under the streetlamp. "As it would be to educate your Mr. McGee."

"Who are *you*?" Glory wanted to know, neck craned out the door and blonde curls askew.

"I'm your sister's catechism teacher, Mrs. McGuire," Faith said, "and you are . . . ?"

"Glory, short for Gloria Celeste Kennedy."

"Well, Miss Gloria Celeste Kennedy, it's very nice to make your acquaintance."

"What's quay-tents mean?" Glory wanted to know, nose scrunched.

"It means it's nice to meet you," Annie explained.

"Do you have any kids I can play with?" The little stinker was suddenly wide awake.

Faith laughed and tugged Glory from the car, hefting her in her arms. "Well, yes, ma'am, I do. My oldest, Bella, is almost nine, Laney is seven going on eight, and Abby is six going on seven who," she said with a tickle of Glory's ribs, "is a little peanut just like you."

"Wow!" Glory said with a giggle. "Is that what you call her, 'Peanut'?"

"That's what my husband calls her because she's small for her age, but quite big in the bossy department, I assure you."

"When can we play?" Glory's eyes expanded so much, Faith chuckled.

"Soon," Faith said, grinning. She turned to Annie. "What do you say? Should we take our girls to story time at the Book-ends Bookstore? My girls love it, and I think Glory would too. Then I can introduce you to my sisters, and the two of us can chat. What do you think?"

"Jeepers creepers, that would be swell!" Glory said with a bounce.

Annie poked Glory in the ribs, eliciting a squirmy giggle. "I don't suppose I have any choice or Miss Gloria Celeste

Kennedy will hound me to death, so thank you." Her gaze connected with Faith's, and somehow she had a feeling this woman would be good for her, not only as a teacher and friend, but as a woman to talk to now that Mama and Maggie weren't around.

"It's settled, then. We'll put a date on the calendar next week, okay?" Faith kissed Glory's cheek and tucked her back in the car. "Good night, Glory, it was nice to meet you."

Annie sneaked a peek at Aunt Eleanor and Mr. Callahan, whose conversation appeared to have risen in tension based on their stilted posture. "I wonder why they don't get along?" she murmured.

"Perhaps they've butted heads on the committee," Faith suggested quietly.

A pucker wedged at the bridge of Annie's nose. "Goodness, he is a decent and honorable man, I hope?" she said with another worried glance at her aunt.

"Oh, absolutely." Faith's smile relaxed the tension at the back of Annie's neck. "Mr. Callahan is a widower who is a pillar of the community and one of the city's best lawyers as well as counsel for the parish."

Relief seeped through Annie's lips. "Oh, thank goodness, because it certainly appears as if Aunt Eleanor doesn't care for him, maybe even a bit afraid, I'd say, which I've never seen before."

Faith patted Annie's arm. "Well, not to worry. It could be something as simple as a disagreement on the Catholic Workers' committee, since both your aunt and Mr. Callahan are board members. But if it worries you, we can always pray about it next week."

"Pray about it?" Annie said, a dizzy sensation swirling through her body at the memory of her father's propensity to pray about everything. Praying together had been as natural as breathing for him, an evangelical pastor who took everything—large and small—to the Almighty. But anyone else? *Unheard of!* "You . . . pray together? With people, I mean . . . one-on-one?"

Faith's smile was gentle. "Every day of my life, whenever I see a need. It's our verbal connection with God, just like you and I are connecting right now." She gave Annie a hug. "I'll see you next week, and we'll put a date on the calendar for Bookends, okay?" She winked at Glory, then turned to extend a hand to Frailey. "Nice to meet you too, Frailey." She grinned. "And, oh, how I wish I could bring you home to Luke."

"'Tis a shame I'll not have the opportunity to educate the boy. Good night, miss."

"Indeed," Faith said with a grin. With a wave, she hurried back up the church steps.

A moment later Aunt Eleanor strode toward the car with a pinched look, her disagreeable business obviously concluded. "Frailey, I have a dreadful headache, so do hurry us home."

Annie's stomach clenched when Aunt Eleanor bulldozed her into the backseat with a grim-lipped expression, prodding with the back of her hand. Both slid into the car, and Frailey shut the door.

"Aunt Eleanor—are you all right?" Annie asked, voice tentative.

"Yes, dear, I'm fine. Frailey, please stop at the Woolworth's on Main. I took the last of my aspirin this morning, and we'll need to pick up some more. They're open till nine, correct?"

"Yes, ma'am."

"Good. I'm sure this would be a migraine come morning if I don't attend to it tonight." Aunt Eleanor closed her eyes and laid her head on the back of the seat, a silent dismissal of her niece.

They rode to the store and then home in silence, and Annie couldn't help but reflect on the difference between her aunt and Faith McGuire. Probably only a few years older than Faith, Aunt Eleanor lived life as if she carried the weight of the world on her shoulders. She seldom smiled, seemed addicted to aspirin, and possessed no joy or fun despite a beautiful home and healthy bank account. Faith McGuire, on the other hand, radiated something different—joy, peace, and an unmistakable confidence. Not to mention a fabulous marriage to an incredibly handsome man, judging from how he'd kissed her at the door when he dropped off the lesson plan she'd forgotten at home.

A faint smile lifted the corners of Annie's mouth even as her heart swelled with hope. Oh, to have a love like that! To have a man look at you like Faith's husband looked at her . . . like Daddy had looked at Mama. She sighed. No, there was no mistake about it. Somehow Faith McGuire had learned the secret to being happy and fulfilled, while Aunt Eleanor—with all her money in the bank, lofty board positions, and countless charitable auctions she'd chaired—had not.

The thought made Annie sad, hopeful, and determined, all at the same time. Sad for Aunt Eleanor that she'd spent her life bound up in bitterness, never learning how to love. Hopeful that maybe—just maybe—Faith McGuire knew something Annie did not. And determined that if Faith McGuire did, indeed, possess special knowledge that put that glow in her face, then Annie wanted it too. She opened her eyes, jaw set as she peered out the window into a moonlit sky. *And the sooner the better* . . .

"Whoopee—Annie's the old maid!" Sitting Indian-style on the parlor rug next to Mr. Grump, Glory kicked stubby legs in the air, displaying pink lacy underwear in all of its glory. Lumbering up, Mr. Grump resettled by the French doors, where the scent of jasmine drifted in from a brick garden patio along with the silence of an elite neighborhood deprived of stickball or the chatter of children. Somewhere a tree frog twittered, heralding the arrival of dusk as a pink haze settled, a perfect complement for Glory's drawers.

"Gloria Celeste Kennedy!" Annie dove across her neat stacks of playing cards to tickle Glory's neck, prompting the little dickens to squeal in delight. "Not only is it bad manners to make fun of the loser, you little stinkpot, but one does *not* display her underwear in public!"

Squirming away, the youngster managed to pop up with a delighted shriek, flapping the front of her skirt with a giggle to reveal dimpled knees. "You're not public, Annie, you're my sister." She twirled around, unveiling another glimpse of pretty pink lace. "My *'Old Maid'* sister!"

Annie shot up and snatched her in the air with a spin. "I'll teach you to call me an old maid," she said, pausing to slobber Glory with kisses. High-pitched laughter rolled through the parlor when Annie burrowed into Glory's neck, blowing raspberries against her sister's skin.

"Good heavens, Susannah, how is that child ever going to learn to behave as a proper young lady if you persist in acting more juvenile than her?" Aunt Eleanor stood at the parlor door, gaze flitting to where Mr. Grump lay sprawled in front of the open French doors. Wrinkling her nose, she marched over to shoo him away, yanking the doors closed with a not-so-subtle reminder she preferred them shut to keep out the flies. She cast a wary glance at the girls on the floor as she made her way to her favorite blue brocade wing chair by the fireplace. Retrieving her needlepoint from a cherrywood chest, she settled in with another cumbersome sigh and put her reading glasses on. "I wish you'd act your age rather than playing the hooligan with your impressionable sister," she said, the stiff lines of her face highlighted by a tulip lamp that stood guard over her chair.

Allowing a stone-faced Glory to slip to the floor, Annie forced a smile despite her own pale reflection in the gilded mirror over the hearth. She took a deep breath, determined to forge some kind of connection with her aunt. After all, she was both blood and benefactor, her mother's estranged sister who could've easily turned her back on them in their time of need. Annie smoothed the pleats of her cream paneled dress. "Sorry, Aunt Eleanor, I do behave in public, I promise."

Plopping down on the floor, Glory tugged her abandoned baby doll, the Queen of Sheba, into her lap while she glanced up at her aunt, eyes wide. "We're playing Old Maid, Aunt Eleanor—wanna play?" Her expression was almost angelic. "I bet you'd be good at it."

Annie stooped to pick up the cards, eyes narrowed in warning.

Eleanor looked up from her needlepoint canvas, the downward tilt of her lips lifting slightly as if she might actually smile. But the hazel eyes behind wire-rimmed glasses remained aloof, reflecting the cool green of her prim silk dress. "No, thank you, dear." Her gaze returned to Annie, her tone slightly sterner. "You'll be eighteen in less than a month, Susannah. You need to set an example. Your sister looks up to you and will mimic you whenever possible."

Annie caught her breath, her aunt's mention of her birthday reminding her of Peggy's plea to celebrate her eighteenth out with the gang. *"But I don't want to celebrate my birthday at Ocean Pier,"* Annie had argued, no desire to spend time with Joanie, Ashley, and Erica, or Steven O'Connor for that matter. "How 'bout just you and I go out to dinner?"

Peggy had groaned, her elfin face crimped in pain. "But you're going to be eighteen, Annie Lou—*a woman!* You need to have a party—with people!" She grabbed Annie's hand. "Okay, no Ocean Pier, but at least let us take you to dinner to celebrate, okay? Please?"

Of course Annie had relented. What trouble could she possibly get into at a restaurant?

With a skim of her teeth, she stood and took a step forward, fiddling with the filigreed silver ring Maggie had given her for Christmas. "Uh, Aunt Eleanor? About my birthday . . ."

Her aunt peered over the rim of her glasses, a crevice at the bridge of her nose. "Yes?"

"Peggy and her sister would like to take me to dinner. Would that be all right?"

The crease deepened as she removed her glasses. "I was

hoping to have a birthday dinner for you here, with your sister, but I suppose you may invite Peggy and her sister as well."

Joanie? *With Aunt Eleanor?* Panic jolted like a brain freeze after too much Rocky Road. "Oh no, not to our family dinner," she said, desperate to steer her aunt away from sure disaster. "I only want to celebrate with you and Glory on my actual birthday." She hesitated, licking her dry lips. "This would be the Saturday night after, with Peggy, her sister, and friends."

Aunt Eleanor stared, wheels turning as slowly as the ponderous thud of Annie's heart. "And how old, exactly, are Peggy's sister and her friends?" she asked, her tone measured.

Annie blinked, trying not to swallow. "Well, Peggy's eighteen, of course, and Joanie and her friends, a few years older, I believe."

The greenish hazel eyes narrowed ever so slightly. "How many years older, dear?"

There was no stopping the gulp this time. "They're . . . twenty-five," she whispered.

A heavy sigh parted from Aunt Eleanor's lips as she put her glasses back on. "I'm sorry, Susannah, but I'm just not comfortable with a young woman your age roaming the streets at night with older girls. Heaven knows what type of morals they have, coming of age during such a promiscuous time." She proceeded to pull fibers through the canvas in her lap. "It's my responsibility to see to your best interests, as it is yours to become the kind of role model your sister needs, a young woman of grace and refinement. *Which* you can begin right now by selecting a less rowdy game to play at the table instead of sprawled on the floor."

"Yes, ma'am." Annie's chest deflated. She bent to retrieve the cards and gave her sister a sad smile. "How 'bout we play Hearts instead?" She nodded at the table. "Over there."

Glory trudged to her feet as if she were rotund instead of a bitty little thing. Her tiny brows bunched in a thunderous scowl while the Queen of Sheba dangled from her fist in a most unregal manner. "I'd rather play Old Maid than Hearts," she muttered under her breath, sliding Aunt Eleanor a scowl while she sulked to the table. "The 'old maid' should play—she could use one."

Broiling her sister with another look, Annie took the chair facing the hearth so her aunt wouldn't see Glory's nasty look.

"Lemonade, per your request, Miss Eleanor." Frailey entered the parlor with a tray in hand, head high and body stiff, his stride almost a glide except for the faint indication of a limp.

Eleanor looked up, face in a frown. "Goodness, Frailey, it's almost June, and your arthritis is still acting up?"

"No, miss, not too badly."

The glasses came off. "Don't try to pull the wool over my eyes, Mr. Frailey, you're limping more today than I've seen in a while." Her daunting tone couldn't mask the concern in her eyes. "Are you trying the cider vinegar and honey concoction I told you about?"

Frailey offered her a lemonade, bending slightly at the waist. "No, miss."

"Well, I suggest you do so right now, is that clear?"

"Yes, miss."

Before he could turn away, she reached to brush his hand, almost a caress to gnarled fingers as they held the tray. Her voice was low, as if she didn't want anyone to hear except Frailey, and so fraught with pain that Annie paused. "You mean the world to me, Arthur, you know that. Please—for me—take care of yourself. When you're in pain, I'm in pain."

"Annie, it's your turn," Glory said, shaking Annie's arm.

She startled and returned her attention to the game, stunned at her aunt's depth of concern for her elderly butler. Never once had she known Aunt Eleanor to express emotion of any kind, even when her only sister had passed away. Mama told her once that she and her little sister "Ellie" had been close growing up—Eleanor a vivacious and bright-eyed little girl and Mama the older sister she idolized. But everything changed when Mama quit Radcliffe to elope with Daddy, not only alienating her parents by marrying outside the church and moving to Chicago, but estranging ten-year-old Ellie as well. But for all her anger and bitterness over her older sister leaving the Church to marry a minister and her disdain for the offspring of that union, Eleanor Martin *had* reached out. First to Maggie in providing a top-notch education at Radcliffe, and now to Annie and Glory.

"Thank you, Frailey," Annie said, reaching for the lemonade he offered.

"My pleasure, miss."

She took a sip, peeking at Aunt Eleanor through lowered lids, noting she had returned to her stitching with a porcelain expression that meant all emotion was safely tucked away. Unbidden, Annie's throat tightened at the sadness that engulfed her aunt, as potent as the tart lemonade that now wrinkled her nose. And then, in the rise and fall of her breath, Annie saw beyond clipped responses and cool gazes into the eyes of a woman who desperately needed love in her life. And a touch from God to heal her soul, just like he'd done for Annie. *Oh, Lord, help me to connect with this woman whose blood I share.*

"Thanks, Frailey." Glory took a gulp of her lemonade, face puckered like a prune. "Mmm . . . nice and sour." Her rosebud lips went flat, voice sinking to a mutter. "Just like Aunt Eleanor."

Annie nudged her with her foot under the table, suddenly comprehending for the first time just why Aunt Eleanor was so bitter. Mama had told her that Ellie's fiancé had broken her heart when he cheated on her days before the wedding, so she'd called it off. And then Mama's parents had perished in a rail accident on their way to New York four years later, leaving Aunt Eleanor broken and alone as the sole heir of a lucrative estate. Aunt Eleanor became a shell of a woman at twenty-six: beautiful, educated, wealthy . . . and so very alone. And as lifeless as the artificial flowers she placed on her parents' graves.

"Ouch!" Glory rubbed her shin, her narrow gaze fusing with Annie's. "Why did you kick me?"

"I did not kick you, young lady," Annie whispered with a stern look, "I just don't think we should be talking about Aunt Eleanor that way."

"Anything else, miss?" Frailey asked with a stiff bow to Aunt Eleanor.

"No, thank you, Frailey—just tend to that leg, all right?"

"Yes, miss."

Annie watched the kindly butler leave, his regal bearing more in keeping with royalty than servitude, and all at once she wondered about this man who had devoted his life to the Martins. Mama said he had come from Manchester, England, and swore that Arthur Frailey had blue blood in his veins. But if he had an aristocratic heritage in Britain, Mr. Frailey never let on. "A love affair gone awry," Mama suspected, never understanding why her beloved butler, with whom she corresponded until her death, never opted to marry.

"Aaaaan-nie," Glory moaned, "you have to start, remember?"

"Oops, sorry." Annie snapped from her reverie to select three cards from her hand and push them forward. "I wonder why Frailey never married," she mused out loud.

"Think about it," Glory whispered in her typical sage-in-a-five-year-old-body mode. "If you worked for Aunt Eleanor, would *you* want to marry a woman?"

"I think she's just really sad," Annie said softly. "Which is why we both need to try harder to be nice to her and do what she says without complaining." Annie leveled a pointed look. "She's Mama's sister, after all, and she's been good to us."

A surprisingly low grunt erupted from Glory's lips. "If you call jail good." She slapped three cards on the table while moisture glistened in her eyes. "I miss Daddy."

Annie squeezed her little hand. "I know you do, baby. I do too . . ."

"Excuse me, Miss Eleanor, but you have a visitor. Mr. Callahan is at the door."

Aunt Eleanor looked up at Frailey, her skin suddenly as white as the milk-glass tulip lamp that highlighted the gold in her hair. Nervous eyes darted to a gilded bronze clock on her Tudor oak writing desk. "At this hour?" Her voice rose to a crack. "What does he want?"

Frailey's eyes softened. "I believe he has papers for you to sign, miss."

She rose with a disgruntled sigh, the set of her shoulders a clear indication the visit would be short. "Well, show him to the library, Frailey, and for pity's sake, don't take his coat."

"Very good, miss." With a stiff bow, Frailey hurried from the room.

Placing her needlepoint aside, she removed her glasses and glanced in the mirror, hands shaky as she smoothed ash-blonde curls. Her flustered gaze collided with Annie's in the glass, and she whirled around, back straight and head high. "Susannah, it's late, and you girls should be asleep. Since Mrs. Pierce left early, I'd appreciate it if you put Glory to bed tonight, please."

"Yes, ma'am." Annie bit back a sigh. She gathered the cards, countering Glory's jutting lip with a sympathetic smile. "We'll play tomorrow night, okay?" she whispered, squeezing her hand.

"No we won't," Glory muttered, golden curls as limp as her mood. "*She'll* still be here."

"I heard that, Gloria," Aunt Eleanor said as she strode by, a storm raging in her eyes. "And, yes, I'll be here, young lady, rest assured, but *you* may not be if an orphanage is more to your liking."

Glory shrank back, tears pooling. She clung to Annie. "I want my mama," she whispered.

Eleanor spun around at the door, her eyes glinting with both tears and torment. "Stop it!" she rasped, hysteria rising along with her chin. "She's gone, do you hear? She left you just like she left me, like she left Mama and Papa—with a broken heart and a life full of pain. Why should *you* be any different?" she screamed, fists clenched white.

Air seized in Annie's throat while her body chilled to stone. She clutched a sobbing Glory to her side, both of them shivering from the shock of their aunt's hateful words. "Shhh, baby, let's go upstairs," she whispered, "and we'll snuggle for a while, okay?" She ushered her out, inching past their aunt, who stood at the door, head in her hands.

Annie flinched when Aunt Eleanor halted them with a quivering arm, face averted to the wall and voice hoarse with repentance. "Forgive me, I . . . I don't know what came over me. I didn't mean it . . ." Her voice broke on a shuddered sob. "I suppose . . . I miss your mother too . . ."

Throat swelling with sympathy, Annie laid a tentative hand on her aunt's shoulder, giving it a gentle squeeze. "It's okay, Aunt Eleanor," she whispered. "We understand."

At least I do, Annie thought with a heavy sigh as she mounted the stairs with her sister weeping in her arms. Glory was young enough to forget most of the pain of losing Mama and even Daddy, but Annie certainly wasn't, something she obviously shared in common with Aunt Eleanor. Determined to forge more commonalities with the woman who now shared their lives, Annie purposed to reach out to her aunt.

"But I need the Queen of Sheba," Glory insisted after Annie tucked her in and said prayers. "She's on the floor in the parlor, and I can't sleep without her."

"Okay, I'll get her, sweetie. Close your eyes, and I'll be right back." Planting a kiss to her sister's cheek, Annie hurried downstairs to rescue the Queen of Sheba. Bobbling the rag doll in her hands, she turned to head back upstairs when a shout halted her at the parlor door.

"Never!" her aunt shrieked. "I could never trust you again—ever! Please leave—now."

Annie stared, her back pressed hard against the green silk wallpaper of the foyer wall, gaze frantic as it darted to the half-open library door. She was paralyzed, desperate to flee, but a thunderous slap rooted her to the floor as surely as the palms that were rooted in brass containers at the foot of the stairs. Her aunt's hysterical shouts to "get out" sent Annie flying to the library door where she skidded to a stop, the next words leeching the blood from her face.

"I've never stopped loving you, Ellie, and I never will. I was a stupid fool, too young and weak and full of myself to see the hurt I would cause. Please . . . you have to forgive me."

Mr. Callahan loved her aunt? Annie's body fused to the wall behind a potted palm, her aunt's wrenching sobs keeping her from flying back up the steps. Hoarse, muffled words told her Mr. Callahan was attempting to comfort her, but it seemed to no avail as her weeping continued . . . until a telling silence. Too scared to move or even make a sound, Annie stood fixed, eyes sealed as if that would alleviate guilt over invasion of her aunt's privacy.

"Marry me, Ellie," he said, his voice urgent and low. "Let me make it up to you so we can have the marriage we were meant to have."

Annie stifled a gasp, unable to escape for the shock grafting her shoulder blades to the wall. *Mr. Callahan was the fiancé who'd broken her aunt's heart?* The next thing Annie knew, Mr. Callahan stormed out of the library without so much as a glance back, the slam of the front door jarring both the beveled glass panes and Annie's nerves. Heart banging against her rib cage, she tiptoed to the stairs and stopped, the sound of weeping drawing her back. Slowly moving to the library door, she peeked in, and tears pricked at the sight of her stern and stoic aunt slumped over the love seat, body heaving with every painful sob. Without a second thought, Annie hurried to her side, hesitating only a moment before dropping Glory's doll to embrace her aunt in her arms.

Eleanor startled, head lunging up to reveal a face swollen with tears. She pushed a damp strand of hair from her eyes, voice hoarse. "What are you doing?" she whispered, her glazed look only adding to the tragedy of her manner.

Kneeling before her, Annie tenderly took her aunt's hand, giving her a faltering smile as moisture welled in her own eyes. "Sharing your grief, Aunt Eleanor," she whispered. "That's what families do, you know."

Mouth parted in shock, Aunt Eleanor stared like sodden stone, seconds passing before her lips began to quiver. With a fresh swell of tears, she collapsed into Annie's arms, clutching tight while Annie stroked her hair with the same tenderness she reserved for Glory. Head bent against her aunt's, she silently prayed for God to heal her hurt, and in one frail shiver of her aunt's body, a rare peace began to settle. "I'm not sure what Mr. Callahan said or did to hurt you like this, Aunt Eleanor, but once when my best friend moved away, I remember Mama comforting me, holding me just like I'm holding you. She said something I didn't really understand at the time, but I remember that it gave me a lot of peace when she said it."

Aunt Eleanor sniffed and pulled away, swiping a limp handkerchief to her eyes. "What was it?" she asked, her words waterlogged and nasal.

Annie ducked to smile into her aunt's eyes like her mother had done so many times for her. "She said, 'Susannah, I know it hurts like the dickens now, but God promises that "weeping may endure for a night, but joy cometh in the morning." ' " Annie swallowed hard, the memory of her mother's comfort pricking her eyes. "So we prayed, and you know what?"

"What?" Aunt Eleanor whispered, eyes rimmed raw and looking a lot like Glory.

Annie caressed her aunt's arm, a rush of love filling her heart. "Within one month, the best friend I ever had moved in next door."

Aunt Eleanor caught her breath, fingers pressed to her mouth. Rare wrinkles bunched beneath squinted eyes that appeared on another onslaught of tears. Blinking hard, she attempted to smile, clutching Annie's hand in a quivering grip. "She was lucky, your friend," she said with a heave, blinking hard as if to dispel more water from streaking her face.

"Oh no, Aunt Eleanor, I was the lucky one," Annie said. She leaned to press a light kiss to her cheek. "Just like now."

"Susannah . . ." Aunt Eleanor's throat shifted before she swallowed Annie in a ferocious hug, her whisper trembling with emotion. "Thank you *so* much."

A grin tipped Annie's lips over her aunt's shoulder. "You're more than welcome, Aunt Eleanor." She closed her eyes, wishing this moment could last forever. "Can I . . . I mean would you . . . allow me to pray with you? It's what Mama would do if she were here, you know."

The breath in Annie's lungs stilled as she waited, Aunt Eleanor silent in her arms. Finally she felt her aunt nod, and her breath slowly seeped from her lips. Tears stinging, she prayed just like Mama and Daddy would pray—calling upon the God whose mercies were new every morning, along with his joys. She asked God to give her aunt peace in the midst of this storm, to heal her soul and bring her joy. When she was finished, she pulled away, giving her aunt's hand a final squeeze before reaching for Glory's doll. Rising to her feet, she smiled, her face as blotchy as her aunt's, no doubt. "Well, I better take this to Glory before there are tears on the second floor as well as the first." She bent to kiss her aunt's cheek. "Good night, Aunt Eleanor. I love you."

"Good night, Susann—" Aunt Eleanor stood, her demeanor calm once again. She tugged on her dress, gaze low as she attempted to straighten it while muscles jerked in her throat. "I mean . . . *Annie*. Thank you." Pink tinted her cheeks. "And I love you too, dear."

Annie smiled and turned to leave, joy leaping in her chest.

"I . . . I'd like you to go with your friends."

Annie stopped, easing around with a kink in her brow. "Pardon me?"

With a firm lift of her chin, Eleanor finally met her gaze.

"Out to dinner for your birthday, dear, and I'll give you funds to pick up the bill."

Annie couldn't help it—her jaw dropped. "Thank you, Aunt Eleanor, but that's not necessary to buy dinner for my friends, truly. I'm not sure if they'll pick someplace a little more expensive or not, but even so, there will be four of them in addition to me, so that's too much."

"No it isn't, Annie," she whispered, moving forward to extinguish the light. "Nothing's too much to repay your kindness." Cupping a tentative arm to Annie's waist, her aunt gave her one of the first genuine smiles she'd ever seen on her face. "And to be honest, my dear," she said, a tremor in her tone, "dinner for a thousand wouldn't be enough."

Flinging the door wide, Luke McGee stormed into his four-story brownstone on Commonwealth Avenue, the subsequent slam of the front door a perfect match for his mood. Usually the seven-block walk from the Boston Children's Aid Society was a pleasure this time of year, when May was just burgeoning into June. There was nothing Luke loved more about summer than shooting a hoop or two with dirty-faced urchins who clamored for his attention, while mothers strolled with toddlers and neighbors jabbered from yard to yard. But tonight, the chatter of tree frogs and scent of honeysuckle were the farthest things from his mind. No, tonight his thoughts were first and foremost on his wife. Katie Rose, the sass and love of his life . . . and the woman with a penchant for secrets when they suited her cause.

With two abrupt jerks, he loosened his tie and bolted up the worn oak steps to his second-story flat like he hadn't just worked a thirteen-hour day. Adrenaline pumped through his veins along with more than a little anger. Even at the late hour of ten o'clock, the smell of fried chicken from somebody's supper still lingered in the hall along with the scent of his neighbor's pipe, a docile man whose wife refused to allow him to smoke in their flat. Luke's lips leveled in a tight line. Why would Mr. Tuttle allow his wife to wear the pants in the family, for pity's sake? Didn't he know women needed—no, *wanted*—a strong man they couldn't ride roughshod over? That if given the chance, some women had no problem batting their baby blues while taking an inch and pushing a mile? Free as a bird to flit wherever they wanted?

Like my wife. Suit coat slung over his shoulder, he grunted and fished his key from his pocket, thinking tonight might be a good night to clip a few wings.

Key in the lock, he paused, reflecting on the last time Katie Rose pulled a stunt like this almost a year ago when they'd been newlyweds in the throes of wedded bliss. She'd enrolled in law school without telling him, and Luke had been so mad, he'd slept on the couch for a solid week. They'd had their fights since then, but nothing like that. He ground his jaw. *Till tonight.*

He blasted out a noisy breath, knowing full well he needed to calm down. He was tired and hungry and just found out his wife was cavorting with her old boyfriend behind his back—not a good combination for a happy home. Hand on the knob, he closed his eyes, determined to give Katie the benefit of the doubt. She'd probably run into Jack and forgotten to mention it. He exhaled and hung his head, his conscience a little heavier than before. Just like he'd "forgotten" to mention working nights with the wealthy intern Carmichael foisted on him for the summer.

"Hey, Boss, forgot to tell you I saw your wife at the Harvard Law Library this week," his pretty new intern had said before she'd left tonight.

"What?" Luke had looked up from his desk, staring as if she had just tossed the cup of coffee she was holding into his face. He blinked. "You know my wife?"

"Not personally," the brown-eyed beauty had said, nodding to Luke's wedding picture in the bookcase against the wall. "But I recognized her from your picture." She offered a shy grin. "My brother's at Harvard Law, and sometimes I go to the law library with him."

He nodded, trying to remember if Katie mentioned a night class or seminar this week. "Did you talk to her?" he asked, the collar of his shirt suddenly too warm over what Katie might say about him working late hours with a pretty intern.

"Nope." She deposited a stack of typed letters and the cup of fresh coffee onto his desk. "I didn't want to interrupt—she was talking to some guy." She flicked a strand of platinum hair over her shoulder, adjusting a dress on a shapely body Luke had never really noticed before.

Heat climbed up the back of his neck as he averted his eyes, snatching the letters to scrawl his signature at the bottom of each one. "Probably the Dean of Portia Law School or maybe one of her professors," he murmured, feeling the clamp of his jaw. "Distinguished older gentleman, slight build, thinning on top?" He kept signing letters, trying to appear nonchalant.

Her hesitation made him glance up, and she shook her head, nose scrunched. "No, this guy was pretty young, about her age or a few years older. Tall, dark, well dressed." She shrugged. "Probably just a friend from Harvard Law."

He froze, pen stalled midsignature, its point gouging until a tiny pool of ink bled onto the paper. *Jack.* He scratched the rest of the signature with way too much force. *Sweet mother of Job, she was hobnobbing with her old fiancé?*

"Well, I better go," she said quickly, as if suddenly aware Luke was clenching his jaw. Glancing at her watch, she headed for the door, sending a smile over her shoulder. "Unless you need me to get those letters out tonight, that is, which I can do. It's just I promised my mom I'd be home early." She smiled. "At least before ten this time."

He waved her out the door. "No, go—please. I appreciate all your help, Lauren, I could have never done it without you, especially with Gladys on leave and Bobbie Sue out with shingles." He slumped back in his chair and pinched the bridge of his nose, suddenly feeling way older than his twenty-five years. He managed a tired smile. "And thanks for the coffee. You're a wonder. Haven't seen an intern work this hard since my wife before we got married."

Lauren spun at the door, hands clasped to her chest and brown eyes suddenly aglow. "Oh, your wife was an intern at the BCAS too? How romantic! Is that how you met?"

A smile tilted the corners of his mouth as he thought of Katie's first day as a volunteer. She had been a royal brat, just like when she was a kid, but he'd fallen in love with her anyway. "Basically. I knew her as a kid, of course, but she was such a snob, we never really got along."

Lauren sighed, sagging against the door. "Golly, I sure hope that happens for me when I go to Radcliffe this fall." She grinned and wiggled her brows. "Harvard men are such sheiks!" She stood up straight with a shy tug of her lip. "Uh, you are a Harvard man, right, Luke?"

Luke squeezed the pen so tight, the tip punched through the paper. "Nope. Fordham."

"Oh," she said, the stars dimming in her eyes. "Well, I'm sure that's a very good school."

His smile was as cinched as his grip on the pen. With a final flourish, he signed the last letter and tossed it on the pile. "Thanks again, Lauren, you're a lifesaver." He stood to his feet and stretched, hoping he sounded casual. "I'll tell Katie you saw her chatting with someone." He paused, weighing his words. "Or did you say they were studying?"

Her lips pursed as she attempted to recall. "Studying, I believe, or at least that's how it looked. They were sitting next to each other pretty close, I think, poring over some ridiculously big book." She flopped a hand in the air. "Well, anyway, g'night, Luke. Don't stay too late or Katie will throw you out of the house."

He smiled and waved, despite the tic in his jaw. *If I don't throw her out first.*

"Hand stuck to the knob?"

"What?" Luke wheeled around, the key flying from his hand and clinking to the floor.

Mr. Tuttle smiled, a sheen of perspiration spanning up and over a bald spot while he puffed on the pipe between his teeth. "You've been standing there so long, I thought maybe you were plum tired, asleep on the knob." A fog of smoke clouded the hall, and the distinct smell of almonds from his neighbor's sweet cavendish reminded him he'd gone without dinner. The old gentleman glanced at the pocket watch looped to his vest and grimaced. "Uh-oh, after ten. Still working the late hours, I see." He grinned. "Thought the little woman changed the lock."

Luke awarded him a stiff smile. "Nope, just lost in a train of thought, I'm afraid." He sighed and picked up his key. "G'night, Mr. Tuttle. Better head in before she bolts the door."

The old man chuckled. "Yessiree, Bob, those little women can sure get riled up when things don't go their way."

Yeah, like tonight. Luke jammed the key in the lock. *Only it'll be me riled when things don't go her way.* Opening the door into a dark parlor, he tossed his coat over the faded blue armchair rather than the brass coatrack Katie insisted he use, knowing it would ruffle her feathers. He intended to ruffle more than her feathers if she didn't come clean, explaining just why she was cozying up to Jack. He peered toward their bedroom, where a shaft of light spilled down the dark hall, and then paused to suck in a stabilizing breath. He would give her every opportunity to confess, of course. He didn't want to go off half-cocked like she would if she found out about Lauren. Besides, working late with an intern to prepare for the biannual board meeting when Bobbie Sue and Gladys were out of commission was a *lot* different than chumming it up with an old boyfriend.

"Luke—is that you, I hope?" Katie called, her voice groggy, like she'd fallen asleep.

"It better be," he said, strolling into the bedroom with a wry smile. He sat on the bed to give her a quick kiss before removing his shoes and socks. "Unless maybe you were expecting somebody else?" He rolled the dirty socks in a ball and aimed it at the hamper across the room, where it ricocheted into a corner. Ignoring his faulty throw, he started unbuttoning his shirt.

She reached her arms overhead in a lazy stretch and yawned, an open book flat on her lap. "Nope, my boyfriend couldn't come over tonight, so I figured I'd wait up for you."

Not funny, Katie Rose.

She delivered a sassy smile, her sleepy blue eyes and mussed blonde hair lending a sweetly seductive look that both annoyed and triggered his pulse at the same time. She leaned to glance at the clock on the nightstand, letting loose a low whistle. "Goodness, McGee, anyone would think *you* had a girlfriend, working as late as you do."

Blood gorged his face, prompting him to rip the half-unbuttoned shirt right over his head, tie and all, hoping to deflect the heat in his cheeks. Crumpling it, he stood and sailed it and the tie toward the hamper, missing it by a mile.

Katie chuckled. "Gee, you're zero for two. Hope you're not losing your touch."

He turned to face her, not missing the swell of breasts straining her nightgown when she reached to angle the clock. His mouth went dry, reminding him the last thing he wanted to do was to lose his "touch." "Hope not," he said with a faint smile, trying not to focus on her gown.

"So . . . are you hungry?" She sat up. "Because I can warm up the stew . . ."

"No." The late hours he'd worked all week had certainly heightened his appetite . . . but not for food. He studied her while he unbuckled his belt, wishing she didn't look so darn sexy in his bed when he had a bone to pick. He dropped his trousers and folded them before hanging them in the closet, then slipped into the bathroom to brush his teeth and change into pajama bottoms. Returning, he flipped off the light and crawled into bed, pulling her into his arms as he sucked in a deep breath. With a gentle kiss to her head, he exhaled his stress, praying the encounter with Jack was only by chance. "So . . . how's Kit?"

She snuggled in, teasing the smooth skin of his chest with soft, little kisses that almost pushed Jack from his mind. *Almost.* "Well, she learned all her colors this week and drew a picture of you and me under a rainbow with her crayons, so she's real excited to show it to you."

He sighed. "I can't believe she's going to be three," he said, grateful Katie had bonded so closely with his adopted daughter. "Seems like she was just a baby."

"Well, she's not a baby now," Katie said with a grunt, "and she'll spit in your eye if you tell her so. She's even taken to selecting her own clothes, refusing to wear anything I suggest. Today she wore a striped romper with a plaid blouse. I thought my eyes were going to cross."

He chuckled, thinking for the hundredth time what a good mother Katie was. He suddenly thought of Jack, and his smile went flat. Now to make sure she remained a good wife . . . "How's school?"

"Draining, especially the seminar Monday night. I was spent when I finally picked Kit up from Lizzie's." She trailed a finger over his bicep and down his arm, slowly circling his palm with her thumb. "I felt like you with all the hours you work. I don't know how you do it, Luke." She nuzzled his neck. "When's the board meeting over again?"

"Three weeks," he said, his voice a near croak. He forced himself to focus on the problem at hand rather than the thrum of his body. "So . . . other than the seminar Monday night, what have you and Kit been doing with the rest of your evenings?"

Her thumb ceased. "Nothing much, lots of books, games, walks—you know, the usual."

He paused, fiddling with the strap of her gown. "So you just stayed home all week? Didn't go anywhere else, like your parents' or Lizzie's?"

Her chest expanded and released with a heavy draw of air before she responded. "Well, I did go out last night," she said slowly, voice breathless. "Mother watched Kit while I went to the law library."

The air eased from his lungs. "Alone?"

She hesitated a moment too long. "Yes, of course. Meg couldn't go."

"Aw, you hate studying alone." He massaged her arm. "Run into anybody you know?"

He felt the shift of her throat when she swallowed hard. "Uh . . . yeah." She rushed to kiss him full on the mouth, swaying her lips against his. "Mmm . . ."

Heat jolted, and he rolled her over, kissing her thoroughly before trailing his lips to her throat. "Who?" he whispered, the scent of her almost making him forget that he cared.

She moaned softly, ignoring his question while she tunneled fingers into his hair. His lips wandered lower. "Who, Katie?" he asked again, and her body went completely still. He looked up, heart thundering. *Tell me the truth, Katie—please.* "You all right?" he asked quietly.

Her mouth opened and closed as if she wanted to speak, but nothing came out, blue eyes blinking so fast, he thought she might cry. All air wedged in his throat. *Please, Katie, don't lie . . .*

"Luke," she began with a chew of her lip, "you know how I've struggled with contract law and you've been too busy to help?" She avoided his eyes. "Well, I . . . ," a shaky breath quivered out, "accepted someone's offer to tutor."

He didn't breathe.

She stared for several seconds, eyes clouded and teeth grating her lip in a way that meant she was weighing her options. Disappointment stabbed when she lunged to take his mouth with hers, pulling him down. "I love you, Luke McGee," she whispered, "and I missed you so much, it hurt."

Yeah, I know the feeling. Tempering his frustration, he gently fondled her lips, taking his time with a languid kiss that

146

made her go soft beneath his hold. In a slow and measured tease, he explored her mouth with his own, eliciting a moan deep in her throat when he gently tugged at her lip. "Who?" he whispered again, mouth straying to the lobe of her ear.

"What?" Her eyes were closed and her breathing shallow.

His mouth meandered to the curve of her throat, keeping pace with his hands as they skimmed the curve of her body. "I was wondering who helped you?"

Her body tensed beneath his lips and he knew this was it—the moment of reckoning. When Katie would tell him the truth or lie through her teeth. Taut with both passion and anger, Luke coaxed, trailing her collarbone with kisses while toying with the strap of her gown . . .

She shuddered beneath his lips, voice barely audible and as soft as a guilty thought. "Jack."

His lips stilled on her skin. The lids of his eyes weighted down with relief before heat surged that had nothing to do with the lure of his wife's body. "Jack?" he rasped, the word more of a hiss than a name. He jerked to a sitting position, shocked at the venom that flowed in his veins. "You asked *Jack* to tutor you?" He pierced her with a gaze that made her squirm.

Wincing, she shot up, hand clutched to his arm. "But you told me to get help . . ."

His mouth went slack. "From your *teachers*, Katie Rose," he ground out, "not your former fiancé." He slashed taut fingers through his hair, feeling the tug of the couch. "Oh, I'll just bet old Jack is flying high over this one, worming his way back in."

"He is *not* worming his way back in, Luke, he's helping an old friend." Her eyes sparked, matching a tone way less conciliatory than before. "*Because*," she said with tight emphasis, "her lawyer husband can't find the time to come home, I might add, much less tutor his wife."

He leaned in, lips compressed along with his jaw. "Yeah, well, I work for a living, Katie Rose, *which*, I might add," he said, mimicking her words, "apparently allows my wife the time and luxury to dally with her old boyfriend."

"*Dally?*" she breathed, all color blanching from her face. Her petite body rose up several inches to slant in, meeting him nose to nose. "My GPA in contract law has gone from near failing to dean's list, you Neanderthal, and no thanks to you."

She may as well have bopped him with his own club—heat blasted his face. *Translation: My old boyfriend was there when my husband wasn't.* He swallowed hard, guilt the perfect stabilizer for jealousy. "You're on the dean's list?" he said quietly, pride battling the angst in his gut.

The jut of her lip softened, catching his eye, stirring his pulse. She folded her arms with a grunt. "Yeah, well, I guess all that 'dallying' must have paid off."

He exhaled heavily, hands mauling his face before they dropped to the bed where his fingers strayed to circle her thigh. "I'm proud of you, Sass," he whispered, "really I am, and I apologize for not being here when you needed me." Cupping her face, he bent to brush a tender kiss to her lips, then pulled away, eyes locking with hers. "But I have a right to know, Katie—did you ask him, or did he offer? And where and how long has this been going on?"

She stared at her fingers, now laced with his. "Four months," she whispered, muscles tugging in her throat. "At the law library. I ran in to him one day and he offered to help."

"Oh, I just bet he did." His fingers nudged her chin till her gaze connected with his. "*Four months?*" he repeated. "You've been meeting with that clown for a whole semester?" He expelled a noisy breath, torn between kissing her senseless or shaking her silly. He opted for the first and pushed her to the pillow hard, descending with a kiss meant to restake his claim. "Never again, Katie Rose," he whispered when he finally came up for air. "Jack is out of our lives for good, is that clear? No tutoring, studying, or dallying of any kind beyond hello and goodbye. The next time you need help, you come to me, no matter how busy I am, understood?"

She nodded, eyes glazed and chest pumping. Her gaze strayed to his mouth, and his blood heated by several degrees, but he restrained himself to drive the point home. "It's just not smart, Katie, for a married woman to spend time alone with a man unless he's the dean, a blood relative, or a priest."

Or an intern? The thought singed the back of his neck, setting his jaw. *Lauren's different,* he argued in his mind, *an employee and nothing more. And hired by Carmichael, not me.*

A soft smile tilted her beautiful lips. "You're right, and you have my word—I'll never spend time with Jack again." Her eyelids lowered to half mast, delivering a smoky look that tingled all the way to his toes. She licked her lips, mouth parted and words breathy. "I'm sorry, Luke, I know how I'd feel if you did that to me . . ."

Luke swallowed.

Issuing a seductive smile, she trailed fingers down his bare chest. "From now on, you're the only tutor I need." She tugged him down until his mouth mated with hers. "But it's only fair to warn you, Mr. McGee," she said, breathless against his skin, "with extra classes this summer, I may need a whole lot of work."

He descended, settling in with a broad grin. "No problem, Sass," he whispered, his mouth playing with hers. "You can depend on me to work you hard till you shine. But just to make sure . . ." Lips skimming her jaw, he eased his way down, dislodging the strap of her gown with his teeth. "We better begin tonight . . ."

7

 o . . . how was the wedding?" Joe laced up his boxing
shoes and shot a quick glance at Steven, the smile
on his lips easing into a cocky grin. "Give you cold chills?"

Steven wrapped his fingers in a soft cloth before tugging
a padded leather glove on with his teeth. "Nope, not as long
as Erica doesn't get any cockamamie ideas that she and I are
more than friends. She needed a date, so I helped her out.
End of story."

"Or the beginning," Joe said with a stretch, pumping his
elbows back and forth to get warmed up. His lips slid to the
right. "The woman's been lovesick over you since that fling
you had with her when you broke up with Maggie the first
time."

Steven exhaled loudly and stood to his feet, jaw stiffening
somewhat. "I know, Joe, but trust me, I've made it perfectly
clear that I'm not interested in anything more this time."

Joe flexed his fingers, his smile sobering considerably. "You
mean other than dancing or necking?" he said casually, his
glib demeanor doing nothing to soften the conviction of his
words. "Which is better than before, I guess."

Eyeing a free boxing bag, Steven gave a curt nod to the

150

far side of the gym and started walking fast, sweat rag over his shoulder. Joe's reference to his heated affair with Erica made him itchy to pound the stuffing out of anything he could, and better Pop Clancy's bag than his partner's face. Lately Joe had been coming at him a lot about Erica, and Steven was tired of it. The last thing he wanted to do was relive memories of a past that made him feel like dirt, from a time when he'd used Erica to get over Maggie. Not that it worked, he thought with a twist of his lips. He'd picked right back up with Maggie the next year, which devastated Erica, even though he'd ended it with her months earlier. He skirted a ring where a Jack Dempsey hopeful was pummeling a guy twice his size, and Steven wished he could do the same with his past. Annihilate his guilt until it no longer ate at his soul, setting him free from this albatross around the neck of the man he wanted to be.

A man of honor and truth. A man people could trust. A man *he* could trust.

"Hey, wait up." Joe sprinted behind, stopping Steven with a hand to his arm. "No reason to go off half-cocked." He switched hands on the jug of water he carried.

Steven faced him head-on, hands slung low on his hips. "Look, Joe, I thought you *wanted* me back in the game, having some laughs, seeing women again, right? So what's your beef?"

A weighty sigh wavered from his partner's lips. "Yeah, I did, Steven. But lately, seeing you with Erica, well," he tunneled a hand through sandy hair, "I guess I'm worried you're having some laughs with a friend who won't think it's so funny when you break her heart."

Steven slacked a hip, eyes narrowing at Joe's veiled implication that he was using Erica. "What are you talking about, Walsh? Erica knows exactly where I stand and yet she still comes around—her decision, not mine. Believe me, I couldn't be clearer if I sent her a telegram."

"Yeah, well, I think maybe you could," Joe said quietly, his somber expression indicating his concern for their mutual friend. "You could cut her loose altogether, not string her along with dancing and occasional kisses on the dance floor at the Pier."

Heat scalded the back of Steven's neck. "It's a few harmless kisses, Walsh. For pity's sake, it's not like I'm taking her to bed."

Joe sighed and positioned himself behind the bag. "You may as well be, Steven. Erica's crazy about you, and every kiss only makes it worse. I thought at first maybe she'd be good for you, you know? Get you back in the game and maybe you two could really have something together. But the harder she falls, the farther away you seem to get, and I just hate to see a good friend get hurt. We both know there are plenty of girls who'll accommodate you, girls who are out for nothing but laughs just like you and me." He girded the canvas bag with muscular arms, leg braced. "Hate to tell you this, O'Connor, but Erica's not one of 'em."

Steven closed his eyes and pawed at his temple with the bulky glove, the old, familiar guilt slithering back in, as hot and uncomfortable as the sweat crawling down his chest. Deep down inside, he'd known it, hated himself for giving in to the temptation Erica always posed—attractive, willing, comfortable . . . *safe*. Holding her, kissing her, made him feel alive again, like his body could respond to love even if his heart couldn't. She'd made it perfectly clear he could take it as far as he needed, but what he *needed* was distance from a past that haunted him, not giving in to passion that would only take him down once again.

His chest expanded and released. "You're right." He opened his eyes to face the friend who never pulled any punches except at the gym, a man who cared about others as much as he did Steven. "Sorry, Joe, never meant to hurt Erica, you know that. Just figured kisses would be safe with somebody who didn't have a hold on me, but I guess not. At least not for her." His mouth edged into a sheepish smile. "Got a little too caught up in being with a woman again, I suppose. I've been on hold for a while, you know, while you've hobnobbed with the ladies."

Joe grinned. "Nobody 'hobnobs' better than you, O'Connor, when you set your mind to it." His grin slanted into a dry smile. "That is, when you're not too busy playing it safe."

"Well, trust me, 'safe' is the last thing I'll be playing tonight, Walsh, you can bet on that." He tossed the sweat rag on the bench and tugged the gloves tighter while he gave Joe a goading smile, moving to face the bag. "Beginning right now."

The bag hammered Joe's jaw without mercy while Steven vented every frustration he had. Over Erica, over guilt he couldn't forget, and over memories of a woman he wished he could. *Maggie.* Worlds away and yet always as close as the next thought, she was a two-edged sword, reminding him not only of the kind of love he craved but the kind of destruction a love like that could inflict. No other woman had ever touched him at the core like Maggie, made him feel and care like she had, and Steven missed that. Sweat streamed down his body as he spent his fury on the bag, wondering if he'd ever feel that way again. If any other woman could even come close.

Annie. With a choking heave, he sagged against the bag with eyes shut, trying to catch his breath, both from exertion and thoughts of someone he had no business thinking about. He hadn't seen her at Ocean Pier since his big-brother talk, but her wholesome memory ratcheted his pulse even higher while the canvas soaked up his sweat. He was drawn to her, no question. Her clean, natural look, her sweet naïveté, her childlike candor. *Her innocence.* He winced, taunted by a truth he knew all too well—innocence he would destroy if he ever got ahold of it.

"Feel better?"

Steven's eyelids inched up while he huffed, cheek to the bag. "Not sure."

Joe studied him. "You were a whole lot less serious in college, you know that?"

Steven grabbed the jug and upended it, biceps bulging from

the effort. He swiped the side of his mouth, giving Joe an off-center grin. "Naw, I've always been the serious one, Walsh, and you know it. Heaven knows one of us had to be. Did you even study once?"

The twinkle returned to Joe's hazel eyes as a crooked grin lit his face. "Didn't have to—my best friend was a brain and a straight arrow when it came to the books." He snatched the jug and took a swig. "Still don't know how you did it, burning the candle at both ends—fraternity president, parties till dawn, obsession with Maggie. And *still* on the dean's list without even trying." He winked and guzzled more water. "Plus keeping Maggie happy through it all."

"A little too happy," Steven muttered, nabbing the water.

"Yeah, I have to admit, that always surprised me. You have more drive and willpower than anybody I've ever seen, Steven, in college, at work." His lips went flat. "Except with Mags."

"Don't remind me." Steven's smile faded into a scowl.

Joe set the jug down. "To tell you the truth, there was a time I was glad to see the hold Maggie had over you. Since first grade, you've been this perfect kid—smart, calm, in control, nothing ever slipping you up. Then you meet her, and *boom*—all that golden willpower and control flies right out the window. Weirdest thing I ever saw—hard-nosed and unflinching about grades or work, but put you in a car with Maggie Kennedy, and you couldn't say 'no' to save your life."

Steven flinched while his eyes trailed into a stare. *Or my soul.*

Gripping the bag, Joe leaned to keep his chin clear of the battering zone. "Hey, I met a doll last week, and she's got some good-looking friends. Why don't you go tonight?"

"Sorry, Joe, can't." Two minutes of bullet-fire blows had Steven heaving till it hurt, his body drenched from the effort. He collapsed on the bench, wet head plastered to the wall. "Promised Gabe a night of ice cream and checkers," he said, gasping for air. He swabbed his face with the towel before gulping another swig of water.

Shaking his head, Joe sucked air through clenched teeth.

"Gosh, you're starting to worry me, O'Connor, opting for checkers with a kid on Saturday night instead of a good-looking doll."

Steven grinned. "At least I won't be dragging my body into church after burning the midnight oil *or* in need of a confessional when I finally do show up."

A bit of the devil sparkled in his partner's eyes. "But, oh, so worth it, O'Connor, trust me. I think I may be in love this time." He grabbed the jug and took a long swallow. "Even so, I won't be in need of a confessional any more than you. You're not the only one who's changed since college, you know. I'm looking to keep my postgraduate reputation pristine."

Steven unlaced the gloves and tossed them at Joe with a grin, rising to position himself behind the bag. "Well, well, now, would you look at us—two squeaky-clean altar boys with halos aglow."

With a low chuckle, Joe wrapped both hands before tugging on the gloves, his freckled face beaming. "Yeah, but *my* halo will be comfortably off-kilter while yours, buddy boy, will be as flat and stiff as your love life." He winked. "Hmmm . . . wonder who'll have more fun?"

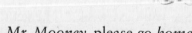

Mr. Mooney, please *go home!* Glancing at the clock on the wall, Annie chewed on her lip, absently collecting catechism texts from each desk. Her eyes strayed to where Vincent Mooney regaled Faith McGuire with his latest ventures as a romance writer for *Love Story Magazine,* and her hopes sank along with her shoulders. Trudging to the cabinet to put books away, she prayed for a moment alone with Faith before Aunt Eleanor's board meeting was over, but it didn't look promising. *Not with Mr. Mooney "mooning" over their teacher!* Annie sighed. She was desperate to discuss—and pray—about uneasy feelings plaguing her since she'd made peace with her aunt. But . . . apparently not tonight. Reaching for her purse, she slowly rose, her eyes meeting Faith's for the briefest of moments, but apparently it was more than enough.

Retrieving her own purse from the drawer of the teacher's desk, Faith quickly shook Mr. Mooney's hand, her smile as warm as the woman herself. "Congratulations, Mr. Mooney, on yet another sale. It's not easy getting a story published. I know—I've been trying for years and only sold one." She glanced at her watch. "Goodness, my husband'll send out a posse if I don't get home soon."

Mr. Mooney took the hint nicely. "Thank you, Mrs. McGuire, for your encouragement, as always." A twinkle in his blue eyes matched the silver in his hair. "Mr. McGuire's a lucky man."

Faith laughed, slipping her sweater off the back of the chair. "Not if I don't get home in time to put my daughters to bed. He's a bit of a softie when it comes to his girls, I'm afraid, and they bamboozle him into piggyback rides and way too many bedtime stories. So the man gets a wee bit cranky if I'm late." Straightening the teacher's desk, her gaze connected with Annie's. "Oh, Annie—you're still here. Good. I need to ask you something before I go."

"Well, good night, Mrs. McGuire," Mr. Mooney said, making his way to the door.

"G'night, Mr. Mooney. See you next week." The gentleman disappeared down the hall and Faith sat down in the first row with a pat on the next desk. "Sit, Annie—you look like you need to chat."

Annie glanced at the clock. "But don't you need to get home?" she asked, concern flitting in her stomach like so many fireflies. "I don't want your husband getting 'cranky.'"

"Soon, but not before we talk . . . *and* set a date to take the girls to story time at Bookends." She winked. "And don't worry about Collin. I'll get home in plenty of time to ward off cranky, I hope. Or late enough that he'll already be fast asleep."

Smiling, Annie plopped down in a desk, grateful for this

gentle woman who in some ways reminded her of Mama—patient, kind, and a personality that went from empathy to sparkle in the utterance of a prayer. "Thanks, Faith, I do have something I need to discuss." Her gaze darted to the clock and back. "But I don't have much time."

"Then tell me quickly." Faith shifted to get comfortable.

Puffing out a sigh, Annie fidgeted with her nails, eyes fixed on her hands. "It has to do with Aunt Eleanor," she began, gaze lifting to offer Faith a weak smile. "She and I had a huge breakthrough last week after you and I prayed, so I can't thank you enough. But now . . ." Annie swallowed hard. "Well, now, I'm feeling guilty about all the things I did behind her back when I first came to Boston." She took a deep breath. "Things like sneaking out of the house, going to Ocean Pier when she told me not to, and even getting involved with questionable guys."

"Involved?" Faith said slowly.

Annie's cheeks pulsed with heat. "Well, not like it sounds. I suppose one guy, actually, and only one kiss at that. But I have to be honest, Faith . . ." She peeked up beneath lowered lashes, her reluctant confession making her squirm. "This particular boy—well, man, really—turned my insides to mush so much that I . . . well, I wished it could be more."

"We all do, Annie," Faith said with a squeeze of her hand, sympathy radiating from her eyes. "It's how God made us as women, to crave a man's touch, his love. Trust me, I had many a battle when Collin came into my life—both with myself and with him, especially after we were engaged." Her smile went soft. "But the good news is both you and I are blessed enough to know the truest and surest way to win the right man's love and respect is God's way, not ours." She grinned and gave a little shiver. "Although a kiss from a man who turns our insides to mush can certainly make a girl wish—and do—a lot of things she shouldn't." She hesitated. "Are you still seeing him?" Her smile crooked. "This mush-maker?"

Heat traveled clear to the tips of Annie's ears. "Oh no, no

. . . I stopped going to Ocean Pier, and that's where I would always see him before." She exhaled, relief and regret merging in the shaky sigh that escaped from her lips. "Remember the letter I told you about, the one my father wrote me before he died? Well, it changed everything, Faith. So, between God's conviction and the mush-maker's insistence that I was 'too special' of a girl to be part of the wild crowd—"

"Wait . . ." Faith sat up. "This mush-maker was trying to *keep* you from going down the wrong path?"

Annie nodded, her smile sheepish. "Over and over. In fact, he only kissed me that once to scare me off, he said. To teach a lesson that the wrong guy would take advantage of my innocence." A wispy sigh floated from her lips. "But the truth is, Faith, much to my shame, he made me feel like I *wanted* him to take advantage. Which is why I stopped going to the Pier altogether. I knew it was wrong, not only defying Aunt Eleanor, but feeling that way."

"Good girl," Faith said, patting Annie's arm with a smile. "But, I have to admit, this guy sounds pretty special, so no wonder you were smitten. Still . . . ," she leaned forward to fold her arms on the desk, "God will honor your obedience, Annie, he always does. Now . . . suppose you tell me about your problem with Aunt Eleanor?"

"Well, I've been thinking lately that since Aunt Eleanor and I have gotten closer, maybe I should confess all the things I did behind her back."

"No!" Faith sat up, brows high and lips parted in a definite "O."

"No?" Annie blinked in confusion. "But, why not? I thought confession was good for the soul, being a sacrament of the Church and all."

"Good for *your* soul, maybe, but not Aunt Eleanor's. Yes, honesty is crucial in our walk with God, for sure, but the Bible tells us that although some things are lawful, not all are profitable or edify. It's the rule of love God is so partial to—let no one seek his own, it says, but that of the other.

Which means," Faith said with a pointed look, "we have to weigh every word out of our mouth. Although what we want to say may be the truth, if it doesn't lift the person up, encourage, or set free, more than likely we need to keep it between God and ourselves."

Sucking in a deep breath, Annie nodded. "Okay, that makes sense, so problem solved. Now . . . I just have one more."

"Yes?" Faith arched a brow.

"My friend Peggy's older sister and friends are a bit on the wild side, and Peggy told them my eighteenth birthday is coming up. Now they want to take me to dinner, and at first Aunt Eleanor said no. But then she changed her mind and wants to pay for everyone's dinner."

"How nice," Faith said.

"Yes, it is." Annie hesitated. "Except for this uneasy feeling I shouldn't go."

"Why? It's just dinner, right?"

"Yes."

"Well, then, I think you should just go, enjoy yourself, and then go home."

"You do?"

"Sure. But if there's a check in your spirit, we can pray about it. When that happens to me, I just pray for wisdom, close my eyes, and think about each option. Now, you have to be really seeking to follow God's leading rather than your own, mind you, but if you are, one of the options will usually give you more peace than the other. And that's the one I generally choose."

"Really?"

"Really." Faith smiled.

With a giggle of relief, Annie gave Faith a hug. "Perfect! Thank you so much." She smiled, eyes warm with admiration. "How'd you get so smart anyway?"

A chuckle rumbled from Faith's lips. "Well, actually, God's the smart one because his Word tells us how to live in order to reap blessing, and I was lucky enough to learn that early. So when I applied his precepts to my life—things like praying for people who hurt me or staying pure in my relationship with Collin before we married—well, blessings overtook me. Before long, it became a lifestyle of the heart, giving me a wisdom about life I never had before."

Annie sighed, hope springing in her chest. "Oh, Faith, I want that more than anything!"

Faith grinned. "Then I have the perfect prayer for you—a prayer I've prayed daily for years. But a word of warning, Annie," she said with a hint of mischief. "Don't pray it unless you're prepared for God to answer, because he *will*."

"What is it?" Annie breathed, adrenaline surging.

"Psalm 139:23–24. 'Search me, O God, and know my heart. Try me and know my thoughts. See if there be any wicked way in me, and lead me in the way everlasting.'" She squeezed Annie's hand. "But don't say I didn't warn you."

Just the sound of Faith's words triggered Annie's pulse. *Oh yes, God, please!*

"Annie? Are you ready? Glory is waiting in the car with Frailey."

Annie glanced up to see Aunt Eleanor in the doorway, a smile on her face.

"Miss Martin, so nice to see you again," Faith said, rising. "We're just finishing up." She turned to Annie. "All except a date to take the girls to story time. How does this Saturday sound? Ten o'clock at Bookends, followed by cookie baking at my mother's house? Fair warning—you'll meet my sisters and their kids, which may be more than you bargained for."

Annie laughed. "Wouldn't dare miss it—Glory would wring my neck." Looping her purse over her shoulder, she joined her aunt at the door. "Good night, Faith. See you Saturday." Her lips tipped in a sassy grin. "And if 'you know who' is 'cranky,' I hope he's asleep."

Not likely, Faith thought with a wave and slow burn of her cheeks, recalling the gleam in Collin's eyes when he'd kissed her goodbye after dinner. A warm shiver traveled her bones. The same gleam he'd worn for the last six months in his quest for a son.

"You best come straight home tonight, Mrs. McGuire," he'd whispered, his voice husky with warning. Hooking her close, his teeth had nipped at her earlobe, lips wandering her neck until she'd been as limp as the spaghetti she'd fixed for dinner. Without question, Collin McGuire had been her "mush-maker" since the fifth grade when he'd defended her from a bully on the playground, and a day didn't go by she didn't thank God for this man in her life.

Her eyes drifted closed as she gently caressed her abdomen, cherishing the seed of his child that grew in her womb. A child her husband didn't know about yet, but could very well be the son whom he craved. Taking a deep breath, she discreetly let out two more notches of her belt, grateful she'd moved the buttons on her skirt. She sighed, warmth invading her chest at how elated he'd be after five years of trying. Guilt niggled. *That is . . . if he knew.*

"I'll tell him, Lord," she whispered, slipping her sweater over her shoulders, "soon." Turning out the lights, she hurried down the hall and out the door, mind in turmoil over the news she needed to share with her husband. She was almost in her fourth month now, but she'd kept it from him because she was afraid. Afraid to dash Collin's hopes if something went wrong.

And afraid he'd forbid you to teach this class?

Her brisk pace down the street slowed considerably. Maybe a little, she conceded, but that wasn't all. Collin was such an emotional man, she couldn't bear to see the hurt in his eyes if she miscarried. Shame wormed its way in over how desperately she'd wanted to teach this class . . . *and* to continue to do so.

Especially now. For the first time since her copywriter job at the *Boston Herald* before Bella was born, she felt alive again, someone who contributed to the world outside of being a mother. She quickened her pace, thoughts of her daughters plucking her heart. Not that she didn't love being a mom. No, it was the most important job in her life. But now that the girls would all be in school, Faith needed more than an empty house to clean. She understood Katie and Charity more than ever before, Katie wanting to be a lawyer and Charity longing to work at the store. But like Luke and Mitch, Collin felt a woman's place was in the home, which was fine, she thought with a twist of her lips. If the poor woman wasn't stuck in an empty house eight hours a day.

Eyes fixed on the stoplight at the curb, she tapped her toe impatiently while she waited for the light to change, debating when to tell Collin his child was on the way. *Next week? The week after?* The light turned green, and she darted across, realizing it would have to be soon. Palming a hand to her stomach, she felt the burgeoning mound. "Soon, God," she promised.

She scampered up the steps of the tiny brownstone she and Collin called home, gaze darting to the second story where their bedroom window was dark. A ridge creased her brow. *Goodness, he's asleep already?* She eased the knob of the front door, letting herself in as quietly as possible, thankful Collin had left the parlor light on. Locking it again, she moved to turn off the light and stopped. There sprawled on the gold brocade sofa was her husband, sound asleep with feet bare and a newspaper bunched on his chest. Love swelled in her throat, and she tiptoed to where he lay, heart thudding as always when she could watch him unobserved.

Hands down, Collin McGuire was the most handsome man she'd ever met, never failing to trigger her pulse whenever he entered a room. Chestnut hair rumpled from sleep fell over eyes that boasted the longest lashes she had ever seen. Her gaze wandered from a chiseled face shadowed by a day's growth of beard down muscular arms relaxed in sleep, and a rush of emotion filled her till tears pricked her eyes. *God, I never tire of thanking you for the gift of this man.* Bending over, she pressed a soft kiss to his cheek, and then squealed when she tumbled on top of him after he hooked an arm to her waist. "Collin McGuire, you scared me to death!" Smacking his chest, she squirmed to break free.

"Serves you right for keeping your husband waiting," he groused, burying his lips in her hair. "Apparently I didn't make my intentions clear when you left tonight, Mrs. McGuire, so let me rectify that right now." In one fluid motion, he had her flipped on her back with a mischievous glint in his eye. "You owe me, Little Bit," he whispered, "make no mistake." Her breath caught when he nuzzled her throat. "Three baths . . ." His lips trailed to her collarbone. "Four bedtime stories . . ." Warm palms fondled her shoulders while stray fingers teased along the collar of her blouse. "And six piggyback rides' worth, to be exact." He took her mouth with a vengeance, trapping a soft moan in her throat before his lips wandered south.

"Collin, you'll wake the girls," she breathed, giggles rising at the tickle of his beard.

Gaze shuttered, he pinned her with both a wicked look and possessive hands while that slow smile she loved went to work. "Not if you succumb peacefully, Mrs. McGuire."

A squeak caught in her throat when he swept her up in his arms. "What on earth . . ."

He strode to the staircase, a man on a mission. "Did you lock the door?" he asked.

"Yes, but my purse is on the floor by the—"

"Leave it," he ordered. "Not foremost on my mind right now." Huffing on the landing, he eyed her with a quirk of his brow. "Either I need to ramp it up at the gym, Little Bit, or you and Abby have been snacking on too many cookies." He repositioned her with a grunt and proceeded down the hall, butting their bedroom door closed before placing her on the bed. "You may be eating more cookies," he said with a roguish smile, "but it's going in all the right places."

He crawled in beside her and she giggled, slapping his hands away. "Collin McGuire, will you please show some restraint? I need to get ready for bed."

163

She started to get up and he rolled her back, kissing her soundly. "Sorry, Little Bit, but I used all my restraint when we were engaged."

Batting his hands away, she shimmied free and popped to her feet, tossing an impish smile over her shoulder. "Absence makes the heart grow fonder, my love, so hold that thought."

He lumbered to his feet, his tone a near growl. "Any fonder, Little Bit, and you're going to see a grown man cry." Following her into the bathroom, he snatched his toothbrush and squeezed a curl of toothpaste to brush behind her in the mirror. "You're definitely the civilized one in this family, Faith, just shy of prim and proper." Lips sloped in a wry smile, he lifted a lock of her hair to plant a foamy kiss scented with peppermint, and she gave a little squeal.

"I'll show you civilized," she said with a mock glare. She pinched a glob of toothpaste on her hand and lunged, slashing him with a clump of cream that oozed down his neck.

Eyes circled in shock, he stared, toothbrush limp in his mouth. Slamming it in the sink, he grinned, capturing her from behind. "So you want to play dirty, do you?" he whispered. And with a playful flick of his tongue, he murmured hot words in her ear, their intent disarming as much as his actions. Hands skilled at lovemaking traveled her body with a gentle caress, and her eyes drifted closed while heat shimmered her skin. *Oh, Collin . . .*

All tease faded away at the warmth of his touch. "I love you, Faith," he said quietly, his voice husky and low, "and I've been craving you since you walked out that door." Sweeping her hair aside, he grazed the curve of her neck with his lips, unleashing a soft moan from her throat. Renegade hands roamed to her waist where gentle fingers tugged her blouse from her skirt. The warmth of his palm slid to her stomach and stopped . . . His eyes met hers in the mirror, and she swallowed hard as the truth dawned in their depths. "Your stomach is usually flat, Little Bit . . . ," he whispered, a muscle shifting in his throat. "Are you . . . is it possible . . . could you be pregnant?"

Tears welled in her eyes and she nodded.

"Oh, Faith . . ." Swallowing her in his arms, he began to laugh, the sound tender and reverent and mixed with his tears. With trembling hand, he gently palmed her stomach again, his silent heaves shuddering against her back. "Oh, God, thank you, thank you," he said softly, the intensity of his emotion vibrating against her hair. "We'll gladly take whatever you send, but oh, Lord, my soul longs for a son . . ."

Turning her to face him, he cupped her cheeks in his hands, nuzzling her lips with such tenderness that tears spilled from her eyes. "I love you, Faith, more than anything in this world." He clutched her close, his breath warm in her ear. "When?" he whispered.

Her heart stalled. "I . . . haven't been to the doctor yet, so I'm not certain."

He pulled back, his face that of a little boy at Christmas. "Your best guess, then. February? March? Come on, Faith, I'm gonna be a father again—give me something to go on."

She worried her lip, heart thudding against her ribs. With a hard gulp, she slowly raised her eyes to his. "After Thanksgiving," she said quietly.

Silence. The drip of the faucet sounded deafening as Collin stared, mouth open and jaw slack. The joy that glimmered in his eyes before glinted into a hard veneer beneath dark brows dipped thunderously low. "Thanksgiving?" he repeated, the shock of his tone embedding her guilt even deeper. He stepped back, eyes scanning her body as he was often prone to do, but this time, his desire seemed as cold as the porcelain sink digging into her back. "You've been pregnant for three months or more . . . and you didn't tell me?"

Her body chilled to ice, except for the heat in her face. "Collin, I didn't want to get your hopes up if something happened," she said quickly, circling his waist. "I wanted to make sure."

His gray eyes narrowed to slits of pewter, and a muscle cramped in her stomach when he moved farther away. "You mean 'make sure' you can teach your all-important class, don't you?"

Her breath caught. The truth of his statement hit dead on, her words to Annie sealing her guilt. *"It's the rule of love God is so partial to—let no one seek his own but that of the other."*

Taut muscles in his face eased almost imperceptibly when the dark slash of brows sloped into hurt. *Oh, Collin, forgive me!* She struggled to talk, but her tongue was as thick as the paste on her hand. "You're right," she whispered. "I was being selfish and putting myself before you." She looked up, tears burning her eyes over what she had done. "Will you forgive me, please?"

The lines of his face softened a degree, but the damage she'd caused still darkened his eyes. "You deceived me, Faith. That's my baby as well as yours, and I had a right to know."

She stepped forward, fingers shaking when she twined them with his, his hand cold and still. With a heavy heart, she moved in close, arms to his waist and head to his chest. Eyes shut, she breathed in his scent—musk and soap and the sweet hint of talcum powder he used on the girls. She heard the beat of his heart, steady and strong, a heart that beat fiercely for her, his family, and the God they all served. Fingers clenched, she dug into the rigid muscles of his back, her voice a grieved whisper. "Will you forgive me?"

He exhaled and she realized she'd been holding her breath. "I forgive you, Faith, but I'm hurt. We promised to tell each other everything."

"I know." She stood on tiptoe to brush her lips to his, well aware his arms remained slack for a man with a one-track mind when it came to his wife.

He held her away, his cool look chilling her skin. "Forgiven, Faith, but not forgotten. You knew how much this baby would mean to me, yet you withheld it. It's going to take some time for my anger to cool." He released her abruptly, the absence of his touch leaving her bereft. Reaching for his toothbrush, he rinsed it off and put it back before shoving past her.

Her heart tripped. Clutching his sleeve, she begged with her eyes. "Collin, please, don't do this! Our love has produced a child—can't we embrace that?" Desperate for reconciliation, she clutched him close, resorting to Charity's tactics with a hand grazing his thigh. "Collin, please—make love to me," she whispered.

With an unnatural calm, he quietly removed her hand from his leg, his look as icy as his touch. "I'm sorry, Faith, but I'm just not ready." He turned to go, taking her heart with him.

Sagging against the sink, she put a hand to her eyes and wept. A man of unbridled passion, Collin had seldom turned her away in over thirteen years of marriage, and Faith mourned the loss of his touch. With a swipe of tears, she plucked a tissue from the box on the commode and blew her nose before brushing her teeth and washing her face. She slipped out of her clothes, donned her silk nightgown, and turned out the light, silent in the dark as she slid into bed. Collin lay on his side, his bare back a muscled wall. More tears pricked and she curled into a ball on her edge of the bed, silent prayers soft on her tongue. *Lord, this isn't how I'd hoped to celebrate the news of our child.* But if Collin needed time to heal, then she'd give it, no matter the hurt in her heart. Long moments of heavy silence passed and she drew in a deep breath, finally willing to risk his rejection with a stroke of his shoulder. "I love you, Collin—"

She froze when he gripped her hand, the intensity in his tone stealing her air. "Don't ever, *ever* do this again, Faith," he whispered, turning to face her. "Keeping something from me that I have a right to know. Do you understand?"

Chest heaving, she nodded, his face a mere blur through a curtain of tears.

"That's my son or daughter in there," he whispered in pain, his voice and hands softening with a skim of her stomach, cradling it before his arms cradled her. The clock ticked away the precious moments as he held her, her gratitude filling the silence until he finally pressed a kiss to her hair. Easing her back on the bed, his eyes fused to hers while his hand caressed her belly as if it were the very child in her womb. In slow and deliberate motion, he leaned in, fondling her mouth with a kiss so exquisitely tender, she quivered beneath his touch. "We're one flesh, Faith," he breathed. "My seed, your womb, God's blessing." He kissed her again, slowly, reverently, fingers tucked to her chin while his thumb trailed her jaw. "We need to talk tomorrow about the prospect of you teaching, but for now—tonight—" He swept her hair back from her face with a solemn gaze and a gentle hand. "Tonight," he said quietly, eyes moist and his whisper brimming with awe, "I'd like to celebrate the hope of a son."

⁓

"Last one to the tree is it!" Gabe tore out of Faith's mother's back door, a blur of freckles and curls flying in the breeze, coaxing a smile to Annie's face. Faith's foster sister reminded her a lot of a grown-up Glory—smart, tough, and a bit of the dickens.

Annie sighed. Just one day with Faith's family and already they'd become as big a blessing to Glory as Faith had become to her. The smell of fresh-mown grass drifted into the cheery kitchen, merging with the aroma of warm sugar cookies. A contented sigh parted from Annie's lips as she tied Glory's shoe, the feeling of family as sweet as the smudge of icing across her sister's cheek.

"Annie, hurry—I'm gonna be last . . ." Glory's tiny fist shook Annie's shoulder while a horde of cousins darted behind Gabe, limbs and shrieks slashing the air.

"Oh no you won't, sweetheart," Charity said with a snag of Henry's shirt.

"Thanks, Mrs. Dennehy, you're the best!" Glory shouted, her angelic smile gliding into a smirk as she tore past Henry with a giggle.

"Hey, no fair!" Henry groaned, Charity's ten-year-old twin

son clearly a master at melodrama. Face screwed in agony, he attempted to twist free. "You always make me go last."

"That's because you're a handsome young man who has to learn ladies go first." Charity wrestled an arm to his waist, managing a kiss to his cheek before he dashed out the door. Her lips slanted. "At least till a woman marries, and then heaven knows it's all downhill from there."

"Hush, Charity," Faith teased. "You'll give Annie the wrong idea about marriage."

"Oops." Charity winked. "I *meant* till a woman marries a stubborn Irishman."

Annie giggled, the easy camaraderie between sisters a balm to her soul. She'd known from the moment she'd met Faith's sisters at Bookends this morning, and then their mother upon arrival at the house, that this was the kind of family she'd always longed for. The kind she'd been destined for before Maggie left for college and her mother'd taken ill. A sliver of grief edged the corners of her mind and she pushed it away, unwilling to allow a shadow to fall on one of the best days she'd had in a long time. "So, you all married Irishmen, then?" She scanned the faces of Faith's sisters as they sipped tea around their mother's table.

"'Fraid so," Charity said, teacup in hand and a leisurely smile on her face. Her elbows sank onto the table as perfectly manicured brows angled in tease. "Lady-killers, all—giving a whole new meaning to the word, because trust me, they're as stubborn as they are good-looking."

Katie chuckled. "Right down to the man who gave us life, right, Mother?"

Marcy turned at the counter with a smile, mixing ingredients for a final batch of cookies. "Oh mercy, yes," she said with a shake of her head, the occasional silver strands in her blonde bob one of the few indicators she was Faith's mother and not an older sister. "And his two sons? Goodness, it's as if he spit them out of his mouth, although Sean isn't too bad I suppose, is he, Emma?"

Faith's sister-in-law smiled. "I'm afraid the jury's still out on that one, Marcy." Emma's gray eyes twinkled. "Although I suspect he might be the least stubborn of the lot."

"Humph," Charity said, chomping a cookie, "he's certainly not the most thickheaded, I can tell you that." She swiped a dab of stray frosting with her tongue. "Mitch has a lock on that."

"Well, don't worry, Annie," Marcy said with a crinkle of laugh lines around clear blue eyes, "just steer clear of men from the Southie neighborhood for Italians from the North End."

"Oooo, I hear Italians are romantic." Lizzie stirred cream into her tea with a dreamy sigh.

"Uh-oh, it's not almost two-thirty, is it?" Katie jumped up with a final swig of tea. "I'm supposed to meet Meg at Harvard Law at two-thirty to study criminal justice, and I wanted to surprise Luke with some cookies at the office on my way."

"To soften him up before you tell him about studying with Jack?" Charity licked the remains of frosting from her finger while giving Katie a devious smile.

Katie hiked her chin, a pretty shade of rose blooming on her cheeks. "Already told him, if you must know, and he took it rather well."

"Oh, Katie, I'm so relieved." Marcy delivered bowls of cookie dough to both sides of the table and plopped in a chair, commencing to fan herself with a well-worn recipe card. "I wasn't sure how Luke would react." Her lips tilted as she glanced at Annie. "Something else to consider with Irish men, I suppose—stubbornness compounded by temper."

Katie dropped several sugar cookies into a paper bag, then tucked it in her purse, rounding the table to give her mother a kiss. "To be honest, Mother, I was relieved too, given Luke's penchant for drama. But all I had to do was promise to stop studying with Jack, and all is well in the McGee household once again." She dispensed hugs to her sisters. "Thanks, Lizzie, for keeping Kit tonight. I owe you. With Luke working so many late hours, my studying time has been slim to nil, so a night at the library is a godsend." She extended a hand. "Annie, it was wonderful meeting you and Glory. I hope we'll see you again soon."

Annie squeezed Katie's hand. "I would like nothing better, Katie, trust me."

Retrieving a massive book from the counter, Katie sauntered to the back door and tossed a smile over her shoulder. "This was fun, but duty calls—first to deliver cookies to the love of my life, then on to study a subject that might actually teach me how to deal with my husband."

"Manslaughter?" Charity asked smoothly, lips curving into a wicked smile.

Katie chuckled. "Nope, bribery." Waving, she pushed the screen door open. "Toodle oo."

"Goodbye, dear. So, Annie," Marcy said, not missing a beat as she spooned cookie dough onto a baking sheet. "Faith says you live with your aunt, Eleanor Martin. We've never met, but I've heard wonderful things about what she's done for the parish, so you must be very proud."

Annie glanced up. She'd never thought of Aunt Eleanor in terms of being proud of her, but since the two of them had grown closer, Annie discovered a warm glow spreading through her chest. "Why, yes, I suppose I am, Marcy," she said slowly, still hesitant to call Faith's mother by her first name as Marcy insisted. "I won't lie, it was a shock when Glory and I moved here. You see, our family was estranged from Aunt Eleanor, so when Daddy died six months ago, almost two years after Mama, it was an adjustment. Not only for my sister and me, but for Aunt Eleanor too, given a long-standing feud between our families."

"Oh, I'm so sorry to hear that," Marcy whispered. The kindness in her eyes caused moisture to well in Annie's. "Faith told us about your mother and father, which absolutely broke my heart." She gave Annie's hand a gentle squeeze before returning to the task before her. "But it seems as if God has certainly provided for you and your sister."

"Yes, he has," Annie breathed, swiping her eye with the back of her wrist. Her gaze connected with Faith's, who watched her with the affection of a big sister. "Especially when he brought your daughter into my life at a time I was struggling with both my faith and my aunt."

Marcy smiled. "Yes, Faith has been blessed with wisdom and passion for God, which has seen all of us through many a trial, I can tell you that. It seems to be her gift." Her gaze rounded the table, eyes soft as she beheld each of the women in the room. "But then each of my daughters and daughter-in-law have unique gifts that have blessed my life."

"Ooo-ooo, what's mine?" Charity asked, blue eyes sparkling as she leaned on the table.

"Making grown men cry," Faith said with a grin.

"Hey, only my husband," Charity said with a thrust of her jaw, "and it's been awhile." Her nose scrunched in thought. "I think."

Chuckling, Emma smiled at Annie. "I understand you're from Badger, Iowa. Did you live there all your life, or does your family hail from Boston?"

"My younger sister and I were born and raised there, but my older sister was born in Chicago. My mother, Aunt Eleanor's sister, was born in Boston." Annie smiled, her tone suddenly edged with melancholy. "When Mama fell in love with Daddy, apparently it caused quite a ruckus in the family. You see, Mother was Catholic and Father was a Protestant minister, so they left Boston to raise a family in Chicago and then moved to Badger." Her sigh was heavy. "I don't think Mama's parents ever forgave her before they died and Aunt Eleanor seemed to follow suit." Her smile returned as she glanced at Faith, breaking her bittersweet reverie. "But, that's all changed now because of Faith's counsel and prayers, hopefully to end the feud forever between the Martins and Kennedys."

"Kennedy?" Charity asked over her shoulder, checking on the cookies in the oven. "You wouldn't by chance be related to . . ." She paused and shook her head. "Naw, of course not—

you're from Iowa. Although you do remind me of someone," she said with a squint, causing Annie's stomach to flip-flop as Charity sized her up. Shooting her a smile, Charity plopped back into her chair. "Don't worry—it'll come to me sooner or later, I'm sure."

"Annie!" An apple-cheeked Glory flew into the kitchen with a squeal, her blonde Shirley Temple curls damp and disheveled. "Can we stay for dinner, please?" she said, barely able to catch her breath. "Gabe invited us and we're going to play Sardine's Ghost!"

"Glory, no—" Annie began, blood warming her cheeks at her little sister's boldness.

"Of course you'll stay for dinner," Marcy insisted, popping up when the timer buzzed. She set the cookie sheet on a rack to cool before putting a new one in, then grabbed a cookie from the plate and handed it to Glory with a hug. "You look like you could use this, Glory."

Annie was mortified. "Marcy, honestly, about dinner—we can't impose."

Glory spun around, eyes wide. "Sure we can, Annie. Aunt Eleanor won't be home till late, remember? Please, can't we stay, *please*?"

"Say yes, Annie," Faith said with a chuckle. "Tonight's the only night Brady and Collin can work out at the gym and Mitch is working late too, so Lizzie, Charity, and I are staying. Besides, I'd love for you to meet my father and brothers."

Annie glanced from Marcy to Faith while Glory tugged on her arm. "Puh-leeeeez, Annie? We're having so much fun with Gabe and the others. I'll die if we have to go home!"

"Well, we can't have that, I suppose," Annie said with a crooked grin.

"Yay!!" Glory squealed and raced out the door.

"Thank you, Marcy," Annie said. "And Faith, I'd love to meet your father and brothers."

Charity elbowed Faith in the ribs. "Not as much as we'd like you to meet them." She plopped her chin in her hand and stared at Annie with a mischievous smile. "I have a brother who could sure use a sweet girl like you in his life."

"Charity, enough," Marcy said, offering Annie an apology with her smile. "I'm afraid Charity is the matchmaker in the family, so just ignore her."

"Like we try to do," Faith said with a grin.

Charity's lips went flat. "And my husband . . ."

"Do I smell cookies?" The screen door opened wide, and a tall, sandy-haired man in his midthirties strolled in with a hungry gleam in his blue eyes. He made a beeline for Emma to give her a kiss before nabbing several cookies. With a quick peck to Marcy's cheek, his gaze landed on Annie, his boyish grin and freckled face reminding her of a grown-up Huck Finn.

"Sean, this is Annie, a friend of mine from catechism class," Faith said, clearing the table. She playfully pinched the back of his neck. "And this is my big brother, Sean."

"Nice to meet you, Annie." Sean shook her hand with a smile that was easy and warm.

"Likewise, Sean," Annie said with equal enthusiasm, reaching for a cookie.

He tugged Emma from the chair and kissed her soundly. "Ready to go, Mrs. O'Connor?"

The cookie wedged in Annie's throat. *O'Connor?* Her gaze darted from Marcy, Faith, and Charity to Lizzie and Sean, and alarm curled in her stomach at a sudden glimpse of Steven in their features. The straight lines of a classic nose, the familiar shape and depth of expressive eyes. She started to cough, and Charity slapped her on the back. "Goodness, you okay? Sean has that effect on people, I know, but he's not too bad once you get to know him, right, Emma?"

Annie struggled for air while Emma blushed. "Nope, not bad at all."

"Newlyweds," Charity said with a bored sigh, shooting her brother a dry smile. "I'm afraid the poor guy was a bachelor so long, he doesn't know how to behave in public."

"Or maybe I do and you're just jealous since I'm here and Mitch isn't." Sean tweaked Charity's blonde bob as he passed, Emma in tow.

The smile on Charity's lips veered sideways. "Is it really that obvious?"

"Yes," Sean and Emma said in unison, laughing on their way to the door. "See you Sunday, everyone," Emma called, blowing Charity a kiss.

Annie gulped her tea, mouth dry and hands shaking so much the liquid sloshed in her cup. "Y-you mentioned t-two sons, Marcy," she whispered, her voice nearly hoarse. "Sean and . . ."

"Steven," Marcy said, rising to put the last tray of cookies in the oven.

The cup slipped from Annie's fingers to rattle against the saucer and spill, Earl Gray pooling on the table as quickly as dread pooled in her chest. *God help me, I have to go . . .* She bounded to her feet, almost tripping over her chair to retrieve the dishrag from the sink. "Goodness, forgive me, I am so clumsy!" Near breathless, she attempted to clean up. "I . . . we . . . should go. You don't need two extra mouths to feed . . ."

Eyeing her with concern, Faith took the dishrag from her hands. "Sit, Annie, it's no big deal, truly. Mother has a vat of chili prepared and salad in the icebox, so we have plenty to eat."

"Absolutely. We won't take no for an answer," Marcy confirmed with a warm smile.

Annie's hands started to sweat. "No, really I should go."

"May as well give in." Charity gave Annie's neck a playful squeeze on her way to wash up the dishes. "If there's one thing we O'Connors are famous for, it's our powers of persuasion."

Yes, I know. The image of Steven pushing her to the wall with a kiss suddenly scalded Annie's cheeks. "B-but . . . but . . . Cook has probably already started dinner . . ."

"Then call her," Faith said calmly, steering Annie to the

phone with a gentle prod. She handed her the receiver. "It's unanimous—we all want you to stay."

Not all, Annie thought, the mere mention of staying causing her stomach to lurch.

"Besides, I want you to meet my father. Stubborn and Irish to the core, but one of the men I love and respect most in the world. I just know you're going to love him too. Oh, and my brother?" Faith flitted her fingers, indicating for Annie to hurry and dial the phone. "Steven's a real sweetheart as well, so don't worry—you're going to love him to pieces."

Worry? That she wouldn't love him to pieces? Annie gulped. *No problem there.*

~~~

Katie skittered up the steps of the Boston Children's Aid Society, a flood of memories catching her off guard. It'd been almost a year since she'd quit working part-time at the BCAS to return to law school and almost a year since she'd become Luke's wife. She pressed an impatient finger to the elevator button, unleashing creaks and groans from antiquated pulleys. A smile flickered across her lips. *But, oh what a year!* Never had she believed she'd fall as hard as she did for a man as pushy as Luke McGee, but fall for him she had, pigheadedness and all.

The elevator door creaked open, and she hurried in, thinking how wonderful he'd been when she'd told him about Jack. Absently tapping the button, she leaned against the wall while the elevator jerked and shimmied to the second floor. Amazingly understanding, patient, kind, forgiving, especially for a man whose workload had spread his patience quite thin. And gorgeous, to boot! The model husband, actually, the memory of his wise words underscoring what she already knew to be true. *"It's just not smart, Katie, for a married woman to spend time alone with a man unless he's the dean, a blood relative, or a priest."*

The elevator jolted open and she fished the bag of cookies from her purse. The man was a saint, no doubt about it, working long hours alone while Bobbie Sue was sick and Gladys out of town. A twinge of guilt tightened her chest. And all while his wife "dallied" with her old fiancé, studying or no. Without question, Luke McGee deserved these cookies and more. A soft smile curved on her lips. And, oh, how she looked forward to giving him "more"!

She tiptoed toward his office, giddy at the prospect of surprising the man who could warm her blood by just walking into a room. Adrenaline rushing, she peeked in, and in the catch of her breath, that same blood went from warm to subzero.

"I owe you another dinner, Lauren. These reports are top drawer." Luke scanned and shuffled papers while a young woman beamed over his shoulder, hand casually on the back of his chair. Platinum curls obscured her face with a peek-a-boo style while her expensive crepe blouse and button-down pencil skirt revealed curves Katie could only dream about.

The fashion plate gave Luke's shoulder a casual squeeze, and Katie's jaw dropped. "If you keep buying me dinners, Luke McGee, I'll be the most spoiled intern in Boston."

Intern? Sweet chorus of angels, he has an intern?? Katie's lips compressed, thinking she'd like to do a little "spoiling" of her own—first Luke McGee's evening, and then his face.

"Trust me, Lauren, you're worth every penny. The best intern I ever had."

Excuse me? Fury boiled up, spilling over. "Really, darling? I thought that was me."

Luke glanced up and went pale so fast, his freckles looked like buckshot. "Katie . . ." The voice that cracked was no more than a croak. "W-what are you doing here?"

"Interrupting, apparently," she said coolly, striding forward with a tight smile. Extending her arm, she held the paper bag over his desk, fingers pinched like it was one of Kit's soiled diapers. "Gosh, hon, I felt so bad about you working *alone*, that I brought you some cookies." She promptly let go, cookies landing with a splat.

Ever the professional, Luke shot to his feet with a clear of his throat, the cool of his tone belying the heat in his eyes. "Katie, this is my intern for the summer, Miss Lauren Hill," he said with restrained patience, those blue eyes piercing as always when he wanted the upper hand—calm, calculated, and in control. A silent demand for dignity and decorum. *Yeah, fat chance.*

Katie offered a hand with a plaster smile, tone as tight as the muscle quivering in Luke's jaw. "Yes, sweetheart, I heard. The best intern you've ever had."

With a nervous slash of his white-blond hair, Luke had the grace to blush outright while Miss Hill's arm inched forward with the barest hint of a tremble. "It's g-good to meet you, Mrs. McGee. Your husband speaks of you often."

"Really?" Katie's gaze veered to Luke's with a saccharine smile. "Over dinner, darling?"

He fisted the papers and shoved them at Lauren, steering her around the desk. "Will you give us a few moments, please? I'd like to speak with my wife."

"Yes, sir." Lauren bolted for the door, shutting it behind her.

He wasted no time on damage control, hooking Katie close as he propped himself on the edge of his desk. "Thanks for the cookies, Sass, but next time you need to call before you come."

She jerked away and stepped back, crossing her arms to keep from smacking his face. "Why? So you can hustle your pretty intern out before I step foot in the door?"

"Come on, Katie . . ." He reached to pull her back, but she slapped his hand away.

"Don't you 'come on, Katie' me, not when you're buying dinner for some upper-class coed night after night." She glared, incensed that even as worn as he looked, tie jerked loose and shirtsleeves rolled up, those blue eyes could still quiver her stomach. She warded off the attraction by focusing on his deceit. "How dare you call me on the carpet about studying with Jack when you've been 'dallying' with some, some . . . socialite?"

"Intern," he emphasized carefully, the tic in his temple evidence of a temper he worked hard to rein in. "Hired by Carmichael, not me, as a favor to the board." He folded muscled arms, his voice soft but his point sharp. "An employee, Katie Rose, not a woman I was engaged to in the past."

His parental air struck a match to her temper. She thrust her chin out, hands on her hips. "Oh, really? Well, to paraphrase a statement, you blind baboon, 'it's just not smart for a married man to spend time alone with a woman unless she's the dean, a blood relative, or a nun.'"

He rose to his full six-foot-three height to intimidate her, no doubt, arms propped loose on his hips. The thrust of his bristled jaw matched hers, a sure sign her statement found its mark. "It's-not-the-same-thing, Katie Rose," he ground out, "so don't give yourself airs. Lauren's an employee, not an old fiancé, and if I need to work with her from now to kingdom come to get the work done, then I will." He took a step forward, teeth clenched. "Case closed."

Tears pricked, but she fought them off, suddenly not a bit attracted to the blockheaded bully staring her down. "Case closed? *Fine*. Then the door's closed too—the one to the bedroom where you used to sleep at night." She seized the bag of cookies. "And I'll give these to Jack."

He jerked the cookies from her hand and hurled them down with a rabid look she'd seen only two other times, evidence of a dormant temper about to blow. "Look, Katie, I'm tired, worn, and worked to the bone, so *don't* threaten me. I've got hours of work ahead with an intern as overloaded as me, so I'm warning you right now—if you lock the door, I'll just break it down."

Katie blinked, shades of the snot-nosed hooligan Luke McGee used to be staring her down, reflecting none of his promise "to love and cherish till death do them part."

179

Which may be sooner than he thinks.

Exhaling heavily, he drew her to his chest against her will, voice softening as he rubbed her back with weary motion. "Katie, I'm sorry, but I'm tired and crabby and overworked, and the last thing I need right now is a jealous wife."

She lurched away, mouth gaping. "Is that supposed to be an apology?"

"Come on, Sass." He tugged her back, his tone a tired plea. "I need your understanding now, like I gave you with Jack."

Her two palms slapped flat to his chest, shoving him away. "Sure, McGee, I'll give you all the understanding you gave me, once you send the coed packing."

A scowl flitted across his face. "Either you trust me or you don't. It's as simple as that."

"Oh, like you trusted me?" she asked, head cocked and arms locked to her chest.

"It's-different," he enunciated slowly, teeth gritted and tone even worse.

"I'll say—you're a bully who wants his own way, and I'm the fool who almost let you get it."

He snatched the cookies up and slammed them in the wastebasket, storming around his desk to sit in his chair. "I don't have time for this," he muttered. "We'll hash this out at home."

"*If* I go home." Spinning on her heel, she charged for the door, jerking it open.

"Katie!" His voice had a dangerous edge so out of character for the man she loved. "Don't even think about turning me out of my bed."

Without so much as a glance back, she slammed the door so hard it rattled the hinges along with her nerves. *Turn him out of my bed? Maybe not.* She thundered through the outer office, ignoring the openmouthed shock on the intern's face.

But my heart?

Oh, you bet.

8

"ncle Steven!" A brown-eyed moppet hopped off the swing and flew at him, giggling as she wrapped stubby legs around his trousers. "Can we have a piggyback ride, please, please?"

Wiping the sweat from his eyes with the sleeve of his T-shirt, Steven rolled his basketball toward the porch steps, then hiked his niece up in the air, unleashing a chorus of giggles and squeals. "Hey, what are you doing here, Abby-kins?"

"Daddy and Uncle Brady are boxing tonight and Uncle Mitch has to work, so Grandma said all the cousins get to eat dinner here. Will you sit with me?"

"You bet, squirt. Where are the others?" Steven asked, setting her back down. He eyed a shy, curly haired blonde staring from a few feet away. "And who's that pretty little thing?"

"That's my new friend, Glory," Abby said. "She just moved here and we're her very first friends." There was a note of pride in her tone. "All the other kids are playing school with Gabe in Grandpa's den, but Glory and I wanted to swing instead, didn't we, Glory?" Abby hopped up and down, flapping the side of Steven's pants. "Hey, can you give her a piggyback ride and carry me too? And take us inside to get a cookie?"

"Sure, kiddo." Squatting, he shook Glory's hand. "Hi, Glory, I'm Steven. Ready to fly?"

She nodded shyly, finger in her mouth.

"Okay, up we go." He positioned Glory on his shoulders, then crouched low to scoop Abby into the crook of his arms. "Now . . . where are those cookies?"

"Inside!" Abby shouted while Glory giggled and hung on, hands plastered over his eyes.

"Mama, Mama—Uncle Steven's strong!" Abby breathed, legs pumping with excitement as he carried them through the screen door.

"Well, if it isn't our own personal jungle gym," Faith said at the sink.

"Oooo, can I have a ride too?" Charity asked with a wiggle of brows.

Steven groaned, trying to peel Glory's fingers from his eyes. "Don't think so, sis," he said with a chuckle. "I'm strong, not stupid." He sniffed. "Is that chili, I hope?" He bent to give his mother a kiss at the counter before peeking inside her bowl. "And cornbread too? Yes! Tell me we have honey butter—please."

"Yes, dear, honey butter and salad and noodles for chili mac." Marcy wrinkled her nose. "But I suggest you wash up, Steven, because you're not coming to the table smelling like that."

"I guess I am pretty ripe," he said with a chuckle, muscles straining as he put Abby down, then Glory. He tugged on her curl. "Say, you're pretty cute—who do you belong to anyway?"

"To her," Abby said loudly, pointing to where his sisters prepared a salad at the table.

He threaded a hand through damp hair and turned, and the sweat froze on his body.

"Hi, Steven." Annie's smile was weak. "I had no idea you were Faith's brother, honest."

"You know Steven?" Faith's tented brows indicated surprise equal to his.

But not quite. He stared, mouth slack and heart thumping like the basketball he'd just dribbled on the St. Stephen's school yard. Glory and his nieces squealed in an impromptu game of tag in the kitchen, but all he could hear was the pound of a runaway pulse in his ears.

His lack of response dusted Annie's cheeks with a shade of pink that made her look all the more innocent and even younger than she was. *At least from the neck up.* Male instinct drew his eyes to the soft waves of strawberry-blonde hair that skimmed creamy shoulders, evident in a sleeveless butter-yellow blouse that molded to curves he remembered all too well. He quickly forced his eyes up to her face, and his stomach tightened. The face of an angel, unfortunately, with peaches and cream skin setting off green eyes that threatened to swallow him whole. The muscles in his throat shifted out of pure reflex when she peeked up beneath a sweep of long lashes. "Yes, I . . . well, *we* . . . met a few times at the Ocean Pier Ballroom."

Faith blinked, gaze flitting from Annie to Steven and back again, her eyes going wide. "Ocean Pier Ballroom?" she repeated slowly, head dipped in question.

Annie's cheeks nearly deepened to the soft rose of her bare lips. "Yes," she said quietly—emphatically—her tone almost breathless as her eyes locked with his.

A smile played at the edges of his sister's mouth. "Well, well, Steven," Faith said, looking as if she were privy to some deep, dark secret. "You do get around."

"Wait—what's going on here?" Charity demanded, a talent for digging up dirt that would put a steam shovel to shame.

Steven ignored her and inched away, a lump the size of a basketball wedged in his throat. "What are you *doing* here, Annie?" Voice hoarse, he shifted, well aware his T-shirt was sweaty and dirty, hair damp and disheveled, and face void of blood beneath a layer of dirt.

"Annie's in my catechism class," Faith explained easily, giving each of the little girls a cookie before shooing them outside. "We've become good friends, so I invited her and her sister to story time at Bookends, then to bake cookies, and now she's staying for dinner." She sauntered over to where Steven stood and pressed a quick kiss to his cheek before nudging his jaw up with her thumb. "Close your mouth, Steven, it's rude to stare."

Annie continued to shred lettuce beyond recognition, obviously ill at ease. "I'm sorry, Steven. If I'd known this was your house, I wouldn't have come."

"Oh? And why is that, Annie?" Charity said with a grin, bumping Steven's hip with her own as she sashayed past to wash several carrots at the sink. "Because of the way he smells?"

Heat blasted Steven's cheeks. "Knock it off, Charity," he said in a near growl, not sure what made him more nauseous—the situation or the rank smell of his body. He swallowed hard, struggling to recover the nonchalance he'd fine-tuned with his sisters—not an easy thing to do when his heart was pumping faster than his sweat glands. "No, it's fine, really. You took me by surprise, that's all. I'm just home to shower before heading out again for burgers with Joe."

"Liar." Charity poked him in the ribs on her way back to the table. "You wouldn't miss Mother's chili for all the burgers in the world. Face it, you're not going anywhere." She tapped his chest with an annoying thump. "Except up to the shower before you sit down for dinner."

Steven opened his mouth to object, but his mother stopped him with a firm look. "I suggest you get a move on, Steven. Your father will be home any minute, and dinner's at six." A knowing smile edged her lips. "We're having the chili *you* begged me to make, if you remember."

The air escaped from his lungs in one slow, reedy breath. His jaw hardened to rock on the way to the door. "Sorry, Mom, forgot," he said, avoiding Annie's eyes. "I'll just sit with the kids in the kitchen because I promised Abby."

"Uh . . . as much sense as it makes for you to sit with the children," Charity said with a drawl, "I think it's time for you to sit at the big table, don't you?" Her jibe ground him to a halt, and he shot her a withering look, palm stiff against the swinging door. She gave him a sassy wink. "Besides, Annie will think you don't like her."

"I like her fine," he said through a thinly veiled smile that felt like cardboard. His eyes flicked to where Annie sat at the table, shoulders slumped and eyes focused intently on the lettuce she was reshredding, and he realized his attitude stunk as much as his body. He blasted out a sigh of surrender. "Look, Annie, I'm sorry—it's no reflection on you, really. You just caught me at a bad time, that's all. Trust me, a cold shower will do wonders for my mood."

And my body. He shoved through the door and strode to the stairs, heat suddenly scorching his face at the implication of his words. "Real bright, O'Connor," he muttered, taking the stairs two at a time, knowing full well he needed a cold shower bad—and not because of the obvious heat of summer. To shock his system out of this stupor, to slow this annoying throb of his pulse, and to purge an image he wanted to forget—a girl chatting in his kitchen as if she belonged there more than he did. No, a kid, really, turning the tables to make him the tongue-tied little boy.

Jerking a clean towel from the closet, he slammed the bathroom door hard and ripped his T-shirt off before hurling it at the hamper. He stared in the mirror, his jaw dark with bristle and a muscled chest reminding him he was no little boy. No, he was a man with needs, something he'd forgotten until Annie came along. He leaned hard on the sink, head bent and heart heavy, his body humming with a desire he hadn't felt in a long, long time. Oh yeah, he needed a cold shower all right, he thought, stepping into the tub and cranking the faucet all the way to the right. Sucking in a sharp breath, he allowed the cool water to pelt his skin while he lathered with soap, scrubbing hard. He shivered as he rinsed, grateful for the water that battered his body like sleet.

And God help him, it wasn't near cold enough.

Lips twitching with a mischievous smile, Charity slid into her chair across from Annie and leaned in, elbows flat on the table and eyebrows dancing. "Cold shower, huh? Mmm, good idea—both for the summer heat *and* the heat in the kitchen."

"Charity, hush," Marcy said, loading a tray of corn muffins into the oven. "You're embarrassing Annie with talk like that."

Annie's cheeks steamed as much as the noodles boiling on the stove.

Marcy shot her a sympathetic smile. "My apologies, Annie. I'm afraid Charity tends to be a bit pushy, so don't pay her any mind." Her eyes softened. "Would you like some iced tea?"

"That would be lovely, Mar—" She gulped, painfully aware that *this* was the mother of the man who turned her insides to mush. "Uh, I mean, Mrs. O'Connor," she finished weakly.

Marcy filled a glass with ice, then poured in fresh tea before handing it to Annie, her voice gentle. "Now don't you dare backtrack on calling me Marcy, young lady. When my daughters and I get together, I'm just one of the girls, understood? Lemon and sugar?"

"Yes, please," Annie said, releasing a shaky sigh. She chanced a tentative look at Steven's sisters. "Goodness, I think I was more shocked than him."

"I wouldn't bet on it," Faith said with a chuckle. She eased into the chair next to Annie. "But I have to be honest—it's not just Charity's imagination running away here. I've never seen Steven so off-kilter in front of a girl before. Since college, he's always had the advantage with women, calm and collected, impossible to fluster, and totally in control. Trust me—we haven't seen *this* Steven O'Connor since he was a shy little boy with his head in a magic book. Whatever happened at Ocean Pier, you obviously had quite an effect on him."

"I'll say," Charity piped in, "I haven't seen him that ruffled since Mag—"

"*Please* believe me," Annie said in a rush, stomach churning at the mention of her sister. Her voice came out strained, heart racing at what this family would think if they knew she was related to Maggie. "Steven has no interest in me that way, I promise."

Faith braced a hand to Annie's arm. "What about you?" she asked quietly. "Do you?"

Heat crawled up Annie's neck.

"I knew it!" Charity shouted, victory ringing in her tone. "I have a sixth sense about these things, and the minute you two looked at each other, the sparks could have simmered the chili."

Faith leaned in, eyes locked with Annie's. "We don't mean to embarrass you, Annie, truly, and I don't normally jump in with Charity so quickly, but I have to admit you had Steven rattled, which leads me to suspect he has more than a passing interest in you."

"Oh, Annie, you and Steven would make such a darling couple," Lizzie breathed. "And Ocean Pier is so romantic!" Her eyes lit. "How did you meet? Did Steven ask you to dance?"

Annie shook her head, peeking up to see Steven's family studying her. "He rescued me from a guy with a bad reputation." Her shoulders slumped as her eyes trailed into a blank stare. "He warned me to stay away from guys like that." She glanced up, her smile sad. "Including him. I even told him I liked him, but he claims I'm too young. Sees himself as a big brother and nothing more." She sighed. "I guess I am—I'm not eighteen until next week."

"Horse feathers," Charity said with no little scowl, grating a carrot into the salad bowl. "That sure didn't look like the reaction of a big brother to me, so don't you believe it. And you are *not* too young. In fact, you're exactly what we've been praying for—a sweet girl from a good family. Besides, Mitch is sixteen years older than me and we have a dream marriage."

"Well, you do, anyway," Faith said with an evil grin.

Charity's eyes narrowed. "I beg your pardon—the man's crazy in love, and you know it."

"Yes, we'll give him 'crazy,'" Marcy said with a chuckle.

"Mother!"

"Sorry, dear, couldn't resist . . . any more than that crazy husband of yours can resist you." Marcy hefted a stack of plates and bowls and handed them to Charity with a concilia-tory kiss on the cheek. "Here, make yourself useful instead of badgering this poor girl. If there's interest between Steven and Annie, Mother Nature will handle it without any help from you."

"Wanna bet?" Faith collected utensils and a stack of linen napkins from the drawer. She winked. "Trust me, Annie, this one makes Mother Nature look like an amateur."

Charity grinned, plates and bowls stacked to her chin. "Ac-tually, Mother Nature and I make a great team—she strikes the match, and I fan the flame."

No doubt about that. Annie gulped and took a swig of her tea.

"Charity Katherine Dennehy!" Marcy's voice halted Char-ity midpush through the door. Hooking an arm to Annie's shoulder, she arched a brow. "You will not meddle in this young woman's relationship with Steven unless she gives you express permission, is that clear?" She patted Annie's hand. "Just give me the word, Annie, and we'll lock her down."

Four sets of eyes converged on Annie's face and she blinked, barely able to believe Steven's family wanted to help. Would it be the same if they knew she was Maggie's sister? She drew in a shaky breath, well aware she needed to tell Faith privately . . . and soon.

Her heart slowed to a thud. But could they be right? Did he have feelings he wasn't willing to admit? Her pulse took off at the prospect, and she glanced up at Marcy and then at each of her daughters, a shy smile blooming on her lips. "The truth is, Marcy . . . I've been drawn to your son from the moment I met him, and I haven't been able to think of anything else. But . . ." She locked gazes with Faith, completely certain what she needed to do. "If it's okay with all of you, I'd like to pray about it first, just to make sure we're doing the right thing."

"Sweet saints, *now* I know who you remind me of!" Charity said with a sag of her jaw. Her gaze flicked to Faith and held while her lips curved into a smile. "She reminds me of you!"

Annie laughed. "You do realize you people will have a hard time getting rid of me with compliments like that *and* treating me like family?"

"Well, if we play our cards right—" Charity began.

"Charity . . . ," Marcy warned.

"Hurry," Faith said, prodding Charity through the door. "We need to pray before Steven returns." She smiled at Annie. "You're sure, now? 'Cause there's no stopping once she gets started."

Annie nodded, skitters in her stomach. "All I care about is praying first, and then give the woman full rein and throw away the key."

Charity literally preened, chin high and her expression a near smirk. "Well, you all heard her. She's obviously a woman with a good head on her shoulders who knows how to get what she wants." Butting the door with her hip, she shot Annie a wink. "You and me?" she said with a scrunch of her nose. "We're going to get along just fine."

"Steven."

"Huh?" Steven blinked, his father blurring into focus from across the chessboard.

Patrick O'Connor leaned forward, arms folded on the table and a hint of a smile in gray eyes that scrutinized his son with deadly accuracy. His mouth crooked. "If I'd wanted to win with my eyes closed, I'd be playing with Sean."

"What?" Steven said again, his eyes on his father but ears

on the fun and revelry going on in the next room. His brow wrinkled. "What are you talking about, Pop?"

"The game, Steven," Patrick said with a thin smile, "your mind's not in it." His father leaned back in his chair, gaze shrewd as he studied his son. Despite dark curly hair glinted with silver at the temple and the sag of facial muscles that indicated a long day at work, Steven knew that Patrick O'Connor missed nothing when it came to his family. Sliding a glance over his shoulder into the dining room where Annie played dominoes with his mother and sisters, his father looked back with a knowing smile. "At least, not this one."

Heat braised Steven's cheeks and he shifted, downing half his iced tea. "I'm just distracted tonight, Pop, that's all." He attempted to focus hard on the board, but all he could see was Annie at dinner, laughing with his family, chatting, teasing . . . just like she belonged. His jaw went stiff. She'd been so close he could smell her, a mix of honeysuckle and shampoo that hit him full force, like he'd taken a shot of aged whiskey—smooth, warm, tingling his senses till he wanted more. Her fingers had brushed his when she'd passed the cornbread, and he hated how every nerve had vibrated as if pure adrenaline coursed his veins instead of just blood warmed by her touch. She's too young and vulnerable, he reminded himself, and yet she seemed older here, confident, relaxed, easy to talk to. Despite his efforts to ignore her, she'd drawn him in over and over to conversation that indicated a keen mind, engaging his brain as well as his body.

After dinner Henry had begged him to play kick ball, and Charity had shooed Annie out, claiming she needed to help Glory play the game. Regrettably, Steven had never enjoyed himself more, laughing, teasing, running bases with Glory on his shoulders while Henry cheered him on. An athlete like Sean, Steven had taken pleasure in watching Annie run the bases, her grace and ability evident in every stride. Consumed by the game, she was a beautiful tomboy with legs pumping and hair flying. Her cheeks were flushed and her green eyes sparkled so much, he could barely stop staring. Apparently competitive to the core, she was a ruthless coach, almost stealing the win. But not quite. A hint of a smile edged his frown.

Blasting out a sigh, he glared at the board, grateful his father had saved his hide with a game of chess because every minute with the kid was proving to be deadly. A competition that went well beyond kick ball—his will vs. his mind and body—and at the moment, his will was in sorry shape. No matter. He was a man who prided himself on his will of iron, or at least till Maggie came along. Well, never again. He shook off thoughts of the kid and forced a smile he hoped would derail his father. "Distracted, maybe, but don't count your win just yet, Pop, because I'll get over it."

"You sure about that?" Patrick rolled the sleeves of his white shirt and then loosened his tie, the heat of a summer night obviously taking its toll. He gave a quick nod toward the next room while he assessed his son with a keen eye. "She's a pretty little thing, Faith's friend. Smart, sweet, and obviously a very nice young woman. It's no crime to look, you know."

Steven huffed out another sigh and moved his pawn forward. "She's too young, Pop, only seventeen, and you're beginning to sound a lot like Charity, you know that?"

"Maybe," Patrick said with a diagonal move. "But she only interferes because she cares about you, as do I." He captured Steven's pawn, calmly removing it from the board. "Sorry."

Steven's lips went flat. "Yeah, I can see how much you care. Good move."

"It was, wasn't it?" Patrick said, his smile almost smug. He leaned back in the chair, eyeing Steven with affection. "That young woman might be a good move too—I like her. And given your distraction with the game in the other room, I'd say you do too." He chuckled. "And right now your chances for a win are a lot better with dominoes than they are with chess."

"I smell chili . . ." Collin burst through the front door with

Brady on his heels, the two of them as sweaty and worn as Steven before his shower.

"Thank God," Patrick boomed. "Fresh blood."

"Nothing fresh about it," Collin said with a grin, "but you'd lose anyway, by sheer asphyxiation."

"Daddy! We're playing Sardine's Ghost—wanna play?" Abby barreled through the swinging door and flew across the room to collide into Collin's legs with a giggle.

Swooping her up, he slobbered her with kisses before tucking her under his arm. "Nope, Peanut, it's late and we need to get you and your sisters home and into bed." He put her back down and popped her on the bottom. "Go round 'em up, okay?"

"Okay." Abby whooshed through the kitchen door.

"How 'bout you, Brady, up for a quick game?" Patrick eyed him like a shark who smelled blood, the lure of victory bright in his eyes. "Steven's proving to be a disappointment."

Steven flushed. "Hey, Pop, just figured you had a rough day so I was going easy on you," he said, deflecting his embarrassment with a cocky grin at his brothers-in-law.

"Oh, sure, sure . . ." Patrick parried with a chuckle, rising to give his sons-in-law a wink. "And distraction had nothing to do with it whatsoever."

"Oooo, distraction?" Charity honed in neatly, eyes fluttering wide as she strolled into the foyer from the dining room. "And just why is that, Steven?"

"Just never you mind, you little vulture," Patrick said with a grin. "What do you say, Brady? I can make it a quick, painless game where you'll never know what hit you."

Brady ambled to where Lizzie sat at the table with Molly asleep on her shoulder. His lips eased into a dry smile. "I'm afraid I'd be as worthless as Collin or Steven tonight," he said, massaging Lizzie's shoulder before lifting his sleeping daughter onto his own. "And I'd rather be fresh when I take you on, Patrick, if you don't mind." He kissed Molly's head. "I refuse to steal Sean's thunder as the most pitiful chess player in the family. Ready, Lizzie?"

"Sure, Brady." Lizzie lumbered up, a palm to her pregnant belly. She deposited a peck on his cheek before heading to the kitchen to retrieve her son from the backyard.

Patrick sighed. "You're off the hook, Steven. If I want pathetic, I'll wait for Sean."

Faith tugged Annie to where Collin stood, stopping a few feet shy of her husband. "Collin, this is Annie, the good friend I've been telling you so much about."

Collin flashed a smile, arm extended. "Hi, Annie. Faith talks about you all the time." He shook Annie's hand, then hooked Faith's waist, bussing her cheek.

"Not near as much as she talks about you, I bet," Annie said with a chuckle.

Steven fisted his tea, Annie's laughter doing odd things to his gut. *Go home, kid, and leave me alone.*

"Collin McGuire, take your hands off me right now," Faith warned with a squeal, lunging from his hold. "No hugs or kisses till you're squeaky clean, mister."

He threaded fingers through damp hair, giving Annie a wink. "Now there's incentive if ever there was." Collin glanced at Marcy. "Don't suppose there's any chili left?"

"I thought you two were going to grab a bite out?" Faith asked, clearing dirty glasses from the dining room table.

"We did." Brady helped Faith push in chairs while Charity put the dominoes away. "But the man's a bottomless pit, Faith. You should know that by now."

Marcy's smile was apologetic. "Sorry, Collin, I think Steven finished it off."

"Yeah?" Collin leered at Steven. "And exactly how many bowls did you put away?"

Steven grinned and upended his tea. "Not more than four or five, I promise."

Collin groaned as Lizzie returned from the backyard with cousins in tow.

"You need Steven to run you home?" Patrick asked.

"Nope, it's a nice night, a few blocks won't kill us," Brady said, waiting for Lizzie to dispense hugs before leading her and their little ones out the door.

Annie glanced at her watch. "Goodness, it's after nine. Aunt Eleanor will have my head. Do you mind if I use your phone to give Frailey a call?"

"Oh, don't bother," Charity said sweetly, "Steven will drive you home."

The tea pooled in Steven's mouth before going down the wrong pipe. He began to hack.

Faith slapped him on the back while Charity slipped an arm through Annie's. "It's silly to call Frailey when Steven can run you home." She smiled at Steven. "You don't mind, do you?"

Clearing his throat, Steven glanced at Annie, minding way more than he was willing to admit. He managed a smile. "Sure, if the kid needs a ride, I can do it."

"Who needs a ride?" Mitch asked, brows arched. Closing the front door, he strode in and brushed his lips to Charity's. "Plenty of room in the roadster."

"Great!" Steven said in relief. He nodded toward Annie. "The kid needs a ride home."

"No!" Charity said too loudly. "Because Faith and Collin need a ride too, right, Faith?"

"Not a problem," Mitch said. "Everybody can squeeze in since Faith and Collin are just a few blocks away." He nodded at Annie. "You're Annie, I guess? Hi, I'm Mitch."

"Nice to meet you," Annie said shyly, "and thank you for your offer of a ride."

"Unfortunately that won't work, darling," Charity said sweetly, sending a look of concern to where Glory played jacks with the cousins. "You see, Annie's sister needs a ride too."

Mitch blinked. "Oh. Well, I can just run Faith and Collin home first."

Charity yanked on his arm to whisper in his ear, and Mitch's mouth crooked up. "On second thought, the roadster might be a little cramped." He slapped Steven on the back, his smile dry. "Don't look now, Steven, but she's got you in her sights."

Patrick chuckled and moved toward the stairs. "It's late, Marceline, let's head up." He fished keys from his pocket and tossed them at his son. "Steven, lock up and then take Annie and Glory home. Annie, it was a pleasure meeting you, and I hope you'll come back soon." He angled a brow at his foster daughter. "Gabe, upstairs—now."

A painful groan issued from her throat.

"Come on, darling," Marcy soothed, ushering Gabe to the stairs. "I'll fix you a nice, warm bath because I'm afraid you don't smell much better than Collin and Brady." She shot a bright smile over her shoulder. "Don't be a stranger, Annie, you hear? Good night, everyone."

"Good night, Mr. and Mrs. O'Connor, and thank you!" Annie called. Her gaze collided with Steven's, and she chewed at her lip. "Sorry for the inconvenience. I can call Frailey, really."

He felt like a louse. But then innocence like Annie's always made him feel that way. He sighed and buried his hands in his pockets, offering a polite smile. "Nope, I'll be happy to give you a ride. I need to stop by Joe's anyway."

"Good, then it's all settled." Charity gave Annie a hug. "Hope to see you soon."

Husbands and kids bolted out while Annie linked arms with Faith to follow behind.

Steven expelled a weary breath, and Charity gave him a quick hug. "Come on, Steven, open your eyes," she said with a pinch of his waist. "You're smart, good-looking, and employed, but what good is it? You're one of the loneliest men I know."

He diverted her concern with a laugh. "Single doesn't mean lonely, sis. Trust me, there's nothing lonely about me."

She studied him, eyes suddenly too serious for Charity. "Haunted, then," she said quietly, a solemn look reflecting deep love often obscured by tease. "And you've been that way too long now." She patted his cheek. "Do something about it, will you?" The sparkle returned to her eyes. "Because face it, Steven—miserable is not a good look for you."

He grinned. "I don't know, it works for Mitch."

She smacked his shoulder. "For your information, you little brat, Mitch is one of the happiest men around."

"Yeah?" Steven cocked a hip. "And how do you know that?"

"Simple." She tossed her hair back and sashayed out the door, slipping a grin over her shoulder that included a wink. "Because I tell him so every day."

9

"So . . . Annie tells me you're an officer of the law." Glory sat in the front seat of Steven's father's Model T like a tiny adult, legs crossed at the ankles and hands folded in the lap of a polka-dot dress carefully fanned out. She glanced up, tone matter of fact. "Do you carry a gun?"

He studied her out of the corner of his eye while he shifted gears, a grin easing across his face. "Sometimes."

"Have you ever killed anybody?"

"Gloria Celeste Kennedy, that is an awful question!" Annie pinched her leg.

Kennedy? Steven's palm froze to the wheel.

"Ouch, that hurts," Glory moaned, pinching her sister back. "I'm just curious is all, 'cause Steven's the only person I ever met with a gun."

Glancing over his shoulder, Steven eased into the next lane before peering at Annie, his tone sharp. "Kennedy? Joe said your name was Martin." Even in the dark, he saw her blush.

"Martin is my aunt's name," she said quietly, staring straight ahead, throat shifting in silhouette. "I guess Peggy told Joe I lived with my aunt, so maybe he just assumed."

"Yeah, maybe." Steven braked at a stoplight, his mind shifting as fast as the Model T.

"Steven?" Her voice was tentative.

"Yeah?" He waited, finally looking over when she didn't respond.

She opened her mouth, but nothing came out.

He squinted. "You okay?"

"No, not completely." She paused, her face as pale as the moonlight streaming through her window. "There's something I need to tell you, but I'm not ready." She exhaled. "But I will."

He nodded, studying her with a crimp in his brow. "Okay." Sucking in a deep breath, he slowly released it again and stared straight ahead, allowing his thoughts to stray. Kennedy was a common name in Boston, but it always had the same shocking effect, taking him back to Maggie. She had hailed from Chicago as he recalled, and the only sister she ever mentioned was a kid named Gracie Sue, or something like that. Come to think of it, he hadn't really known a lot about Maggie, and he supposed that had been part of her mystique. Mysterious, passionate, sexy.

And deadly.

"So, have you?" Glory persisted, slapping Annie's hand away from her leg.

He could feel Glory's questioning gaze and it edged his mouth into a smile. "Nope."

"Good, I'm glad." Glory smoothed a wrinkle in her skirt with the utmost care.

Turning a corner, he gave her an off-center smile. "Me too," he said with a wink.

A few moments later, he felt a gentle tug on his leg and looked down at the upturned face of an angel. "Would you mind if we came over again sometime, Steven?"

His eyes flicked from Glory's soulful stare up to Annie's cautious look, and he sighed, leveling his gaze on the street ahead. "Sure, why not?"

"I'm glad. Faith said we could come over again after story time next week."

Good to know. Steven took a corner with a slice of the wheel. *I'll make sure I'm gone.*

"We'll see, Glory." Annie's tone was nervous.

"Okie-dokie," she said with a big yawn. Snuggling close, she surprised him when she laid her head on his lap, hand curled over his knee. "Thanks for the piggyback ride, Steven."

"You're welcome, Glory," he said quietly, palm resting on her hair while his thumb grazed her neck. Within seconds her soft snores made him smile.

"Steven?"

He glanced over, and Annie's tentative eyes met his. "I really had no idea you were Faith's brother, and I'm sorry for barging into your life like that. I wouldn't have come had I known."

He exhaled, gaze back on the road. "It's okay, Annie, really."

"No . . . no it's not," she said, shifting to stare straight ahead. Her voice lowered to a near whisper. "I threw myself at you once, Steven, and it was wrong. You tried to warn me, protect me, but I was too stupid and too angry to understand."

He chanced a glimpse, heart stuttering at the moisture in her eyes. "Angry about what?"

She buffed her arms as if she were cold despite the steamy summer night, and when she spoke, her voice was thick with emotion. "At God for taking my parents away, for abandoning Glory and me to an aunt who neither wanted nor approved of us." She paused, head bowed, and he sensed the weight of guilt in the slump of her shoulders. "I was the good girl in the family, you know, the devout one my father counted on, his spiritual pride and joy. But when he . . ." Her voice cracked and without thinking, Steven lifted his palm from Glory's head to Annie's shoulder, giving her a gentle squeeze. She averted her gaze and quickly swiped at her eyes. "When

Daddy died, I . . . wanted no part of God anymore, so when I came to Boston, I made up my mind that since Daddy's love was gone, I'd find love on my own . . ."

Steven expended a quiet sigh. "With any guy who came along . . ."

"Yes," she whispered, eyes fixed on her fingers. "I know Peggy and her sister aren't the type of friends my father would have liked me to have, but I was too angry to care and so I . . ."

He downshifted and slid her a sideways glance. "Threw caution to the wind?"

She swallowed hard and peeked up. "Yes."

"Happens to the best of us, kid," he said, remembering all too well when it'd changed for him, that dark transformation from good to evil, forever staining both his memory and his soul.

"Yes, it does unfortunately . . . only *you* saved me from the worst." Her chest expanded with a heavy breath as she looked away, eyes lagging into a glossy stare over the dash. "So, I owe you an apology and my thanks because I honestly don't know what might have happened if you hadn't taken such a hard stance with me, warned me . . . *protected* me." She turned, eyes awash with gratitude. "You see, Steven, God used you to safeguard me until I could come back . . ."

He coasted to a stop at the light, eyes in a squint. "Come back? What do you mean?"

She paused to take in another deep breath. "Back to *him*. I'm doing things God's way now, seeking the right kind of love with him in the center, not the wrong kind like you warned me about. And you started it, Steven, but it was God who finished it." She smiled, the effect somehow soft and strong at the same time. "You see, he brought Faith into my life to show me what true faith in God can be." Her throat shifted in profile. "And the type of true love that's only available through him." Her chin notched up the slightest bit, almost giving her an air of invincibility. "So trust me when I say it's the only love I'll ever settle for again."

200

The light changed and he gunned the engine hard as if to escape this uneasy feeling in his gut, like God had him in his sights, ready to pick him off. "That's why you've avoided the Pier?" he asked, hoping to steer the conversation away from a subject he neither understood nor liked.

"Yeah, *that's* why I avoided the Pier." She grinned and turned with a little bounce, exuding that innocence he found so attractive. "Because as much as I wanted to see you again," she said, rifling through her purse, "I'm through being that kind of girl." She popped a Life Saver into her mouth, then offered him one. "Peppermint?"

He shook his head, but her words triggered a warm glow in his chest. "I'm glad, Annie."

"Me too," she said with a contented sigh. "So, you see, if I had known I was coming to *your* house, I would have never set foot in the door."

Signaling a turn, he eased onto her street, gliding the car up to the curb in front of Aunt Eleanor's house. He coasted into park before he slipped her a slow grin, allowing the engine to rumble along with the chuckle in his throat. "You make me sound like an ogre, Miss Kennedy."

"Nope, just a hard-nosed arm of the law whom I'm scared to cross."

"Good," he said, turning the engine off, "then my work here is done." Fisting his door handle, he glanced down at the angel drooling on his leg and smiled. "Come on, you little piece of heaven," he whispered. He slipped his hands beneath her fragile arms and draped her over his shoulder before easing out of the car. A smile nudged when her arms curled around his neck, and the scent of Ivory soap and bubble gum caused a sudden ache in his heart. He opened Annie's door and helped her out, and in the flash of a moment, longing invaded his chest. The touch of her hand, the weight of Glory on his shoulder, and he almost felt whole again, as if he deserved the happiness of a good woman, one who would give him children to love . . .

"Thank you," Annie whispered, reaching to take Glory.

"No," he said, unable to resist burying his head in her sweet mass of curls. "I don't mind." Lump in his throat, he kissed Glory's cheek and followed Annie up the steps.

"I can't thank you enough for bringing us home," Annie said, slipping her key in the door. She pushed it ajar, then turned and held her arms out for Glory, her smile warm. "You're a very lucky man, Steven O'Connor, to have the kind of family you do."

He paused, her statement taking him by surprise, as did the realization she was right, something he'd come to learn the hard way when his father almost died. He'd taken his family for granted before that . . . but never again.

Her smile tipped into a soft grin. "Or maybe 'blessed' would be a better word."

It was his turn to smile. "That's certainly what my sisters would say, especially Faith. Come on, munchkin," he whispered in Glory's ear, "time for bed." Gently dislodging Glory's fingers, he leaned forward to pass her to Annie.

"No . . . ," she groaned, her sweet little voice groggy with sleep as her arms inched back to his neck. "I don't want you to go . . ."

He paused, head tucked against hers as emotion thickened his throat.

Annie tugged at her sister. "Glory, Steven has to go home and we have to go to bed . . ."

"B-but will I see you a-again?" she said with a whimper.

He swallowed hard. "Sure, kiddo, anytime you want." His gaze flicked to Annie and back, and suddenly his hopes for distance seemed to be fading.

"We'll see," Annie said, voice and hold adamant as she tried to pull Glory away.

"Okie-dokie." Glory loosened her grip, then patted a fat little palm to his cheek. "You're itchy," she said with a giggle, then deposited a sweet, tiny kiss on his mouth. "G'night, Steven."

"G'night, Glory." He kissed her nose before Annie managed to pry her away.

"Thanks again," Annie said, inching through the door with Glory in her arms.

"Wait! Aren't you going to kiss her too?" Glory spun around, eyes wide with the innocence of a little girl who had no earthly idea what she was asking him to do.

He blinked, noting the expanse of Annie's eyes.

"Glory, no," she whispered, turning ten kinds of pale.

"Please?" The little troublemaker stared at him with those wide eyes of an angel.

Heart thudding, he did the only thing he knew to do. He kissed Annie right on the tip of her nose. Clearing his throat, he stepped back. "Well, good night, ladies."

"No, silly," Glory said, "like this . . ." She demonstrated with a sweet little peck on her sister's lips as if he were too stupid to understand, then tilted her head. "See? It's easy."

Too easy, he thought with a trip of his pulse. *Way, way too easy . . .*

"Stop it, Glory, Steven doesn't want to—"

"Sure I do," he whispered, his words shocking him as much as Annie. Gaze holding hers, he slowly leaned in, close enough to see the long sweep of her lashes, the pale gold in eyes so green, he felt like he was in Oz, about to be granted a wish. He heard the soft hitch of her breath when she stopped breathing because it coincided with the halt of air in his own lungs. Cupping her face in his hand, his eyelids sheathed closed at the touch of her lips—soft, supple, and just a hint of peppermint from the candy she'd offered him in the car. It was meant to be no more than a peck like Glory had given him, but somehow his mouth wanted to linger and explore . . . He stepped in close, body grazing hers and Glory's till they were one. A little-girl giggle broke the trance, and Annie's lips curved beneath his.

"His whiskers are itchy, aren't they, Annie?" Glory asked, patting his face once again. "Kinda makes you wiggly all over, doesn't it?"

Annie's eyes glowed as she caressed her own cheek. "Very wiggly," she whispered.

"Well," Steven said quickly with a clear of his throat. He chucked Glory beneath her dimpled chin. "I suppose that's enough kisses for one night, wouldn't you say?"

"No!" Glory giggled with a thrust of her chin.

He hiked a brow. "You know what? *You* are going to be trouble when you grow up, little girl." Tapping a finger to Glory's chin, he slid Annie a smile and winked. "Just like your sister."

"I know." She looped an arm around Annie with a pixie smile. "G'night, Steven."

"G'night, Glory." His eyes strayed to Annie and he nodded. "Annie." Without another word, he loped to the car, his thoughts as warm as the summer night. He slipped into the front seat with a faint smile and turned the ignition before shifting into gear with a tentative sigh. His gaze lighted on the passenger seat where Annie had been, and something warm and deep and full of hope expanded in his chest till he thought he couldn't breathe.

"You're a very lucky man, Steven O'Connor," she had said.

Fingers clenched tight on the stick, he downshifted hard, all warmth dissipating the farther he rumbled away from her street. Exhaling slowly, his lips inched into a sad smile. *Don't I wish.*

⸺⸺⸺

"You never get tired of it, do you?" Emma said, peeking up at her husband with a touch of tease in her tone, knowing full well Sean O'Connor *never* got tired of sports.

"Nope. But gosh, Emma, can't you see why? Man alive, what a night!" Sean tucked an arm close to Emma's waist as they strolled home from his game, the trill of tree frogs and locusts lending a buzz of excitement that rivaled that of her husband's voice. A ragtag group of boys was playing kick ball in the street as they passed, soon disrupted by the honk of a horn before they scattered from the path of a Model T. The scent of fresh-mown grass and exhaust mingled with the telltale smell of a Snickers bar as Sean released a contented sigh. He pressed a kiss to her head that tugged a smile to her lips. "I think this may just be my best team yet, don't you?"

Emma's chuckle merged with the sounds of the summer night, Sean's little-boy enthusiasm tickling her as much as the playful pinch of his fingers. "Well, given this is the first season I've attended your games," she said with a hint of brogue usually reserved for a tease, "I may not be the perfect person to ask." She nipped his waist right back, not surprised when her hand met hard muscle. "But yes, Coach O'Connor, I'd say you have a contender on your hands."

At her words, he halted in the middle of the sidewalk and pulled her to him so fast, she let out a little squeak that was promptly swallowed up in a kiss. The heat of embarrassment over his display of affection quickly turned to heat of another kind, confirming that although Sean O'Connor had been a bachelor who avoided women most of his life, he was a natural athlete who excelled in *all* manners of sport. He finally pulled away, but massive hands still anchored at the small of her back, firmly pinning her to a chest as solid as the concrete beneath her feet. "Ah, but you *are* the perfect person, Mrs. O'Connor," he said with that easy grin she loved. "Because there's no one's opinion—" he kissed the tip of her nose—"or kiss I'd rather have."

Hooking her back to his side once again, he relinquished another heavy sigh, a hint of longing creeping into his tone as they made their way to their house on Dorchester Street. "I'll tell you what, I hope our sons have half the ability of Bobby Dalton, because that kid can sure sail a ball over the fence when you need him to."

Emma lowered her gaze, eyes fixed on the cracks in the sidewalk as the smile faded from her lips. Sean continued to chatter while he ushered her up the steps of their traditional clapboard row house with its pretty bay window flanked by azaleas and hostas. Lightning bugs blinked as the glow of dusk gave way to the dark of night. The heavy scent of Emma's fragrant cottage roses on the sunny side of the house filled the air like a rare perfume. But none of the sights and sounds that usually thrilled her could do so tonight, not at the reminder that her husband longed for sons she could probably never give. *But I can still be a mother to our children,* she thought, a glimmer of hope flitting in her heart like the fireflies in the dark.

Adoption.

Turning the key in the door, he glanced up, an edge of concern in his voice. "You've gotten awfully quiet, Emma." He stroked a hand to her cheek. "You feeling okay?"

"Of course," she said, forcing a light tone. She followed him into their cozy foyer where they'd left a small Tiffany lamp lit and waited while he bolted the door. "I think I'm just worn out from a full day with your mother, sisters, and the cousins, that's all."

His chuckle rumbled as they climbed the staircase to the second story. "That'd do it. Charity and Henry alone would wear me out, so I can certainly understand why you're tired." He bent to skim a soft kiss to her lips. "But not too, I hope," he whispered, and Emma's stomach dipped, well aware his Saturday night games usually heightened his yearning for a son.

"I'm going to take a quick shower," he said with a squeeze of her waist, whistling while he ambled down the hall on the way to the bathroom. The door closed with a click and Emma put a shaky hand to her eyes. "Oh, Lord, it will crush him not to have children," she whispered, fighting a sting of tears. She inhaled as if drawing in sustenance, then squared her shoulders and entered their bedroom, reminding herself how God had given her the love of a good man despite a past that didn't deserve it. For mercy's sake, he had set her free from loneliness, shame, and guilt—he could certainly set her husband free from pain over not having a son of his own blood.

Or heal me so he could?

The thought gave her pause, making her wonder how long she should wait before she told Sean the truth, that she had miscarried his babies. How long before she knew with a certainty she would never give him children of his own? She blinked, and her two cats, Lancelot and Guinevere, came into focus on the bed. Her lips curved at Lancelot hogging both pillows, sprawled like a fox collar of orange and cream stripes while Guinevere presided over the middle of the coverlet in a ball of white fluff. Slitted eyes barely lifting, Lancelot seemed to glare, obviously not happy Sean was home to take over the bed. Guinevere emitted a cute, little yawn that sounded like a growl before choosing to ignore the inevitable ousting of the felines, at least until Sean fell asleep.

Kicking off her shoes, Emma spanned across the covers on her tummy, kneading Lancelot's paw while she stroked Guinevere's head, her mind straying to how much her life had changed since Sean had made her his wife. In him she had everything she'd ever hoped for in a marriage. Except for his children, she reminded herself, and the thought prompted her to close her eyes and pray until she heard the bathroom door open. The bed vibrated with the purrs of her former bedmates, bringing a giggle to her lips. "So, how was your evening, your highness and your majesty?" she said with a soft scrub of their fur. "I know you're not pleased my husband steals your snuggle time, but remember, once he closes his eyes, he's gone for the night, so just bide your time . . ."

"Are you conspiring with those cats again, Emma O'Connor?" Sean assessed her with a shuttered gaze, arms folded and hip cocked in the doorway. Sculpted chest bare, he ambled into the room in boxers, blond hair damp from his shower. A slow grin of warning stretched across wide lips as he eased onto the bed to lie beside her. Elbow cocked and head in hand, he massaged Guinevere's rib cage, warming

Emma with a dangerous smile. Leaning close, he grazed her lips, then pulled away, the blue eyes tripping her pulse. "You're next," he whispered, and Emma was certain he could unleash a purr from her throat as easily as Guin's.

"I best get ready for bed," she said, attempting to get up.

A firm wrist gently tugged her near. "Not yet," he whispered, and with the grace of an athlete, he rolled on his back and pulled her along to lie on his chest. His tall frame dominated the bed, prompting Lance and Guin to find elsewhere to sleep while Emma's body relaxed against his. His kiss was slow and sweet, and her eyelids fluttered closed while magical fingers kneaded the nape of her neck to coax her closer. His scent surrounded her, drugging her body as much as his kiss—the clean smell of soap and shaving cream and the taste of mint in his mouth. Never had she felt so alive, so loved, so beautiful as she did in Sean's arms.

"I love you, Emma," he said softly, "more than Snickers and baseball and beating Brady and Luke at sports." The tease in his words faded with another tender kiss, and when he pulled away, he caressed her with a look that nearly stole her breath. Never had she known a man who could make love with his eyes more than Sean O'Connor. "I adore you," he whispered, "and sometimes I wonder how I survived without you."

She trailed fingers along his clean-shaven jaw, heart thudding and tears stinging her eyes. "And I, you. I thank God every hour of every day for the joy of being your wife, Sean."

In one fluid motion, he tumbled her onto her back, descending with a kiss that all but melted her to the bed. "Oh, Emma," he whispered, nuzzling her ear, "I want to give you babies—lots and lots of babies."

Her eyelids closed as moisture welled. *Oh God, please, I can't break his heart.*

"Girls, boys, it doesn't matter," he continued, his husky chuckle warm in her ear. "Although tonight, Mrs. O'Connor—I feel like a son."

She couldn't help it, her body convulsed in a heave.

His mouth stalled on her skin before his head jerked up, face suddenly pale. Skimming the tears from her cheek, he sat up. "Emma—what's wrong?"

She tried, but suddenly there was no way she could contain it—her grief over the death of his children, his dream—and with one agonizing wrench of her throat, she wept. Six months of hope deferred spilled from her eyes—deep, painful tears of mourning for her loss and his.

He cupped her face, thumbs grazing her cheeks. "Emma, please, tell me what's wrong."

"I can't . . ."

Heaves wracked her body, and he swept her up into his arms, head tucked against hers. "Yes, you can. Wherever happens to you, happens to me."

A moan withered on her lips. "I c-can't do this . . ."

He rocked her with gentle motion, palm stroking her hair. "It's okay, Emma," he soothed, "we don't have to tonight if you don't want to, really."

She jerked from his embrace to clutch frantic hands to his arms. "No," she said, his face little more than a blur. "I *can't* give you children . . ."

His ashen face stilled to stone, her words choking the air from the room before they settled on his features like an invisible shroud, proclaiming the death of his dream. His lips parted, but nothing came forth except a frail thread of air, no doubt expelling all hope. Muscles shifted in his throat and he buried his fingers into the hair at her temples. "What do you mean?"

Tears streamed her cheeks while she reached to caress the clean line of his jaw. "I . . . want to give you children, Sean, but I . . ." She paused, eyes flickering closed to stave off more tears before they opened again to reveal her sorrow. "I've miscarried twice since March, and I—"she swallowed the pain in her throat—"don't know if I can ever bring a baby to term."

"Twice?" he whispered, his voice strangled.

"Yes, my love." She clutched his hand, gripping tightly as if she could absorb some of his pain. "Once three months after we wed, but I . . . ," she expelled a frail sigh, "couldn't bring myself to tell you, to dash your hopes, because I'd hoped . . . prayed . . ." She stared at him through the haze of her tears. "But two months ago it happened again . . ."

Seconds passed as he stared, grief welling in his eyes, and she knew he was mourning the loss of their children. And then without a word, he bent to kiss her with all the gentleness she'd come to expect of this man, caressing her with his mouth as he lowered her to the bed. Lying beside her, he held her close, his voice hoarse but stronger than before. "Women miscarry, Emma, don't they? It doesn't have to mean—"

"No, it doesn't mean that God can't give us a child, but . . ." She closed her eyes, drawing strength from the steady beat of his heart. "But I have a history of miscarriage, Sean—four times with Rory and now two with you." Her voice broke and she closed her eyes. "Six babies," she whispered, "precious gifts from God that my violent past has stolen away." A shudder rippled through her. "Which breaks my heart, because I so wanted to be a mother to your children."

His arm tightened at her waist. "And so you will," he said quietly, stroking her hair. She felt the shift of his throat and when he spoke, his voice carried an assurance that seeped into her soul like the warmth of his body against hers. "You are the greatest blessing God has ever given me, Emma, and although my heart mourns over the loss of our babies and the prospect that we may never have children of our own . . . ," he kissed her lips before his mouth tipped in a tender smile, "God created you to be a mother, and I know he will give us children to love."

She sat up in his arms. "But—"

"No 'buts,' " he said with a tender stroke of her jaw. "Whether our children have our blood in their veins or someone else's, they'll still be our children and you'll still be their mother."

She blinked, not sure she'd heard right. "What are you saying?" she breathed.

He studied her for a long while, as if memorizing every nuance of her face. With the barest of smiles, he lifted her hand to his lips, lids closed as he kissed her palm. When his eyes opened, a sheen of moisture accompanied his gaze. "We'll adopt," he whispered.

Her pulse stopped . . . and then in a violent surge of joy, it pounded in her ears until she thought she would faint. "Oh, Sean!" Lunging into his arms, she began to weep again, her sobs in beautiful harmony with his husky chuckles. "I was so afraid—afraid you'd be crushed, afraid you wouldn't consider adoption." She pulled away, pushing the tears from her eyes. "When?"

He laughed outright and tucked a finger to her chin. "Why do I get the feeling you've already thought this all out?"

Heat braised her cheeks, and he pulled her into his arms with another deep chuckle, holding her close. "You're spending entirely too much time with Charity, you know that?" He kissed the tip of her nose and cocked a brow. "When? Well . . . why don't *you* tell me?"

Barely able to contain herself, she bounced up to sit cross-legged, taking his hands in hers. "Well, as a matter of fact," she began in a rush, "Charity and I visited St. Mary's Home for Unwed Mothers a few times—"

"Oh, you have, have you?" Elbow cocked, he slanted back with a ghost of a smile.

She bit the edge of her lip and offered a shy smile. "Just to see the babies sometimes, that's all. Charity and I like to hold them."

He quirked a thick blond brow. "Just hold them, huh, and nothing else?"

She giggled and bent to give him a quick kiss, then inhaled deeply to calm her racing heart, her smile fading. "Oh, Sean, my heart breaks for those little ones, all alone in the world, no family of their own. If we can give our home and our hearts to just a few—"

"A few?" The whites of his eyes expanded. "More than one? All at once?"

She clasped his hands with a smile. "No, not all at once, my love. But . . . if I am truly unable to give you sons and daughters of your own, then yes, more than one." She blinked to ward off the prick of more tears, unable to fight the quiver of her lips any more than she could stem the flow of love in her heart. "Until our hearts and our home are so full of love, we fairly burst with joy." She clasped his hands. "Just think, Sean—a family like your parents gave you, the greatest gift we can give to a forgotten soul who has no family of their own."

In a clutch of her heart, Sean tugged her into his arms before toppling her onto her back to thread gentle fingers into her hair. "And this, Emma O'Connor," he whispered, love glowing in his eyes, "is only one of the many, *many* reasons I had no choice but to fall desperately in love with you." In slow motion, he leaned in to fondle her lips with his own, his kiss warming her skin while his tenderness warmed her soul.

Her arms curled around his neck. "So, you'll go with me tomorrow . . . to see the babies?" The air hushed in her lungs while she awaited his answer.

That easy smile she'd fallen in love with slipped across his lips as he bent to feather her jaw with kisses. "Tomorrow, yes." His fingers trailed down, skimming across the first button of her blouse to loosen its hold. "And tonight?" His lips returned with a languid kiss that quickly focused her mind on the present. "Tonight we work on hedging our bets."

10

"Any questions?" Director Hackett scanned the cramped meeting room, beady black eyes daring anyone to say a word. Most of the Prohibition agents slouched in their rickety wood chairs, faces grim while the director's eyes disappeared into slits, thunderous black brows slashing downward. His bald head gleamed with sweat. "Good. Because the last thing I need right now is the DA breathing down my neck 'cause somebody got greedy."

A loose filament in the tungsten lamp overhead flickered, casting an eerie mirror-ball effect on the man whom no agent with half a brain would want to cross. Especially on Monday morning after a weekend of foiled raids. Sweat stains circled beneath meaty arms propped on rumpled gray trousers as the director continued to glare as much as the light above. "Philly and New York have thrown the book at 10 percent of their force, but if it happens here, on my watch?" His words chewed the air like a buzz saw, their gravelly tone suggesting the man devoured 16-penny nails for breakfast. "You'll go to the slammer, all right, but not until I rip your tonsils out and wrap 'em around your neck, got it?"

Joe elbowed Steven, leaning close with a smirk on his face.

"Almost wish the Hack was on the take himself, so he'd lay off these bribery rants. My eyes are glazing over."

"You think this is funny, Walsh?"

Joe froze in the back row, his face suddenly as pale as the chalk diagrams Hack scrawled across the portable blackboard at the front of the room. "Uh, no sir."

Steven stared straight ahead, lips clamped hard to keep from laughing.

The director folded beefy arms matted with black hair that matched a thatch peeking over a tie loosened so much, it sagged like the bags under his eyes. "That's good, Walsh, 'cause I doubt you'll be laughing if you pull detail this weekend."

A nearly silent groan echoed in Joe's chest. "Yes, sir."

"If you were smart," Hack continued, his tone as surly as his scowl, "you'd take this job a little more seriously, like your partner there. We're not pussyfooting here, Walsh. I need tough federal agents who can get the job done, not a vaudeville act, ya got it?"

"Yes, sir."

"O'Connor." The director cocked his head, lips pursed as he honed in on Steven.

Steven sat up, spine rigid and jaw tense. "Yes, sir?"

"You're the brains on your team—use 'em. I expect you to rub off on Walsh, not the other way around, understood?"

A reedy sigh escaped Steven's lips, his suit coat stifling his air. "Yes, sir."

Hackett back-fisted the blackboard. "Before we break, I need six volunteers for a special assignment this weekend. Rumor has it there's a frat shindig in Duke's County Friday night, complete with stills and wild women, so I'll need one or two pretty faces to pass for fancy frat boys." The edge of his lip curled as he leveled a sharp gaze in Joe's direction. "Not you, Walsh, with that mug, but O'Connor would fit right in, so let me know by five or I'll pick who I want. Saturday night, I'll need six more because we'll be working overtime on the North End. The commissioner's due for inspection in the next two weeks, and I aim to make this a record month. We'll comb the North End all week, paying some surprise visits to a few blind pigs." He rapped the board with his knuckles. "The assignment sheet's posted, so break's over."

Joe waited till the director left before turning to Steven, mouth skewed. "I swear that guy hates me." He slid Steven a narrow look and loosened his tie. "And it's all because of you, O'Connor, always toeing the line. You make Eliot Ness look like a slouch."

Steven slapped Joe on the back, grinning as they strolled from the room. He slipped his suit coat off and slung it over his shoulder, checking the roster on Hackett's door. "Come on, Joe, don't give me all the credit—you have a true talent for making yourself look bad."

"Very funny. And the boss thinks *I'm* the comedian. He's so sure I'm the bad influence on his golden boy, but that's a laugh. Can't even get you to Ocean Pier for some fun." Joe squinted at the list and groaned. "Man alive, we're on the docket with Raby—I can't believe it."

Steven ruffled Joe's hair with a chuckle. "Come on, Joe, grow up. Lee's a good agent and I'd take detail with him anytime."

"Hey, knock it off, 'pretty boy.'" Joe patted his sandy hair back down. "This thatch is hard enough to keep combed without you messing it up, making me look like some country yokel. Not everyone looks like you, O'Connor, so have some respect." He followed Steven to their back-to-back desks and dropped into his chair, propping his feet on the drawers. "And the only reason you like Raby is he's just like you, so straitlaced he's got a rod up his back."

Steven hooked his coat over his chair and sat down to shuffle through papers. "It's called being an exemplary civil servant, Agent Walsh, something that's actually considered a good thing."

"Yeah?" Joe's feet thudded to the ground as he leaned in,

arms flat on his desk. "So be a good influence like Hackett said, Steven—go to Ocean Pier with me this weekend and keep me in line."

"Sorry, buddy, can't—got something else in mind for Saturday night." Steven peered up. "Hey, you remember the address of the speak we raided last week on the North End?"

Joe stared, mouth swagging open. "Yeah, Steven, let me get my typed log where I list every second of every day." He shook his head. "Criminy, I'm surprised you don't keep one."

Steven grinned. "I do—left it at home this weekend when I did paperwork."

Slumping into his chair, Joe dropped his head on the back with another groan. "Come on, Steven, you're my best friend. Don't make me go to the Pier with Zuchek—he hogs all the girls."

Steven laughed, a definite ribbing to his tone. "So do I, Walsh, so what's the difference?"

A grunt erupted from Joe's lips. "Yeah, but you're a nice guy who shares. Besides, you're so gunshy with women right now that you draw 'em like flies, then turn 'em over to me."

"How 'bout Harper?" Steven asked, filling out his report. "He'd jump at the chance."

A wrinkle appeared at the bridge of Joe's nose. "Yeah, but he's so homely, girls don't even come around." He eyed Steven with a dubious look. "I bet you're planning to take on both of those special assignments on Friday and Saturday nights, aren't you? You already got the boss in your hip pocket—why volunteer for every detail there is?"

"I'm not," Steven said with half a smile. "Just Friday night 'cause Saturday night I have plans."

Joe sat up, a plea in his tone. "Come on, you're not going to spend another Saturday night with Gabe, are ya? You spent last Saturday night with the kid, so you owe me."

"*Owe* you?" Steven said with a lift of brows. "How ya figure?"

The smile faded from Joe's face as the tease left his tone.

"Because we're best friends, Steven, and best friends *do* things together besides raid speakeasies. They talk, they go to the gym, they go out with girls." His hazel eyes reflected a hint of hurt that Steven noticed for the first time. "They have fun together." A sigh withered from Joe's lips. "You spent almost three years dodging the social scene and me along with it, and to be honest, I'm worried about you. And it's not just 'cause I miss the fun we always had, even though I do." He snatched his time sheet from his drawer and started filling it out, pausing to glance up while concern shaded his eyes. "You haven't been yourself since college—quieter, more introspective, almost like you're far away. I thought once I got you back to the Pier again, you'd get back to normal. I was even encouraging Erica to go for you because I thought you needed a woman in your life, but that hasn't worked. And I sure don't want to see Erica hurt any more than you, but I gotta tell ya, buddy, you need to get back in the game and start seeing women again."

A heavy exhale gusted from Steven's lips as he sagged back in his chair. He mauled his face with his hands and then looked up. "I'm sorry, Joe. And you're right, I have been a bore, but I promise that's all going to change. I'm ready to move on and start dating again, so you and I will be able to double like old times." He drew in a stabilizing breath and locked gazes with his partner, a hint of a smile on his lips. "And I already have somebody in mind, which is why I can't go to the Pier Saturday night."

Joe's mouth went slack, along with the pen in his hand. "Good grief, O'Connor—you holding out on me?"

Steven shook his head. "Nope, just too stupid and scared to realize something I should have figured out before now."

"Yeah?" Joe leaned in, interest piqued. "And what's that? You'd make a lousy priest?"

Steven laughed, giving his partner a wayward smile. "Uh, yeah, I'd say that's pretty conclusive—celibacy is not my idea of happily ever after."

"I'll go along there," Joe said with a grin. He cocked his head, eyes in a squint. "So who's the doll? You got me on pins and needles here. And how exactly did this revelation hit?"

Steven glanced at the clock on the wall, aware Lee Raby would be rounding them up before long. He inked more specifics onto his report. "Saturday night when I drove her home."

Joe's jaw dropped. "Hey, you told me you were spending time with Gabe."

"I did, Joe, honest, but *she* was there too—at my house." Steven tunneled through his hair, cheeks warming at how adamantly he'd denied his interest in Annie. He'd given Joe his word there was nothing between them nor ever would be. But somehow that kiss they'd shared when he'd driven her home had him tossing and turning all night long and befuddled all the next day. Thoughts of her had been relentless—laughing in his kitchen, sitting at his table, mixing with his family— haunting him every waking hour until he finally realized that, seventeen or no, he wanted to see Annie Martin again. He pinched the bridge of his nose. No, make that *Kennedy*. He glanced up at Joe and gave him a sheepish smile. "Turns out she's cozy with her catechism teacher, who just happens to be my sister, which she claims she didn't know."

Joe blinked, mouth in a sag. "Well, who the devil is she? Steven, you're killing me here!"

Steven tossed the pen on the desk and leaned back. "You're not gonna believe it."

"Try me." Chin raised, Joe dared him with a curious smile.

Exhaling loudly, Steven peered up, a slow grin traveling his lips. "Annie Martin."

It was a contest as to which faded first—Joe's color or his smile. "Tell me you're joking."

A frown ridged Steven's brow. "Come on, Joe, I know I said I had no intention of fooling with the kid, and I meant it at the time, I swear." The seeds of a headache pulsed in his temple and he kneaded it with his fingers. "But she spent the evening with my family and we laughed and had a good time

218

and I took her home and . . ." He swallowed hard, realizing how fickle he must sound, bent on avoiding the kid one minute, dating her the next. Heat climbed his neck. "The truth is . . . I kissed her, and now I can't get her out of my mind."

"No?" Joe said with a sharp hike of his brow. "Well, I can."

Steven's eyes narrowed. "What's that supposed to mean?" His headache began to throb. "You said it yourself—the kid would be good for me."

"That was before I knew who she was."

"What are you talking about, Walsh?" Annoyance threaded his tone as he leaned in, forearms flat on the desk. "You got something to say?"

Joe studied him for several seconds before he answered, a wariness in his eyes. "Yeah, Steven, I do, and I can tell you right now—you're not going to like it."

"O'Connor, Walsh, Luepke, Hanson, and Lewellen." Raby inclined his head to the door. "On the dock, five minutes."

Steven glanced up, every muscle in his body as stiff as the nod he gave Raby. He stood to his feet, double-checked his Smith & Wesson Model 10, and slipped it back into his shoulder holster before grilling Joe with a glare. "You better spit it out, Joe, or so help me . . ."

"Her name's not Martin, it's Kennedy."

"Yeah? Well, she already told me that, so what?" Steven snatched his time sheet.

The hesitation in Joe's manner prickled the back of Steven's neck before his partner finally exhaled and stood to his feet, eyes locked with his in a show of sympathy. "So she's Maggie's little sister, Steven—Susannah Grace Kennedy."

Steven blinked, body numb as if Joe had just cold-cocked him with his own Smith & Wesson. *Gracie Sue* . . . He swallowed hard, struggling for air, but all he could muster were shallow breaths through a throat as dry as the paper in his hand. "How do you know?" he said, his voice a croak as his gaze dropped and drifted into a vacant stare.

"Peggy let it slip last week at the Pier while she and I were dancing. Joanie gave her too much giggle water and the kid got plastered, tongue as loose as a hooker on Ann Street." He sighed. "Begged me not to tell anybody, so I promised I wouldn't, but your interest in Annie changes everything. I figured you had a right to know."

Dazed, Steven nodded. He pushed in his chair. "We better go. Raby'll have our hides."

Joe scrawled his name at the top of his time sheet and nabbed it before following Steven to the door. "What are you going to do?" he asked quietly, his concern clear in his tone.

"Nothing." Steven tossed his time sheet into the bin and stopped to pop his head into Hackett's office. "Boss, I'm in for both Friday and Saturday nights."

Hackett looked up from his paperwork, a half smile, half scowl on his face. "I knew I could count on you, O'Connor, but honestly, don't you have a life?"

Heat crawled up Steven's neck. He gave the director a thin smile. "Apparently not, sir." Ducking out, he shoved through the double doors, striding for the back exit, eyes straight ahead.

"Steven, wait—" Tossing his sheet in the basket, Joe hustled after him, slowing his pace with a hand to his arm. "So, you gonna start seeing her anyway?"

A nerve pulsed in Steven's jaw, a nice complement to the throbbing pain in his head. "Nope." He slammed through a door on the way to the dock, cracking it against the wall.

"Look, Steven, she's a nice kid. Maybe she didn't know about you and Maggie."

"She knew." He fairly spit it out, jaw compressed at the memory of her words in the car. *"There's something I need to tell you, but I'm not quite ready."* Fisting the knob of the steel door to the dock, Steven hurled it open, and a blast of summer heat slammed him in the face, as hard and hot as the temper boiling inside.

"Steven, I'm sorry."

Striding to where the other agents waited, Steven was in

the perfect mood for a raid, itching to take somebody down. "Yeah, Joe," he said, lips pinched in a thin line. "Me too."

~

"Come on, Annie Lou, it's your birthday—live a little!" Peggy ducked to peer into Annie's vanity mirror, a plea in her tone and eyebrow pencil in hand. "Just a little makeup, please?" Her lower lip bulged in a pout, and Annie laughed.

"You are nothing but a little girl, Peggy Pankow, you know that?" Annie shook her head. "One who never got over playing with dolls."

Two pencil-drawn brows did a Groucho Marx as Peggy gave her an imp of a smile. "Especially the male kind," she said, tilting copper curls against Annie's shoulder-length waves. "Come on, Annie, please? You're just so much fun to doll up with those big green eyes and that strawberry-blonde hair. Besides, you're finally eighteen—don't you want to look it for once?"

The satin bodice of the lavender dress Peggy talked her into shimmered when Annie huffed out a sigh. "Oh, all right. But just this once because dressing like this makes me feel so . . . so . . ." She squinted in the mirror, not completely comfortable with the seductive sway of blonde hair over one eye that Peggy had fixed in the latest Garbo style.

"Wicked?" A blue eyelid winked as Peggy bumped a hip to Annie's. "Move over."

"Yes, as a matter of fact." Annie faced her friend with eyes closed so shadow could be applied. "And a little dangerous too, if you know what I mean." She drew in an uneasy breath, not completely comfortable going to dinner with the gang. She sighed, grateful she'd drawn the line at going to the Pier after, especially the way she looked tonight. "A little too much like a woman," she muttered. "The kind who gives men the wrong idea."

"Yes, I know what you mean, but it's okay to give men the

wrong idea just once, as long as you don't give 'em anything else." Peg bent to line Annie's shadowed lids, then applied the finishing touch with Pink Passion lipstick. She straightened. "Perfect!"

Annie looked in the mirror, and a soft rush of rose added to the dusting of rouge Peggy applied over ivory powder that diminished all freckles. Her green eyes went wide. "Mercy me, how can a little shadow, powder, and liner make such a difference?"

"You're just a natural, Annie Lou, one of those faces that can go either way." She shook her head, assessing the finished product. "From innocent to vamp in the snap of a finger."

Annie sighed. "Not if 'vamp' isn't what I want. A touch of lipstick suits me just fine."

"Oh pooh, you're just not used to dolling up in small-town Iowa, but you're a city girl now. You have to look the part, at least on your birthday." She reached in her purse for something that put a devious smile on her lips. "And look what I have," she said in a sing-song voice, waving a long tube in the air. "The latest movie star craze—Max Factor's X-Rated Lip Gloss, guaranteed kissable lips the next time you tangle with the law . . ."

Annie's rouge had nothing on the blood in her cheeks. "Peggy Pankow—stop! I have no intention of 'tangling' with the law, kissable lips or no."

Glossing her own lips and then Annie's, Peggy gave her a wink. "Yeah, and if Steven O'Connor tries to kiss you again, you're going to shoo him away, right?"

Annie stared in the mirror at lips that were shiny and wet— lips caressed by Steven O'Connor, not once but twice. She blinked, fully aware that she wanted him to do it again . . .

"I thought so," Peggy said with a smirk, tossing her makeup into her purse. "Face it, Annie, good girl or no, you're a goner when it comes to Steven O'Connor, and I'm pretttttty certain if he wanted a taste of your lip gloss, you're not going to tell him no." She hooked the strap of her purse over her shoulder. "Are you sure you won't change your mind and go with us to the Pier after dinner? Because you-know-who might be there . . ."

Chin firm, Annie tucked her clutch under her arm on her way to the door. "Nope, I already told you, Peg, I'm steering clear of the Pier." She glanced at her watch. "We better run."

Skittering down the staircase with Peg on her heels, Annie hurried to the library to tell her aunt and sister goodbye. She smiled at the sight of Aunt Eleanor on the floor with Glory, playing Old Maid. Nose in the air, she sashayed in and took a spin. "So . . . how do I look?"

"Holy-moly, Annie, you look like a movie star!" Glory's blue eyes bugged wide, her rosebud lips curling into a grin. "Boys are gonna think you're gorgeous!"

Annie chewed the edge of her lip when her eyes lighted on her aunt's shocked face. "What do you think, Aunt Eleanor?" she asked shyly, pushing the hair from her eyes as she peeked at her aunt through lashes thick with Peggy's mascara. She fingered one of the loose curls grazing her shoulders, giving it a nervous tug. "Is it too much?"

Rising to her feet, Aunt Eleanor opened her mouth to speak, but nothing came out. Instead, a sheen of tears glazed her eyes while shaky fingers fluttered to her throat.

"Aunt Eleanor?" Annie took a step forward, placing a hand to her aunt's arm.

With a short shake of her head, her aunt clutched Annie's hand, finally giving it a maternal pat. "Forgive me, dear," she whispered, her voice thick with emotion as she awkwardly swiped at her eyes, "but I don't think I ever fully realized how much you look like my sister . . ."

Annie's throat constricted, and with a short little heave, she gave her a tight hug. "Oh, Aunt Eleanor, you couldn't have given a finer compliment. I adored my mother."

A pitiful sob choked into a chuckle as Aunt Eleanor gripped her niece tightly, her blonde hair tucked against Annie's. "I did too, Annie," she whispered. "I just didn't know how much until you girls came." Giving her a final squeeze, she pulled away, hands braced to Annie's arms as she studied her face. "It's more makeup than I like you to wear and certainly more than you need, but you do look beautiful." With a hike of her chin, she brushed the tears from her eyes and dipped in her pocket for a wad of bills she pressed into Annie's palm, gently fisting it closed. "This is to celebrate your birthday with your friends." She kissed Annie's cheek. "Happy birthday, dear—I'm so very grateful you were born."

"Oh, Aunt Eleanor." Annie embraced her again, hardly believing this was the woman she disdained not six months ago. She slipped the money in her purse. "I can't thank you enough."

"You look very pretty too, Peggy," Aunt Eleanor said, noting Peggy hovering at the door.

"Thank you, Miss Martin. We're taking Annie to Lorenzo's in the Italian Quarter."

Aunt Eleanor nodded. "The North End's not too far, but I don't believe I've heard of Lorenzo's. Do you need Frailey to give you a ride?"

"It's new," Peggy said with a smile, "or at least that's what my sister says. It was her idea. And thanks for the offer of a ride, but we'll walk, then my sister's friend will bring us home."

"Have a good time, then, but not too late, Annie, all right?" Aunt Eleanor released a sigh, eyeing Glory on the floor. "Are you sure you wouldn't be more comfortable at the table, dear?"

Annie bussed Glory's cheek. "Let's try the table," Annie whispered. "Shall we?"

"Okay, but you'll kiss me when you come home, right? Even if I'm asleep?"

"Yes, ma'am." Annie blew a kiss on her way out the door. "Good night, all."

Strolling down the sidewalk with Peggy, she breathed in the heady scent of honeysuckle as excitement bubbled in her veins. "Oh, what a beautiful night—balmy temperatures, the scent of flowers, and Italian food." Annie sighed, quite certain this was the perfect night for a birthday dinner. "And as if that isn't enough, I'm finally eighteen." She giggled, hurrying past the tiny city park outside Louisburg Square where jazz floated in the air from a concert on the lawn. "I'll tell you what, Peg, it doesn't get much better than this."

"Sure it does, Annie Lou," Peggy said with a mischievous gleam. "Who knows, if you go to the Pier tonight, you may just meet some tall-dark-and-handsome with a gun and a badge."

Annie paused at the red light, almost tempted. A group of boys on bicycles flew past on the street, earning honks from passing cars while little girls played hopscotch on the sidewalk. She sighed. "Sorry, Peg—can't. Even if I wanted to, I can't lie to Aunt Eleanor. Besides, I already told Steven I wasn't going to the Pier anymore, and if he saw me there . . ."

The light changed, and Peggy tugged her across. "He might be glad, you know, especially after that kiss last week when he drove you home. Sounds like he's warming up to you."

"Oh, I hope so," she said softly, praying she'd run into Steven at his house next time she was there. The thought put an extra bounce in her step.

When they arrived, Peggy opened the door of a charming brick building on Hanover Street, and the spicy smell of basil and oregano merged with exhaust fumes from the street and the tang of sea air just a few blocks away. Lush flower boxes of red and white petunias flanked either side of the red, white, and green striped awning where two old-fashioned streetlamps lent a cozy glow. "See? Isn't this nice? Aren't you glad I talked you into dinner with the gang?"

"I suppose," Annie said, still gun-shy about spending time with Joanie and her friends. Inside, the aroma of Italian spices rumbled Annie's stomach as she blinked to adjust to the dim atmosphere where candles flickered in wine bottles on white-linen tables. Waiters in ties and white aprons bustled through a maze of crowded diners like bees in a hive, delivering platters of food that watered Annie's mouth. The room was filled with smoke and people, laughing and dining to the lively tune of a string quartet. Following on Peggy's heels, Annie scanned the restaurant for any sign of her sister and friends. "I don't see them," she said with a squint, "so maybe we better put our name in for a table."

"Nope." Peggy grabbed Annie's hand to lead her toward the back of the restaurant to a long hall with a rear door. "They reserved a table downstairs, Annie, in honor of your birthday."

"But this is so nice up here . . ." She shot a look of longing as Peggy dragged her through the cozy restaurant where waiters hurried by with sizzling steaks and steaming bowls of pasta.

"Yeah, but downstairs is *extra* special." She eased the door open and led Annie down creaky stairs to another ornate wooden door with a small leaded-glass window. The walls pulsed with the sound of jazz, and Annie's heart thudded when Peggy knocked on the door. The little window wheeled open with a gravelly voice that gave Annie the shivers. "Password?"

"Al Jolson," Peggy whispered on tiptoe with a hand to her mouth.

The voice on the other side grunted and opened the door, ushering Annie into a world that effectively took her breath away. Eyes spanning wide, she was Alice in Wonderland, mouth ajar as she stumbled along behind Peggy, who wove through the crowd in search of her sister. A haze of smoke hung in the room so thick with people, she could only stare as they passed an endless burlwood bar where patrons perched on red leather stools. The room throbbed with life—Lindy Hoppers whirling and kicking on a circular dance floor in the center of a room while musicians gleamed with sweat, lost in the rhythm of jazz and swing.

"Over there!" Peggy shouted over the noise. Annie followed, ignoring men's glances and whistles as she wound her way through the mob to where Joanie waved from a booth at the back.

"Happy birthday, kiddo—you look like a million bucks." Joanie scooted over.

"Yeah, kid, happy birthday." Erica raised a toast with a glass of what looked like 7UP. "Here's to the best birthday ever, and a night you'll never forget."

"Here, here!" Ashley and Joanie clinked drinks on the table twice, then took a swig.

Annie leaned close to Peg, panic in her tone. "Is this . . . a . . . ," she gulped, "speakeasy?"

"Yep, isn't it the bee's knees? Joanie's been to lots of them, but this is my very first one." She patted Annie's hand. "Don't worry, just get Dr Pepper like you always do, okay?"

Annie nodded dumbly. She sagged against the booth, a buzz in her brain without ever taking a drink. *I am SO stupid!*

"So, what'll it be?" Erica said with a smile. "Joanie, Ashley, and I are buying your first drink—Annie's for her birthday and Peg's, just because."

"Pick something you think I'll like," Peggy said, hooking an arm to Annie's shoulder. She gave her a squeeze. "But Annie just wants Dr Pepper, okay?"

"You got it." Erica handed out menus with a wink. "Figure out what you want and I'll be right back."

She hurried away and Annie's eyes fluttered closed. *Stay calm, then just eat and run . . .*

"My name is Rudy and this is Vince. Any of you ladies care to dance?"

Annie's eyes popped open, pulse catching at the sight of two men, easily in their thirties. "Rudy" offered a lazy smile, gaze circling the table till it landed on Annie. "How 'bout it, doll?"

Muscles quivered in her throat. "Uh, no thank you," she whispered, cheeks aflame.

"Ashley and I will," Joanie said, jumping up so fast she

almost toppled her drink. She tugged Ashley with her, and the two couples made their way to the floor while Peggy powdered her nose.

"Hey, where'd everybody go?" Erica handed a glass of what looked like lemonade to Peggy and Dr Pepper to Annie before she slid in the booth.

"Joanie and Ashley are dancing." Peggy took a sip of her drink. "So, what is this?"

"It's called a daiquiri and you're gonna love it, trust me."

"And this is . . . ?" Annie sniffed, quite sure "trust" was not something Erica inspired.

"Dr Pepper, sweetie . . . just what the doctor ordered." Erica lifted her glass. "To Annie."

More than a little nervous, Annie sipped the Dr Pepper to authenticate its purity. It tasted like it all right, but still . . . She sipped again. "You sure, Erica, because it tastes a little different."

Erica rolled her eyes. "Of course it does, kid—it's from a soda fountain, not a bottle."

Satisfied it was only pop, Annie took a swallow and then another, closing her eyes to allow the music to seep into her limbs while thoughts of Steven O'Connor seeped into her mind.

"Annie!"

"Oh!" She almost dropped her drink, eyes popping open. "What?"

Peggy grinned. "Oliver wants your order."

Blood warmed her cheeks as she offered a smile of apology to the waiter, fumbling the menu. "I'm sorry, Oliver, I'm afraid I haven't even looked yet."

"Whew, that was fun," Joanie said, back from her dance.

"You know what you want?" Erica made room for Ashley with a nod at the waiter.

"Anything without garlic," Joanie said with a chuckle, eyeing the menu.

"Oh, I forgot to tell you guys." Annie looked up. "I'm

picking up the bill because my aunt wanted to buy everyone dinner for my birthday."

Ashley blinked. "How much did she give you, Annie, 'cause Lorenzo's is pretty steep?"

"I . . . don't know—let me look." Digging through her purse, she pulled out the money Aunt Eleanor had given her. Her mouth went slack when she counted out eight twenty-dollar bills. "It's . . . it's a hundred sixty dollars," she whispered, moisture pricking her eyes.

Erica cut loose with a whistle. "Well, in that case, I'll have the filet mignon," she said with a chuckle, handing the menu to the waiter. "Your aunt's a dream, Annie, you know that?"

"Oooo, I'll have the filet too," Peggy said, glass raised in the air. "To Aunt Eleanor!"

"To Aunt Eleanor," the others echoed, and Annie giggled, upending her drink with everyone else.

Oliver took their orders, then paused. "Another round, ladies?"

"Oh, I like a man who thinks ahead," Erica said with a smile. "Daiquiris all around, except for the birthday girl." She winked at the waiter. "Dr Pepper—heavy on the Dr."

Oliver smiled with a slight bow at the waist. "Very good, ladies."

A slow song began, and Peggy and Erica left to dance. Annie sighed and rested her head on the back of the booth while Joanie and Ashley chatted away, her mind as mellow as the flow of the music. She closed her eyes, the last of her Dr Pepper going down smoothly as thoughts of Steven curved her lips into a smile.

"Care to dance?"

Joanie jabbed an elbow into Annie's side, and she startled. "He's asking you to dance, Annie," she said with a jerk of her head, indicating a nice-looking man with an easy smile.

"The name's Eddie." He nodded to the dance floor. "What do you say . . . Annie, is it?"

She blinked, her body suddenly so heavy, she wasn't sure she could stand up.

Joanie prodded her out. "Come on, Birthday Girl, the man's asking you to dance."

"But—"

"No 'buts,' please," Eddie said, giving her a boyish smile. "You're too cute to sit out." He led her onto the floor, and all at once, she felt afloat as he pulled her into his arms, her body wonderfully limp. Closing her eyes, she felt the warmth of his hands at her waist, and when he tucked his head to hers, his scent reminded her so much of Steven, her heart began to race.

"Mmm . . . this is nice," she whispered, and Eddie pulled her closer.

"Make a wish, Annie," he said, whirling her with a heady spin. "And I'll make one too."

People pressed in on all sides, yet for Annie, everyone disappeared but the man who held her in his arms. "Here's hoping both of our wishes come true," he breathed, and tipping her chin, he kissed her softly on the mouth.

A glorious warmth traveled her body as the room began to spin. "Oh, me too," she whispered, and with a languid sigh, she returned Steven's kiss with a gentle one of her own.

11

*J*oe looked at his watch and sighed. "Man, I'm whipped. Two raids tonight and one yet to go. And to think I could be dancing with the girl of my dreams right now at the Pier." He loosened his tie and wiped the sweat from his face with the sleeve of his coat. "Life isn't fair."

"Sure it is," Steven said with a half smile, eyes closed and hat tipped low while resting on the backseat of the bureau vehicle driven by Lee Raby. "You were home free till you pulled that stunt this week. You're lucky you got this detail instead of Hackett pulling your badge."

Joe shot a glance at the front seat where Raby was in deep discussion with Donze, then lowered his voice. "Hey, I was just trying to assess if it was booze in those milk jugs, or water."

One of Steven's eyes edged up. "By upending it in front of the director?"

Joe grinned. "So I was thirsty," he said, poking Steven with his elbow. "Besides, how was I supposed to know Hack was in the head?" He braced an arm along the open window, hand splayed to catch the breeze. "I'll tell you what, O'Connor, about broke my heart pouring that moonshine down the toilet—smoothest stuff I ever had." He chuckled, pulling

Wrigley's Doublemint from his pocket. "Talk about white lightning! Made the rotgut we cooked up in college taste like Clorox." He popped a piece in his mouth, then offered one to Steven. "Gum?"

"Yeah, thanks." Steven plucked the piece from Joe's hand and unwrapped it, shoving it into his mouth before pocketing the crumpled wrapper. He looked out his window, eyes glazing into an emotionless stare at the mention of the bathtub gin they used to brew in college. Yeah, it was Clorox, all right, he thought with a clamp of his jaw, pure poison that traveled a man's bloodstream until it had him by the throat, stealing both his will and his conscience.

And sometimes his life . . .

Steven's eyelids weighted closed, guilt surging his system as naturally as booze once surged his veins. The same booze that had killed a kid on his watch. No, he hadn't poured the rotgut down Vinnie Logan's throat, but he may as well have. He was fraternity president when Vinnie died, so much hard stuff inside he passed out and choked on his own vomit. Vinnie's rich family hushed it up with little more than a suspension for the fraternity, saving Steven's hide.

Except with his father. *And with my conscience.*

"O'Connor!"

He jerked at the sound of Joe's voice, facing him with a pinch of brows. "What?"

"You haven't heard a word I've said, have you?"

Steven exhaled loudly. "Sorry, Joe, my mind was somewhere else."

"No joke. And I bet I know where."

Steven slid him a narrow gaze. "Bet you don't."

"So you weren't thinking about you-know-who?"

For once, no. His mouth took a slant. "Nope, but thanks for the reminder."

Hat angled low on his forehead, Joe laid his head back, giving Steven a sideways smile. "Sorry, buddy, but I just spent the last few minutes talking to myself, so I figured it was a safe guess." He folded his arms and closed his eyes. "Hard to believe she's Maggie's sister, isn't it?"

"Yeah," Steven said quietly, suddenly seeing the resemblance in ways that hadn't been obvious before—in the almond shape of the eyes, the golden hair color, or that certain sparkle that Maggie always had. Steven's lips tightened. Only Maggie had been a flirt, seductive. Not innocent and naïve like Annie—or like Maggie *used* to be. His mouth thinned. *Before me.*

"She seems so different than Maggie, a sweet kid with a conscience. I don't know, if it were me, I think I'd give her a shot, Maggie's sister or no. Girls like her don't grow on trees."

Steven's smile went stiff. "That's for darn sure. Until jokers like you and me pluck 'em off." He exhaled. "Nope, already ruined one Kennedy's life. No sense in ruining another."

"O'Connor, you got the layouts?" Raby shot a glance over his shoulder before coasting to a stop in front of the curb two blocks from Lorenzo's, a speakeasy they'd cased earlier in the week. Two more bureau cars eased in behind them, headlights fading to dark.

"Yeah, Boss, right here." Steven pulled several papers from his suit coat and handed them over. "According to my source, the speak's in the basement and it's a class joint, not a blind pig like the last dive we hit. It's brand-new, so it's pretty sophisticated—three exits with reinforced doors, buzzer alarms behind the bar, and shelves that button-flip to dump the booze down a shoot into the sewer. We either have to break in or one of us goes in legit, with a dame on our arm, which is what I suggest." He leaned over the front seat and pointed to several spots on the diagram. "This is the main entrance with access through the restaurant, then exits at either side of the bar on the south wall, including one that tunnels to the hat shop next door."

Raby pushed his fedora up and glanced in the rearview mirror, prompting Steven to look behind. A steady stream of squad cars and paddy wagons made their way down the street. "Okay, Brennan's boys are here, so let's move it. O'Connor, you think you can pick up a dame inside or do we need to break out the axe?"

Joe grunted with a roll of his eyes.

"Sure, Boss. Give me five minutes, and I'll flag you at the door."

"Make that two," Joe muttered with another grunt.

"Walsh, you and Donze flank the wall for O'Connor and make a beeline for those exits as soon as you get in. Savarino and Flannery's men will be waiting with Brennan's cops right behind." Raby handed sheets to Donze and Walsh. "Pass these out when you brief Rimmel and Flannery, and I'll take care of Brennan. O'Connor, once you flag, don't make a move till I give the signal, understood?" He hurled his door open and swung out while each of the men followed suit. "Okay, we've got plenty of paddies to fill up, so let's make Hackett proud."

Steven watched Joe, Donze, and Raby make their way to the other vehicles while he slid his suit jacket off. He slipped his badge and two sets of handcuffs into his trousers' pocket, then folded his coat and laid it on the backseat before rolling up the sleeves of his crisp white dress shirt. Closing his door, he removed his hat and made a quick pass through his hair to disrupt the groomed, slicked-back style before tapping it back on. He buttoned his suit vest to hide his firearm and straightened his tie, then buried his hands in his pockets and strolled the two blocks to Lorenzo's. A quarter block away, the front door wheeled open, and a group of five young women exited, their laughter mingling with the sound of a string quartet. Steven picked up pace, eyeing each of the girls, then zeroed in on the redhead who glanced up and held his gaze. He smiled and noted the pretty blush that crept into her cheeks when she smiled back.

Their chatter died when he approached, and he flashed some teeth, eyes scanning their faces before fixing on the redhead. "I hear this place is new, so tell me, ladies—how's the food?"

"Wonderful," they agreed in unison with a few nervous giggles and several bold stares.

Steven nudged his fedora up. "Dining upstairs, downstairs, both? What do you suggest?"

"I think there's only one level as far as I know," a petite blonde said.

The redhead nodded, gaze fused to Steven's. "But there's plenty of seating, so you should get a table." She paused, eyes twinkling. "Goodness, you're not eating alone, I hope?"

He smiled and reached into his vest pocket. "I'm not eating at all, but I am going in, and I'd rather not go in alone if I can help it." He flipped his badge open, and the redhead's eyes practically doubled in size. "I'm Agent O'Connor with the Prohibition Bureau and you ladies are . . ."

A lump bobbed in her throat as she peeked up. "I'm Josephine Moncado," she said with a shy smile, then nodded to the others. "And this is my sister, Carol, and our friends Emily Reilly, Kayla Hughes, and Eileen Jo Legat."

"Ladies," he said with a nod before refocusing on the redhead. His smile eased into a grin, deepening the blush on her cheeks. "Well, Miss Moncado, I was wondering if you would do me a favor that won't take much of your time. You see, I need a lady on my arm for about five minutes in Lorenzo's. Are you game?"

"Five minutes?" she said with a tilt of her head, her smile warming.

He raised his palm. "Scout's honor. And the federal government will be forever indebted."

"Well, I certainly don't mind assisting the government," she said. "When do we start?"

Glancing at his watch, he squinted over his shoulder where Raby's car was now parked one block down. He waved, and headlights blinked on and off while Joe and Donze got out of the vehicle and headed toward them. Steven turned back with a smile. "Right now, as a matter of fact. Ladies—Miss Moncado will rejoin you in a few moments, and I thank you for your patience."

Steven nodded to Joe and Donze before ushering Josephine

into the restaurant, hand pressed to the small of her back while his eyes adjusted to the dim lighting. He bent close to her ear as he steered her toward the back of the room and down a dark hall to a rear door. "Josephine, we're going downstairs to a speakeasy, and I'm going to put my arm around you and pretend to be real cozy until they open the door." He hesitated. "Will that be all right?"

Her smile was shy. "You don't have to pretend, Agent O'Connor," she said with a blush.

He grinned. "Appreciate that, Miss Moncado." He shot a quick glance over his shoulder to make sure Joe and Donze were following at a safe distance as inconspicuously as possible, one at a time. He hooked an arm to her waist and led her down the stairs, lips to her ear. "As soon as they open the door, I want you to hightail it out of here, understood?"

With a nervous nod, she glanced back when Joe and then Donze eased down the steps and stood to the sides of the door, backs pressed to the wall.

"You get all the fun, O'Connor," Joe whispered, giving Josephine a wink.

Steven draped a loose arm over her shoulder and knocked on the door, tugging her close to nuzzle while music thundered on the other side of the wall.

The window slid open. "Password?" The word was a low growl.

Taking his sweet time, Steven pulled away from Josephine with a lazy grin. "Al Jolson," he said, promptly returning to whisper in Josephine's ear. "A fine job, Miss Moncado. Thank you."

Beady eyes narrowed on the other side of the door. "I.D.?"

"Sure thing." Steven smiled, producing his driver's license. He passed it through the window, then gave Josephine a casual kiss before he heard the grind of a lock. The door swung open, revealing a scowling giant at least a head taller than Steven with a coal-black mustache and a jagged scar. In the catch of Josephine's breath, Steven nudged her toward the steps and strode in, flashing his badge. "Federal agents," he said quietly, "this is a raid."

Joe and Donze pushed past, racing to the two exits at the back of the room.

"*Raid!*" the bouncer yelled, scrambling to hurl the door closed and trip the alarm.

Steven lunged, adrenaline pumping as he slammed him to the wall. "I wouldn't if I were you," he hissed, the bouncer's hand mere inches from a buzzer mounted behind the door.

Shoving back, the man took a swing, and Steven deflected with a straight right that thudded the goon against the door. Jerking him around, he cuffed him just as Brennan's cops clattered down the stairs, ready to swarm the room like an army of ants after a weeklong picnic.

Music blared and Steven knew crucial seconds ticked by as he pushed his way through the crowd to the bar. Several bartenders looked up, squinting at the exits. A silent curse wedged in Steven's throat when bells clanged and buzzers groaned, replacing the jazz of musicians who now frantically packed up to go. The grind of gears could be heard as rows of bottles disappeared from shelves that flipped upside down. *Blast! There goes our evidence . . .* The sound of breaking glass added to frantic shouts and female shrieks while bottles crashed into chutes leading to the sewer. Adrenaline surged when Steven spotted a lone bottle of bourbon that had obviously tipped off the shelf onto the counter. Vaulting over the bar, he lunged for it at the same time as one of the bartenders. The strong stench of alcohol filled the room as Steven rammed him against the back counter so hard, an empty shelf splintered and dropped.

"You don't have anything on us," the bartender said with a sneer, and Steven cuffed him.

"Sure I do, wise guy." He thrust him at a cop, then wielded the bottle of booze. "This is all the proof I need."

"Steven!" Joe huffed up, face flushed and sweat on his brow. "We got trouble."

"What kind of trouble?" Bottle in hand, Steven hurdled the bar with little or no effort. He wiped his forehead with his sleeve while his gaze swept the room, spotting Raby and Brennan spilling out orders as furiously as cops spilling out glasses of booze. Disgruntled patrons were pushed to the wall, some griping and some too glazed to even utter a word.

"Girl trouble," Joe muttered, eyes flitting to the far side of the room. "Joanie, Erica, Ashley, and Peggy—down there, against the wall."

Steven cursed under his breath, a rarity that was quickly becoming habit. "What the devil are they doing here?" he said, his gaze following Joe's.

"A birthday party for somebody you don't even want to know."

The minute the words were out of Joe's mouth, every muscle in Steven's body tensed at the sight of a girl next to Erica, sobbing in some guy's arms. Fury pulsed in his veins when the pretty boy kneaded the girl's back, stroking strawberry-blonde curls Steven would know anywhere. Her small frame shuddered as he comforted her, and Steven's jaw calcified to stone.

"What do you want to do?" Joe asked, his voice low. "We can't let 'em go to jail."

"Why not?" Steven's tone was as hard as the bottle in his hand. "Serves 'em right."

"Because they're our *friends*," Joe said with emphasis. "Friends don't arrest friends."

"They do when they break the law," Steven shot back.

"Even an agent as stiff-necked as you, O'Connor, would never do that to his friends."

"I didn't," he said through clenched teeth, "they did it to themselves."

Cuffing his shoulder, Joe shot another glance at the girls, who watched them with pleas in their eyes. "Come on, Steven, Prohibition is as good as dead after the election anyway, and we both know we're not going to let our friends go to jail."

Steven's jaw felt like rock. "So help me, Walsh, if Raby catches us, your butt is on the line, you got that?"

"Yeah, I got it, you hardnose," Joe said with a chuckle. "I'll handle Joanie, Peggy, and the kid, and you can take care of Erica and Ashley."

"No," Steven bit out. "The kid's mine. I've got a few choice words for her."

"Yeah, well, you're not gonna have time for a chat, Steven, if we hope to get 'em out without Raby the wiser."

"Wanna bet?" Steven pushed the bottle at Joe. "You play decoy and I'll get 'em through the side alley to the front. We're off duty after this bust anyway, so tell Raby something came up and I left, okay?" Not waiting for Joe's answer, he strode to the other side of the room where police were moving everyone out. With a curt nod at the officer guarding the back door, Steven burned Erica and Ashley with a glare before yanking Annie from the pretty boy's arms.

She cried out and stumbled against his chest, dropping her purse. He steadied her with a rough hold, and her red-rimmed eyes spanned wide. "S-steven?" she said, swaying on her feet.

Plucking the purse from the ground, he pulled Erica from the line and then Ashley, pushing them forward. "Come on, ladies, I'll see to it that you get a prime seat in the wagon."

"Hey, wait a minute," the bozo with Annie said, grabbing her arm. "She's with me."

"Not anymore, you lowlife." Steven prodded Erica and Ashley toward the door, tightening his hold on Annie as he glared at the man. "One more word and I'll throw you in the brig for resisting arrest, public drunkenness, and anything else I can make stick, ya got that?"

Eyes hard, the creep eased back against the wall. "I'll see you at the station, Annie."

Steven dragged her out, shoving all three girls to the side while several officers filled a paddy wagon in the back alley. He thrust Annie's purse at her and scowled, hands loose on his hips. "You ladies are in a lot of trouble," he said, his loud rebuke meant to imply a verbal thrashing. Joanie and Peggy faltered through the door with Joe behind, and Steven nodded, sending Joe toward the officers by the wagon to make a ruckus about somebody in the van.

In a split second, Steven had all five girls scurrying through the alley between the restaurant and hat shop, arm hooked to Annie's waist to hurry her along.

"Steven, thank you for this," Erica said over her shoulder, words thick with remorse.

"Yeah, well, this is your last 'get out of jail free' card. After this, you're on your own."

"W-we're so s-sorry, Steven," Peggy said, voice wavering. "All we w-wanted was to celebrate Annie's eighteenth birthday with a b-bang."

"Well, you certainly accomplished that."

Annie tripped, and Steven caught her, halting when he noticed the glazed look in her eyes. His stomach dropped along with his jaw. "Are you drunk?" he demanded, shock raising his tone several octaves. He gripped her hard, giving her a shake that bobbled her head.

Tears welled. "No, I p-promise, Steven, I dinn't drink," she said with a distinct slur.

Another colorful word parted from his lips, and the sound of it ricocheted in the alley, confirming that after tonight, he'd need to wash his mouth out with soap.

Erica peeked up, gaze hesitant. "I think that guy she was dancing with must have bought her some drinks, Steven. That's the only thing I can figure, right, Ashley?"

Ashley traded looks with Joanie and Erica before she nodded. "I think so."

Annie started to cry as Steven propped her to the wall. "Cut the act, kid, I'm not buying it." He gave her shoulders a firm shake, then angled her chin. "Stay here, is that clear?"

She continued to weep with no response to his question, and his temper flared, furious at what could have happened to her if he hadn't been there. *Brainless kid!* He tightened his hold. "I said, *is that clear?*" His voice was a hiss, jolting her sobs into a whimper as she gave him a shaky nod. Releasing her, he pushed past the others and paused at the alley entrance with a final glare over his shoulder. "Erica!" His whisper was harsh. "When you see me talking to the officers, I want you to lead everyone but the kid out of the alley—*calmly, understand?*—then down the street in the opposite direction. And if anybody calls or comes after you, run like the devil—you got it?"

They nodded and Steven strolled into view, badge flipped as he approached a group of officers herding people into the wagons. "Any of you men seen a tall ugly mug with a black mustache and a scar? He took a swing at me, and I think he's on one of these two wagons."

"I remember him," a young officer said, glancing back at the two vehicles parked several feet down the curb. "But I'm not sure which wagon he's in."

"Mind checking the second while I check this one?" Steven asked, moving forward.

"No problem, Agent O'Connor," the officer said while the other two followed to prod the last of the speakeasy patrons into the van.

Glancing over his shoulder, Steven watched the girls slink from the alley before he peered in the van, spotting the bouncer with a surly look on his face. "That's the one," Steven said. "Can you see to it he's charged with both assault of a federal agent and liquor violation?"

"Sure thing." The officer nudged the last two into the van and slammed the door.

"Thanks." Steven ambled back to the alley where Annie was still crying, slumped on the ground with her back to the wall. Head bowed and knees tented to her chest, her fragile silhouette shuddered with heaves that wracked his heart as well as her body. Some of his anger softened and he squatted in front of her, picking her purse up from the ground.

"Annie," he whispered, "come on—I'm taking you home."

Tugging her to her feet, he handed her the purse and braced her waist, a faint smile tipping his lips when she swiped her face with her bare arm.

"Here," he said, handing her a clean handkerchief. He waited while she blew her nose.

She slipped the handkerchief in her purse. "Thank you. I'll wash it and give it back."

It was barely a whisper, ragged and nasal and so much like a little girl, he found his anger flagging, replaced by the desire to hold her, comfort her. Resisting the urge, he hooked her close and walked to the entrance of the alley, making sure the officers were occupied before he ushered her to the sidewalk and down the street. Two blocks away, a neon sign caught his eye, and he steered her forward, lured by the smell of fried food. Glancing through a window crowded with grease-pencil menus, he opened the glass door to a noisy clash of bells and the growl of his stomach. The diner was empty except for a booth of teenagers at the far end, horsing around and a couple with eyes only for each other. Bing Crosby's velvet voice crooned from a jukebox in the corner, lending a cozy intimacy to a place that smelled of burgers and chicken fried steak.

"What are we doing?" she asked, voice hoarse and husky as if she were a chain-smoker.

"Getting some coffee into you before I take you home. Trust me, you're in no condition to face Aunt Eleanor right now." He steered her into a brown padded booth before taking a seat on the other side, its polished maple table scarred and etched with initials and hearts.

"Thank you," she whispered again, hands and eyes fused to the purse in her lap.

He leaned in with elbows flat, his voice softer than before. "Annie . . . look at me."

She shook her head, a shimmering curtain of silky blonde hair falling over one eye, making her appear both innocent and sexy all at the same time.

Puffing out a sigh, he reached to lift her chin. "I need you to look at me, Annie, please?"

A frail heave quivered through her and she slowly looked up, eyes spidered with red.

"Why did you go there tonight?" he said quietly.

Her throat shifted before she answered. "P-peggy said J-joanie and the others wanted to take me out for my b-birthday, but I thought they just meant d-dinner . . . at a nice restaurant." Tears flooded her eyes. "I . . . didn't know . . . it would be a speakeasy, Steven, I s-swear."

"I believe you," he said, relief seeping out on a quiet sigh. He sat back and folded his arms, head cocked as he studied her through slatted eyes. "But why did you drink the booze?"

"Hi, folks, what'll it be tonight?" A waitress too perky for the way Steven felt pulled a pencil from behind her ear and a pad from her apron pocket, brows arched in question.

"Two cups of coffee, please, as hot and strong as it comes." He squinted at the menu, encased in a plastic holder on the wall of the booth, then glanced at Annie. "You hungry?"

She shook her head and he ignored her response, ordering two hamburgers, two orders of French fried potatoes, a piece of peach pie, and a glass of milk. "Cream in your coffee?"

"Please," she said quietly, fingers fiddling with the leather fringe on the flap of her purse.

He smiled at the waitress. "One black, one cream."

"Coming right up." Miss Perky tucked the pencil back behind her ear and disappeared.

"So . . . ," he said, a bit more bite in his tone, "I'm going to ask you again—why did you drink tonight? Was that whole spiel about you turning back to God just a put-on?"

Her head shot up in a flash of green eyes. "No, of course not! I meant every word."

He planted arms on the table, hands loosely clasped and eyes pensive. "Then why?"

Color burnished her cheeks and she shifted, clearly ill at ease as her hands shrank to her lap. "You won't believe me."

"Try me," he said, lips flat.

She drew in a deep breath and peeked up, the color heightening in her face. "I think Erica may have spiked my drink, only I didn't know it."

"You didn't know it," he repeated dully, his suspicion on the rise once again. His voice edged toward curt. "You didn't taste it? Smell it? Feel woozy when the booze took effect?"

"See? I knew you wouldn't believe me," she said with a jut of her chin, temper obviously prickled. "And no, I didn't smell or taste it, and by the time I suspected anything, it was too late."

"What kind of drink was it?" He waited while she paused, his eyes narrowing a tad.

She swallowed hard. "Dr Pepper."

"Did you see Erica or anyone pour anything in?"

"No, of course not," she said in a huff. "Do you really think I would drink it if I did?"

"I don't know, Annie," he said, leaning back against the booth with a fold of his arms. "You're not exactly the most honest girl I know."

The green eyes blinked wide. "And what's that supposed to mean?"

His smile went stiff as his anger resurged, every syllable as pointed as the look in his eyes. "I don't know, you tell me . . . Susannah-Grace-Kennedy." A muscle twitched in his jaw. "And while you're at it, why don't you give me an update on how my old girlfriend's doing?"

"Here you go, two coffees—one cream, one black, both piping hot. The burgers are about up, so I'll be back in a jiff." The waitress set the coffees and utensils down before flitting away.

Annie didn't move or blink while she stared in her cup, crimson bleeding into her cheeks.

His coffee spilled when he jerked up his mug, the liquid scalding his fingers like her deception scalded his temper. "You have nothing to say?"

A knot jerked in her throat and she looked up, almost a square to her shoulders as she steeled her jaw. "I was wrong, Steven, I should have told you. But I never expected—" She lowered her gaze to blow on her coffee, obviously in an effort to stall.

"Never expected what?" he asked sharply, glaring over the rim of his cup. She took a timid sip while a full range of emotions flickered across her beautiful face, from hesitation and worry, to vulnerability and shame. And something deeper that raced his pulse and tightened his gut all at the same time.

She drew in a deep breath before forging on, her gaze finally rising to meet his. "I never expected to . . ." Her voice trailed off until it was barely audible. "Fall in love with you," she said quietly, the truth hovering in the air like the steam from the coffee.

She may as well have tossed it in his face—it burned all the same. His jaw went as firm as his will. "You're not in love with me, Annie."

A frail sigh withered from her lips while a sheen of sadness welled in her eyes. "I wasn't sure either," she whispered, "until you kissed me that night when you took Glory and me home."

He bent forward, palms clutching the table and his tone so harsh and cutting, he saw her flinch. "That was a mistake."

"Yes," she whispered, tears giving way to glints of anger, "it was, Steven, because that night you planted the seed of hope that someday you might feel for me what I feel for you."

He slammed his fist on the table, spilling his coffee. "Blast it, Annie, you're too young."

"That's just an excuse, and we both know it."

His mouth went slack. "For the love of all that's decent— you're Maggie's kid sister! Do you really think I can do this with you?"

She hoisted her chin, blinking back her tears. "I not only think you can, I think you do, but you're too stubborn to admit it."

He gaped, shaking his head as he dropped back in the seat,

arm draped over the top. His lips parted in a hard smile meant to convey his disbelief. "You're out of your mind, kid, you know that? Drink your coffee," he ordered, "the alcohol's still muddling your brain."

She did what he said, eyes averted and manner calming as if every drink she took braced her for battle. When she finished, she carefully laid the mug down and folded her hands neatly on the table, looking for all her eighteen years and tear-splotched face as if she were the adult and he was the pie-eyed kid on a bender. "What are you afraid of, Steven?" she whispered.

That did it. "You want to know what I'm afraid of?" he demanded. "I'm afraid of this—some kid still wet behind the ears thinking it's smart to fool around with a guy like me."

"I have no intention of 'fooling around' with you," she said quietly, the strength of her words belying the softness of her tone. "No matter how I feel about you."

He stared openmouthed, heat scalding his neck at the audacity of her statement. His pride prickled. Who did she think she was? Women threw themselves at him all the time. For pity's sake, her own *sister* threw herself at him! And she thought she'd be different? He folded his arms on the table and leaned in. "Don't be so sure, little sister," he said, a trace of anger in a voice that was husky and low. "You Kennedys don't have the best track record, you know."

He heard the sharp catch of her breath and took satisfaction in the blush that broiled her cheeks. And then she opened fire like one of Capone's thugs, gunning him down with a flash of her eyes. "Well, this is a different Kennedy, Agent O'Connor, *and* a different sister, and you know what? I think you're running scared. You can deny your feelings all you want, but the truth is, you kissed me—not once, but twice, not to mention interfering in my life at every turn—"

"*Interfering* in your life?" His voice rose along with his blood pressure.

She defied him with a hard thrust of her chin, eyes glittering. "Yes, first with Billy Brubaker, then Joe and Dale Brannock, and now Eddie tonight when you dragged me away."

"*Dragged-you-away?*" He blinked, barely able to believe he was wasting good breath arguing with a kid who was obviously as thick as she was tipsy. "I should have let them throw your carcass in jail, you brainless brat, and then you'd be Aunt Eleanor's problem, not mine."

"Exactly," she snapped, as if he'd just proven her point. "But you didn't. You risked your job and your reputation to haul me out of there tonight, so if we're going to talk 'brainless,' Agent O'Connor, then I suggest you look in the mirror, because unless I miss my guess, you are one dim-witted man with his head in the sand."

Miss Perky chose that moment to light on the booth, as welcome as a plague of locusts. "Here you go—two burgers, two orders of French fried potatoes, a slab of peach pie, and a glass of milk." She dazzled them with a grin. "Anything else?"

Steven forced a smile, jaw clenched so tight his teeth ached. "Just the check."

"Sure thing." She placed the bill on the table and patted it for good measure. "Enjoy!"

Grinding his jaw, he grabbed his burger and bit in hard, singeing Annie with a glare.

She didn't seem to notice, annoying him to no end. Lips pursed, she carefully cut her burger in half and took a dainty bite while perusing the menu with apparent fascination.

Halfway through his sandwich, he expelled a noisy breath. "Why are we arguing?"

She turned, chin elevated and brows raised. "Because you're dim-witted and scared?"

He hurled his half-eaten burger on the plate. "Don't start with me, Annie."

"All right, Steven, how 'bout I finish with you instead? Just because I'm in love with you doesn't mean you can bully me around like some . . . some snot-nosed kid fresh off the farm."

"You *are* some snot-nosed kid fresh off the farm," he hissed.

"Fine. Have it your way. There are plenty of guys who see me otherwise."

A harsh laugh erupted from his throat. "Oh yeah, I've seen the kind of jokers you attract. Like that clown tonight with his hands all over you."

She pushed her burger away, the anger in her tone matching her eyes. "He-was-consoling-me, you dimwit, and at least he's man enough to take a chance on a girl that he likes."

Her statement barbed, discharging his temper with another stony smile. "Sure, why not when he knows he can get what he wants?"

Her breath hitched, and he regretted the words the moment they left his mouth, but it was too late. Her face sagged from anger into hurt. Chin trembling, she silently rose, hands shaking while she groped for her purse.

"Annie, look, I'm sorry—"

Taking a step forward, she hauled off and slapped him so fast he never saw it coming, bells clanging in his skull as loudly as those from the door when it slammed hard behind her.

Muttering under his breath, he hurled payment and tip down before striding outside, finally spotting her running a half block away. "Blast it, Annie . . ." He took after her in a sprint, ignoring the stares of the few people who passed him on the way. He was heaving when he finally caught up with her, her heels clicking just a few feet ahead. "Annie—stop! I'm sorry . . ."

"Leave me alone!" she screamed over her shoulder, almost tripping in her effort to flee.

"I can't do that," he said. Breathing hard, he grabbed her from behind, and his gut cramped when a cry wrenched from her throat. She twisted and kicked like a wildcat and he pinned her close, restraining her until she finally went limp in his arms. Crickets crooned and cars whooshed by while couples laughed and music drifted, filling the steamy night with the rhythm of the city. But all he could hear was the sound of her weeping as her body shuddered against his, and he closed his eyes, heartsick at hurting her like he had.

Head tucked to hers, he gently stroked her hair, breathing in the clean scent of her shampoo and the pull of perfume that triggered his pulse. "Annie, I'm sorry," he whispered. "I'm an idiot, and that was a rotten thing to say. Please forgive me."

Her weeping slowed, and he kneaded her back, jaw clenching at the thought of Eddie doing the same. Shaking the thought off, he pressed a kiss to her hair and pulled back, hands grazing down her arms to hold her at bay. "Can't we put this behind us and still be friends?"

Friends? Annie's gaze slowly rose to meet his, her eyes raw, but nothing compared to her heart. She stared, bleeding at the concern etched into every muscle of his chiseled face, the intensity in blue eyes that told her he was a man of integrity and passion. Her gaze followed the line of a hard-sculpted jaw that conveyed a quiet strength and iron will, full lips that made her ache for the want of them, and she knew "friends" would never be an option again. She stroked a hand to his face and felt the bristle of beard that now shadowed his skin, and her heart ached at the only choice she had. Shoring up with a deep breath, she released it again in one long, quivering sigh. "I forgive you, Steven, and yes, we can put this behind us . . ." She shook her head and stepped out of his hold. "But if it's all the same to you, I don't think I can be your friend right now. My feelings for you are—" her throat shifted—"deep, and I need some time and distance."

Swallowing hard, he buried his hands in his pockets and she suddenly saw the shy, introspective boy he must have been so long ago. "I understand, Annie, but can I at least walk you home?"

She nodded and he slipped a gentle arm to her shoulders, drawing her close on the few blocks to Aunt Eleanor's house. Neither spoke, and she was glad. She was tired of crying and there was really nothing more to say. Hand to the small of her back, he guided her through the iron gate to the half-moon brick portico where lush impatiens and ivy spilled from graceful stone urns. A brass sconce overhead cast a pale glow softer than moonlight while the music of tree frogs and crickets welcomed her home.

Fitting the key into the lock, she opened the door, leaving it ajar as she lifted her gaze. "Thank you for rescuing me tonight, Steven—*again*." A pitiful smile trembled on her lips. She pulled the handkerchief from her purse and dabbed at her nose, her smile giving way to a weepy grin. "I suppose you're right—I *am* a snot-nosed kid fresh off the farm. I'll get this back to you, I promise."

"No hurry," he whispered, grazing her cheek with his thumb. "Good night, Annie."

"Good night, Steven." Turning away, she pulled her key from the lock and quietly stepped inside, desperate to shut the door before more tears could slip from her eyes.

"Wait." It was a whisper, urgent and husky.

Her heart stopped, afraid she'd only imagined it. But when he blocked the door with his hand, her breath heaved still in her throat. "W-what are you d-doing?" she stuttered.

With a heavy exhale of air, he pulled her back through and prodded her to the brick wall, looming so close she almost felt the nerve that pulsed in his jaw. His voice was strained. "The last thing I want to do is get mixed up with a sweet kid like you. I'm no good for you, don't you get that?" He backed away, stabbing at his hair while he paced and mumbled under his breath, a stream of garbled words she couldn't decipher. Turning to face her again, he gripped her arms and gave her a shake. "I don't want this," he rasped, "don't you understand that?"

She shrank back with a shaky nod, not really sure what else to do.

"Blast it, Annie, you've got me so crazy, I'm about to lose my mind." He stared at her hard, almost wild-eyed, and then with a mutter, he wrenched her close and kissed her so thoroughly, her knees went to jelly. Breaking away with a groan, he butted her shoulders to the wall with a pained look in his eyes. "See? This is exactly what I mean. You're this naïve and innocent kid, and I'm so crazy for you that if we ever got together, I wouldn't be good for you, I swear. I know what I'm like. I'd push and push—"

"Crazy for me?" she whispered, heart thudding while a smile trembled.

He huffed out a loud blast of air, eyes fixed on her lips before rising to capture her gaze, lids heavy with a look that heated both her skin and the goose bumps on it. "Yeah," he whispered, "and I have no earthly idea what I'm going to do about it."

She didn't dare breathe while he studied her intently for several moments, a muscle twittering in his cheek as if a battle waged in his mind.

His chest expanded and released with a slow, weary breath before he cupped her face in his hands. "But, God help me, kid, I think I'm about to find out."

As soft as the summer breeze feathering her skin, he bent to nuzzle her lips, his touch so tender that it stole the breath in her lungs. "I want to start seeing you, Annie," he whispered, his mouth warm against her ear, "but you have to promise me something." Her breathing shallowed when he fondled her mouth with his own, so slow and deliberate that she had to stifle a moan. "Promise you'll be strong, that you'll stay innocent no matter what I say or do."

Heart thundering, she tore herself away to lay her head on his chest. She could hear the wild beat of his heart, smell his familiar scent that never failed to trip her pulse, and joy pumped inside at the prospect he might someday belong to her. "I promise," she said in a quiet tone that belied the frantic clip of her heart. "And not just you, Steven, but God too."

His heavy sigh tickled her ear, and for the first time all evening, she sensed a peace had settled on his soul. "Good girl." Pressing a kiss to her head, he reached behind and opened the door, nudging her through with a smile that fluttered her stomach. "Then I guess we're officially dating now," he said with an off-center grin, cuffing the back of his neck. He released a quiet breath. "G'night, Annie—I'll give you a call tomorrow." Shoving his hands in his pockets, he turned to go, wheeling halfway on the top step to shoot her a narrow gaze. He slipped a hand from his pocket to level a finger, his tone a playful threat. "Don't make me regret it."

She couldn't help it—she slid him a sassy grin. "The only thing you're going to regret, Steven O'Connor," she said, brow arched while she eased the door closed in his face, "is that it took you so long to wise up."

Okay, it was official—he was an idiot. Luke stripped his T-shirt off and tossed it on top of the hamper, ignoring it when it slid to the floor. He stepped out of his boxers and into the shower, turning the faucet all the way to the right till the water pelted, as hard and cold as he could get—he deserved it. Feeling dirty, he picked up the soap and scrubbed his hands with a vengeance, wishing he could do the same with this guilt that sullied his conscience.

Katie had been right. He should have been working alone, not with some starry-eyed coed who had the skill of flirting down to a fine art. He closed his eyes, letting the icy water freeze his body while her memory frosted his mind.

"Luke, I need your help," she had said, smiling over her shoulder, tiptoe on a chair. In natural reflex, he'd scanned up mile-long legs, past the curve of her hips to the stretch of her torso as she tugged a heavy box of files off a top shelf.

"Lauren, what are you doing?" he had yelled, dashing to her rescue. But he'd known *exactly* what she was doing the moment he'd taken the box and helped her down. Fingers trailing from his neck to his arms, she'd slipped them to his waist while her body slid against his.

"Goodness, your body is like rock," she'd whispered, a sense of awe in her tone, and not even the sleet raining down on him now could chill the warmth of his blood at how that had made him feel. Like a lightning bolt out of nowhere, temptation struck hard, reminding him how long it'd been since he'd made love to his wife, and how long he and Katie had been warring. No, she hadn't turned him out of her bed for the last several weeks, but she may as well have. Barely talking, cool smiles for Kit's sake, and then studying late till he was asleep before she'd slip into their bed. And even then, her body was as cold and unwilling as if she hadn't been there at all. Making it easy—*so easy*—to feel the heat of Lauren's hands at his waist, to hear the shallow breathing from parted lips, to see the hope in eyes so blatant with desire.

I am SUCH an idiot . . .

He'd always known women were attracted to him, but he'd prided himself on self-control and a level head. Hadn't he proven that with Katie before they got married? And, yes, he supposed he'd noticed Lauren's occasional stares or the playful banter that broke the grueling monotony of long days and nights, but he had almost the same thing with Bobbie Sue and Gladys, so why was this different? He closed his eyes with a silent groan, welcoming the punishment of the icy cold. Because deep down inside he'd had his suspicions, but he'd been too preoccupied with work, too grateful for the help, and too blasted cocky to think anything could trip up the invincible Luke McGee. But this, he was reluctant to admit, *this* had caught him off guard. Something evil and sinister he'd never seen coming—an invitation in a smile, drawing his lips to hers like a lamb to the slaughter. A blood sacrifice of his marriage vow on the altar of lust.

He swallowed hard, eyelids weighting closed from the burden of guilt. Not guilt over giving in, because he hadn't. No, his anger had risen up inside so fierce, he'd literally pushed the woman away, toppling both her and a vase of flowers when she bumped into her desk. Carmichael's friend or no, he fired her on the spot, sending her packing with her baggage and all.

And now he had baggage of his own.

He'd been so convinced Katie was wrong and he was right, seeing Jack as the proverbial speck in her eye while he completely missed the plank in his own. A man so proud, he'd trusted himself more than he trusted his wife, dead sure he was beyond temptation.

Yeah, right . . .

Yes, he'd turned Lauren away, but reality slapped him hard in the face when the "impossible" happened. Moral, upstanding Luke McGee, the man who loved God and adored his wife and family, came face-to-face with the ugliness of lust. And deep in his soul he had to live with the fact that in the single space of a heartbeat, he'd been attracted to a woman who wasn't his wife. "Your body is like rock," said the spider to the fly. His mouth went flat. *No, that would be my skull.* The cold water continued to badger and he washed his hands again, almost feeling the residue of temptation sticky on his palms as needles of ice prickled his skin.

Katie, forgive me . . .

Lauren had fled with the slam of a door, and he'd wandered into his office like a zombie, slumped in his chair with his head in his hands while his pride lay as shattered as the vase on the floor. And then in the innocent jangle of the phone, what was left of his pride had been neatly ground in by a call from his wife.

"I have my orals tonight and Lizzie can't watch Kit. Can you be home by six?"

Not *hello . . . how was your day? . . .* or even *Luke, I need a favor.* And yet, somehow it didn't matter, because it was the most important call he'd ever had, reminding him just how much he loved his wife. *And* how much she had a right to be angry. Because at the end of the day, when all the slivers and pieces of his pride were picked up and swept away, the truth was that she was married to an idiot . . . and a pompous one at that.

Turning the water off, he reached for his towel and stepped

out of the tub, chilled by both the frigid shower and the prospect of a frigid night when he told his wife the truth. "Correction," he said, lathering his jaw with Barbasol. "*If I tell my wife the truth.*" All Katie really needed to know was he was wrong and he was sorry, and not anything more. In his mind he'd already committed an unpardonable sin—a moment of lust—and the last thing he wanted was to hurt the woman he loved. Razor to skin, the blade nicked and he winced, staring at the blood on his cheek. He sighed and hung his head. *Because heaven knows I'm bleeding enough for us both.*

The clock in the parlor chimed nine as he slipped into his pajama bottoms and spiked fingers through his hair. Wiping down the sink, he tossed his towel over the rack and his clothes in the hamper, peeking in on Kit on his way to the kitchen. Chugging a glass of milk, he heard the front door open and close, and instantly it pooled in his mouth. He set the empty glass in the sink and sucked in a swallow of air, ambling down the hall as if it were a walk in the park.

She was bent over the coffee table with a stack of books in her hands, and his eyes automatically roved from shapely legs to the gentle curve of her hips, imparting a heated awareness of just how much he'd missed his wife. Gulping back the knot of pride in his throat, he folded his arms and slacked a hip to the wall. "You hungry? 'Cause I can fix you a sandwich."

Emitting a tiny squeak, she whirled around so fast, half the books spilled on the floor. She slapped a hand to her chest, voice hoarse. "Good night, McGee, why don't you just hide behind the door and jump out—you scared the living daylights out of me!"

Tamping down a smile, he strolled in and retrieved her books. "Sorry, Sass, but I do live here you know, as unappealing as that may be at the moment."

He leaned over to kiss her, but she quickly turned away. "How's Kit?" she asked over her shoulder on the way to their room. "Did she go to bed without a fuss?"

"Yeah, if you don't count three glasses of water and six stories a 'fuss.'" He followed her down the hall, eyeing her from the door as she unbuttoned her blouse. "How'd your orals go?"

"Fine." She glanced up, color staining her cheeks as he watched her take off her blouse. Shifting her hip, she clasped the blouse closed with a tight purse of her lips. "Do you mind?"

No way could he stop the lazy grin that slid over his face. "Not at all, Sass, you go right ahead."

Blouse bunched, she angled a brow. "Well then, do you mind turning around?"

He crossed his arms and leaned against the door, the slightest bit of edge to his tone. "Actually I do. You're my wife, Katie Rose, and I can look all I want."

Emitting a noisy breath, she snatched her nightgown and started for the bathroom.

He blocked her way with palms flat to the door, softening his tone. "Come on, Sass, can't we talk this out, please? I have something I need to say."

She parked her hands on her hips, blouse dangling at her side. "Well, unless it's an apology, McGee, you'll be talking to yourself." She paused, tilting her head to the right. "Or as your wife, is listening something *else* I'm expected to do?"

He exhaled, feeling the heat of his pride creeping up the back of his neck. "It is," he said quietly, "an apology, that is. Not something you're expected to do." His smile was contrite.

That seemed to take the wind out of her sails—her chest expanded and contracted in a slow release of air before her chin inched up. "All right . . . I'm listening."

He pried a hand from her hip and led her to the sofa, easing her down before sitting beside her. Replenishing his air, he took both of her hands in his. "Katie," he whispered, forcing the words from his throat, "I . . ." He swallowed hard, cleared his throat, and tried again. "Katie, I . . . well, I owe you an apology," he said in a rush. There. It was out, and he wasn't even annoyed by the drop of her chin. Thumbs grazing her palms, he forged on. "I was wrong to yell at you in the office, and I apologize." He released a reedy breath. *Okay, that wasn't so bad.*

She arched a brow. "And?"

Without realizing it, he began to grind his jaw. *"Aaannd . . . ,"* he said, dragging the word out as long as he could, "I want you to know I respect your opinion regarding the situation with Lauren, and I won't be working with her again."

"Why?"

He blinked, a muscle spasm adding to the grind of his jaw. "Because . . . she's gone, so you have nothing to worry about."

"Gone?" she said, the question as flat as the press of her lips.

"Yes, gone."

"Why?"

"Because she just is."

She leaned forward, eyes laying him bare. "Gone to lunch, gone across town, gone on vacation? I want facts, McGee, not single syllables."

He blasted out a sigh. "For pity's sake, Katie, I fired her, okay?"

She nodded her head. "I see. And why exactly would you do that?"

He gulped, nearly choking on the words caught in his throat. "Because . . . you were right . . ." His eyelids flickered briefly as he pushed the rest of the sentence off the tip of his tongue. "And . . . I was . . . wrong."

Her smile could have blinded him, which given the superior gloat in her eyes, might be a good thing. "Ahhhhh . . . words I never thought I'd hear from the sanctified lips of Luke McGee." She sat back with a fold of her arms, the smile suddenly nowhere in sight. Her voice was clipped. "And when exactly did this revelation occur?"

It felt like fire ants were swarming his neck, which, based on the dangerous look on Katie's face, would have been his first option. His voice was a croak. "Uh . . . recently."

She cocked her head, brows lifting to new heights. "Really. How recently, would you say? Last week, this week, yesterday, today?"

His voice cracked. "Today."

She leaned forward, and he was pretty sure her eyes burned more than the ants. "Why?" she whispered, her voice akin to the calm before the storm.

Avoiding her gaze, he opened his mouth, but nothing came out. He swallowed hard, tried again. Still nothing.

Lunging forward with wildfire in her eyes, she jerked his chin up, index finger and thumb pinching his skin. "So help me, Luke McGee, you better spit it out right now, what you or that woman did to get her fired, or I will launch on you like a bad case of measles scratched raw."

Teeth clenched, muscle spasms in his face had a field day as he slowly removed her hand from his jaw, biting the words out. "She-made-a-pass-at-me, okay? Are you satisfied?"

"Deliriously. What happened?" she snapped.

He shot to his feet and started to pace, practically gouging his hair by the roots. "Nothing, I swear. She was on a stool, pulling a box from a shelf, and needed help." He reinforced his lungs with more air, then dove right back in as he mauled the back of his neck. "The next thing I know, I'm helping her down and she . . . she . . ."

Katie's eyes narrowed, stretching two syllables into four. "She-e wha-t?"

He stopped, suddenly too exhausted to worry anymore. Venting with a sigh, he plopped on the couch and put his head in his hands. "She slid down the front of me and put her hands to my waist. Said my body was like a rock."

Nothing. He waited, not sure he wanted to see her expression. A giggle floated in the air, and he glanced up, a pinch of hurt between his brows. "You think this is funny?"

Lips pursed to ward off a smile, she shook her head in a series of tiny little shakes before her eyes widened with a grate of her lip. "Are you sure she wasn't talking about your head?"

His eyes narrowed into a squint. "This isn't funny, Katie Rose, and I think you're being awfully cavalier about another woman flirting with your husband."

She sobered quickly, a tender slant to her brows. "No, darling, I don't think this is funny. I'm just venting with humor so I don't scratch your eyes out."

"Oh," he said, discreetly scooting a few inches away.

"Did you kiss her?"

He jerked up as if he'd been shot. "Kiss her?!" he rasped, nearly dislocating his jaw. "For the love of all that's decent, Katie, are you crazy? No, I didn't kiss her—I pushed her away!"

Her lips twitched. "And she didn't kiss you?"

He shook his head hard. "Of course not! I wasn't about to let it get that far."

"And you fired her?"

"Absolutely—right on the spot."

She took his hand in hers, ducking to peek up at him. "Then what's the problem, Luke? You admitted I was right and you were wrong, you apologized, you resisted temptation, and you sent the hussy packing. All in all, I'd say that's a pretty good day."

He shot her a sideways glance, mouth sagging that she was taking it so well. His lips clamped as a sliver of hurt prickled. *Too* well. "Aren't you even a little jealous?"

She shimmied close to tuck an arm to his waist. "Not really, because unlike *someone* I know," she said with teasing emphasis, "I trust you, which—" she poked his shoulder—"is *not* carte blanche for a married man *or* woman to spend time alone with the opposite sex unless they are the dean, a blood relative, or clergy." She pressed a lingering kiss to his cheek. "But that said, I've watched women ogle you since my first day at the BCAS, Luke McGee, and heaven knows I've done my fair share. So it's no great surprise to me that women find you to be a dangerously handsome man. But I also know you love me, you love God, and you love your family with a

259

vengeance, and in every single situation I've ever seen you in with a woman—me included—you've proven yourself to be one of the most honorable and decent men I've ever known."

A slow grin traveled his lips. He slipped an arm to her waist, pulling her close. "Really?"

"Really." She scrunched her nose. "Of course, your thick head and caveman mentality does cancel a lot of that out, you know."

His grin faded to soft as he caressed her cheek, weaving his hand into her hair. "I love you, Katie Rose," he whispered, a prick of wetness in his eyes. "Thank you for loving me."

"You're welcome, Luke," she said softly, grazing his jaw with the tips of her fingers. The barest hint of a twinkle lit in her eye. "It's not too hard, you know—*most* of the time."

He zeroed in on her lips, and his mouth went dry. "Dangerously handsome? Caveman mentality?" Prodding her back on the couch, he gave her a grin that had trouble written all over it. "You're putting ideas into my head, Sass," he whispered, taking his time to suckle her ear.

"Wouldn't take much, McGee," she said, voice breathless. "You tend to have a one-track mind when it comes to your wife."

The grin ramped up to perilous. "Glad you noticed. I'd be in a sorry state if you hadn't." In one seamless move, he eased her legs up on the couch and stretched out beside her, playfully tugging her lip before delving into a kiss that made them both groan. "I wonder," he whispered, her skin warm against his mouth, "should I utilize my caveman skills and carry you to bed over my shoulder or . . . ," he nuzzled his way down the curve of her throat, "just make love to you right here?" His ragged breathing matched hers to a heartbeat as he placed wispy kisses along the delicate line of her collarbone. His hungry hand swept the length of her, pausing to play with the button of her skirt. He looked up with a half-lidded smile. "Any suggestions?"

"Just one," she said, voice hoarse and breathing even worse.

She lassoed his neck and pulled him down hard. "Shut up and kiss me."

⌇⌇⌇

Cabinets clattered in Marcy's kitchen as Steven whistled up a storm, luring a smile to Faith's lips while she and her mother and sisters sewed on the back porch. The earthy smell of cut grass and fresh mulch drifted on a warm summer breeze, along with the chatter of a mockingbird and children's laughter. Sprawled on the lawn, Gabe and the cousins were harmonious for once, enjoying Popsicles from the Good Humor truck in a backyard manicured by Uncle Steven.

Charity leaned toward Faith, muffling her whisper with a hand to her mouth as she nodded toward the kitchen. "Saints almighty, what's going on? Did Steven take a job as the Good Humor man . . . or do my matchmaking instincts detect Annie's involved?"

Peeking at the kitchen window, Faith grinned when Steven broke into a chorus of "I'm in the Mood for Love." "Close," she said softly, ready to break into song herself. "Annie told me Thursday night our boy has finally asked her out for a movie tonight."

The shirt Marcy was mending dropped along with her mouth. "Oh, I knew it!" she whispered. "Of course Steven's been as tight-lipped as a tomb, but I suspected something with all his humming and whistling this week, kissing me every time he comes in the room and even laughing when your father humiliated him at chess." She shook her head, a grin curving her lips. "I tell you what, the boy's been downright giddy, and now I know why." Her sigh was pure contentment. "Oh, I do hope Annie can reel him in—I like her."

"Me too," Emma said softly, gray eyes twinkling. "After all, it's not often we see the buttoned-down Agent O'Connor off-kilter over a girl."

Lizzie all but glowed, absently caressing the increasingly

cumbersome mound beneath her blue maternity shift. "And soooo romantic . . ."

Charity assessed the skirt she was sewing, face in a squint. "Oh, she'll reel him in, all right, if I have anything to say about it," she said with grunt.

Katie leaned in, her voice a whisper. "Not if he catches wind we're pushing it. Growing up, all I had to do was let the little brat know I wanted him to do something, and he did the exact opposite. And frankly, I like Annie too much to risk that."

"Don't you worry about that," Charity said with an air of confidence. "Steven may be a brick wall when it comes to emotional involvement, but with all of us praying and my superior matchmaking skills, the man has no choice but to fall in love." She held up a hem she'd just basted, eyeing it for accuracy. "Mark my words—the boy's a goner."

"Who's a goner?" Steven asked, ambling through the screen door with a glass of lemonade. He upended it, then wiped his wet forehead with the side of his arm while he perched on the wood railing. Drenched with sweat and riddled with grass stains, his sleeveless T-shirt revealed tan, muscled arms, and a smooth, solid chest.

"Henry," Charity said without missing a beat, "who else?"

Steven chuckled, white teeth gleaming in a face dark from outside sports and lawn work. He ruffled fingers through damp hair that was such a deep chestnut, it almost looked black. "What's the boy done now?" he asked, taking another drink.

"Oh, you know, the usual—smoking Father's pipe, worms in his sister's bed, building an armory with rocks, mud balls, and persimmons for a game of Civil War."

"That's not so bad." Steven set his glass on the railing. "All boys like to play war."

Charity's brow spiked. "In their father's brand-new Ford Model A Roadster?"

"Ouch." Steven grinned, biceps taut as he folded his arms. "Poor Mitch. Bet that hurt."

"Not as much as it hurt Henry. Mitch went off like a rocket's red glare. Haven't seen the love of my life lose it like that since . . ." She paused to think, head cocked and hand to mouth. "Well, I guess since yesterday when he cut his face with the razor I used on the neighbor's dog." She scrunched her nose and shivered. "Beggar's lice and skunk. Don't ask—it's not pretty."

Faith laughed, shaking her head. "I'll tell you what, sis, I swear Henry is God's comeuppance for all the trouble you gave me growing up, and now Mitch."

"Oh no you don't," Charity said with a thin gaze. "The good Lord said, 'I will be merciful to their iniquities, and their sins will I remember no more.' Trust me, I'm hanging my hat on that one." She chewed the edge of her lip, eyes in a squint. "Although it is awfully suspicious I live with both Mitch and Henry." She waved her hand. "Oh well, it's not important. All that matters is Henry is punished for what he did to Kelsey Raber."

Steven tipped his glass for a piece of ice. "Uh-oh, what'd he do to Kelsey Raber?"

Charity arched a brow. "The worms-in-the-bed stunt?" She nodded, mouth in a wry slant. "Kelsey Raber spent the night with Hope. Poor kid crawled into bed and screamed, giving a whole new meaning to the term 'night crawlers.' "

"No!" Emma put a hand to her mouth, a smile peeking through while her sisters chuckled, shaking their heads. Steven just laughed and popped more ice while Emma threaded a needle, brows in a crimp. "But I thought you said Henry had a crush on Kelsey."

"He does," Charity said with a scowl. "And that's his way of showing it. Completely ignores her except for stunts like that." She glanced up at Steven, mouth kinked. "Maybe you can tell me, Steven—why do men ignore a woman they obviously like?"

Mid-drink, a spray of lemonade misted the air as Steven choked.

Faith jumped up to pat him on the back while he hacked, his cheeks as red as the kids' cherry Popsicles. "You okay?" She bit back a smile. *Goodness, Annie, what have you done to the boy?*

Steven nodded hard, palm in the air.

"Personal experience?" Charity asked with a devilish smile.

He shot up, waving Faith away. "No!" he said with a hoarse clear of his throat. He bolted for the door. "See ya. Just remembered something I need to do."

The screen door slammed, and Marcy quirked a brow. "See what I mean? A tomb, and one buried six feet under at that. Lips and pride sealed tight and scared to death somebody's going to break in."

"Well, don't you worry, Mother, I'll get the scoop from Annie come Thursday." Faith tugged a torn pair of trousers into her lap, lips squirming into a mischievous smile. "Because Steven's lips may be sealed tighter than a tomb, but trust me—it's his pride we're gonna bury."

12

Cards exploded in the air while Annie dove for a spoon a split second after Steven snatched the last from the pile. Teeth clenched as tight as her fist, she yanked with all her might, ignoring Steven's grin as they played tug-of-war on Aunt Eleanor's parlor floor. With Glory cheering him on, he gave Annie a slow wink before easily jerking the spoon from her grip, leaving her with bright red fingers and cheeks that were even worse.

"Whoop-eee! Annie has S-P-O-O-N and we win!!" Glory bounced up and down on Steven's lap, her giggles ricocheting off the walls when his fingers became "Tickle Monster."

He slid Annie a lazy grin over the little girl's wild blonde curls. "Sorry, kid," he teased, "but face it—you're just not that fast."

She collected her cards with a smirk, reaching around Mr. Grump to retrieve a few strays. The basset lay oblivious, surrounded by a sea of board games. "Not that fast . . . mmm. I suppose that might be considered a good thing if dating you, wouldn't you say, Agent O'Connor?"

His grin broadened considerably. "Oh yeah," he said, warming her with a smoky look.

She lowered her head, hoping to hide the blush she felt by focusing on collecting more cards, well aware Steven O'Connor had a disastrous effect on her. *Particularly* now after dating two months. One look, one kiss was all it took to send her pulse into overdrive, and Annie was grateful he appeared to be taking it slow. He'd been the perfect gentleman so far, no lingering in the car and nothing more than a safe kiss at the door.

Safe? Annie gulped, watching him horse around with Glory, biceps bulging while pumping her up and down in the air. Who was she kidding? Every moment spent with him just meant she fell a little more in love, and although the kisses at the door started out gentle and tame, Annie sensed a change that felt anything but "safe." The last time he'd said good night, he'd butted her to the portico wall with an urgency in his kiss that both excited and alarmed her. A warm shiver skittered as he wrestled with Glory, and she couldn't help but worry that sometime soon, she might be doing some wrestling of her own.

"Let's play dominoes," Glory shouted, plopping down on Steven's back.

"Sorry, dear." Aunt Eleanor looked up, needlepoint in hand. "It's almost eight, and after traipsing through the zoo with Steven and your sister all day, you'll need a bath before bed."

"But I'm not tired," Glory moaned over Steven's shoulder, "and Steven's still here."

"But leaving soon, Glory Girl," he said emphatically, flipping her little body over his head before laying her down flat.

She squealed and scampered back up, hanging onto his legs after he jumped to his feet. "But why do you have to leave so soon?" she asked, blue eyes peering up.

He hoisted her up in his arms to deposit a kiss on her nose, lips curving into a soft smile. "Gotta go to work, little girl. Special assignment."

"But when are you coming back?"

He gave Annie a lidded smile that doubled her pulse. "That's up to your sister."

"Soon," Annie promised. She tugged Glory from his arms.

"Not soon enough," he whispered, his wayward fingers straying down her arms.

"Come on, squirt," Annie said, "I'll let you use my honeysuckle bubble bath."

"And wear one of your silky nightgowns too?" she asked, the glow of hope in her eyes.

Something bittersweet plucked at Annie's heart at Glory wanting to follow in the path of her big sister. *Just like I used to with Maggie.* Fighting a stab of melancholy, she nuzzled Glory's nose. "Absolutely." She slipped Steven a smile. "Do you have time to wait till I get her in the tub, Steven, or do I need to say goodbye now?"

"I'll wait," he said, the look in his eyes doing funny things to her stomach.

Aunt Eleanor removed her reading glasses and placed them on the table. "No, Annie, I'll take care of Glory tonight." She put her needlepoint aside and rose. "Steven'll be leaving soon, dear, so I'll let you see him out." She bent to rumple Mr. Grump's ears before tugging a yawning Glory away from Annie. "Come on, Mr. Grump, you can finish your nap upstairs." Her smile was warm. "Good night, Steven, thank you for giving my girls such a wonderful day."

My girls. Annie's throat thickened as she gave Glory to her aunt with a grateful smile.

"My pleasure, Miss Martin," Steven said, squatting to gather the games from the floor.

Annie ruffled Glory's hair before they left the room with Mr. Grump toddling behind. "Thanks, Aunt Eleanor, I'll be up shortly to take over. And don't overdo it with my bubble bath, you stinkpot," she called with a playful threat, "or I just may join you in that tub and give you some dunks."

"Now there's a mental picture I'm pretty sure you don't want me to have."

Annie spun around, cheeks aflame at the implication. She knelt to help put away the games, avoiding his eyes. "Uh, no, I'd rather you strike it from memory, if you don't mind."

"Done," he said with a chuckle, stretching out on his side to stack dominoes in a box a few inches away. His smile turned rogue. "Although not without repercussions, I'm afraid."

She peeked up. "Repercussions," she repeated, battling a smile. "Such as?"

"Such as thoughts of you in nothing but bubbles," he whispered, voice husky as he reached to tug her close, nudging her back on the carpet with a hazardous smile.

"Steven!" Her whisper was hoarse as he lay beside her, head propped in one hand while his muscled arm pinned her with the other. She wiggled to get back up, to no avail. "Stop it. What if Aunt Eleanor were to walk back in?" she whispered, voice frantic.

The blue of his eyes deepened. "Come on, Annie," he said softly, inching close. His tease faded to a whisper. "You can't expect us to spend the day together without a single kiss and then taunt me with that image of you in the tub."

"Steven, I—"

Her bones melted into warm honey when he kissed her right there on the carpet, and for several mind-numbing moments, nothing mattered but Steven's mouth exploring hers or the warmth of his hand gliding her hips. A silent moan trapped in her throat when he pressed in close, lips skimming her jaw to nip at her ear. "Oh, Annie, I never met a girl like you . . ."

"Oh, babe, I never met a girl like you . . ."

She froze, Brubaker's words hot in her ear. Heart racing, she pushed him away hard, her breathing as ragged as his when she stumbled to her knees. She suddenly felt cheap, and her anger flared. "No, I suspect you haven't if you think I'm going to fall for a line like that, Steven O'Connor . . . or should I say, Billy Brubaker?"

He stared, shallow breaths heaving from parted lips. The smoky glaze in his eyes glinted into anger. "I'm not Billy Brubaker," he said, his whisper more than harsh.

"Then don't act like it," she snapped, repeating the very words he'd once said to her.

She'd never seen Steven blush before, but he did so now, a dangerous shade that bled all the way up his neck. His jaw was like rock as he rose to his feet, and his blue eyes were almost black. "I have to go, but please thank your aunt for dinner." He strode toward the door and turned, tone clipped and gaze hard, displaying a temper she didn't even know he had. "If I get a chance, I'll give you a call, but don't hold your breath, kid." He turned to go.

"Steven!" She jutted her chin, incensed he was turning the tables on her, making this her fault instead of his. "Just so you know," she called, stopping him at the door as he glared over his shoulder, "don't bother calling if you plan to pull this again. Because if you do—it's over."

"*If* I call." He jerked the front door open and slid her a granite gaze, a muscle flickering in his cheek. "Get this and get it good, little girl—no woman, much less a kid barely eighteen, is going to dictate to me, ya got that?" The door slammed hard, both on its hinges and in her heart, and she winced, praying the bathwater was running and Aunt Eleanor couldn't hear.

Steven stormed to his father's car and hurled the door open, heaving it closed again with a deafening bang before grinding the ignition. The engine roared to life, rivaling the fury in his gut, and he was sorely tempted to squeal away from the curb. He punched the dash with his fist before slumping over the wheel with a hand to his eyes, desperate to control a temper he seldom lost. Every nerve in his body was on edge, tight, and ready to snap. Who the devil did she think she was? She was just some kid still wet behind the ears who thought she was going to tell him how it was going to be. Well, he had news for Miss Susannah Grace Kennedy, there were plenty of women who would accommodate him with a few kisses and more, and they certainly wouldn't be naïve enough to compare him to vermin like Brubaker.

"*Oh, babe, I never met a girl like you . . .*"

The words suddenly stabbed in his brain, and his eyelids

sank shut, all air heaving still in his chest. Like the shift of a kaleidoscope, the pieces fell into place and he suddenly saw just what Annie had seen—Brubaker pressuring a woman to get what he wants.

"He doesn't care like I do," he hissed, but even as he said it, he could see the old Steven coercing his way, looking for pleasure with a woman he cared for until she gave him her all. Pushing, teasing, breaking her down . . . just like he'd done with Maggie.

"Oh, Annie, I never met a girl like you . . ."

But the truth was, he had, and he'd ruined her—just like he was trying to do to Annie.

Sagging back against the seat, shame burned all anger away while bile climbed in his throat. Because deep down inside, he realized he wasn't much different than Brubaker, and somehow he couldn't live with that thought. *God, help me, I am such a jerk . . .*

He flung the car door open, then slammed it again and loped up to the porch, pressing the buzzer so hard that his thumb ached. Peering through the thick, beveled glass, he thought he saw Frailey in the foyer, but his heart thudded to a stop at the approach of a woman instead.

"Steven?" Eleanor Martin blinked, hand on the knob. "Did you forget something?"

"Yes, Miss Martin, I did. I . . . forgot to tell Annie something." Striving for nonchalance, he plunged his hands in his pockets and smiled, his voice calmer than he felt. "Is she still up?"

"Certainly." Eleanor stepped back. "Why don't you come in, and I'll get her."

"No," he said too quickly, palm raised in the air. "I mean, I can't stay. I just forgot to tell her something, so if it's all the same to you, I'll just wait right here."

"All right." A furrow wrinkled her brow. "She'll be right down."

"Thank you, ma'am." He exhaled his relief when she closed

the door. Minutes later, Annie descended the steps, and when it wheeled open again, his heart climbed in his throat.

"You have something to say?" Her voice was cool and her eyes, cautious.

He swallowed hard, painfully aware that for the first time in his life, a girl had him by the throat. *No, not a girl*, he decided with a shaky exhale, *a woman*. A strong, beautiful woman who at eighteen was more mature and steady and smart than he could ever hope to be at twenty-five, and the realization humbled him considerably. And, he thought with a hard shift of his throat, diminished the years between them as well. He sucked in a fortifying breath, determined to squash his pride and do the right thing.

"Yeah, I . . ." His hands began to sweat, making him feel all of ten again. "Well, I wanted to apologize, Annie, for losing my temper and for . . . ," he licked his lips, tongue so thick, he thought he would choke, "trying to . . . push you . . ." His voice trailed off as he stared at her, scared to death he was falling in love. Those pale green eyes and that fresh-scrubbed face dusted with freckles bewitched him like no other woman ever had, even Maggie. Beautiful inside and out, a gentle spirit and innocence he could drown in . . . and a body that could threaten it all.

Annie, please—give me another chance.

Taking a risk, he quietly hooked her fingers with his own, gently tugging her out on the porch. He closed the door till it was ajar, then released her and shoved his hands in his pockets with a tentative smile. "So, what do you say, kid—can you forgive me for being a jerk?"

He waited, unable to breathe while she assessed him through pensive eyes, lips pursed as if she couldn't decide. And then he saw it, the barest tilt of assent flickering at the corners of her beautiful mouth, and with a boyish smile, the air slowly seeped from his lungs. He took her hand in his and grazed her knuckles with his thumb. "Please tell me that's a 'yes.' "

She nodded, and he inhaled deeply, releasing it again as he slowly drew her into his arms.

"I'm really sorry, Annie, for losing my temper, but the bottom line is I'm so darned attracted to you, I have trouble keeping my hands to myself."

She pulled back to search his face, a tinge of sadness lining her smile. "It's not easy for me either, Steven, because it's no secret I'm in love with you, and when you kiss me like that . . . touch me like that . . ." Moisture glazed her eyes while her voice softened to a whisper. "I want to give you my all, but I can't, because it doesn't belong to you. My body may crave your touch and I may want to give you mine, but that's not love, even if it seems like it at the time. True love always wants the best for the other, and although you may not agree, the best is only available through the hand of God." She drew in a deep breath and released it slowly. "Which means, if you want a relationship with me, we'll be doing things God's way, not ours." She cupped his bristled jaw with a soft smile, reeling him in with every breath that she took. "Because, *my* bottom line is I care about you too much to hurt you that way . . ."

He exhaled loudly, one edge of his lip crooking up. "His way or the highway, huh?"

She patted his cheek. "His way *is* the 'high' way, Agent O'Connor," she said softly, lips sliding into an imp of a smile. "And as a federal agent who prides himself on toeing the line, I suggest when you're with me, you keep all toes *and* hands from inching over, okay?"

"I can't help but notice there was no mention of lips," he said, a bit of the rake in his tone while his mouth hovered over hers. "Something for which I am *most* grateful." Before she could respond, he bent to kiss her, a tender wisp of his lips against hers—gentle, soft, innocent—like Susannah Kennedy herself, and so chaste it almost felt reverent. Eyes closed, he reveled in the taste of her, the scent of honeysuckle and Tabu creating a magical moment unlike any he'd ever known. He wanted to tell her he loved her, but he refrained, because the truth was, he wasn't sure. Not sure it wasn't lust like with Maggie, and unsure he could trust himself with a love as tender as the girl he held in his arms. Breaking the connection, he stepped away and exhaled, mouth crooking into a smile. "Well, you haven't stomped on my toes yet, so I guess that was okay."

"More than okay," she whispered, the sweet blush in her cheeks making him want to kiss her all over again. Her lips trembled into a smile. "I love you, Steven."

He stared, throat muscles working hard to fight a similar response. He cupped a palm to her cheek. "Have a good night, Annie," he whispered. "At least, as good as you made mine." Slipping his hands in his pockets, he sprinted to the street, grinning all the way to the car. Because *his* bottom line was—"good" didn't even come close.

Exhausted, Steven glanced at his watch before veering his father's Model T onto Worth Street, where except for the buzz of locusts and the glow of streetlights, silence and darkness prevailed at one o'clock in the morning. Shifting gears, he sagged over the wheel as he drove, the cross from St. Stephen's spire catching his eye, reminding him of Annie. His smile sloped sideways. But then everything reminded him of Annie these days, it seemed.

He rubbed his bristled jaw as he coasted to a stop at the stop sign, wondering how on earth an innocent kid of barely eighteen could disarm a twenty-five-year-old federal agent who raided speakeasies for a living, tangled with disgruntled bouncers, and carried a gun. But disarm him she had, reducing him to a stammering sixteen-year-old with overactive hormones all over again. He blasted out a weary sigh. And to be painfully honest, he wasn't all that sure he liked it.

Oh, he liked Annie all right, and heaven knows he liked the attraction she stirred—a little too much according to her— but he had to admit a part of him felt uncomfortable with the control she wielded. Since senior year in high school, he'd always called the shots with women, held the reins, gotten his way, but not this time apparently. Even as free-spirited as Maggie had been, Steven had always known she'd go to any lengths to keep him around. And she had. His gut tightened. But, that wasn't what he wanted from Annie.

Was it?

A familiar guilt crawled in his chest, thinning his air, and he knew it wasn't, not deep down. But on the surface? Oh yeah . . . desire waged a war Steven had fought too many times before . . . and lost. But Annie was different, he argued, and a part of him was desperate to keep her that way. Unfortunately, it was at war with the part of him that didn't want to. The part of him that wanted to hold her, kiss her, express his love in a way that seemed to control him as much as he wanted to control her. A way that felt so right and good at the time, but then ate away, both at his gut and the relationship he longed to have. Annie's innocence and purity had captured him from the start, a glimmering oasis in a parched and thirsty wasteland littered with his own mistakes. From the very beginning, all he'd wanted was to protect her from men who would taint her, marring the very beauty that drew them. Steven downshifted at another stop sign, guilt stabbing anew. *But who's going to protect her from me?*

Exhaling heavily, he glanced at St. Stephen's church, squinting over at the dimly lit school yard where a group of guys were involved in a game of moonlight basketball. A grin tugged and he pulled the Model T to the curb, arms draped over his door to hail his older brother. "Hey, O'Connor!"

Sean turned, a flash of white teeth in a tan face gleaming with sweat. He jogged over to the car with a basketball under his arm, muscles slick from exertion on a September night far too steamy for basketball. Leaning in, he rested damp arms on the open window, thick blond brows arched high as he assessed Steven's loosened tie and rolled-up sleeves. "The graveyard shift again? I thought you'd be out tonight with Annie or Joe."

"Special assignment," Steven said with a twist of his lips, remembering how much he'd enjoyed Saturday night detail before Annie. "Spent the day at the zoo with Annie and her sister, then dinner and games at her aunt's before duty called."

An easy grin tipped his brother's lips. "Mmm . . . zoo with the kid sister and dinner with the family—sounds serious."

Steven's mouth quirked, his brother's probing statement prickling more than expected. The last thing he wanted was his family knowing how he felt about Annie. "Yeah, well, what it sounds like and what it is are two different things," he said, tone defensive. "I like the kid and we have fun together, but don't read any more into it than that." He paused, gaze flicking to the group of guys on the court. "But talk about serious—you guys are way over the top if you're tossing a ball around in this steam bath."

Glancing over his shoulder, Sean swatted at a mosquito. "Yeah, the guys are pretty crazed when it comes to midnight basketball games." Sean turned back with a grin. "But then they're single and don't have to raid speakeasies on Saturday nights, so the poor slobs have to burn excess energy off some way, I guess."

Steven shook his head, his smile flat. "I'll tell you what, Sean, you sure lucked out with Emma. Can't imagine many women who'd stand for midnight basketball with the guys."

"She's one in a million all right, but then luck didn't have a whole lot to do with it."

Somehow the statement nettled, and Steven fought off a scowl. All of his life, Sean had been the older brother he'd looked up to, the man he respected, and the bachelor he wanted to emulate. But when he'd abandoned his buddies and bachelorhood to fall in love with Emma last year, Steven suddenly felt alienated from the brother who'd always commiserated with him on religion and relationships. Overnight, Sean had gone from avoiding both like the plague to an all-out allegiance to God and marriage, happily committed to a woman and a faith that had transformed him into a new man. A weary sigh seeped through Steven's lips. A man who obviously wouldn't understand the struggles Steven now faced with Annie.

Or would he?

"Hey, you need a ride home?" Steven squinted, a sudden urge to talk to his brother.

A slow grin worked its way across Sean's face. "Sure." He tossed his basketball onto the seat and called over his shoulder, "Hey, guys, I'm calling it a night. See you next week." Rounding the car, he slipped in on the other side and slammed the door, gingerly rolling his neck with a groan. "Man, I'm getting too old for this."

Steven eyed the ball on the seat. "So you can take your ball and go home, just like that?"

"Why not?" Another grin creased his lips. "I've got someone to go home to—these poor clowns don't. Besides, Joe brought his, so they'll be another hour or so." He tapped the roof over his door. "Fifteen thirteen Dorchester, and take the scenic route." Positioning an arm over the back of the seat, his easy grin faded enough for Steven to notice. "So . . . what's on your mind?"

Steven shook his head, wondering how his older brother did it. From childhood on, it seemed as if Sean had always been able to read his thoughts, hone in when Steven was in turmoil, know when he needed to talk. *A bloomin' mind reader,* he thought with a quirk of his lips. He slid him a sideways smile, nervous about revealing his weakness with Annie. "What makes you think something's on my mind?"

Another gleam of teeth put Steven at ease, his brother's easy manner taking the edge off an awkward subject. "Well, if the knuckled grip isn't a dead giveaway, the tic in your jaw is."

Steven glimpsed in the rearview mirror, shaking his head as he headed down the street. "I swear, you always did have a sixth sense."

Sean hiked a well-worn Ked to the dash, leg jiggling along with the vehicle. "How do you think I managed to stay single so long? I could smell trouble a mile away, especially the female kind."

"Yeah, well, me too," Steven said, taking a corner with a zag of his lips, "which is why I'm looking for advice."

The jiggling stopped. "This about Annie?"

Heat ringed Steven's collar as he veered onto Sean's street before coasting to a stop in front of his house. "Yeah," he said, shifting the vehicle into park. He turned off the ignition and exhaled a noisy breath, sagging over the wheel. "I guess I like the kid more than I'm letting on, Sean, but I sure in the blazes don't want anybody else to know, *especially* our mother or sisters." He shook his head, gaze straight ahead. "That would be a living nightmare."

"Well, they won't hear it from me, if that's what you're worried about." Sean paused. "But when you say you don't want anybody to know . . . does that include Annie?"

Leaning back to rest his head on the seat, Steven closed his eyes. "Yeah, it includes Annie, but I think it may be a little late for that, especially after tonight. The kid may be naïve, but she's smart. I'm pretty sure she can spot a sucker in love when she sees one."

"Are you?" Sean studied him while he idly tossed the ball from hand to hand.

Steven slid him a sideways glance, hackles prickling again. "A sucker in love? Heck, no," he emphasized with a press of lips, unwilling to admit Annie controlled the relationship. "Or at least I don't want to be. I mean, I like Annie a lot . . ." He rested his arm on the open window, thumb tracing the leather casing. "But I'm not a guy who likes the girl to call the shots."

"When you say 'call the shots' . . . ," Sean said slowly, "what do you mean, exactly?"

Steven stared out his window, his comfort level sinking along with his stomach. "I mean controlling the relationship, telling me what I can and cannot do, you know—things."

Sean's pause was too long to suit. "You mean sexual things, like keeping you in line?"

"Yeah," Steven said, suddenly feeling as big a jerk in front of Sean as he had in front of Annie. He peered at his brother. "Look, Sean, I'm not talking about going too far or anything like that, but the kid about had a conniption tonight when I kissed her, telling me if it happened again, we were through."

A low whistle parted from Sean's lips. "Over a kiss? That must have been some kiss. You don't find many women like that around anymore. Did you cross the line or something?"

Fire singed the back of his neck. "Are you kidding? In her aunt's house? Not on your life. It was just an innocent kiss on the floor, nothing more."

The ball froze midair. "On the floor?" Sean's voice climbed an octave. "As in stretched out . . . the two of you . . . side by side?" He whistled again. "Gotta tell you, Steven, that's asking for trouble."

"Yeah, well, apparently she thought so too, 'cause she read me the riot act, tripping my temper so fast, I wanted to wash my hands altogether."

"Why?"

Steven stared, jaw gaping. "Why? Because I'm a grown man, that's why. An adult who doesn't like some kid telling me how it's going to be."

"Wait—aren't you the one always complaining how loose the women are today?" Sean asked, the ball back in action. "I would think a girl like Annie would be a breath of fresh air." He hesitated, the ball slowing again. "Unless, of course, that's not really what you're looking for . . ."

"I'm not looking for anything," Steven said too quickly, "except spending time with a girl I like and maybe having a little fun—period. I'll tell you one thing I'm *not* looking for, though, is getting serious now or anytime soon."

"Sounds like your idea of 'fun' might conflict with Annie's, then." Sean quietly placed the ball on the seat between them. "And God's."

Steven slid his brother a narrow gaze. "Come on, Sean, you're not going to sit there and tell me that you didn't do your fair share of necking before Emma, because I know better. And that's all I'm talking about here, nothing more."

Sean released a weighty sigh. "No, I'm not going to tell

you I didn't get off track a few times, because I did, which is something I'm not proud of. But . . . that's exactly why I know your idea of 'fun' could lead to way more than you bargain for, Steven. You should know that better than anyone after your relationship with Maggie."

Steven pinched the bridge of his nose, his tone defeated. "I know," he said quietly, "which is why I'm worried. I like the kid a lot and the last thing I want to do is mess this up."

"Then Annie's the perfect girl, because it doesn't sound like she'll let you."

Steven grunted. "Maybe not now," he said with a harsh laugh. "But trust me, when I fall for a girl and she falls for me? I have this uncanny ability to push until we both regret it."

"Then don't."

The corner of his lip cocked up. "Easier said than done. When I was crazy in love with Maggie, it was just second nature to express it." He studied Sean out of the corner of his eye. "Did you and Emma struggle with that? You know, before you two got married?"

Sean's chest rose and fell as he peered out the windshield, a faint smile on his lips. "Surprisingly no, but only because I loved her so much, I never wanted to hurt her that way."

His brother's words stung. "I loved Maggie too," Steven said too sharply, "but I still couldn't keep my hands off of her, and she couldn't keep hers off me."

Sean slipped him a sympathetic smile. "I know, it's near impossible when God's not a part of the equation, as I discovered before Emma." He exhaled. "But with Emma, doing things God's way was so important to her, that it became important to me too. Even so, I never could have done it without God's help, because as you discovered with Maggie, when you love someone, you crave that closeness. A closeness God fully intends between a man and wife, not a couple who are dating or even engaged. And with good reason."

"Yeah, and what's that?" Steven asked, more than a little cynicism creeping in. The tendons in his jaw automatically tightened at the mention of God. Faith in God might be a big part of his brother's life now, but to Steven—and Sean, not so very long ago—God was little more than an hour in a pew once a week and an occasional pass through the confessional, no matter how much his family depended on him.

Sean sized him up through pensive eyes, as if contemplating whether Steven would receive what he had to say. "Because God wants us to have the best marriage and relationship possible, and he knows that can't happen without him. He built it into the process, Steven, when he created us—blessing based on obedience, kind of like a spiritual gravity." Flipping the basketball into the air, he caught it again with a practiced palm. "You throw a ball in the air, and it falls back down." He tossed the ball back on the seat, eyes locked with his brother's. "It's the same with God's precepts—apply them, and blessings fall on everything in your life. And when you apply them in a relationship with a woman you care about?" His gaze was steady and firm. "Not only does it deepen and enrich your relationship with God, but with the woman you love. Suddenly everything in the relationship is stronger—the emotional bond you share, the trust you have with each other, and your own self-respect. Not to mention a peace and joy you never dreamed possible."

"I don't know, Sean," Steven said slowly, "sounds too good to be true." He snatched the ball and rotated it with his thumbs, eyes fixed on the movement.

Sean scratched his sandpaper jaw. "Yeah, I know, and trust me, I wouldn't have believed it either if I hadn't experienced it for myself. But I'm telling you, Steven, it's the only way to fly." He cuffed his brother's shoulder. "So if you really care about Annie like you say, why on earth would you risk cutting her off from God's blessings to gratify your own desires?"

Steven stared, the truth of his brother's statement hitting him square in the chest. "I guess I wouldn't," he whispered, slowly lowering the ball to his lap. He sighed and handed it over to his brother, his voice quiet. "I'm just not sure I have the same control you had with Emma."

Sean bobbled the ball in his hand. "You can . . . but only with God's help."

"Yeah, well, that might be a problem." Steven rubbed the back of his neck. "Don't get me wrong—I believe in God, but I don't have a whole lot of trust in him, at least not like you."

Sean grunted. "Yeah, well, neither did I . . . before Emma. And nobody knows that better than you." Opening the car door, he got out and closed it once again. He leaned in then, ball under his arm and palms on the windowsill, an intensity in his eyes belying the calm of his face. "You know, Steven, you've always been the kind of kid searching out answers wherever you could—first with science and magic as a boy, then with girls and booze in college. Even as a federal agent, you drive yourself harder than anybody I know, but it's never enough. Whether in school, with Maggie, or even in your job, you've always been restless—a man on the hunt for some elusive happiness you've never been able to find." The semblance of a smile shaded his lips. "This is it, Steven, this is what you've been looking for all of your life—a faith in God that will bring you true joy. Don't be stupid like me and let ten years go by without it, because the truth is . . . you *can* trust him." He stood up straight and tapped his palm twice on the roof. "G'night, kid—thanks for the lift."

Steven watched his brother's shadow disappear into the house, and although Sean's words brought him a sense of peace, he still felt that restlessness stirring inside. It just seemed all too easy, too pat, especially for someone who didn't really deserve the kind of peace his brother mentioned. Turning the ignition, he shifted into gear and eased down the road, not sure if he was ready to invoke the help of some invisible deity he'd defied more than once.

You can trust him, Sean had said, something Steven might actually consider at some point in time. His lips slanted as he headed for home.

Because God knows he couldn't trust himself.

13

nnie? It's always great to see you, of course, but
. . . why aren't you in school?"

Annie gave Faith a weak smile, a stack of textbooks in her
arms. "My last class was cancelled, so I took a chance you
might be home." She drew in a deep breath and released it
again with a quivering sigh, gaze flicking from the wash basket
on Faith's hip to the quiet house beyond. "But if you're busy,
I can come another time."

"Don't be silly." Shifting the basket, Faith tugged Annie
into the house with her free hand. "This is perfect timing
because I don't have to pick the girls up from school for
another two hours, so I have plenty of time for girl talk and
tea." She wiggled her brows. "And I have cookies . . . ," she
said in a singsong voice that brought a smile to Annie's face.

She closed the door and ushered Annie down a hall emblazoned with pictures of Collin and the girls. Annie stopped
midway, heart swooping at an old family photo of the
O'Connors when Steven was small. He looked so sweet and
serious, probably no more than eight at the time, hands shoved
deep in his pockets like he was often prone to do. The walls
of her throat thickened as she studied him, tracing a finger

from the rumpled dark hair that fell into shy eyes, down the plaid suit that couldn't hide a little boy's spindly frame.

"He was always such a sweet kid," Faith said over her shoulder, affection softening her tone. "I swear, the patience of Job in dealing with Katie, and never a lick of trouble . . . or at least not till college."

Annie's smile faded. "You mean till Maggie," she said quietly, grateful she'd finally confided in Faith that Maggie was her sister.

Faith braced Annie's shoulder and led her to the kitchen at the back of the house where the heavenly smell of snickerdoodles wafted in the air. "It takes two, Annie," she said, steering her into a spindled oak chair at a well-worn kitchen table. She set the laundry basket down and filled a kettle for tea. "Maggie wasn't the first girl Steven got involved with, you know, only the one he dated the longest, so he was no angel when they met, trust me. The trouble started when he and Joe fell in with a fast crowd the summer before college, and everything changed after that. But I will admit, he and Maggie were not very good for each other."

The sound of Faith's words caused Annie to slump in the chair. "Well, that's actually one of the things I wanted to talk about, Faith." She sucked in a calming breath. "I'm not sure Steven and I are good for each other either."

Faith turned at the pantry where she was rifling through a selection of tea. "What do you mean?" she asked with a frown. "You're perfect for my brother, Annie—we all think so."

"Maybe not," she whispered, cheeks warming from something other than the heat of the oven. "Your brother's wearing me down, and I'm not sure how strong I can continue to be."

With a blink of green eyes, Faith tossed the box of tea bags onto the counter and immediately pulled out a chair, leaning forward to place a hand on Annie's arm. "But you said he stopped pushing after your ultimatum—that if he ever got fresh again, it was over."

"Yes . . . ," Annie said slowly, "and he's been wonderful ever since—nothing more than a chaste kiss at the door." She sat up with a shaky sigh, picking at her nails. "Until Saturday night, that is. All during the picture show he played with my hair, not even aware of what he was doing. Fondling my ear-lobe, grazing my palm with his thumb . . ." She shuddered. "I swear, Faith, I was ready to crawl out of my skin."

Faith sat up with fire in her eyes. "For pity's sake, why didn't you slap his hand away?"

She swallowed hard, peeking up with a nervous chew of her lip. "Because I liked it, that's the problem. It was so innocent and casual when he began, I never even thought anything about it till my body started to tingle, and then it was too late because by that time, I . . . ," a shallow breath quivered from her lips, "*wanted* him to do it." She hesitated, avoiding Faith's eyes. "Which is why we kissed in the car for a while before he walked me to the door . . ."

Faith slammed a palm on the table, causing Annie to jump. "See? This is exactly what I've been talking about. When men are courting women, they seem to have a one-track mind."

"No," Annie said quickly, rising to Steven's defense. "I don't think Steven was even aware how he was affecting me. It's me I'm ashamed of, Faith, for responding like I did."

Faith folded her arms, gaze thinning along with her smile. "Oh, sure, and when Collin and I were engaged, the poor man had no earthly idea kissing my neck would weaken me at the knees, either." She grabbed Annie's shoulders and gave her a little shake, green sparks all but flying from her eyes. "Poppycock! This is exactly why you have to keep my brother in line, Annie. He's older than you and has a lot of experience with women. Trust me on this—Steven knows *exactly* what he's doing, just like Collin." Annie's head bobbled back and forth as Faith gave her another shake before she sagged back in her chair with a huff. She slapped her arm on the table, fingers drumming. "Oh, I wish Steven were here right now, so I could shake the little brat silly for turning into such a . . .

a . . . ," she flailed a hand in the air, a storm brewing in her eyes, "man," she finished with a clipped tongue.

Annie blinked and then giggled. "Goodness, I've never seen you so . . . volatile."

The hard line of Faith's mouth edged up while she peered at Annie through a sliver of eyes. "That's because nothing lights my fuse like this, Annie—men who say they care about you, then disrespect your wishes. Sweet saints, it's hard enough to stay pure until marriage without a man who supposedly loves you making it twice as difficult to say no."

Annie sighed. "I wish Steven loved me," she said sadly, "but I don't think he does."

"I was talking about Collin," Faith snapped, eyes squinted in a hard stare as if recalling her past. "The man was so good when we were engaged, and then—BOOM! The month before we married, had to fight him off with a crowbar." She looked up, gaze shrewd. "I don't know if Steven loves you, Annie, but I do know this—he cares about you more than he's cared about any girl in a long time. So you have to stand your ground if you want God to honor you with the kind of relationship you want with my brother." She leaned in, jaw firm. "Before marriage is the only time a woman has control, so she has to use it wisely. After she's married, God calls her to submit to her husband, so you may as well take advantage of keeping Steven in line now. Which means," she said with a hike of her brow, "a good night kiss is fine, but when the flutters and tingles escalate, nip it in the bud, 'cause if you give 'em an inch, they'll take a mile, understood?"

Moisture smarted in Annie's eyes. "Yes, I understand, but I have to tell you—this is the hardest thing I've ever done. I'm so in love with Steven, just one look makes me weak all over, and so help me, Faith, when he tells me he cares about me, I literally melt in his arms."

Faith released a quiet sigh, eyes tender. "I know, Annie, I remember loving Collin so much I wanted to give myself to him, body and soul. One night he stirred me up more than usual, and I argued with God in my head that we'd be married in mere days, so what could it hurt? But the truth is, real love denies self to give those we love God's best. So I said no to Collin and yes to God, and I truly believe that's why our marriage is so wonderful today. Because the Bible is clear—God honors those who honor him."

"But what if . . . ," Annie swallowed hard, "I say no, but Steven persists?"

Faith stared at her for several seconds before she answered, her gaze soft. "Then you tell him it's over, just like you warned him in the beginning."

"But . . . what if he leaves forever?" She blinked, heart stalled in her chest.

"He won't," Faith whispered, rising to the whistle of the teakettle, "but if he does, then he's not the right man for you, and God has spared you further heartbreak."

Annie stared hard at the floor, her breathing uneven before she lifted her eyes to Faith's. "All right," she whispered, "but I'll need lots of prayer." She hesitated. "And, Faith?"

"Yes?" Faith turned at the counter, where she was pouring their hot water for tea.

"Steven needs prayer too," Annie said quietly. "Not just about us, mind you." She drew in a shallow breath, eyes locked with Faith's. "His faith in God—I don't think it's very strong."

Faith's chest wavered with a heavy exhale as she carried steaming cups of tea to the table. "Yes, Annie, I know. Oh, Steven believes in God and he goes to mass every Sunday, but I'm afraid he's a lot like my brother Sean used to be."

"How's that?" Annie said, taking a cookie when Faith offered the plate.

Setting the plate on the table, Faith sat to steep her tea. "Good men who believe in God, certainly, and that he sent his Son to save them, but no real passion for it. A sort of long-distance relationship comprised of church once a week and grace at dinner. But . . . ," she reached for a cookie, "the good

286

news is, all that can change if a man really loves a woman, which is what happened with Sean. Emma's faith ignited his, and to be honest, Annie, that's what I've been praying for with you and Steven. You have the kind of faith to set Steven's on fire, but it's going to require adherence to God's precepts to do it, which is another reason you have to be strong."

A wispy sigh parted from Annie's lips. "I know. I've tried a number of times to talk about my faith with Steven, but he always changes the subject." She glanced up, trepidation in her eyes. "So I know it will be my actions that speak rather than my words."

Faith smiled. "Ah yes, the immortal words of St. Francis of Assisi—'preach the gospel at all times and when necessary, use words.'" Her eyes twinkled as she took a sip of her tea.

Annie tilted her head. "I never heard that before, but it's so true."

"Yes, it is." Faith set her cup down to take Annie's hand, chin firm. "Which means when it comes to Steven, you'll have my daily vigil of prayers, beginning right now."

Annie nodded, her heart lighter at the thought . . . but not completely. "Faith?"

"Mmm?"

"Can we pray about something else too? About Maggie?"

"Absolutely," Faith said with a squeeze of her hands. "What about Maggie?"

Annie hesitated, the words difficult to say. "I . . . haven't told her yet."

It was Faith's turn to pause. "That you've been seeing Steven?"

She gave a wooden nod. "I wrote her I was dating, but was afraid to tell her who."

A reedy breath seeped through Faith's lips. "I see. Because you feel guilty . . . or because you're afraid she'll be angry?"

"A little of both, I suppose." Annie pulled her hands from Faith's to buff her arms, goose bumps popping from a sudden chill. "I never thought for a moment anything would ever happen between Steven and me, but now that it has, I worry Maggie'll be hurt."

"But that was three years ago, Annie, and your sister's in love with somebody else now, engaged to be married. If she does harbor any hurt, I'm sure she'll get over it quickly, especially if we pray about it." Faith's smile was gentle. "But you do need to tell her soon, okay?"

Annie nodded.

Faith extended her hands. "But right now, we have bigger fish to fry, young lady."

"We do, don't we?" Annie placed her hands into Faith's with a sheepish smile.

"Yes, ma'am, we do. Because if you're going to land my brother in the proverbial boat," Faith hiked a brow, a "Charity" smile sprouting on her lips, "we'll have to set the hook hard." She winked. "Right after he swallows the bait whole."

Marcy glanced at the clock on her nightstand with a nervous eye, wondering what in the world was taking Steven so long to lose at chess with his father. "Sweet saints, Steven," she muttered under her breath, "just push a pawn or sacrifice a queen or even touch the wrong piece, but for sanity's sake, let your father win!" Her hands shook as she slapped at a page in the magazine she wasn't reading, her stomach in knots as she waited for Patrick to come to bed.

Calm down, Marceline, or he'll sense something is up.

Resting her head on the headboard, she closed her eyes to heed the silent warning, forcing a calm she didn't feel. She and Patrick communicated about everything—everything *except* the thing nearest and dearest to Marcy's heart, adopting Gabe. Since Patrick's heart incident four months ago, Marcy had laid low, avoiding the subject of Gabe as deftly as her husband. But with another paperwork deadline tomorrow, she no longer had the luxury of waiting. And as much as she despised manipulation, her guilt couldn't keep pace with her longing to call Gabe one of their own. Tonight she needed to sway Patrick as never before, and if that meant softening him up with good news, good food, and calculated affection . . . well, so be it.

Her gaze strayed to the clock again, tongue gliding across her teeth. Half past eleven. Hopefully he'd be buoyed up by a win and not too tired either to talk or whatever else was needed to ensure the papers were signed. Chest expanding, she exhaled, confident everything was in place for a win, not only for Patrick in chess, but for his very patient wife who was a mere signature away from her dream. Hands trembling, she slipped two papers from the back of the magazine, the final forms that would declare Gabriella Dawn Smith an O'Connor by Christmas . . . and Marcy a mother of a precious street orphan who just needed to be loved.

She went over her plan for surely the hundredth time, quite certain there would never be a better time. This very week, the board of the *Boston Herald* hired another editor to replace the two they'd lost, which meant Patrick and Mitch would actually be home with their families on Saturdays, and this on top of a rise in circulation! She'd been almost giddy when Patrick walked in the door whistling tonight—*whistling*, for heaven's sake, a rarity in itself during a depression that had all but sucked the good humor from her husband. The moment he'd sauntered into the kitchen with that handsome grin, she'd known it was confirmation from God.

Tonight was the night.

She prepared a favorite meal—chicken and dumplings, not too fancy that he'd notice, but definitely high on the list of meals he loved, and then threw caution to the wind with coconut cream pie, a dessert that always put a smile on his face. And praise be to God, Gabe's report card had actually shown improvement with a hint of praise from Sister Mary Veronica herself! Hope flickered in Marcy's chest as a tremulous sigh drifted forth. Could it get any better than this?

"Yes, Lord," she said with another nervous glide over her teeth, "a win at chess would be lovely, and Patrick's signature on the dotted line even better."

Slipping the papers in the magazine, she absently toyed with the strap of her satin gown, the one she seldom wore because it was Patrick's favorite. Since his heart incident months ago, she'd discouraged romantic pursuits, worried sick it would trigger another attack. But it had only triggered his temper instead, resulting in a row that had scared her half to death.

"Blast it, Marcy, I'm a man, not an invalid, and I need to make love to my wife."

"Patrick, please, you were pale as death just last week, and Dr. Williamson said—"

"The deuce with Williamson," he'd shouted, grasping her shoulders to give her a sound shake. "I will not allow fear to ruin my life, Marceline, do you hear?"

"No, but you'll allow your death to ruin mine," she said, body trembling.

A nerve had pulsed in his cheek as he'd stared long and hard, finally cupping her face in his hands. He'd leaned in to gently brush his lips against hers, his touch tender. "Loving you won't kill me, Marcy," he'd whispered with grief in his eyes, "but not loving you will."

So she'd given in, finally letting go of her fear. She learned to trust God to keep her husband safe—now she'd trust him again to change Patrick's mind. Inhaling deeply, she adjusted her lace nightgown, praying it would coax him in more ways than one. The scent of his favorite perfume rose from the cleft of her breasts, reminding her how uncomfortable she was playing the vamp. But Gabe was too important and Marcy too desperate. Age and heart aside, Patrick O'Connor was still an amorous man and never more so than when she took the lead.

She heard his whistle long before he entered the room, and her stomach looped, pulse skittering as she quickly turned on her side, idly flipping pages of the magazine that harbored her plan.

"You know, darlin', it's downright criminal to humiliate one's own flesh and blood so thoroughly," he said as he strolled into the room, the flash of white teeth a stark contrast to the dark shadow of his bristled jaw, "but I suspect it's even worse to feel good about it." He glanced up, fingers paused on the third button of his shirt as his gaze traveled her body. With a wayward smile that suggested trouble, he ambled over to sit on the bed, leaning in to skim his lips against hers. The silver at his temples gleamed like the tease in his eyes. "So you decided to wait up and read, did you?" His thumb played with the strap of her gown while his lips played with the lobe of her ear. "Tell me, Marceline, can you read my mind right now?"

Her chuckle wavered when he eased her back on the pillow with a kiss. "I believe I could be blindfolded and still read your mind, Patrick O'Connor," she said, studying the man who held her heart in the palm of his hand. She threaded her fingers through the salt-and-pepper curls at the back of his head and delivered an off-center smile. "It's not difficult, you know."

He pressed a quick kiss to her nose and pushed up with a grunt. "Not when you're wearing a gown like that, darlin'," he said with a grin. "Let me get dressed for bed, and you and I can 'read' together." He stripped off his shirt and tossed it on the hamper on his way to the closet, snatching his pajamas off the back of the door. "I was certainly relieved to see Gabe's grades on the upswing," he said casually, removing his trousers to hang them over the press. "Sweet heavens, we might actually be making some progress with the girl."

Marcy's heart leapt. "Oh, we are, Patrick, I just know it!" She slipped under the covers, anxious to push the discussion in the right direction. "She's been good as gold lately."

"And just as expensive," Patrick reminded with a slant of a smile. "I'm still paying for Victor Kincaid's jaw, if you recall."

"But at least she didn't break any teeth—"

"Hold that thought, Marceline, while I go brush my own," he called on his way to the bathroom, and Marcy sucked in more air that did little to quell the jitters in her stomach.

Nerves twitching, she heard the water running in the bathroom while she stared at the door, finally opting for some last-minute prayer. "Please, Lord," she whispered, thinking of the little girl down the hall, "soften his heart to say ye—" The prayer died in her throat when Patrick appeared in the door with neckties in hand and a tic in his jaw.

"I believe we were discussing expense," he said, striding forward to toss three of his best neckties onto the bed. Marcy's heart sank along with the ties. Each was knotted several times, apparently makeshift headbands for Indians at war, with war paint that looked suspiciously like lipstick and feathers stabbed through. "I found these stuffed behind the hamper."

"Patrick, she's just a child . . . ," she said weakly.

He snatched the Indian gear back up and shook it in her face. "No, Marcy, she's not just a child, she's a wild Indian. Three of my most expensive ties—ruined just like my good mood. I swear the child is in league with the devil, out to destroy my sanity." Hurling the ties toward the hamper, he jerked the covers aside and plopped down, jostling the bed along with her nerves.

"Patrick, she just needs to be loved."

"She needs more than love, she needs a muzzle and a chain, and if she were mine—"

His words stilled when she touched her hand to his mouth. "That's just it, my love," she whispered, her eyes pleading with his. "She can be. And, Patrick, she should be . . ."

His lips parted in shock. "Marcy, no—"

"Patrick, she needs us, and we need her—"

He jerked his pillow and punched it several times, then repositioned it with a hard clamp of his jaw. "She has us, darlin'—for pity's sake, we've opened our home to her."

"But not our hearts, Patrick. She needs to be family."

"She *is* family! We've given the girl a home, an education, and a family that genuinely loves her. What else could she possibly need?"

Wetness stung Marcy's eyes. "A name," she whispered. "A name that tells the world she's neither an outcast nor an orphan taken in out of pity. A family she can call her own, with a mother and a father, siblings who may not be blood but are joined all the same . . . by a name."

Patrick was shaking his head before she even finished. "Adoption?" He issued a harsh grunt that indicated his opinion of the idea. "Sweet saints, Marcy, we're way too old for that."

She clutched him tightly, and a tear slithered into the crease of his neck. "No, Patrick, we're not. We're young and vital and just what Gabe needs. She adores you and you her . . ."

"I love the girl, Marcy, I do . . . but *adoption*?" He pulled away to gouge shaky fingers through unruly hair. "For the love of sanity, woman, she's a terror at ten. Can you imagine what the teenage years might bring? I'm not sure either of us can survive."

Marcy kissed his cheek, the scruff of his beard rough against her lips. "We'll survive, my love, and our hearts will grow in the process. And then, every day thereafter—you mark my words—we will get down on our knees and thank God we opened our hearts to one of our own."

He sat up, his jaw tight with tension and his eyes piercing hers with a sobriety that gave her pause. His voice was gruff. "I really don't have much say in this, do I, Marceline?"

She blinked, thinking how important this was to her. And then in the depth of his gray eyes, she saw the intensity of his love shadowed by the barest hint of resignation, reminding her once again just how important *he* was to her. She leaned to press her lips to his, her words warm and soft against his mouth. "Oh, you have say, Patrick," she said quietly, "because my love for you guides every decision I make. And you have my word—if you say no, it will not happen."

With a firm hand, he lifted her chin, allowing his thumb to graze the curve of her mouth. "You're wrong, Marceline, I have no say whatsoever. Because if I say no, I break your heart . . . and mine in the process. I'm not ready for this, Marcy, not by a long shot . . ." He flopped back on the pillow with a heavy sigh. "But I suppose it wouldn't hurt to consider it."

"Oh, Patrick!" Tears stung her eyes, and she flung herself into his arms. She besieged him with kisses that prompted a low moan from his throat. She pulled away to swipe a tear from her eye. "I swear, Patrick, I never believed it possible, but I love you more every day."

His husky laughter rumbled in the dark. "Only because I get older every day, too tired to do naught but give you your way." He kissed the tip of her nose. "I'll look into it next week."

No! In a violent beat of her heart, she retrieved the papers from the magazine on the nightstand along with a pen, breathless when she handed them over. "No need, darling—the papers are filled out and awaiting your signature." Her tongue skated her teeth. "Due tomorrow."

He sat up in apparent shock, eyeing the papers with a slack of his jaw. His lips compressed in a hard line that mottled his chin, and instantly, she knew she was in trouble. Her euphoria popped like one of Gabe's four-inch Dubble Bubbles, stifling her air with a sticky goo. Sweat glazed her body at his tone, deadly low. "If I say no, it won't happen, eh?"

Her stomach cramped. "Patrick, I—"

He stood, eyes smoldering as he snatched his pillow from the bed. "Spare me, Marceline," he said, his tone clipped and cold. "There's nothing you can say or do to convince me you haven't played me for the fool—not fix a fancy dinner, make my favorite dessert, or cozy up to me in bed." He cocked his head, lips curled in a harsh smile. "And if I have my guesses right, I suspect the game I won so handily tonight was your doing also."

Guilt heated her face. "Patrick, please . . ." She rose to follow.

He thrust a hand out, as if to ward her off, the hard muscles of his arm as defined as the anger in his face. "No! Not this time, Marcy—not tears nor pie nor easy wins can save you tonight. Not when you try to manipulate me and then enlist my own son in the effort. After all these years, I thought we'd forged a relationship on trust and communication, not cold, calculated scheming to force my hand regarding decisions you've already made on your own." He wedged the pillow under his arm. "I now see where Charity gets her manipulative skills."

He strode to the door, and her heart climbed in her throat. "Patrick, please—talk to me!" But his posture was as hard as the night Sam O'Rourke had come to town years back, upending their happy home. She'd seen the same cold anger that she saw now, and shame slithered in to join forces with fear, icing her skin. She'd promised then never to keep the truth from him again, never lie, never deceive. Never withhold information he had a right to know in order to manipulate her own way, and never put her desires before the integrity of their marriage. She swallowed hard. Before the integrity of the man before her, whose pride she'd wounded *again*.

She ran to his side, her remorse as real as the tears on her cheeks. "Patrick, I'm sorry! Adopting Gabe means the world to me, it's true, but not as much as our marriage. I was wrong for not discussing this with you, wrong for trying to force your hand, and I'm sorry." She placed trembling fingers to his arm, eyes pleading with his. "Please forgive me and come back to bed."

A nerve flickered in his cheek as he stared, his anger appearing to ebb despite the resolve she saw etched in his face. "Empty apologies won't win my favor this time, Marcy, but I appreciate the fact you can admit you were wrong." He gripped her chin, the softening of his tone an indication they were on the mend. "I love you, Marcy, you know that. And because of that love, I was willing to forego my reservations regarding Gabe. You didn't need to calculate or manipulate to get your own way. My love should have been enough." His fingers slid from her chin to the side of her face, cupping her head at the back of the neck, his strength gentle but firm. "And your love for me should be enough as well—to trust me as the head of this family regarding decisions affecting my life as well as yours . . . and this family's."

A sigh wavered from her lips as she nodded. "You're right, Patrick, and I apologize again for not discussing this with you sooner. And for shamelessly resorting to both feminine and culinary wiles to force my own way." She drew in a deep breath. "I truly mean it, that if you say no to this adoption, then the decision is done."

He studied her through wary eyes that held a hint of regret. "That said, darlin', your apology may have diffused my anger, but your actions haven't exactly shored up my trust. I can't help but suspect that although you say I have the deciding vote, those may be mere words from someone who still expects to get her own way." He sighed and pulled her into his arms. "Which means, darlin', that although I may be inclined to sign those papers in the future . . . ," his hold stiffened, as if to brace himself for her volatile reaction, "I'm not inclined to do so tonight."

Her eyelids wavered closed, all hope for Gabe to be an O'Connor by Christmas as out of reach as her husband's trust. But not forever, she reminded herself, grateful that Patrick had left the door open . . . Exhaling her resignation, she sank against his chest, putting her dream for Gabe into the hands of God—a God who had ordained her husband as the head of this family.

She drew in a cleansing breath and released it again, along with her right to be angry. "I understand, Patrick, and as I said before, this decision is done." Pulling away, she retrieved the adoption papers and returned to his side, standing before him with shaky resolve. "And to prove your trust is more important than any desire I might have to adopt Gabe *and* that I mean what I say, let's put this to rest right now." With a firm set of her jaw that belied the sting in her eyes, she ripped the papers in two and then again before crumpling them in a ball. Marching over to the waste can, she tossed them inside before squaring her shoulders. "Now, can we go to bed, please?" she said with a catch in her throat. "I'd very much like for you to hold me."

He stared, mouth ajar. "I don't believe it," he whispered.

Marcy staved off the inclination to bristle with a jut of her chin. "What? You think I'm so inflexible that I can't accept when God tells me no?"

A boyish grin eased across his face as he slowly moved to where she stood with her hands on her hips. He latched a sturdy arm to her waist and pulled her close, teasing her senses with a whiff of musk soap. "So I'm God, now, am I?" he said, trailing her jaw with kisses.

She slapped at his chest, dodging his lips when they dove for her neck. "Hardly, Patrick O'Connor. God is a God of mercy, not some Irish tyrant who bullies his wife."

He chuckled as he held her at bay, one brow angled high. "*Bullies* his wife? You mean the same wife who 'bullies' her husband through blatant manipulation?"

Her smile slanted as she tilted her head. "If it was 'blatant,' you stubborn Irishman, you would have seen through it with the pie. I despise coconut cream, and you know it."

His laughter was warm against her ear when he swallowed her up in his arms. "Despise my pie, yes, but you love me, so I just assumed there were no strings attached, Marceline." He kissed her neck and shocked her when he swooped her up in his arms.

Her breath caught. "For heaven's sake, Patrick, what are you doing?"

He carried her to the bed. "Just following orders, Marceline. You wanted to go to bed and you wanted me to hold you. Your wish is my command."

The edge of her lip crooked. "If my wish was your command, Patrick, I'd have signed papers tucked in my drawer right now." She sighed and leaned against his chest, allowing his arm to reel her in close. Moisture suddenly misted her eyes. "Do you realize the last time you carried me like this was over the threshold of this house over thirty years ago?"

His voice was tender and husky with emotion. "Lightest burden I've ever had."

She sat up, the makings of a pout on her lips. "Oh, so now I'm a burden, am I?"

The grin on his lips softened into a smile. "Loving you has never been a burden, Marcy, even on our worst day." His smile veered off center. "Perhaps 'challenge' is a better word."

She started to swat him, but he disarmed her with a chuckle and a firm hold, tugging her back before shifting her to face him again as they lay side by side. With a tender stroke of her jaw, he leaned to kiss her, his touch almost reverent. "I can't imagine my life without you, Marcy—ever. You have brought me more joy than I ever dreamed possible, more joy than I ever deserved."

"Except for tonight," she whispered, her heart swelling at the look of love in his eyes.

"Especially tonight," he said softly, brushing his lips against hers with a kiss that quickened her pulse. He gave her a tight squeeze and then bounded from bed. "I need water. Do you want anything while I'm up—water, another fan . . . new husband?"

She sighed, head propped on her elbow. "Water would be nice, thank you, but hurry up, please. I believe you're cutting into my holding time."

He disappeared down the hall and she lay back, staring at the ceiling with a melancholy smile. "You say 'all things work together for good to them that love God,' so I'm going to hold you to that. Because if ever there was a demonstration of my love for you and Patrick, Lord, this is it." She closed her eyes and waited, finally hearing Patrick's bare feet padding down the hall. He closed the door, then returned to the bed to deliver the water.

She sat up. "Thank you," she said, brows knit in a frown when he turned on the light. She blinked, hand to her eyes. "What are you doing?"

Ignoring her, he proceeded to the wastebasket, where he fished out the crumpled papers.

"Patrick, what on earth are you doing?" she repeated, the crack in her voice conveying her shock. She blinked and pushed the hair from her eyes when he sat on the bed and unraveled the papers, smoothing them out. Her breath hitched at the tape he held in his hands. "W-what are you d-doing?" she whispered, barely able to breathe.

He glanced up, the look of love in his eyes bringing her to tears. "You tore it up to win my trust; I'm patching it to win yours." He caressed her cheek with his fingers, his voice rough with emotion. "Because God knows, Marceline, when I see you give up the desire of your heart to honor me, I will move heaven and earth to give it back."

Oh, God, just like you . . .

She stared in disbelief as he repaired the papers with awkward strips of tape and then reached behind him for the pen on the nightstand. Her heart caught in her throat when he signed and handed them back, lips cocked. "Your signature has already been applied, I believe?"

She blinked, feeling as if this were a dream, and then with a broken sob, she lunged into his arms, knocking him flat on the edge of the bed. "Oh, Patrick, I have never loved you more!" She smothered his neck with kisses, now salty from her tears, then squeezed him as if she would never let go. "I just knew it! I knew you would never disappoint me, because you, my love, are man with a voracious need to give to those he loves."

"Mmm . . ." Nestling his lips in the crook of her neck, he drew her body flush with his. "Voracious appetite, indeed." He pulled back to study her with a twist of his lips. "Even so, I think you're a little too sure of yourself, woman."

She sat up, clutching the rumpled document to her chest

with another sweet sting of tears. "Oh yes, my love, I am—quite sure I'm one of the luckiest women alive."

He plucked the papers from her hand and placed them on the nightstand with a perilous smile. Tugging her close, he smothered her throat with soft, lingering kisses. "And I'm quite sure that tonight, at least, I'll be one of the luckiest men alive." He prodded her back on the pillow, voice husky with intent as he nuzzled her mouth. "Make love to me, Marceline," he whispered, "before Gabe makes me too old to enjoy it."

Marcy cupped his jaw with eyes full of love. "Only if you admit Gabe keeps us young."

His eyes drifted closed as he bent to suckle the soft flesh of her ear. "Mmm . . . maybe a wee bit, darlin'," he whispered. His lips trailed the curve of her jaw, hovering before he slid his mouth firmly against hers. "But you? In my bed like this?" He feathered a finger along the lacy strap of her gown. "Makes me feel all of twenty again . . ."

14

*S*he was hopelessly in love and knew it. Annie relinquished a contented sigh, sneaking a peek at the man of her dreams as he regaled her with a comical tale of Joe's deathly fear of carousels after retching on a merry-go-round with his three-year-old niece. Despite the chilly autumn night, she felt warm and gooey inside, totally relaxed against the front seat of Steven's father's car as they drove home from dinner and the movies. She studied his handsome profile, the clean line of his jaw, and another wispy sigh floated out. *Oh, Lord, if only he felt the same . . .*

It certainly seemed as if he did, at least given the last four weeks, which had been the best of her life. Phone calls during the week and dates on the weekend had not only given her glimpses into a deep and honorable man who gave his all to every task—at work, in his family, and with her—but also hints of the shy and endearing little boy who was curious about life and bent on conquering it. From moonlight strolls on Revere Beach to picnics in the park to fishing with Glory and Gabe, Steven possessed both a quiet strength and a mischievous humor, a man who was at home wrestling with her sister on the floor or discussing politics with her aunt. Other than their date last week when he'd kissed her in the car rather than walking her to the door, he'd been the perfect gentleman and most definitely a man who could turn her insides to mush with the crook of his smile. She tugged on her lip. *Or too many heated kisses in a car?*

He turned and gave her an easy smile, and it may as well have been a heat wave in July. Swallowing hard, she responded with a shy one of her own, her pulse skipping when he reached for her hand. "Great movie tonight, wasn't it, *Trouble in Paradise?*"

"Mmmm . . . I love romantic comedies, but then I love romance in any form," she teased. "As long as I'm with you."

He squeezed her hand. "Good to hear," he said with a grin, tingling her skin when he slowly grazed her palm with the pad of his thumb. "I sure don't want any trouble in our paradise, Annie, because things are too good the way they are."

"I agree," she whispered, casually slipping her hand from his when the tingle from his touch triggered a warm shiver. She deflected with a reach into her purse to pull out some gum. "Juicy Fruit?" she asked, unwrapping a piece and offering it to him.

"Thanks." He took it and popped it into his mouth. "You cold?" he asked, extending an arm as an invitation to snuggle close."

"No, not really."

"Yes you are—I just saw you shiver." He patted the seat, then tugged her over. His muscular arm looped over her shoulders and butted her close. "Now . . . isn't this better?" he asked, fingers gently skimming her throat.

Annie gulped. *Um . . . yes and no . . .*

He stopped at a red light, stealing her breath when he casually slid her hair aside to kiss her neck. "You drive me crazy, Annie," he whispered.

The light turned green, and she started breathing again . . . until his fingers traced to the hollow of her throat in gentle exploration. She closed her eyes, feeling her body beginning to hum. "We should stop . . . ," she whispered, totally unaware she'd spoken aloud.

"Mmm?" His voice sounded husky and dazed while his hand roved up to graze the lobe of her ear. "You say something?" he asked, maneuvering the corner with one hand before easing the car to the curb in front of her house.

Relief whooshed from her lungs when he downshifted and turned the engine off, and before he could touch her again, she scooted over and reached for her purse. She gave him a feeble smile, fingers white on the knob. "This w-was a w-wonderful evening, Steven, thank you so much," she said, words tumbling over each other as she waited for him to open his door.

Only he didn't. "Don't go yet, please," he whispered, curling an arm to her waist with a smoky look in his eyes. "I need to tell you something."

"Steven, it's late, and I should go in . . ."

He glanced at his watch. "It's only eleven, and your curfew is midnight, remember?"

A lump shifted in her throat.

He turned her to face him, fanning her hair away from her face while his thumb grazed the edge of her jaw. "Annie, please, I'm crazy about you and I would never hurt you," he said softly, bending to brush her lips with his own.

Her eyes fluttered closed while her breathing quickened, and the caress of his mouth, the scent of his aftershave, weakened her resolve.

"I think I may be falling in love with you," he said quietly. Taking her hand, he slowly lifted it to his mouth and kissed her palm, his gaze locking with hers. "I have something I want to give you, to let you know how special you are to me." He reached into his pocket and placed a delicate silver chain in her palm with a ring attached. "It's only my college ring, Annie, but I want you to have something of mine now to show my intent. And then someday, if things work out, I hope to give you the real thing."

"Oh, Steven!" Her heart soared in her chest. "Do you mean it?"

He grinned. "What do you think?" he teased, gently nuzzling her lips before easing her back to deepen the kiss.

Oh, Faith, he loves me! As if they had a mind of their own, Annie's arms slipped around Steven's neck, and she returned his kiss while a heady warmth invaded her body.

"You are so beautiful," he whispered, his voice almost hoarse as his hands swept the length of her hips, skimming her thigh and quivering her stomach.

"A good night kiss is fine, but when the flutters and tingles escalate, nip it in the bud . . ."

Faith's words broke through the haze and she gently shoved him back, her breathing as labored as his. "Steven, I should go," she said, "before we get carried away."

He smoothed disheveled curls from her eyes, cradling her face with his palm. "I'm in love with you, Annie," he whispered, a tinge of hurt in his eyes. "Doesn't that mean anything? I've been on my best behavior for months now, so please—can't I just hold you awhile?"

She shook her head. "I don't think we should. The more we kiss, the harder it is to stop."

"That's normal," he said, gaze tender. "When two people feel the way we do, it's natural to want to be close, natural to want to give of ourselves to each other. Because that's what love is." Grazing her jaw with his thumb, he slowly leaned in, mouth hovering over hers. "Let me love you, Annie," he whispered, skimming her lips, "just for a while . . ."

Real love denies self to give those we love God's best.

Faith's words drifted in her brain, causing her to shudder. "No, that's not what love is," she said quietly, nudging him away once again. "I can't allow myself to be intimate with you, Steven, and we would, because when you touch me, kiss me, even a little, I feel myself losing control, and I love you too much to risk that." She steeled her resolve, painfully aware she may well lose him. "And if you truly loved me," she said, her voice a pained whisper, "you'd honor my wishes for a kiss at the door instead of pushing for more."

He blinked, the barb of her words obviously triggering his temper. "And if you really loved me, you'd trust me with *more* than a kiss at the door." A nerve flickered in his angular jaw. "Which is why I didn't want to get involved with someone as young as you in the first place."

She stared, jaw slack before her ire flared. "You mean someone as young and 'innocent,' as I recall, which certainly wouldn't be the case for long if you had your way."

She may as well have slapped him, given the sting of heat in his face—her words slammed against him with all the force of his guilty past. She didn't trust him, and with good reason, but the reality of her statement stripped away any self-respect he'd earned in the last three months. He'd worked hard to meet her demands, deny himself any desire he'd felt to kiss her, hold her, touch her, and for what? So she could fling it in his face once again that he couldn't be trusted, that he would use her like he'd used her sister. The injustice of it was like a blow to the chest, joining forces with the fear in his gut that said she was right.

His anger swelled, all hurt calcifying into wounded pride. "Yeah, well, maybe I need a woman instead of a little girl who can't trust herself any more than she can trust me."

He flinched when she slapped him so hard, it echoed in his ears. "How dare you?" she whispered, wet anger sparking in her eyes. "When you were the very one telling me how special and innocent I was and 'not to throw it all away.'" She grappled with the door, hands trembling as she bolted from the car. She peered in, tears streaming down her face. "But it's okay to 'throw it all away' with you, is that it, Steven? Well, maybe you do need a woman who'll give in to your every whim, because I won't no matter how much you *claim* you love me." With a shaky heave, she threw the ring on the seat, chin angled high. "And when you find her, be sure to give her this to show her just how 'special' she is, because that's the only way she's going to know."

"Annie, wait—"

The door slammed in his face, heels clicking as she ran up the steps and disappeared into the house before he could even get out of the car. He stared, body numb and heart thudding, stunned at the turn of events. One minute he's professing his love, and the next, she's slapping him silly. He touched his hand to the ignition, then slumped back in the seat, eyes glazed. *What just happened?*

But he already knew. The same thing that happened dozens of times before when he'd pushed, prodded, and coaxed his own way with Maggie and others. Only this was the one woman who'd finally pushed back. He rubbed his jaw where she'd slugged him, fully aware he'd deserved it. Deep down he'd known exactly what he was doing, what he was hoping for, where he was leading her. No, he'd never intended to go as far as he had with Maggie, but he certainly felt entitled to more than a kiss at the door.

Why?

"Because I love her," he hissed.

"If you really care about Annie like you say you do, then why on earth would you risk cutting her off from God's blessings to gratify your own desires?"

His brother's words sucked the wind from his anger, distilling the truth in his mind. "Because I want her," he finally whispered, painfully aware that although he was falling in love with Annie Kennedy, at the moment, his lust was far greater. Just like it had been with Maggie, overpowering his love until there was nothing left but the shame.

Then honor her, the thought came.

And therein was the rub, because he wasn't sure he could. All of his life, he'd worked hard to win people's trust—with his parents, at school, at work—giving him a false sense of security that he was a man to be trusted. But Maggie had changed all that when he'd discovered just how weak he really was, unable to trust himself when it came to her love.

The same weakness he felt now, falling for Annie.

Could he honor her?

Exhaling heavily, he turned the ignition and shifted into gear, knowing at the moment there was only one way he could. He'd keep her safe, far away from a man she couldn't trust, at least for a while. Until he could trust himself.

If that was even possible.

~~~~~

This isn't the way it's supposed to be.

Annie shivered in her bed while she stared at the ceiling, eyes raw and pillow wet, the light of the full moon a hazy blur as it spilled into a bedroom where sleep was nowhere in sight.

Just like Steven O'Connor.

She turned on her side and clutched the pillow to her chest while she curled in a ball. She hadn't heard from him since their last date four weeks ago, and she was beginning to lose hope.

"Give him time," Faith had said, giving her hand a squeeze when they met at Bookends with the children two weeks ago. "He just needs time to cool down."

She sniffed. "Any more 'cooling down,' and the relationship will be stone cold," Annie muttered, arms folded across her chest.

"Trust me, he's been a real grouch lately," Faith assured her, "which means he misses you as much as you miss him."

"Then why hasn't he called?" she'd asked, brows sloped in concern.

"Because men have more pride than common sense, sweetie." Charity patted her arm, sympathy edging her tone. "Don't they teach you anything at Radcliffe?"

Faith laughed, looping an arm to Annie's waist while Katie chuckled and Lizzie offered a shy grin. "Charity's right, you know. Steven needs to stew a little before he comes to his senses."

"Could be awhile," Katie said with dry smile. "On those

rare occasions when Steven pestered me instead of the other way around, it'd take him forever to apologize, even when Mother threatened to pitch his Mysto Magic set." Her lips sloped to the side. "And don't forget the head-butting he did with Father during college."

"He'll be back," Faith had said, tone adamant.

"Maybe not," Annie whispered, lying in the gloom of her room. She closed her eyes while the clock ticked away the minutes of another restless night. She thought of Maggie and more tears slithered her cheeks, grateful she'd put off telling her about Steven. Now her sister need never know the man who had broken her heart . . . had also broken Annie's.

"Annie—are you crying?"

Shoving tears from her eyes, Annie sat up in bed, squinting in the dark to see Glory at the door. "Just a little," she whispered. She sniffed to clear the nasal tone from her throat and glanced at the clock, which registered after midnight. "Honey, why are you still up?"

Her little sister padded in with her doll dragging behind and crawled up on the bed, slipping under the covers. "I woke up," she whispered, a tremor in her tone. "I had a dream."

"A nightmare?" Annie asked, her worries about Steven suddenly forgotten as she cuddled Glory close, stroking rumpled blonde curls.

The little girl nodded. "I dreamt about Steven."

Annie blinked. *Yep, that'd be a nightmare, all right, one I have every night.*

A frail sigh shuddered through her little sister's body. "I miss him, Annie."

Annie sucked in a deep breath. "Me too, sweetie."

"Doesn't he like us anymore?"

Annie swallowed hard. "Sure he does, honey, but sometimes people have to leave for a little while before we get to see them again." *If we see them again.*

"Like Maggie?" Glory asked, her childlike question plucking at Annie's heart.

Annie's smile was melancholy. "Yes, honey, a lot like Maggie, as a matter of fact."

"Does that mean that we won't see Steven till Thanksgiving or Christmas, like Maggie?" Glory lay back on the pillow, shimmying beneath the covers to fold tiny hands on her chest.

Annie paused, remembering Maggie's visit at Easter when she mentioned she wouldn't be back until Christmas. "Maybe . . . but it will be fun to see our big sister again, won't it?" she asked, anxious to divert Glory's attention from Steven. "Maybe she'll stay longer than a month this time, and we can do all the fun things we always do."

Glory hopped up with a squeal. "You mean like shopping at Filene's and muffins at Jordan Marsh?"

Annie tapped her nose. "And slumber parties with fancy negligees, playing dress-up and beauty parlor."

Glory launched into Annie's arms, knocking her back on the bed. "Oh boy, I love Maggie being a movie star," Glory said in a rush, "even though we don't get to see her too much."

"Me too." Annie tucked Glory close, lips tipping into a smile at Glory's pride in her older sister. Maggie'd landed a few bit parts and was engaged to a director, but the status of movie star had yet to materialize. "How 'bout we snuggle in and dream of Maggie coming home to play?"

"I say YES," Glory shouted and tunneled under the covers to nestle in, the warmth of her little body a sweet comfort. Breathing in the fresh scent of talcum powder from her sister's bath, Annie closed her eyes, ready to drift off to sleep.

"Annie?"

She jolted, Glory's voice pulling her back from near slumber. "Mmm?"

"Can we say a prayer for Steven? So he remembers we love him and comes back soon?"

Moisture welled beneath Annie's closed lids. "Yes, sweetheart, we can, and I think that's a wonderful idea. Do you want to pray or should I?"

"You," Glory said with a big yawn.

"Okay." Annie drew in a deep breath, her thoughts returning to their usual focus of late. "Dear Lord, Glory and I miss Steven a lot and we were wondering if you would let him know he misses us too. I don't know if he's the right man, Lord, but if he is, will you please bring him back to me?"

"To us," Glory insisted, her voice drowsy with sleep."

Annie's lips tilted. "To us," she corrected, kissing her sister's head. "And if it's all the same to you, Lord . . . ," she closed her eyes, sleep mere seconds away, "the sooner the better."

~~~~~

The mantel clock chimed nine, and Patrick paused in his game of chess—if that's what you'd call it given Steven's comatose state—to peer at Gabe reading funny papers on the couch.

"Time for bed, sweetheart." Marcy set her knitting aside and rose from her chair, shooting her foster daughter a peaceful smile.

Sprawled on her tummy in a most unladylike pose, Gabe flapped skinny legs in the air while a wad of Dubble Bubble rolled in her mouth, rivaling a bad case of the mumps. Her legs ceased flailing while freckles scrunched in a scowl. Brown eyes suddenly connected with his, and in a bob of her throat, the scowl melted into a shaky smile that forced Patrick to bite back a grin.

"Yes, ma'am," she said, lumbering up from the couch with a heavy sigh. She started to toss the newspaper on the floor and stopped, eyes meeting Patrick's once again. Lips flat, she carefully refolded and placed it on the table before heading over to give him a kiss, her manner as stiff as her smile. "Good night, Mr. O'Connor," she said, obviously not comfortable yet with Marcy's request to show appreciation to her new father-to-be.

Steven broke from his stupor long enough to slip Gabe one of the first smiles Patrick'd seen on his face in a month. "Hey, squirt, you can practice calling him 'Pop' now, you know."

310

Gabe's eyes flicked to Patrick's with a glimmer of something soft he'd never seen, and the sensation tightened his throat. "Okay. G'night . . . Pop," she whispered. She turned away, and then with a sudden brim of tears, she wheeled around to fling scrawny arms around his neck.

For a sliver of a second, he was paralyzed to the chair, and then in a sharp catch of his breath, he swallowed her up in his arms with such ferocity, moisture welled in his eyes. "Good night, Gabriella Dawn," he whispered.

She clung to him for several seconds before awkwardly pulling away, gaze on the floor and hands creeping into her pockets. "Thanks again, Mr. O'Connor . . . ," she paused while a giant knot shifted in her throat, "I mean . . . 'Pop' . . . for giving me a chance to be part of your family."

Emotion nearly sealed his throat. Tucking a finger to her chin, he captured her gaze. "You've always been a part of this family, Gabe. Now you'll just have the name to go along with it." He tickled her jaw in a tease. "It's a good name, darlin'—don't abuse it, you hear?"

She grinned. "No, sir." With a peck on his cheek, she ran to give Marcy a hug at the door.

A sob broke from Marcy's lips along with a giggle, and in that single, solitary moment when her watery gaze met his, Patrick felt as if he might break down and cry himself. A rush of joy rose up that nearly stole his breath and flooded his eyes, so overcome with gratitude was he for this woman and the God who'd given her. "I love you, Marceline," he whispered, and more tears sprang to her eyes as she nodded, apparently too overcome to speak.

Gabe glanced up at Marcy before shooting a crooked grin over her shoulder. "You were right, Mrs. O'Connor—oops, I mean, Mother," she said with an imp of a wink, "he's a *lot* nicer when he wins."

His lips zagged in a droll smile. "You should see when I have a daughter who behaves."

"Come on, darling," Marcy said with a soggy grin, "I'll

311

teach you all you need to know to stay on his good side." She blew him a kiss. "Good night, Steven. Patrick, don't be long."

"I wouldn't worry, Mother," Steven said, "he's about to bury me here, so he'll be up soon. G'night, squirt. Don't forget I'm taking you to Robinson's tomorrow night if you're good."

"Whoopie!" Gabe did a little hop in the air. "Annie and Glory too?"

"Nope."

At Steven's clipped tone, Marcy shot Patrick a pleading look before heading upstairs.

He sighed, ready to end the game but hesitant to humiliate someone already so low. Clearing his throat, he focused on the board. "So, how long is this going to continue?"

"Not much longer," Steven said, "given your affinity for a clean and quick kill."

Patrick glanced up, his tone as dry as Steven's. "Not the game, son, we both know where that's headed. I mean this funk you're in that makes Mitch look like the Good Humor man."

A scowl creased Steven's face as he made a move that had Patrick questioning his intelligence along with his mood. "I'm fine, Pop, just under the gun at work, that's all."

"Yes, well, that happens when one volunteers for every weekend detail." Patrick squinted at the board, tempted to throw Steven a bone with a poor move. "Contrary to the poor example I've given you at the *Herald*, Steven, there is more fulfillment in life than a job well done."

Steven eased his pawn forward in an obvious attempt to apply pressure to Patrick's queen. He exhaled a burdensome sigh and sat back, arms folded. "Yeah, well, that must have been the lesson I missed, Pop, while we were both working Saturdays the last seven months."

"Touché," Patrick said, eyes on the board. He contemplated a pity play, using his queen as expected rather than setting Steven up for the fall with his king's bishop instead.

Steven pinched the bridge of his nose, expending another

weary sigh. "Look, Pop, I'm sorry, but I know where you're headed and I don't want to talk about it, okay? Let's just chalk my work mode and mood off to me being a chip off the old block, all right?"

Patrick peered up, his pity popping faster than one of Gabe's eight-inch Dubble Bubbles. With a press of his mouth, he moved his king's bishop four spaces. "Well, I'll give you that. When Sean was young, I thought I was home free with a compliant boy, grateful he'd gotten Marcy's genes instead of mine." He leaned in, elbows on the table. "Then you came along, Steven, and for all your compliance as a youngster, I knew you were my comeuppance."

"What's that supposed to mean?" Steven asked, tone gruff as he studied the board. He moved his pawn forward and looked up.

Patrick's lips leveled. "It means you're a chip off the old block in more ways than you think, which I admit always worried me a wee bit. I never cottoned to the idea of you following in my footsteps as a young man, but the die was cast, I suppose, given the mistakes I made."

The blue of Steven's eyes deepened as he assessed Patrick with a cautious gaze. "Mistakes? I doubt that, Pop, given your life now. Great marriage, a close family, a job you love." Steven shook his head, tunneling through the neatly trimmed hair at the back of his head. "Nope, you got it all, so whatever mistakes you made, they obviously didn't hurt."

For the second time that evening, Patrick's chest expanded with gratitude as he reflected on Marcy and the change she'd made in his life for the better. He paused to consider his son's statement, fingers skimming the sides of his queen. "I'm afraid the credit goes to your mother, Steven, a woman who changed the course of my life." He drew in a deep breath and looked up, fingers resting on the board. "Not unlike your Annie."

Steven glanced up, a nerve twittering in his cheek. "She's not 'my Annie,' Pop, and I already told you, I don't want to talk about it."

Easing back in his chair, Patrick crossed his arms in a mirror pose of his son, noting for the first time how much Steven resembled him as a man. The blue eyes were definitely Marcy's—a deeper, stormier blue to be sure, serious and intent like his wife's when something was on her mind. But from there on, he was Patrick to a T at twenty-five—thick dark hair, angular jaw, and a stone-fierce countenance that hinted at a deep-hidden temper few ever saw.

Like now.

Patrick exhaled slowly, aware his son needed to hear what he had to say whether he wanted to or not. "Hard as it is to believe, Steven, I was a lot like you growing up—diligent, hardworking, focused on schoolwork . . . and determined to win my father's approval. You might say I was almost rigid, so intent was I on everything I set my hand to. Then my best friend, Sam, and I took a turn in high school, and life as we knew it changed, just like it did for you in college. The same passion I poured into everything before, I now channeled into having a good time." Patrick's smile thinned. "Exploring the wonders of women and alcohol, just like you."

Steven shook his head, a faint smile shadowing his lips. "Sean mentioned once you had a jaded past similar to Collin's, but I have to admit, Pop, I couldn't see it. You're such a straight arrow now, it's hard to believe you were ever like me."

"Yes, well, now you understand why I rode you so hard in college." Patrick scratched the back of his head, remembering with painful accuracy the times he and Steven came to blows. "My father did the same, I'm afraid, and it ruined our relationship just like it ruined yours and mine." Arms crossed, Patrick propped a fist to his mouth while he drifted into a blank stare. "Only I never got the chance to make amends like you, Steven, the chance to restore my father's trust and approval." He closed his eyes to ward off the moisture that threatened. "And I regret that, I really do. But I was just a young man when he died, and so I became a tortured soul, riddled with guilt and desperate to prove worth I didn't feel I had."

Steven rested his arms on the table, the tenderness of his mother's gaze evident in the slope of his brows. "I'm sorry, Pop. Not just about you losing your father, but that you didn't have the chance—" he paused, a faint heave rippling in his throat. "The chance to make it right, to earn his trust." He released a frail breath. "That must haunt you."

Patrick glanced up, sympathy softening his gaze. "Not as much as it haunts you."

A ridge puckered in Steven's brow. "What are you talking about, Pop? At least I have the chance to make it right with you, to try and restore your trust."

"Steven," Patrick said quietly, "my trust in you was restored the day you broke up with Maggie. I know what she meant to you, how much you cared about her, and yet you offered me the ultimate sacrifice—you surrendered your love for her to honor me." He reached out to grip his arm. "Hear me on this, son—there are few men I trust . . . and respect . . . more than you."

Steven stared, facial muscles sculpted tight as if he were desperate to maintain control.

Patrick expended a weary breath, eyes intent as he rested his forearms on the table. "You've spent the last three years beating yourself up, convinced you'd broken my trust, your mother's, and Maggie's. And, I suspect," he said quietly, "your own."

"But that's just it—I did!" Steven fisted the table, voice harsh. "I ruined your health and Maggie's life for my own selfish needs. What kind of man does that?"

"A man like me," Patrick said softly, tears glazing his eyes. He paused several moments, silently praying that the pain of his past might somehow free Steven from his. "I've never told another soul the burden I carried in my heart after my father died, except for your mother, of course." He closed his eyes then, reliving the pain of the day he'd fought with his father. The awful words spoken that could never be taken back, the blood on his father's face from an accidental fall when his eldest son had shoved him away in a defiant rage. He disclosed it all—to a son who was not only one of the few who would understand but to a man who needed to know that God can purge guilt from any man's soul. Guilt so raw and so deep, that even now, Patrick's stomach wrenched at the memory. At the finish of his sorry tale, his eyelids flickered open to look at his son, chest constricting as it had so long ago. His words were low and rough with emotion. "Two days later, my father died, Steven, from a heart attack the doctors said, but I'm convinced it was brought on by a broken heart caused by his only son who defied him at every turn."

"Oh, Pop . . ." Steven reached across the table, touching his father's arm while a knot shifted in his throat. "I'm so sorry."

"So am I." He patted his son's hand and leaned back, fingers limp over the arms of his chair. "But through it all, I learned a life lesson that changed the course of my life, Steven, and that is that obedience is a ticket to freedom while rebellion is a ticket to slavery. Not just rebellion toward one's parents, but rebellion against God." Patrick sighed, plowing a hand through his hair. "Trust me, I bore the guilt of that rebellion for a long time." His gaze fused with his son's. "But I no longer bear it today. Not guilt, not shame, and not a broken heart over what I did to my father. And I owe it all to your mother."

Steven cocked his head, brows in a wedge. "How'd she get you over it, Pop?"

Patrick drew in a careful breath, praying his son would receive the very lesson that had redeemed his life—and his soul—forever. He exhaled slowly. "By introducing me to her God."

Creases appeared at the bridge of Steven's nose as he leaned in, arms folded on the table. "But I thought you already believed in God, Pop, because you went to St. Mary's, right?"

"Yes, I believed in God," he said, nodding his head. "But I didn't *know* him, Steven, not like Marcy." A smile tilted as his mind drifted back to a wonderful memory in his life.

"She was something, I'll tell you, your mother—a woman who knew her mind and her God. To her, he wasn't just some invisible entity in the sky, he was real and alive and so much a part of who she was that she haunted me." His lips quirked. "*He* haunted me through her until I was so desperate to have her, I'd do anything—even give my life to God in a way I never knew I could till Marcy showed me how. Not only as my Savior, mind you, but as my best friend, my confidence, my strength in good times and bad." He exhaled softly, then cuffed the back of his neck with a sheepish smile. "And I have to tell you, Steven, something happened I never expected. Suddenly God was no longer a wooden crucifix over an altar, a name in the Bible that may or may not be real. He became my friend as well as my Savior, my hope as well as my God." He glanced up. "You remember the skit in the third grade where you played King David as a shepherd boy?"

Steven nodded, lips in a slant. "How could I forget? Sister Laurita made me memorize the Twenty-Third Psalm till I was blue in the face. 'The Lord is my shepherd; I shall not want. He maketh me to lie down in green pastures: he leadeth me beside the still waters. He restoreth my soul: he leadeth me in the paths of righteousness for his name's sake.'"

A chuckle slipped from Patrick's lips. "Yes, well, as King David so aptly put it, God made me lie down in green pastures with a marriage made in heaven, he led me beside still waters that brought peace to my mind . . . and he restored my soul." His gratitude drifted out on a sigh. "A soul badly battered and bruised, now restored by a merciful and loving God who sent his only Son to die for us, Steven—not only to 'restore our souls,' mind you, but our lives as well." Patrick smiled. "If he did it for King David and me, son, he can do it for you."

"I don't know, Pop," Steven said quietly. "Sean said the same thing, but it all sounds too good to be true, and even if it is, I have no idea how to get there from where I am."

Patrick chuckled. "It is too good to be true," he said quietly, his tone suddenly softening into serious. "And yet it is. As real and true as the marriage your mother and I share and those of your siblings." He leaned in then, the intensity in his gaze matching that of his tone. "Ask God to change you, Steven, to become as real to you as he is to your family."

Steven peered up, a glimmer of hope behind the glaze of moisture in his eyes. "Even if I do, Pop, how can I ever trust myself to do the right thing again? I have no faith in myself, no trust that I won't bungle my relationship with Annie like I did with Maggie."

"Well now, that's the beauty of it," Patrick said, lips pursed as he appraised the position of Steven's pawn. "You put your faith in him instead of yourself, because without him, we can't be trusted to do the right thing. But with him?" Patrick moved his queen to capture Steven's pawn with a gloat of a grin. "We can scale mountains. Checkmate."

Staring at the board, Steven shook his head, a slope to his smile. "Mountains, huh?"

Patrick rose and tugged on his vest, pushing his chair in with a crook of his lips. "Mountains, yes." His brows rose. "Chess with your father? Not so much." Stifling a yawn, he extended a hand to his son. "Good game, even though it was difficult to take advantage of my own flesh and blood in such a weakened state."

"No," Steven said with a husky laugh, " 'difficult' would be if you didn't win." He stood and gripped his father's hand. "Thanks, Pop, I'll give what you said some thought."

"I hope you give it more than thought," Patrick said, tone dry on the way to the door, "or we'll be forced to call in a professional. I assure you, Charity is quite experienced at handling sour moods such as yours. Douse the lights and lock up if you will, Steven. Good night."

"Pop!"

Patrick turned on the bottom step, eyeing his son through tired eyes.

Striding forward, Steven clutched him in a tight embrace

that thickened the walls of Patrick's throat. "I love you, Pop, and if gratitude to God means anything, then I'm already halfway where you want me to be. Because I can never thank him enough for sparing your life."

Voice gruff, Patrick slapped Steven on the back. "I love you, son." Heading up the stairs, he stopped to circle halfway. "You know, you might consider giving that young woman another shot, Steven, because I believe God will help you do the right thing. Good night."

Steven watched his father scale the steps, no way to stop the gratitude that leaked from his eyes. He swiped at his face and headed back to the parlor and then stopped, moving to the front door instead with a purposeful gait. Stepping outside, he sucked in a deep breath, thick with the loamy scent of wet leaves and wood smoke. He found himself surrounded by stillness except for drizzle on the roof, the distant yapping of a dog, and the pounding of his pulse in his ears. Hands braced on the porch railing, he stared up into a sky as thick and foggy as his brain had been over the last month and wondered if it were really true, that God could help him be the man Annie needed him to be. The man Steven had longed to be all of his life.

"*I don't know, Pop,*" he had said, "*it all sounds too good to be true . . .*" And yet, what if it *was* true? He trusted his father with his life . . . but what if he could trust God with it as well? Closing his eyes, he thought of Annie and knew she was a woman he could love to the depth of his soul, if only he could trust himself to do the right thing.

"*God will help you do the right thing.*"

His father's parting words opened his eyes, prompting him to search the heavens. "Will you, God? Will you help me to do the right thing—not just with Annie, but with the rest of my life? I . . ." His whisper broke in the dark, hoarse and cracked and so desperate for change that emotion choked the words in his throat. "I-I've made so many mistakes . . . with my father, with Maggie, with you. I'm begging you . . ." A heave shuddered his body. "Forgive me, please . . . and change me like you changed my father . . . and help me to become the man you want me to be."

The steady beat of the rain drummed on the roof while the cold air chilled his body, the cool and damp of impending winter heavy in the air. And yet somehow, Steven felt warm, his breathing shallow as his eyes scanned the sky. There were no bolts of lightning to illuminate the dark nor peals of thunder to herald anything new. Only the still small voice of God in his heart, stirring a flame of hope that brought peace to his soul.

He leadeth me beside the still waters . . . He restoreth my soul . . . He leadeth me in the paths of righteousness . . .

"I don't understand," Steven rasped, eyes brimming with tears. "Why do you even care?"

Because you are mine, the thought came, and Steven bowed his head and wept.

Because for the first time in his life, he finally understood. He was.

15

"Heigh-ho, everybody!" Rudy Vallée's magical voice filled Aunt Eleanor's parlor while Annie sat Indian-style on the floor, attempting to braid Glory's hair.

"Welcome to the *Fleischmann Yeast Hour*," the sultry voice continued, and Glory danced her doll on her lap. "Oh, I just love Rudy Vallée," she said with a giggle, "and Sheba does too." A little-girl sigh drifted out as she hugged the queen to her chest. "He's the bee's knees."

Annie's aunt glanced up from her needlepoint, her tone tender. "Yes, dear, he is, especially tonight with Milton Berle as his guest."

"Popcorn and Coca-Cola, miss?" Frailey strode into the room with a tray, dispensing bowls of popcorn and soda, first to Aunt Eleanor and then to each of the girls.

"Thank you, Frailey," Aunt Eleanor said with a warm smile. She hesitated, hazel eyes harboring a sparkle as the elderly butler headed for the door. "Frailey . . . why don't you join us?"

He turned, back erect and empty tray in hand, as still and pale as the fountain statue in the foyer beyond. Annie grinned when a blush bled into his cheeks. He cleared his throat. "I believe Cook needs my assistance in the kitchen, miss, but thank you."

"Oh, come on, Frailey," Annie teased, "Cook accuses you of being underfoot half the time anyway—listen to the *Fleischmann Hour* with us, please?"

"Please, Frailey?" Glory pleaded.

Frailey's face appeared as stiff as his back . . . until the barest of smiles lighted on his weathered lips. "As you wish, miss and young ladies. I shall make short work of Cook and return promptly." He paused, ear cocked as the doorbell rang. "That is . . . after I answer the door."

Aunt Eleanor frowned. "Goodness, it's after seven—who would be calling this late?"

"It's just Peggy," Annie said with a hop to her feet. "She wants to borrow a dress."

"Excuse me, miss." Frailey reappeared at the door, gaze flitting to Annie before he nodded at Aunt Eleanor. "Mr. Steven O'Connor to see Miss Susannah. May I show him in?"

"Yes!" Glory bounded up so fast Mr. Grump's eyelids flapped like a window shade. Annie froze, body grafted to the floor as she stared, unable to speak . . . move . . . *breathe*.

"Gloria Celeste—halt!" Aunt Eleanor sat up in her chair, chin high.

Without so much as a crack of his face, Frailey scooped the little dickens up at the door when she shot by, stubby legs dangling as he carried her back to her aunt.

"But I want to see Steven," she moaned.

"I know, darling," Aunt Eleanor said with a kiss to Glory's cheek, "but Steven's here to see Annie, so we'll head upstairs for a pajama party with snacks and radio, all right?"

"Really?" Glory squealed. She hopped off Aunt Eleanor's lap and snatched her doll from the floor before whirling around with excitement in her eyes. "Annie and Frailey too?"

Aunt Eleanor laughed. "Well, Annie at least and even Mr. Grump, although he'll sleep on the floor." She peeked at Annie, gaze soft. "I assume you *do* want to see him?" she asked.

Annie stood and nodded, still unable to speak for the shock in her throat.

Aunt Eleanor glanced up. "Well then, Frailey, I believe you can show Mr. O'Connor in, but I fear we'll have to postpone Mr. Vallée to next week unless you're partial to pajama parties."

"No, miss," Frailey said with a ghost of a smile. "I believe my favorite PJs are in the wash. I'll just show the young man in."

"Are you all right, darling?" Aunt Eleanor cupped Annie's waist, pressing a kiss to her cheek. "You look pale, but everything will work out, you'll see."

"Steven!" Glory shot across the room and into his arms. She shrieked with joy when he swooped her up in the air.

"Hey, squirt," he said with a chuckle, tossing her over his shoulder. His eyes connected with Annie's, and her pulse took off. The intensity in their blue depths sent goose bumps across her arms. "You have no idea how much I missed you," he said, staring straight at Annie.

"Hello, Steven," Eleanor said with ease, prying Glory loose. "It's good to see you again."

"Likewise, Miss Martin," Steven said with a sheepish smile. "Please forgive me for barging in without calling first, but I just got off work. And I can tell you with certainty I've missed our games of dominoes and Cook's meals more than I should admit."

"Well, you'll have to come back soon, then, right, girls?" Setting Glory on her feet, she sent Annie an encouraging smile while retrieving popcorn and soda. "Annie, Glory and I will head up to start our pajama party, and you come along whenever you can, all right?"

Annie nodded, still unable to speak while her aunt ushered Glory from the room.

Finally alone, Steven faced her, and Annie could barely hear the radio for the blood throbbing in her ears. He took his hat off and passed a quick palm over dark hair, then fidgeted with the fedora while he stared, smile tentative. "Hi, Annie," he said quietly. "Can we talk?"

She nodded nervously, words still not an option, given the emotion swelling in her throat. Spinning on her heel, she quickly moved to the radio and turned it off, shaky fingers fused to the knob as she stood, her back to him while she attempted to breathe.

"Annie." His voice drifted over her shoulder, and she whirled around with a catch of her breath, heart seizing when he steadied her with both hands. His boyish smile melted her on the spot. "I promise I won't bite," he whispered, leading her over to the couch. He gently prodded her to sit, then sat beside her, tossing his hat on the coffee table before taking her hands in his. He inhaled deeply. "Annie, I'm a total idiot, and I'm sorry."

She blinked several times, eyes wide and tongue so swollen with shock, air could barely pass, much less words. She opened her mouth to speak, but apparently she'd turned off the sound of her voice along with the radio.

"I don't blame you for not talking to me, because I acted like a jerk and I apologize for what I said." His Adam's apple did a quick dunk. "But . . . I was hoping that somehow you might be able to . . . well, you know, forgive me . . . because I'd really like to see you again."

She was nearly hyperventilating now, her breathing shallow and fast, and words failing again, she finally just lunged, pressing her lips to his.

He groaned and swallowed her up, returning her kiss with a fervor that now left her breathless as well as speechless. Chest heaving, he gripped her arms and held her at bay, his eyes searching hers. "Annie, I don't know where this is going, but I sure want to find out and you have my word—whatever you say goes, kisses at the door or no."

Tears sparked and she kissed him again, luring a husky chuckle from deep in his throat. Weaving his fingers into her hair, he cupped the back of her head and slowly bent to graze his lips against hers before distancing himself with a pained smile. One dark brow angled high. "Not sure, but I'm guessing 'kisses at the door' don't include necking on the couch either?"

She released a languid sigh and slipped her arms around him before tucking her head to his chest. "No, but I figured it was okay just this once since this is a special occasion."

He laughed. "What, you got your tongue back?"

"No," she said, closing her eyes to breathe in the clean smell of soap and spicy aftershave. "My good mood."

His chuckle merged with a grunt. "Join the club, kid—my family's about to change the locks on the doors."

The doorbell rang and Annie jolted in his arms. "Oh drat, that's Peggy." She deposited a gentle kiss on his lips. "Do you have time to wait till I get the dress she wants to borrow?"

Steven rose and tugged her to her feet, circling her waist with a smoky look in his eyes. "I haven't seen you in over a month—what do you think?"

A glorious warmth braised her cheeks. "I'd say there's a lot to be said for 'absence makes the heart grow fonder,' wouldn't you?"

Cupping her chin, he gave her a lingering kiss before planting another on the tip of her nose. "Make it quick, kiddo," he whispered. "There's a statute of limitations on my patience."

She delivered a sassy smile on her way to the door. "May I remind you—you're the one who stayed away for a month, not me?"

He grinned. "Okay, so I'm stubborn as well as stupid—just hurry."

Releasing a blissful sigh, Annie practically floated to the door, flashing Frailey a smile as he strode from the kitchen. "I'll get it, Frailey," she said with a wave of her hand, "it's Peggy." She grinned at her friend through the thick, beveled glass, excitement bubbling over the good news she wanted to share. "Took you long enough," she said, wheeling the door wide.

"Tell me about it—I've been on a train for over three days."

Annie blinked, the blood in her face coursing to her toes like the water gushing in the foyer fountain. Maggie grinned, sparkling like a diamond in the dim light, from the glint of her platinum hair and the gleam of lip gloss, to the delighted sparkle of tease in pale blue eyes. All Annie could do was stare, paralysis claiming her tongue for the second time that night.

Maggie's laughter echoed in the foyer as she launched herself into Annie's wooden arms, giggling like Glory while she gave her a ferocious hug complete with squeals. "Oh, Suz—the look on your face is priceless, worth every bump on that miserable train!" She retrieved two suitcases from the front porch and marched through the front door, releasing a contented sigh while her eyes scanned the foyer. "Ah . . . mansion, sweet mansion," she said with a throaty chuckle, dropping her bags on the floor. She twirled around and tugged Annie away from the door before shutting it once again. Taking Annie's hands in hers, she surveyed her head to toe with an approving eye. "I swear, you've become a woman overnight, Suz," she said with a shake of her head, giving her sister a wink that toasted her cheeks. "Boy, oh boy—bet the guys can't keep their hands off you."

"M-maggie, w-what are you d-doing here?" Annie managed, her voice as weak as her air supply. "You're not supposed to b-be here t-till Christmas . . ."

"Oh, I know," Maggie said with a shrug, "but I got bored in L.A. and decided to surprise you guys with an early holiday visit." Forever fashionable, she removed a cream hat to pat short platinum waves tucked behind her ear, then slipped off her coat and looked around, first peeking up the stairs, then glancing toward the parlor. "So . . . where's Glo—" She froze, gaze glued to the parlor door while her coat dangled from her hand, as limp as the muscles in Annie's legs.

"Hi, Maggie," Steven said quietly, his face devoid of blood like Annie's, making the shadow of dark stubble on his chiseled jaw all the more noticeable. "It's good to see you again."

"Steven . . ." It was a breathless whisper from a porcelain goddess, pale cheeks accentuating striking blue eyes and glossy pink lips, full and parted with shallow breaths. Her pale pink satin blouse shuddered with a frail release of air beneath a cream tweed jacket open to the waist, cinched by a cream leather belt that showcased an hourglass figure. A matching tweed skirt hugged slim hips before flaring midcalf with bias-cut pleats, allowing a glimpse at beautiful legs in two-inch cream pumps. "W-what are you doing here?" she said in a near choke.

He nodded toward Annie, fiddling with the hat in his hands. "I came to see Annie."

"Annie?" she said, confusion etched into every pore of her face. Her gaze flitted from Annie to Steven and back, a flicker of hurt registering in luminous blue eyes. "Suz? But why?"

Annie's tongue felt like chalk. "I . . . m-meant to tell you, Maggie . . ."

"Tell me what?" she demanded, a thread of hysteria rising in her tone.

Steven took a step closer, eyes tender but tone taut. "We're seeing each other, Maggie."

Maggie's body seemed to stagger as she put a hand to her chest.

Fingers quivering, Annie touched Maggie's arm. "I wanted to tell you a million times—"

She flung Annie's hand away, anger glinting in her eyes. "Then why didn't you, Suz? I'll tell you why—because you knew it would slice me through the heart."

"Maggie, I'm sorry . . ." Annie clutched her arms to her waist, grief and guilt choking until she thought she couldn't breathe.

Steven strode forward. "It was an accident, Maggie—we didn't mean for it to happen."

"And what exactly has happened, Steven?" she asked with a cross of arms, her tone sharp. "Are you engaged?"

Steven's eyes flicked to Annie and back. "No, just dating."

"I see." She hefted her chin, impaling Annie with a look. "For how long?"

Annie reached out, attempting to touch Maggie's arm once again, but her sister only inched away, sending a shiver through Annie's body. "Three months," she whispered hoarsely, "until a month ago when we broke up." She sent Steven a tearful look before she averted her gaze to the floor, shame broiling her cheeks. "Steven came here tonight to make up."

"I see. Well, how inconvenient of me to visit my family."

Steven moved in. "Look, Maggie, it's been over between us for three years—"

"No, Steven, it's been over for *you* for three years, not me." She singed Annie with a hateful glare. "And I don't care if it's been ten to twenty, Suz, I would have never pegged you to stab me through the heart like this."

A sob broke from Annie's throat as she put a hand to her mouth. "Maggie, please—your life is in California now, and you're engaged . . ."

Maggie hiked her chin, but it didn't stop the tears that bled from her eyes. "*Was* engaged—Gregory broke it off. Apparently I'm not worthy of his love any more than Steven's."

"That's not true," Steven said. He clutched her arms, his tone rough with emotion. "I loved you so much it took three years to get over you, Maggie, but both of us have moved on."

"Yes, well, I guess we have my sister to thank for that."

"Maggie!" Glory stood on the landing in her nightgown, a flush in her face and curls bobbing as she flew down the steps. Flapping through the foyer in her bare feet, she slammed into Maggie's legs with such force that Steven had to steady her. "You came, you came!" she shouted, "Oh, Maggie, I missed you so much!"

Wiping the tears from her face, Maggie hefted Glory into her arms, squeezing with all her might. "Oh, honey, I missed you too, so much that I came home early to spend lots of time."

"Yay!" Glory shouted. "And you're just in time for our pajama party with Aunt Eleanor." She pressed rosebud lips to Maggie's. "With me and Annie." She giggled and put a hand to her mouth, winking at Steven. "But not Steven."

Maggie's smile faded. Her watery gaze met his. "No, not Steven . . . ," she whispered.

Heart writhing, Annie tugged Glory from Maggie's arms.

"Come on, munchkin, we'll go upstairs and wait for Maggie while she and Steven talk."

"Annie, no . . ." Steven's tone was brusque.

"But why do they have to talk?" Glory wanted to know, reaching her arms out to give Steven a good night kiss. He stroked her cheek before she gave him a sweet little peck.

"Because Steven and Maggie know each other really well, and they have a lot to catch up on," Annie said, avoiding Steven's eyes.

"Annie, wait . . ." Steven took a step forward.

"No," she whispered, forcing her gaze to his. Tears welled at the confusion in his face, and she quickly blinked to ward them off. "You two have a lot of air to clear." She glanced at Maggie, stomach cramping at the coldness she saw. "As do I with my sister." Her voice wavered. "I'm sick inside, Maggie, for hurting you like this, and if I could take it all back, I would."

"Annie, please, this will all work out . . ." Steven reached for her arm, but Annie backed away, easing toward the staircase while she cuddled Glory.

"I know it will, Steven, one way or the other—but not till you two talk." Moisture pricked as she stared, heart breaking over the pain she'd caused. "Maggie, we'll see you upstairs." Avoiding Steven's gaze, she fled with Glory, pausing on the landing with tears in her eyes. "Good night, Steven," she called, his face little more than a blur. Sobs heaved in her chest. *And maybe goodbye.*

Steven turned the engine off, stomach churning as much as the roiling whitecaps on the moonless waters of Massachusetts Bay. The last thing he wanted was to be sitting in a car with Maggie at Ocean Pier, one of their favorite haunts, dredging up memories he didn't want to recall with a woman he couldn't forget. The crashing of the waves on the shore filled the silence as he stared straight ahead, eyes fixed on the distant lights of the *Romance*, a steamer returning from a day trip to the shores of Cape Cod. The blare of the *Romance*'s whistle pierced the night, issuing a shrill warning to other vessels to ward off shipwrecks during nights that were black as death.

How fitting. Steven's lips compressed. When his own romance with Annie sailed uncertain waters—waters that could sink his hopes as well as crash his heart upon the rocks.

He heard Maggie shift in the seat beside him, and every muscle tensed. It was hard enough being this close with the scent of her perfume and that of the sea luring him back to a time when her body was an addiction and her lips á drug. Heaven help him, he couldn't look at her too, knowing she'd once been his, full lips that owned him and the face of an angel—seduction with pale blue eyes. He may have relented in bringing her here so they could talk, but he refused to look at her. His jaw stiffened. Looking at Maggie had never produced much talk.

"You're not going to melt into the seat if you look at me," she said softly.

A tic twitched in his cheek as he focused ahead, unwilling to give her a chance to reel him in. Not when his pulse was sprinting overtime and his breathing as jagged as the rocks on the shore. "What are we doing here, Maggie? I can't imagine we have a lot to say."

Her melancholy laugh set him on edge. "But then we never really did have a lot to say, did we, Steven?" she whispered, her tone as softly suggestive as the curves beneath her satin blouse.

His temper heated along with his skin. "I like your sister a lot, Maggie, and I don't want you making trouble."

"You liked me a lot once too, remember?" A vulnerability that pricked at his heart tempered her tone. "And we even thought it was love."

He closed his eyes, hoping to shut out the pull she still had. He could feel it even now—that magnetic attraction that had spelled his doom—and sweat beaded the back of his neck. "If it was love, Maggie," he whispered, "then it's gone."

"I don't believe that."

He looked at her then and saw it—the lost little girl who'd drawn him in like a moth to flame, buried deep beneath the façade of a self-assured woman. There was tragedy in those blue eyes that made his heart ache and then something else that caused it to thud. He quickly licked his lips, mouth going dry when her eyes followed the motion. Palms sweating, he reached to crank the ignition, only to stop when she placed her hand over his.

"Please," she said, her voice a pained whisper, "don't shut me out, Steven. I've already had enough heartbreak to last a lifetime."

He stared at the hand over his for several seconds before trailing up to her face, and when his throat constricted, he suspected he still had feelings for her. Slumping back in the seat, he put a hand to his eyes. "What do you want from me, Maggie?"

She didn't answer right away, but when she did, her voice trembled. "I . . . need to know . . . if you still care at all . . ."

The question sucked the air from his lungs. Did he? Did dreams count, and memories that haunted his soul? Or pulse rate or shallow breaths or one's mind in a fog? Steven swallowed hard, reluctant to respond, afraid voicing it would etch it in stone.

He jolted at the touch of her hand. "I have to know, Steven . . . if there's anything left."

"Why?" His voice was harsher than intended. "We were no good for each other, Maggie, so why even rehash it?"

"Because my life's in pieces, and I need to know." Her tone was bleeding.

Like his heart. He turned, eyes burning as he stared and fist clenched on the seat. Sucking in a deep breath, he pinched the bridge of his nose, seconds ticking away like heartbeats until he finally exhaled. "Yes," he said quietly, "but why does it matter?"

She took his hand in her own, kneading his fingers, grazing his palm, and his eyelids weighted closed at the heat of her touch. "Because that's what I came back to find out," she whispered, and before he could open his eyes, her lips swayed against his.

"Aw, Maggie . . ." His voice was a hoarse whisper. "Why are you doing this?" But he knew exactly why and he was loathe to stop, bewitched by the familiar taste of her mouth, the scent of her body, the touch of her skin. It all came flooding back and he found himself responding with a desire he hadn't expected, his body humming as she deepened her kiss.

He leadeth me in the paths of righteousness for his name's sake.

He thought of Annie and his promise to God, and his body went to stone. "I can't do this," he said, his breathing as ragged as his heart. Chest heaving, he turned the ignition and gunned the engine, hands shaking as he put the car into gear.

"Steven, please—we need to talk . . ."

"We're done talking, Maggie, and anything else you have in mind." With a grind of the gears, he gunned down Atlantic Avenue, his temper resurging once again.

Her words were threaded with fear. "She really dug her claws in, didn't she?"

"Nobody's got claws in me, Mags, least of all you." He turned with a squeal of tires.

"Really? There's still something between us, Steven, why deny it?"

He slid her a hard gaze. "I don't deny it, I just don't want it anymore."

"Because of Suz?" she whispered, and he could tell from the tremble in her tone that his answer would crush her.

He chose to ignore it, grateful her aunt's house loomed at the end of the street. Lips clamped, he sped up, silent until he finally eased in next to the curb. Slamming the stick shift into gear, he kept the engine running and glanced over, a cramp in his chest. "I never meant to hurt you, Maggie," he whispered, "I hope you know that."

Her soulful look slashed at his heart. "I know, Steven. You

were torn between your father and me back then. I guess I just hoped things might be different now, you know?"

His eyes softened. "I know. And things are different, just not in the way you want." He reached to fondle a strand of her hair. "I'll never stop caring about you, Maggie. You were my first love, and a man never forgets that."

"You and Suz," she whispered, "is it serious?"

He studied her profile, beautiful and strong and yet weighted with a sadness that plucked at his heart. "It could be," he said quietly, "when you leave again."

"And if I don't?" She turned to stare at him and he studied her in the soft glow of the streetlamp, almost wishing things could be different.

He drew in a deep breath and took her hand in his to skim her knuckles with his thumb. "It's over, Maggie," he whispered, the pain in his tone matching that in her eyes. "Either way."

"Do you love her?" Her voice was as fragile as the question.

Did he? He sighed. Probably, or at least well on his way. But Maggie didn't need that right now. "Annie and I are good friends," he hedged, "dating just a few months, that's all."

"Is that a yes . . . or a no?"

He exhaled his frustration. "No . . . maybe . . . I don't know," he said, unwilling to hurt her. "All I do know is that I want to see where it takes us, which means you and I can't be."

"Not necessarily," she said, her voice barely a whisper, and with the utmost tenderness, she reached to cup his face with her hand, giving him the softest of kisses.

He remained completely still as she kissed him, eyes closed while a familiar warmth seeped through his body, and then with a gentle hand to her face, he grazed her jaw. "I want to be your friend, Maggie, because I still care about you. But you need to know that as lovers, the past is dead and gone."

With a quiver of her chin she shook her head while tears spilled haphazardly down her cheeks. "Oh, Steven . . . ," she said softly, taking his hand in hers. "Not all of it." A muscle jerked in her throat as she stared with agony in her eyes. "We have a child."

It felt like a migraine coming on, this strange buzzing that traveled his body, numbing his brain, telling him it couldn't be true. Did she mean the miscarriage their senior year? He groped in his mind for the last time he and Maggie had made love, and knew it was impossible. She hadn't been pregnant the six months before she left. His heart beat wildly in his chest. Had she? "No," he said in a stupor, certain any baby couldn't be his. "It's impossible. You were fine until you left for California after graduation. I saw you."

Sympathy gleamed wet in her eyes. "Not after graduation, Steven," she whispered, "the summer of sophomore year, after we broke up and I lived with my godmother in California."

He blinked, remembering the awful breakup they'd had, the hateful words that had been spoken, and Maggie running away to attend school at UCLA. It had been the rawest pain he'd ever experienced, living without her, purging his system of her smiles, her love, the meaning she'd brought to his life. He felt the keen betrayal of her departure even now, and how it had pushed him into the arms of Erica, seeking solace that never came. And then Maggie had returned with a vengeance the summer of junior year and they picked up where they'd left off . . . until it finally ended before Thanksgiving senior year in an argument over his father.

"I don't understand . . . ," he said faintly, barely spoken aloud. "W-what are you saying?"

She took his hand once again, and he let her, too numb to move. "I'm saying I went to California because I was pregnant, Steven, not because I was running away from you." Her head bowed, and when she continued, her voice seemed far away, like a distant memory neither wanted to remember. "Mama forced me to stay with my godmother because Daddy was a pastor, and she didn't want anyone to know." A shiver traveled from her body to his. Instinctively, he pulled her close, staring straight ahead as their unsteady breathing fogged both the windows and his mind. "Mama begged me to give her up, so I did."

His leaden lids shuddered closed as his heart wrenched in his chest. *God forgive me, I have a daughter.* "Do you . . . ," a painful mix of shame and hurt convulsed in his throat, cracking his voice, "know anything about her?" he whispered, terrified to know, but more so not to.

"Yes," she said, a thread of pride in a tone laden with tears. "She's very happy with her new family, they tell me, a beautiful child with a bright future . . ." Her voice broke, shredding him inside. "And I miss her so very much . . ."

A heave swelled in his chest and he held Maggie tightly, tears pricking his eyes as sorrow pricked his heart. "Forgive me, Maggie, for putting you through this. I never meant—" a shudder wracked his body as he fought for control of his emotions—"to hurt you . . . to cause you and . . . our child . . . so much pain." He closed his eyes and tears welled, unbidden and unwanted, like the grief in his mind. Blatant sin, wrapping its tentacles around Maggie, around him, and now their daughter, bleeding into their lives with toxic guilt and shame. He laid his head against hers, voice splintered. Not unlike his soul. "I would do anything, Maggie—anything to make up for my sin, to change the path we took, to make it right." Silent sobs convulsed in his throat as he squeezed her so tightly, their grief became one. "And God help me, I would do anything to hold my daughter in my arms just once."

Her body shivered before she silently pulled away, the effect of their sin evident in the sheen of tears on her face. "You can," she whispered, her eyes pleading with his. His heart stopped when she stroked a quivering hand against the bristle of his jaw. "It's Glory."

16

*S*o, what do you think?" Maggie stood on a small carpeted platform in front of the three-way mirror at Filene's, an angel in a full-length ivory bridal gown shimmering with seed pearls. It hugged her body before spilling to the floor in a cascade of satin and lace, and she glanced over her shoulder at Annie and Aunt Eleanor with a tug of her lip. "Do you like it?"

No. Annie deflected the sharp stab in her chest with a bright smile, strolling around the platform to study the lay of the dress. "It's beautiful, Mags, just like you." She turned, ignoring the strained smile on her aunt's face. "Don't you think so, Aunt Eleanor?"

"Absolutely," Eleanor said. She rose from the chair and circled as well, arms crossed over her herringbone suit. "I do believe that dress was made for you, Maggie."

"I think so too," Maggie said softly, her gaze back on the dress as she smoothed her hands down its sleek lines. Her eyes met Annie's in the mirror. They dimmed enough for Annie to notice before she spun around and clapped her hands with a bright smile. "Well, that's that, then—it's lunchtime! If you would be a doll and unzip me, Suz . . . oops, I mean

336

'Annie.'" She sighed and unbuttoned the lace cuffs of the dress. "I suppose I'll get used to your new name eventually, but I tend to be slow in accepting change."

Me too, Annie thought with a silent sigh as she unzipped Maggie's dress, well aware this was one time she couldn't afford to be slow in accepting change. In one month, Maggie would become Steven's wife, a week before Christmas, and there was nothing Annie could do. Steven had made his decision that fateful night two weeks ago, and he'd chosen her sister. A choice that was—despite the agony that seared Annie's soul—one of the very reasons she loved him so—as Glory's father, it was the right thing to do.

Glory's father. Just the sound of those words paralyzed her heart to a comatose state that dulled her mind, but not the pain. Never once had she suspected the foster child her parents "adopted" was not her sister. No, with her older sister a coast away, Annie had been so thrilled to have a sister again, it hadn't even entered her brain that Glory might belong to Maggie.

And to Steven . . .

Never had her faith carried her more than now, when Annie's only choice was between anger and bitterness . . . or laying it down and letting God heal her heart. And although there'd been moments when she'd wanted to rail and scream, almost wishing Maggie had never been born, Annie had chosen to forgive . . .

But it wasn't easy.

"We'll wait outside while you get dressed," Aunt Eleanor said, ushering Annie out the door. Closing it behind them, Aunt Eleanor nodded at several salesladies while she hooked an arm to her niece's waist. She led her to a chaise against the wall and settled beside her, smoothing a stray curl away from Annie's face. "How are you doing?" she whispered, taking Annie's hand in hers.

Annie leaned her head against the wall, smile fading a tad as she released a tenuous sigh. "Okay, I guess, but I won't lie to you, Aunt Eleanor—it's hard."

"I don't doubt that, darling," Aunt Eleanor said with a pat of Annie's hand. "It's hard for all of us, I'm afraid, and we're not doing it with a broken heart." Her sigh was as wispy as Annie's. "Have I told you lately how proud I am of you, Susannah?"

Annie's lips tipped. "All the time," she said with a squeeze of her aunt's hand. "I honestly don't know how I'd do this if it wasn't for you and Faith." Tears pricked. "And God."

Aunt Eleanor nodded, her own eyes glossy. " 'Blessed are the pure in heart, for they shall see God,' " she said softly, trailing into a faraway stare. She sighed again and pressed a kiss to Annie's cheek. "Never have I believed that more than now, Annie, because of you." She cupped her niece's face. "I'm convinced that your pure heart in the face of this hurt will allow you to see God move in your life beyond anything you've ever dreamed." She paused, her smile tender. "I don't know if I can ever thank you enough for all you've done for me, Susannah." Her pearl choker shifted on her throat. "The example you've set . . . an example that has set me free from the pain of my past." Tears welled in her aunt's eyes. "And my future."

"Your future?" Annie said, her head in a curious tilt. "What do you mean, Aunt Eleanor?"

Aunt Eleanor smiled, a beautiful smile brimming with tears of love and hope and peace. "There's someone from my past who I desperately needed to forgive, Annie, but I just couldn't . . . not until you showed me how . . . and why."

Annie's heart sped up. "Mr. Callahan?"

A chuckle broke on a heave as Aunt Eleanor nodded, the motion sending a tear trailing.

"Oh, Aunt Eleanor!" Annie swallowed her up in a joyous squeeze. "Nothing could've lifted my spirits right now more than this!" She pulled back, hands still braced to her aunt's arms while she studied her, gaze tentative. "Does . . . Mr. Callahan know?"

Biting a thumbnail, Aunt Eleanor shook her head with a

tremulous smile, looking so much like a little girl that Annie laughed. "Well then, are you going to tell him?"

A white glove trembled to her aunt's lips while she gave a jerky nod, more tears welling.

Annie gave her a tight hug. "Oh, Aunt Eleanor, I'm so happy for you." She pulled back with a husky chuckle. "But not as happy as Mr. Callahan will be, I suspect."

With a tearful press of Annie's hand, Aunt Eleanor rose to her feet, cheeks blooming a beautiful shade of pink as she fished her handkerchief from her purse and patted her eyes. She quickly glanced at her watch. "Goodness," she said, tugging on the jacket of her suit, "I almost forgot I have something to order before we scoot off to lunch, so I'm going to take advantage. How about I meet you and Maggie at the car in ten minutes? Frailey will be out front."

"Sounds good," Annie called with a smile, watching Aunt Eleanor scurry away. *Thank you, Lord, and please bless her more than she ever dreamed possible.* Exhaling, she folded her arms and slumped to the wall, reflecting on Aunt Eleanor's words. *Blessed are the pure of heart.* A plaintive sigh drifted from her lips. *Oh, Lord, let it be . . .*

A night that should have been one of the happiest of her life—Steven's return and Maggie's homecoming—had shattered her heart instead, and Annie wasn't sure if she would ever be the same again. Her guilt and shame over getting involved with Steven without telling Maggie had prompted her to push the two of them together. To clear the air, she had said, and put the past behind. Only the "past" was here to stay in the sweet presence of a golden-haired child whom Annie loved as a sister. And in the space of an hour, Annie had lost everything she held dear—the man she loved, the sister she idolized, and the little sister she cherished.

With every tick of the clock that night, her heart had grown heavier as she lay in Aunt Eleanor's bed next to Glory, waiting for Maggie, and when the clock finally struck twelve, she knew she was doomed, like Cinderella at the ball. Her fairy-tale romance with Steven had turned into ashes when her sister stole away the handsome prince they both loved.

"Ready?"

She jolted, blinking up at Maggie at the stroke of her sister's hand to her cheek. "Goodness, Suz—you were somewhere far, far away."

"Naw, just a catnap." Annie jumped up to take Maggie by the arm. "Aunt Eleanor had a quick errand to run, so she said she'd meet us at the car. Are you ready?"

"Actually . . . no," Maggie said, brows tented in apology. "The saleswoman brought in the most incredible dress just as I was leaving, and I was wondering if you'd tell me what you think. It should only take a few minutes . . ."

Annie managed a smile. "Sure, lead away." Swallowing a silent groan, she followed Maggie into the dressing room and closed the door. "Oh my, this is gorgeous," she whispered, eyes drawn to a creamy, champagne satin gown hanging on a hook, its elegant scoop neck encrusted with pearls. Small silk-covered buttons edged Renaissance-style sleeves that gave it a fairy-tale air Annie loved. She smiled at her sister. "Oh, Maggie, it's straight out of Cinderella!"

"It is, isn't it?" Maggie said with a glow in her cheeks. "It looks like something a princess would wear to wed her Prince Charming."

Or mine. The bitter thought rose from nowhere, and Annie turned to slip the dress off the hanger and over Maggie's head. *God, forgive me, and help me to be happy for my sister.* Focusing on fastening the buttons, Annie quickly retreated to a chair by the wall when she was done, blinking often to free her eyes from impending tears. She folded her hands in her lap to keep them from trembling. "I think that may be the one, Mags."

"Me too," Maggie said quietly, her eyes fixed on the mirror. She paused, head bowed and a slight wobble in the creamy line of her throat. "Like Steven," she said. "He's been the one from the first moment I ever saw him, Annie." She pivoted slowly, meeting Annie's gaze. And like a reflection in a mirror, Annie saw the same remorse, guilt, and sadness in her sister's face that she felt in hers. The satin neckline of the gown shimmered when a wavering sigh drifted from Maggie's lips. "I never meant to hurt you, Annie, any more than you meant to hurt me, but the truth is, one of the reasons I came back was to see if Steven still cared."

She removed her veil and stepped down from the platform, sitting in the chair by her sister. Staring straight ahead, her eyes were naked with pain and her voice as unsteady as the veil that trembled in her hands. "When Gregory broke the engagement, I . . . w-wanted to die because it was just another confirmation I . . . w-wasn't worthy of love."

"Maggie, that's not true."

She looked up, moisture glazing her eyes. "Maybe not, Suz, but that's how I feel. Rejection everywhere I turn, never good enough for Hollywood or Gregory or Steven." A harsh laugh tripped from her lips. "And let's not forget about Daddy—"

"Daddy loved you," Annie said quickly.

Maggie squeezed Annie's hand, her smile laced with sadness. "It's not your fault, Suz, that Daddy approved of you and not me. You were the good girl, after all, the daughter who made him proud."

"He was proud of you too!" Annie cried, her heart aching for her sister.

Maggie shook her head, sorrow coating her cheeks. "How could he be? I wasn't even proud of myself . . ." Her eyes trailed off into a glassy stare as her voice droned on, threaded with pain. "When Gregory left, my world fell apart, and suddenly nothing mattered more than seeing Glory and you. Gregory's rejection made me realize how selfish I'd been in what I'd done—allowing Mother to pass Glory off as a foster child whom she and Daddy brought into their home. And for the first time, I felt this driving need to make amends to my little girl, to be a mother to my baby . . . if only . . ." Her hand trembled to her mouth while tears welled in her eyes. "If only I could give her the type of home she deserved."

Her eyelids fluttered closed and moments passed before they opened again, chin elevated as if to give her the strength to go on. "So in the midst of my rejection and hurt, I made up my mind to finally do the right thing, and I purposed to see Steven when I got home. At least when he rejected me, it was because of his allegiance to his father and not because he didn't care." Her smile was wistful. "And if there's one thing I knew for certain, Annie, it was that Steven O'Connor was an honorable man who would do the right thing."

Yes, I know, Annie thought with a twist of her heart.

She took Annie's hand in hers, a wet plea in her eyes. "Oh, Suz, please don't hate me," she whispered, "I couldn't live with myself if you did."

Annie embraced her, eyelids tightly shut. "I could never hate you, Mags—I love you."

Maggie pulled back, a weepy grin in place as she swiped at her cheeks. "And I love you." She stroked Annie's face, trepidation in her gaze. "You . . . weren't lying the night I told you about Glory and Steven, were you? When you said you two were just dating and nothing more?"

Annie shook her head, wondering if the absence of words could be considered a lie.

A smile wobbled on Maggie's lips, and the sun broke through the clouds in her eyes. "I'm glad," she breathed, clasping Annie's hand. The smile dimmed somewhat as she chewed at the edge of her lip. "And you're . . . not angry with Steven, I hope . . . because I love you both, Annie, and it would tear my heart apart if you two didn't get along."

"No," Annie whispered, grateful she could speak the truth out loud. "Not even a little."

Relief eased the tension from her sister's face as Maggie crushed her in a tight hug. "Oh, thank God." She pulled back, her gaze glimmering with hope that caused an ache in Annie's throat. "Promise me, Suz, that you and Steven will be friends who love each other like family."

"I promise," Annie whispered. She wrapped her sister in

a fierce hug, staring over her shoulder as tears pricked her eyes. Friends? Maybe. Family? Without question. Love? Annie swallowed the grief in her throat.

Consider it done.

⁓

"Good grief, O'Connor, I've seen happier mugs on a wanted poster." Joe tossed his keys on his desk and plopped in his chair with a look as sour as his mood the last two weeks, a record for the man with a perennial smile. "Why are you doing this?"

Steven glanced up from the report on his desk with a heavy inhale, bracing himself for another barrage of Joe's well-meaning probes. He managed a patient smile. "Because I want to, Joe. How many times do we have to go over this?"

"Till I'm convinced I don't have to report to Hatch that my partner's lost his mind. And for your information, 'because I want to' is not an intelligent answer. Speaks on the North End 'want to' sell booze too, but that ain't gonna happen either."

Huffing out a sigh, Steven tossed his pencil on the desk and sagged back in his chair, kneading the bridge of his nose. "Come on, Walsh, you're just going to have to bite the bullet and accept the fact your best friend's getting married."

"Yeah, well, I would if I thought it was really what you wanted, but you were in the middle of falling in love with one sister, and now you're marrying the other?" He scowled, snatching a pencil. "This whole fiasco is a bolt out of the blue, biting us both in the keister."

Steven chuckled with a fold of his arms, affection warming his gaze for a friend who was more like a brother who had seen him through thick and thin. "You act like you're the one losing your freedom. Trust me, you're my best friend—we'll still hang out together, and nothing will ever change that. Besides, Maggie was never the possessive type, you know that."

Joe's legs plopped on the desk with a grunt. "Yeah? Well,

you just didn't know it because your head was so far in the clouds, you never noticed." He put the pencil through abuse, absently bending it back and forth. "Do you even love her?" he snapped, searing Steven with a look so out of character, it could have been Hatch dressing him down.

Steven sighed. Did he? *No, but I care about her, and she's the mother of my child—what more do I need?* He leaned in, forearms on his desk and patience wearing thin. "Look, Joe, I've never stopped caring about Maggie, and you know that, so lay off about whether I love her or not. What I want to know is why you've been so nasty ever since I told you? You're turning into a bigger nag than Hatch. Why don't you just come out and tell me what's really eating you? I know this is sudden and all, but I thought you liked Maggie."

"I do like her, Steven. Maggie and I were good friends, but holy blazes, you haven't seen the woman for three years! Then two weeks ago, she shows up out of nowhere and you propose in two blinkin' hours?" He shook his head, flexing the pencil so hard, it snapped. He hurled the broken pieces across his desk. "Not to mention your family hates her? No, there's something you're not telling me, Steven—I can smell it."

Yeah, well, you always did have a nose for dirt, Walsh. Steven launched his feet up on the desk like Joe, grateful it was after eight and most of the office had gone home. He closed his eyes and massaged his temple with his forefinger and thumb, determined to spare Maggie embarrassment by keeping her secret, at least till they were married. But it hadn't been easy. From the moment he'd told him about the engagement, Joe had been like a bloodhound with a burr up his nose, itching to dig it out and downright nasty in the process. As if Steven wasn't bleeding enough over what he'd done, first to Maggie and then to his daughter . . .

My daughter. His eyes drifted closed. *Glory.* Joe's grousing faded away, replaced by the same dull ache that had persisted since Maggie told him Glory was his. No one had known the shocking truth but Maggie and her parents, keeping Annie and Eleanor in the dark all these years, as well as him. Moisture stung beneath his lids as always when he thought about the golden-haired moppet who already owned his heart, and now Steven had the chance to give her the family she deserved. The muscles in his jaw tightened. And he would, even if it meant marrying the wrong sister and forgetting the other.

His throat constricted. As if he could.

Annie. Sweet, young, pure. And yet possessing a maturity he'd seldom seen in a woman outside his family. As hard as he tried to put her out of his mind, she dominated his thoughts and haunted his dreams, heart wrenching whenever he thought of the pain he'd caused. *And* the pain he'd caused himself by falling in love. The malaise of the last two weeks seeped back in with its usual numbing ache. Because if he hadn't been sure before, he was dead-sure now—he was in love with Susannah Grace Kennedy, and it took giving her up to realize just how much.

"Steven!"

He jolted, still in a stupor as he stared up at Joe, who was even starting to look like Hatch, thick brows slashing low. Steven blinked. "What?"

"See? That's what I'm talking about. It's like you're somewhere else all the time, half dead and just biding your time till the other half dies." Joe slipped his legs off his desk and leaned in, his devotion to Steven evident in the squint of hazel eyes dark with worry. "So are you going to tell me the truth or not? *Why* are you doing this?"

Sucking in a deep breath, Steven assessed his best friend with a wary eye, well aware that when Joe was riled up, he was like a pit bull with a T-bone after a forty-day fast, unrelenting until you gave him something to chew on. Steven vented with a noisy breath. "Okay, Joe, the truth is, dating Annie forced me to do some soul searching and, well, I find that I'm . . . changing."

"No joke," Joe said, lips in a twist. He settled back in his chair, some of the strain in his face easing as his gaze locked with Steven's. "What kind of soul searching?"

Steven lowered his eyes to scratch the back of his neck, not sure how to explain that God was now more than a Sunday obligation to a former choir boy who'd never given him much thought. His gaze wandered into a stare. "I don't know, the kind that unlocked the jail cell I've been in most of my life. That ruthless drive to achieve and vindicate a past that made me feel like dirt." He glanced up, hungry to connect with Joe on a spiritual level for the first time in his life. They'd always been there for each other to listen and encourage, but they'd never scratched the surface of the truth that had set Steven free. The truth that God wasn't just a "maybe" but a living, breathing Savior who not only saved lives but changed them for the better.

Steven studied his friend, freckles scrunched with a frown in a comfortable face most women found attractive, although you'd never convince Joe. Hazel eyes usually crinkled with humor now slitted in suspicion, and Steven's heart ached for his best friend. Joe was as lost as Steven used to be, he suddenly realized. The easygoing, fun-loving guy who buried his head in good times as deeply as Steven had buried his in a career, both searching for something to alleviate the burden of sin on their soul. Well, Steven found it, and for the first time, he understood Joe needed it too. He swung his feet off and leveled his arms on the desk. "Look, Joe, I'm a moody son of a gun, and you know that better than anybody, but now I finally know why. I was always beating myself up for not making the grade, whether it was failing Maggie, my father, or myself. I'm a man who thrives on trust and yet I had no trust in who I was as a man."

He picked his pencil up, eyes fixed on it as he idly rubbed it between forefinger and thumb. "When I started falling for Annie, I wanted to treat her differently than Maggie—you know, keep it aboveboard?" His gaze veered off into a pensive stare. "Only I kept messing up, just like with Maggie . . .

and Annie called me on it." A harsh chuckle erupted from his throat. "I'll tell you what, Joe, it made me crazy. Not just because some kid was dictating how things were going to be but because she had way more control and strength of conviction than I could ever hope to have." He looked up, meeting Joe's gaze. "And suddenly I realized I wanted that as much as I wanted her—substance and strength that didn't come from me but from something greater." He eased back in his chair, a peace settling deep in his spirit as he rested his head. "So I talked to Annie and Sean and Pop, and I finally understood the thing I've been searching for all along is not trust in myself . . . but trust in God."

Joe blinked. "God?" he whispered, jaw sagging so much that Steven smiled.

He cuffed the back of his neck, the smile giving way to a grin. "Yeah, well, I guess it does sound pretty crazy, but it's the truth." He folded his arms and cocked his head. "Remember the time Nate Phillips dared us to smoke in the confessional and we got caught?"

Joe grinned. "How can I forget? I was so scared, I thought I'd have to change my pants."

"Me too," Steven said with a faint smile, recalling with perfect clarity how his stomach had plunged when Father Mac opened that confessional door, smoke billowing in his face like a fog. All he could think at the time was what Pop would say, and the mere thought had chilled his blood. "I can still remember how my body went cold, pretty sure my life was over."

Joe chuckled. "And mine would have been had my parents found out. I thought we were dead in the water, but then Father Mac let us off scot-free." His nose puckered in thought. "Never could figure out why."

"Me neither, but he called it 'mercy,' remember? All I know is how incredible it felt when he let us go with just a warning and a promise to never smoke again." Steven glanced up, his eyes intense. "Well, that's how it is for me now, Joe. I've been botching my life up left and right and feeling worse about myself all the time, which is not a good state of mind for somebody trying to be perfect. So I prayed and gave it to God, just like Pop did years ago when he married my mother. My dreams, my desires, my life—all of it. And this is going to sound nuts, I know, but ever since?" He exhaled slowly. "I'm at peace for the first time in my life, not just wanting to be a better man and failing miserably . . . ," his throat clotted with emotion, "but actually becoming one through *his* strength instead of my own."

Joe just stared, mouth dangling open, and Steven couldn't help but grin. All at once Joe started laughing, shaking his head with an openmouthed smile. "So the wayward choir boy returns to his roots, huh? And I suppose you're planning on dragging me along?"

Steven's grin grew. "Why not? You've followed my lead since the first grade, Walsh, helping yourself to my homework, my fraternity, and my job. Why should this be any different? Besides, you need it more than me if you're ever going to settle down with a decent woman."

Joe's smile sobered. "I have to admit, I'm pretty tired of the party scene, and settling down with a decent girl has its appeal." He paused, peering up. "But you still haven't explained yourself. By your own admission, the 'decent' woman here is Annie, so what am I missing?"

Joe's words sucked the peace right out, leaving an empty hole in his chest. He sighed, absently fingering the tip of the pencil eraser, wishing he could erase the pain he'd caused. "Sleeping with Maggie was a mistake back in college, Joe, and I knew it deep down, although God knows I never admitted it. Instead I took advantage of her with the promise of marriage."

"But you loved her, Steven."

He glanced up, gaze pensive. "Yeah, I thought so at the time, but Annie taught me that I really loved myself more." His chest rose and fell with a heavy breath. "I stole Maggie's virtue with a cheap promise," he said quietly, "and now I intend to make good."

"But why Maggie?" Joe said, color rising in his cheeks once again. "We both fooled around with a lot of girls—that doesn't mean we have to marry 'em."

Steven's stomach wrenched. "Yeah, I know, but Maggie's the only one I promised, and if there's one thing you know about me, Joe, I don't break a promise if I can help it."

Joe lumbered to his feet, his look of resignation threaded with sorrow. "I wish you'd reconsider, Steven. Something in my gut tells me marrying Maggie won't make you happy."

An unsteady breath expelled from Steven's throat as he rose and hooked his coat over his shoulder. "Maybe not," he said, slapping his best friend on the back. His smile was somber. "But a clean conscience will."

17

*M*aggie, just so you know—Steven cheats at Pinochle." Charity sent a smirk Steven's way as she dealt the cards, sliding them rapid-fire around Marcy's dining-room table where Thanksgiving dinner had been consumed just three hours before.

Steven shook his head and laughed, determined not to dignify Charity's taunt in a Pinochle game to the death between most of his sisters and their spouses. Brady and Lizzie had bowed out to give Steven and Maggie a turn, opting to fawn over their three-month-old baby, Sara, with Marcy and Emma instead. Giggles carried in from the kitchen where cousins played Old Maid, merging with chuckles in the parlor as Patrick annihilated Sean at chess.

"Is that a fact?" Maggie said with a gleam in her blue eyes. "My honest and straitlaced fiancé, the die-hard prohibition agent? Hard to believe."

"What's hard to believe, Mags," Steven said, perusing his cards, "is that Mitch hasn't put a muzzle on Charity yet for all the tales she spins."

"Don't think it hasn't crossed my mind," Mitch said, earning a raised brow from his wife.

"Only because you prefer my lips free," Charity said sweetly, lashes aflutter.

Steven cleared his throat. "For your information, sis, unlike Collin, I win by skill." He flicked a stray crumb of pie at his sister.

"Hey, so my wide range of talents doesn't include Pinochle," Collin defended.

"Or basketball, or baseball, or chess . . . ," Luke said with a grin.

Collin shot him a mock glare. "At least I don't cheat like you and your partner here." He reached around Faith's chair to thump the back of Steven's head. "With nonverbal communication that puts Braille to shame."

"See, Maggie?" Charity assessed her cards. "Outright cheaters—both of them."

"Can we help it if men are better at Pinochle than women?" Luke asked with an innocent lift of brows. "It's not my fault God gave us keen survival instinct that borders on telepathic."

Katie elbowed Luke in the side. "I think the word you're looking for is 'pathetic,' McGee." She leaned on the table with an angelic smile, chin propped in hand. "But if you did mean telepathic, darling, why don't you tell me what I'm thinking right now?"

"I'll give you a hint, Lukie," Charity said with a chuckle. "It has to do with where you and Mitch'll be sleeping tonight."

"In your dreams, little girl." Mitch seared her with a smoky gaze.

"Oh, I hope so," she breathed, an impish tug of her lip that had Mitch shaking his head.

"Speaking of sleeping . . . ," Faith covered a yawn with her hand, "I think I may need to call it a night." She skimmed a palm across a heavily pregnant stomach and wrinkled her nose. "This little one's been kicking up a fuss since dinner, just like when her sisters came."

"*His* sisters," Collin corrected, caressing her abdomen with a ridge in his brow. "Why didn't you say you weren't feeling well, Faith?" Worry threaded his scold as he helped her to her feet. He kissed her on the nose. "I don't want to take any chances with you *or* my son."

She patted his bristled cheek with a tired smile. "I'm fine, Collin, really, but it could be a girl, you know, so you have to be prepared."

He gave her a soft kiss full on the mouth. "I will love this child with all my heart, and you know that. And if the McGuire name ends with me, I will still die a happy man."

"Not for a while, I hope," she said with a misty smile. "I'll need your help with . . . *Oh!*"

"What's wrong?" Charity shot up, bounding around the table one way, and Katie the other.

"Faith?" Collin's voice rose in volume as blood drained from his face.

"Nothing," Faith said quickly, hand to the small of her back. "Just a contraction, I think."

"You think?" Katie's voice was frantic as she spun around, eyes fixed on her mother in the parlor. "Mother, we need you!"

"Uh-oh . . ." Faith chewed her lip as she looked down at Collin's shoe, now speckled with a cloudy-looking liquid. "I think my water broke."

Steven swallowed hard, his first real exposure to having a baby a bit daunting. He reached for Maggie's hand and stood, pulling her with him as he whispered in her ear. "Did you have that?" he said with a gulp, not feeling overly confident in his pending role as parent.

She grinned. "Afraid so," she whispered. "It means the baby is on its way."

"What's going on?" Marcy rushed in with Lizzie and Emma, eyes on Faith as she cradled her stomach. "Contractions?" Smile tentative, her tone was almost giddy.

"Just beginning, I think . . ." Faith gritted her teeth while Charity eased her into the chair.

Palms pressed skyward, Marcy whipped into action, discharging orders. "Patrick, get your keys—we're going to the

352

hospital. Luke, keep the children in the kitchen till we leave, then divvy them up between you, Sean, and Brady—my girls are going with me."

"I can take a few kids," Mitch said.

Marcy seared him with a look, from loving mother-in-law to drill sergeant in under two seconds. "No! We'll need two of you to drive to the hospital, Mitch, so go wait in your car."

A groan parted from Faith's pale lips as Charity rubbed her back.

Marcy shot Collin a steely look, gaze dropping to his wrist. "Where's your watch?"

He blinked and rubbed his arm. "Uh . . . don't know. Took it off when I helped with dishes I think . . ."

Marcy huffed her impatience. "Then find Faith's coat and purse on the double, will you, please?" She zeroed in on Steven. "What time is it?"

He jerked his cuff back to glance at his watch. "Nine-thirty."

Pursing her lips, she held out her hand, as patient as Mitch on a bad day. "Give it to me."

"What?" Steven stared while Maggie stifled a chuckle with a clear of her throat.

"I need to time the contractions, and Patrick's watch is slow." She glanced over her shoulder where Patrick stood at the chessboard, finalizing a move. "Like your father, apparently. Patrick—we need to go—*now*!" She turned back with a hike of her brow, snapping her fingers.

"Okay, okay," Steven groused. He handed the watch over, scowling when Luke laughed.

Marcy wheeled on Luke with a jut of her brow, taking the starch out of his grin. He stifled a smile with a firm salute. "Yes, ma'am, children packed up, divvied, and contained in the kitchen—got it." He barreled through the swinging kitchen door to corral the kids.

"How long are the contractions?" Patrick asked with all the calm of an experienced father.

Charity glanced over her shoulder. "It's over," she said, gently brushing Faith's hair away from her face while her sister sagged into the chair, body as limp as her stray curls.

Marcy glanced at Steven's watch now gracing her arm. "A minute and a half—sweet saints, Patrick, we need to go!" She glanced up when Collin bolted through the swinging door with Faith's coat and purse after saying goodbye to his daughters. "Collin, put her coat on and get her to Patrick's car, pronto."

"Yes, ma'am." He helped Faith to stand, slipping her wrap over her shoulders. "How you doing, Little Bit?" he whispered, kissing her cheek.

"Crabby." Faith slid him a crooked smile. "I'd steer clear, McGuire—these contractions don't exactly endear you to me, you know."

He chuckled, guiding her toward the front door while her sisters followed behind. "I know, but once that baby's here, you'll be crazy about me again."

"You better hope so," she whispered, her breathing heavy. "Oh . . ." She doubled over, and Marcy shooed him through the front door. "Don't stop, Collin—get her into the car."

"How is she?" Sean asked, his look strained as he trailed them to the door, clutching Emma to his side like it was happening to her.

Marcy slipped her coat on. "She'll be fine, this is number four. It's old hat to Faith."

Emma's smile was tender. "I'd like to come to the hospital if there's room, Marcy, or we can take Gabe home, if you like—whatever you need us to do."

"Why can't Gabe stay here with me?" Steven asked, arm hooked to Maggie's waist.

"Because you have to take Maggie home, and once Gabe hears her cousins are having a sleepover, there'll be no rest. And, yes, Emma, please come because I'm sure Brady and Luke have everything under control." Marcy sighed when something crashed in the kitchen. "On second thought," she said with a quick kiss to Sean's cheek, "maybe they could use your help while Emma goes to the hospital with us, all right?"

"What do you need me to do?" Steven asked, feeling like a spare cog in a finely tuned machine. "Maggie and I can clean up the kitchen, but what else do you need?"

Marcy lifted on tiptoe to buss Steven's cheek. "Nothing else, Steven, a clean kitchen would be lovely." She smiled at Maggie, giving her a hug before cupping her face in her hands. "I'm so glad you came tonight, Maggie. We look forward to welcoming you to the family."

Maggie's smile was shaky. "Thank you, Mrs. O'Connor, for the warm welcome. I . . . ," her throat shifted, "can't thank you enough after all the trouble I've caused in the past."

"Nonsense," Marcy said with a pat of her cheek, eyes as glossy as Maggie's. "You and Glory are family now, so the future is the only thing I'm concerned about."

"Mother!" Charity rushed in the door, breathless. "Father said to hurry."

"Coming," Marcy said, flying out the door.

Emma brushed a kiss to Sean's lips before grabbing her coat and hightailing after Marcy. She paused at the door to shoot a smile over her shoulder. "Oh, and it was wonderful meeting you, Maggie. And Steven, she's beautiful." She blew a kiss to Sean. "Don't wait up, darling—babies are my passion . . . after you, that is."

Shaking his head, Sean shut the door with a smile. "It's not always this wild, Maggie, so I hope we haven't scared you off."

"No, it's been a lot of fun seeing the dynamics of a large family, especially during Pinochle."

Sean ambled toward the kitchen with a grin, hand flush to the swinging door. "Yeah, well, you might reserve your opinion till you play with Charity and Luke for more than an hour or two—it can get pretty ugly." Pushing through, he halted with a grimace over his shoulder. "Steven, if you don't want Maggie to change her mind, you may want to take her in the parlor till we clear out the kitchen. It's a little crazy right now."

"Good idea." Steven steered Maggie to the sofa, then sagged down and tugged her along. She snuggled in, and his arm slid to buff hers, conjuring painful memories of the night his father caught them on this very couch in the wee hours of the morning.

He closed his eyes and exhaled, suddenly worn from the day. Although he'd brought Maggie home to meet his parents again after he'd proposed, today was the first time she'd met everyone else, and it had been draining to say the least. His family couldn't have been kinder or more welcoming, but the shock of seeing Maggie instead of Annie with his sisters was still too raw for them all. Which is why he'd put off giving Maggie the ring after dinner as originally planned. That was something he needed to do with Maggie alone, he'd decided, to spare both his family and her the awkwardness over the turn of events he'd sprung on them all.

A quiet sigh escaped from his lips. Not that his family hadn't reached out, because they had from the moment Maggie walked in the door. And Maggie had sparkled and shined, of course, saying all the right things. Yet somehow she hadn't fit in like her sister had, and Steven suspected they missed Annie too. He sucked in a deep breath and released it. With everyone gone, this was the perfect time to give Maggie his ring and seal their fate—a ring he had hoped to give to Annie some day instead. Exhaling softly, he resolved to make this work and tucked Maggie close, pressing a kiss to her hair. "You gotta be exhausted, meeting so many new people."

"A little," she said, burrowing in, "but this is important, to fit into your family, Steven. For your sake and Glory's as well as mine."

"You have nothing to worry about, Mags. My family loves Glory, they'll love you too."

She paused. "As much as they loved Annie?"

His throat constricted. "More." He kneaded her arm. "After they get to know you."

"Do you really think so?" Her voice trembled like a scared little girl. She sat up to meet his gaze, the tragic look of hope in her eyes causing a twinge in his chest.

He studied the girl who'd haunted him till he'd fallen in love with her sister. The memory of their past, the way they used to feel, tugged at his heart. He smiled. "Yeah, Mags, I do."

She paused as tears welled in her eyes. "Will you?"

The kitchen door flew open with shouts and giggles while Luke, Brady, and Sean herded cousins into the foyer to bundle them up in coats, hats, and scarves.

"Three weeks and counting, you two," Luke called, buttoning coats while kids sparred and giggled. "Enjoy single life while you can."

"Nice meeting you, Maggie, and welcome to the family." Brady glanced up, easily attending to hats and gloves with his baby in his arms. "Sorry, Steven, we tried to clean up, but the ruffians got into the ice cream, so there's a royal mess. Sean's doing dishes now, but the kids had a food fight, so you can guess what the floor looks like."

"No problem, Brady." Steven put two fingers to his teeth and whistled, halting all commotion. "Hey, anybody gonna say goodbye to their uncle?"

Cousins flew into the parlor, giggling while Steven kissed and tickled. Maggie asked for a hug, and the girls obliged. "She's pretty," Abby said, "but I miss Annie and Glory."

The smile withered on Maggie's face, and Steven hooked her close. "Annie and Glory spent Thanksgiving with their aunt Eleanor, but next year Glory'll be with us and maybe Annie and Aunt Eleanor too." Ruffling Abby's curls, he gave Henry a Dutch rub. "You guys didn't eat all the ice cream, I hope, because if you did, somebody's going to pay."

"We did!" they squealed, and Steven jumped up like he was going to chase 'em down.

Bedlam broke loose when cousins shrieked out the front door just as Gabe thundered down the steps. "Steven," she shouted, latching her coat on the way out, "make sure Pop knows it was Henry who blew ice-cream bubbles out of his pipe, okay? Bye!"

Sean sauntered through the kitchen door, pipe in hand and a crooked smile on his face. "Good thing Pop likes butter pecan, or Henry could be in big trouble." Setting Patrick's pipe by his chair, Sean strolled to the front door to put on his jacket, flashing a warm smile. "Great meeting you, Maggie." He nodded toward the kitchen. "Don't let Steven coerce you into mopping up—it's no place for a lady. G'night, all."

The door slammed shut like a vault, leaving nothing but silence and air that was hard to breathe. Steven popped up, preferring to deal with his mother's sticky kitchen instead of Maggie's sticky question. He squeezed her hand. "Mags, put your feet up and relax while I clean up, okay?" He paused. "You want anything? Coffee, soda, water?"

"You?" she whispered with a shy tilt of her head. She twined her fingers in his and pulled him back down.

"Maggie, I—"

She kissed him, and the familiar taste of her mouth reminded him how this very attraction had altered their lives. He pulled back to stroke her cheek. "Mags, I need to get the kitchen cleaned up and then walk you home. Unless you want to call Frailey since I don't have a car?"

"No . . . walking's fine." She hesitated, peeking up beneath sooty lashes. "Steven?"

"Mmm?" He brushed a strand of hair from her face.

"You didn't answer my question," she said softly, blue eyes locked with his. "I know you had feelings for Annie or you wouldn't have dated her, but . . ." She swallowed hard. "You care about me too, right? Enough to make this marriage work?"

He smiled, his eyes softening as he studied her. "I wouldn't have asked you to marry me, Mags, if I didn't. Nobody's that noble."

Her smile wavered. "Oh, I don't know—you seem to be." She tilted her head, her gaze fragile. "You've changed a lot,

Steven. There was a time you couldn't keep your hands off me."

"I know," he said quietly. "But I was wrong, and I regret it." He leaned in to graze his lips against hers. "But trust me, Mags, the chemistry's still there."

"But I need to be sure," she whispered, eyes clouded with insecurity.

He stared, the pull of attraction there to a faint degree, but nothing like it once was. His gaze flicked to her full lips before he slowly leaned in to take her mouth with his, reminding himself that Maggie, not Annie, was the mother of his child and would soon be his wife. His mind clung to the thought, but when she deepened the kiss, alarm curled in his stomach. He nudged her back. "Come on, Mags—I want to keep this aboveboard till we're married."

She sat up with a hurt crimp of brows. "But we'll be married in less than a month, Steven, and all I'm asking for is a few kisses. And it's not like we haven't been intimate before."

He drew in a deep breath. "That was then, Maggie, this is now. I want this marriage to work for Glory's sake and ours, which means we do it God's way, period."

She blinked. "God? Since when are you interested in—" Her eyes flared wide. "Wait—this has to do with Annie, doesn't it? She got to you, didn't she?"

He sighed and rubbed her arms. "I won't lie—Annie's been a positive influence. She started me thinking about God in a way I never have before, and it's changed my life." He lifted her chin, gaze gentle. "Which is why I want to marry you. Yes, I care about you, and yes, I'm still attracted to you, but Glory deserves two parents who love her and you deserve a man you can trust." He drew in a fortifying breath. "A man who promised to marry you when you gave him your all. I didn't honor my promise then, but I intend to now for Glory and for you."

Her eyes drifted closed. "You're in love with her, aren't you?"

He was tempted to lie, but he knew he couldn't. Not anymore. "That's not important."

"It is to me!" Her eyes blazed open, fire and pain burning in their depths. "Are you?"

He studied her, loathe to hurt her but unwilling to deny the truth. "I was on my way."

Hand to her eyes, her body crumpled with a heave, and he scooped her up, head bent to hers as he kneaded her back. "Maggie, it doesn't matter."

"It does," she rasped. With a violent shudder, she angled her chin. "Does she love you?"

"I . . . don't know . . . ," he said, quite sure Annie probably hated him by now—he certainly would. He'd left it to Maggie to explain the situation, avoiding Annie ever since.

"You do know!" she screamed, tears ravaging her face. "Don't lie to me, Steven. Annie said you and she were just dating and nothing more, but I have to know—does-she-love-you?"

He stared for several seconds. "You have to ask her."

She shook his arms, teeth clenched. "I'm asking you!"

He paused. A muscle quivered in his cheek. "I think so."

She sagged back on the couch with a hand to her eyes.

"It doesn't matter," he said, gripping her arms. "All that matters is you, me, and Glory."

A shiver rippled as she shook her head. "It does matter," she whispered. "I love my sister, Steven, and I'm not a monster."

"No, Glory is the only thing that matters now," he said quietly. "Everything else is insignificant next to our daughter."

A low moan trailed from Maggie's lips as her shoulders slumped into a sob. "Not 'our' daughter, Steven," she whispered, her voice barely audible, "mine."

His blood stilled to a crawl. "What do you mean?" he said, voice hoarse.

She looked up then, and he saw it all—her love for him, her grief, her shame. "I lied because I need you, and yes, I care for you . . . but you're not Glory's father."

He shot up, fury stuttering his words. "W-what?"

Bolting to her feet, she grasped his arm. "I thought . . . that if you still cared for me, maybe, just maybe, we could try again and make a home for Glory." She moved in close, slipping shaky hands to his waist. "Steven, I only did it because I love you . . ."

He flung her arms away, eyes burning with fury. "By lying and manipulating? God help Glory with a mother like you! And to think I almost made you my wife."

"It's not like that," she cried, her voice almost shrill. "I was angry at Annie for betraying me and angry at you for telling me the past was dead and gone, because for me . . . ," her eyes met his, brimming with tears, "it isn't, Steven. I could tell you still cared and I certainly knew you were still attracted to me, so I just . . . ," she drew in a shaky breath, "stretched the truth a bit."

"Stretched-the-truth-a-bit?" he enunciated tersely. His jaw sagged in disbelief before it went to rock. "You can't stretch what you don't have, Maggie."

She rubbed her arms, eyes desperate. "I would have never done it if you told me you loved Annie, Steven, but you didn't, and then you proposed—"

"Because you tricked me!" he railed. He paced, bile thick in his throat, then wheeled around. "What kind of woman are you anyway?"

"A desperate one, in love with my daughter!" She moved to where he stood, a tic pulsing in his jaw. "You said you still cared, Steven, and I care about you too, and you said you didn't love Annie, so I just thought . . ." She shuddered, avoiding his gaze. "What did I have to lose?"

"Oh, I don't know—your self-respect?" He clenched his hands for fear he would shake her. "Why would you do that to your own sister if you knew she loved me?"

"Because she told me she didn't!" she screamed, fingers quivering when she pushed the hair from her face. She closed her eyes, shoulders slumping as she turned away. "And because I wanted to be a mother to Glory," she whispered, "and I c-can't do that a-alone."

She started to weep, and he felt his fury fade, but he wasn't willing to let it go.

Not yet.

Striding to where she stood, he gripped her, her tears finally softening his hold. He willed his body to settle down, forcing his temper to calm. "Maggie, we'll get through this somehow," he said stiffly, "but not before you tell me the truth." He lifted her chin with a firm finger, muscles twitching his jaw. "Who's the father?" he breathed.

She shook her head and tried to back away. "It's not you, Steven, so why do you care?"

He jerked her back. "Blast it, Maggie, I care about Glory, and God help me, I don't know why, but I care about you too." He sucked in a halting breath, compelling himself to relax. He lowered his voice. "We were going to be married, Mags, I was going to be Glory's father. I have a right to know who it was and when it happened." He thought of Glory, and his heart wrenched, forcing a crack in his voice. "I *need* to know if there's the slightest chance Glory can know her father." A thought struck, and the air thinned in his chest. *Please, God, not Brubaker or Brannock*, he thought, painfully aware Maggie had flirted with both to make him jealous.

Body wavering, she stared, lids rimmed red and despair bleeding from her eyes. He steadied her with a gentle hold, watching as her lips opened and closed.

His heart thudded in his chest while he massaged her arms. "We'll get you through this, Mags, I promise . . . but first I need to know." He drew in a deep breath and took her hands in his, encouraging her with a light squeeze. "Who is it?" he asked quietly.

Her jaw trembled as she pressed a kiss to his palm, eyes raw with pain. "Oh, Steven, please don't hate me." Her gaze dropped as if she couldn't bear to witness his reaction, but not before he saw the truth in her eyes.

Joe.

18

So, help me, Walsh, you're a dead man. Steven latched the iron gate of Aunt Eleanor's Georgian brownstone and stared at the house where two sisters resided for whom he cared deeply—one he'd planned to marry and one he now hoped he could. He noted all windows were dark, which was to be expected long after midnight. Burying his hands in his pockets, he headed north to Washington Street where his partner lived, the best friend who'd betrayed him with the woman he'd loved. His jaw hardened as he picked up his pace, wounded that Joe never told him how he'd felt about Maggie. Since they'd traded baseball cards in the first grade, he and Joe confided in each other about *everything*—everything but Maggie, it seemed—and Steven felt the sting deep in his soul.

The wind whipped at his unbuttoned coat, but he didn't feel the cold. He was too hot at Joe to even notice, and God knows he needed to cool down. He'd always known Maggie and Joe were close, even spending time together when Steven couldn't, but he hadn't known *how* close. After he'd raged and ranted, he and Maggie had talked for hours before he walked her home. He soon discovered she'd turned to Joe when Steven broke up with her in their sophomore year. His lip curled. A real friend in need: comforting her, supporting her.

Loving her.

Steven never meant the breakup to last for long. He'd only wanted to give Maggie some of her own after she'd flirted and done God knows what else with both Brubaker and Brannock to make him jealous. The two guys he hated most in the world, and Maggie knew it, letting them paw and parade her like some prize trophy. Like she belonged to them, but she didn't. She belonged to Steven, body and soul, and he belonged to her. But in a jealous rage to teach her a lesson, he'd taunted her with Erica, and he and Maggie had paid the price.

And soon, Walsh.

Maggie had left Boston, and Steven had been sick with missing her, his love as potent as the hard grain alcohol that flowed through his veins when he tried to forget her. Looking back, he remembered Joe being in a funk too, but then he and Joe were so close they seemed to share everything— highs, lows, moods, failings. *And my girlfriend, apparently.* It should be Steven marrying Maggie, but now that was impossible. Glory needed her father, not her father's best friend, and Steven was going to make sure Joe Walsh owned up to his responsibilities.

Tonight.

He turned the corner, ignoring a group coming out of Brannigan's, loud and lewd and obviously drunk, no matter the law. Something hitched in his chest, and he realized it was a strange mix of regret and gratitude. Regret because that once had been him . . . and gratitude because it no longer was. Maggie came to mind, and his heart ached for all they'd been through, but he vowed to be there for her even if it wasn't as her husband. He didn't envy her telling Annie the truth, but she'd promised she would in the morning, and his heart skipped a beat.

Annie. The little girl he'd looked down on, the "kid still wet behind the ears," had become the woman who'd set the little boy in him free . . . to become the man he'd always hoped to be. A faint smile softened the hard line of his lips. A man now able to love the kind of woman he'd always longed to have. A woman who not only changed his life for the better but that of everyone she knew, from Glory to Aunt Eleanor . . . and now Maggie. The tightness in his chest eased a bit. Part of the reason Maggie had confessed, she said, was because she'd seen something in her sister that struck hard—kindness, honesty, selflessness—things she'd seldom seen in the star-struck world of Hollywood. And, oddly enough, things she'd begun to crave. She'd been baffled when she sensed the same in Steven, a decency that drew her, and she was stunned to realize she wanted what they had. *Even* if it meant giving up one for the other.

A wavering sigh parted from his lips as he hurried up the steps of Joe's mom's perfectly groomed three-decker home, a few streets over from Steven's in the Southie neighborhood of Boston. Steven had spent as much time on this front porch as he had his own, poring over comic books and playing Mysto Magic, and the memories suddenly thickened in his throat. Joe was the best friend he'd ever had, a brother in every way but blood, and Steven knew he'd forgive him.

Eventually.

He rammed his finger to the doorbell and waited, grateful Mrs. Walsh, a near-deaf widow since a year ago May, would never even wake up. But Joe would, and Steven badgered the button again, fresh adrenaline pumping over what he'd done to Maggie.

The porch light went on, and the door wheeled open. Joe blinked through slits, his stubble as dark as the glare in hazel eyes now blackened to brown. "What the devil are you doing, O'Connor?" he groaned, his voice gruff with sleep. He swiped a hand across a sleeveless T-shirt to scratch a muscular chest matted with sandy hair, then cocked a hip, feet bare beneath plaid pajama bottoms. "For crying out loud, it's past one in the morning."

"Outside, Walsh," Steven ordered, the sight of his half-clad "best friend" boiling his blood when thoughts of him with Maggie flashed through his mind. "Now!"

The scowl on Joe's face faded into confusion as he opened the screen door. "Don't be stupid, Steven, come inside and tell me what's wrong."

Steven jerked the front of Joe's T-shirt and yanked him outside before slamming him to the wall. "Twenty years we've been friends, Walsh, and we swore no secrets, but you didn't keep that promise, did you, Joe?"

Joe shoved him away hard, thrusting Steven against the newel post of the porch banister. He was fully awake now, thick arms corded and ready to take Steven on. "What the devil are you talking about, O'Connor? Are you drunk?"

"Nope, dead sober." Hands itching hot, he bulldozed him to the wall again, two-fisting his shirt to pin him with fire in his eyes. "Just like I was when Maggie told me you slept with her."

Joe froze. Even in the dim lighting, Steven saw the blood siphon from his face as his body went slack. Lids shuttering closed, he lowered his head when Steven flung him away, sagging against the wall with a hand to his eyes. "Why'd she have to tell you?" he whispered, his voice hoarse with shame. "It was only one time, Steven, and it was a mistake."

"I'll say, Walsh. A life-shattering one—*yours*."

He looked up then, eyes glazed with anguish, and Steven saw the truth in his face—the torment of a man who loved both his best friend and the woman between them. Like a zombie, Joe lumbered to the far side of the porch, dropping onto the wooden swing where he and Steven ate Good Humor bars in the summer while they traded comic books and army men. He bent as if he were an old man, shoulders stooped and face in his hands. Moving to the railing, Steven eased down on the handrail, arms crossed as he waited for him to speak. When he did, his voice was so broken and low, Steven had to strain to hear it.

"I . . . never, *ever* intended that to happen, Steven, I swear. We were just friends . . ."

Steven grunted, biting back a curse but not his anger. "Friends don't sleep together, Walsh, nor stab their best friend in the back."

"Blast it, O'Connor, I know that," he hissed, head jerking up and eyes ablaze. "You think this has been easy for me? Knowing I betrayed you both, the friend I'd go to the mat for and the woman I craved? I've died a thousand times over what happened that night, despising myself for being a man so in love with my best friend's girl I was willing to be her best friend too, just to be near her." He sank back into the swing, arms limp as he wandered off into a glassy stare. "But all she ever wanted was you, and I swear, Steven, if it'd been any other man, I would have bloodied him." He glanced up then, resignation sagging every muscle in his face. "But I knew she deserved better than me, and it didn't take a quarter of the brains in my head to figure out that was you. You were always the smart one, the kid the teachers loved, and that blasted guy girls always went crazy for." A sheen of moisture glimmered in his eyes while a muscle jerked in his throat. "But I love you like a brother, Steven, and I swear I never intended for that to happen . . . nor saw it coming."

Steven exhaled slowly, his anger finally drifting out with a billow of air that collided with the cool of the night. "How *did* it happen?" he said quietly.

Joe sucked in a deep breath and massaged the bridge of his nose, his voice as flat and dead as the wood banister Steven straddled. "Maggie didn't act like it in front of you, but she was devastated when you guys broke up. I can't tell you how many nights she cried, and I always gave her a shoulder to cry on and nothing else, I swear." He hung his head, avoiding Steven's eyes as he peered at the floor. "Until the night she saw you kissing Erica at the Pier." He shook his head, grief weighting his features. "I'd never seen her like that before—depressed, crazy, ready to rip Erica's eyes out. So I got her out of there fast. Pop lent me his car that night, so I planned to drive her back to the dorm, only . . ." He licked his lips, fingers fidgeting on the wood slats of the swing. "I was scared because she was talking crazy, acting like she was going to hurt herself to get your attention, and I . . . I wanted to stay . . . make sure she was okay, you know? Only she was bent on drinking to forget and begged me for some of that giggle water you and I stashed, so we drove to Lover's Landing because that's where she wanted to go."

Steven closed his eyes, guilt stabbing. *The same parking spot, the same car as our first time . . .*

Joe inhaled and the air shuddered from his body as he glanced up, sorrow wet in his eyes. "The truth is, we got plastered, Steven, literally fried to the hat, and one thing led to another and the next thing I knew . . . ," his Adam's apple shifted while his voice trailed low, "we're waking up the next morning in the backseat of the car, guilty, awkward, and sick to our stomachs." The edge of his lip crooked. "And I mean literally—Maggie threw up all over me and Pop's car."

"Good," Steven said, fighting to stay mad. His eyes went hard. "So who made the first pass, Walsh—you or her?"

He hesitated and swallowed hard, his face creased and riddled with hurt. "She did, Steven, but I suspected all along she only did it to make you pay and I know I should have stopped it, all of it—the Landing, the booze, the necking in the car."

"The baby?"

The word hissed from his lips before he could bite it back, and he may as well have spit in Joe's face. The whites of his eyes splayed wide while his jaw went slack, and his skin leeched as pasty as if he'd just come off that drunk he'd had with Maggie.

"What?" It was a rasp, shallow and harsh. "What are you talking about?"

Steven stared, and suddenly he no longer saw the buddy who'd slept with his girl but the best friend who'd shared his lunch, his toy soldiers, and his comic books for most of his life. The kid he took a bullet for when Joe ruined his father's tie in a magic trick gone awry, and the kid who'd slammed Wilbur Morrison to the ground after he blackened Steven's eye. They were as close to family as two boys could be, mingling blood via an army knife in a pup tent in the Walshes' backyard. Steven's heart twisted as he swallowed the emotion in his throat, the slice of the blade then as sharp as the blade that severed them now—as brothers, partners, and friends who shared everything but this.

Fatherhood.

And yet, somehow, Steven shared his pain.

Heart heavy, Steven moved to sit on the far end of the swing, head bent and hands clasped on knees splayed wide. He felt Joe's stare burning into his profile and exhaled, eyes fixed on the spindles in the wraparound porch. "Think about it, Joe," he whispered. "Maggie went away for a year shortly after that." He looked over then, meeting Joe's gaze, empathy burning in his chest. "She had a baby girl in California, and she told me it was mine, which is why I proposed." He turned to peer out into the brisk night studded with stars, squinting up into the sky. "Made me promise not to say anything to any of my friends till we got married, especially you."

The weathered wood of the swing groaned when Joe slumped back. Sweat glazed his forehead like the shock that glazed his eyes, and when his fingers rose to absently press at his temples, they quivered as much as Steven's insides at the thought of what lay ahead for his best friend.

His touch to Joe's shoulder produced no reaction as Joe continued in a blank stare, breathing ragged.

Steven gripped his arm. "Joe, you need to know your daughter's in Boston."

That did the trick. Joe's head jerked up, mouth gaping so wide, it could have been a yawn. "What?" Every muscle in his face seemed to work at the same time, cheek twitching, lip quivering, and a spasm in his temple that matched the one in his eyes. His voice was a rasp tinged with awe. "M-my daughter? In B-boston?"

"Yeah," Steven said quietly, cuffing his shoulder. "She's a great kid, Joe, so much life and fun, she's a true chip off the old block."

Moisture stung Steven's lids when a flash of tears brimmed in Joe's eyes. "Y-you . . . you've s-seen her?" he whispered, his throat working hard to push the words from his tongue.

"Yeah, I have, Joe, and I love her like my own."

Sandy brows pinched hard in confusion. "But when? How?"

He squeezed Joe's shoulder once more before letting go, then inhaled for strength. "It's Annie's little sister, Glory."

Joe stared for several seconds, all air suspended, and then, body crumpling, he buried his face in his hands, elbows quivering as he wept.

Steven felt every single heave as if it were his own, and rising to his feet, he distanced himself to give Joe space, hip cocked against the railing and arms folded as he stared into the shadowed street. Moments passed before silence fell, and with the faint squeak of the swing, he turned to face his best friend. "Are you okay?" he asked quietly.

"Yeah," Joe said with a hoarse chuckle, resting his head on the back of the swing. "Although a blow to the gut would have been kinder."

Steven strolled over to sit, lips quirked. "Don't think I didn't consider it." He huffed out a sigh. "So, what happens from here?"

A grunt tripped from Joe's lips. "I'm going to meet my daughter, that's what."

"She doesn't know, Joe. Maggie and I planned to tell her after we married."

Joe nodded. "I know, it's a delicate situation to say the least." He glanced up, a steel glint in his eyes. "But she's my daughter, Steven, my blood, and by God, I will be a part of her life."

A smile flickered at the edge of Steven's mouth. "Never doubted it for a minute."

Drawing in a deep breath, Joe released it again with a shake of his head. "I'm sorry for putting you through this, for betraying you . . ." His chest rose and fell as the barest trace of a smile appeared. "But I gotta tell you, Steven, this might just border on being one of the best things that's ever happened to me." Tears glistened in his eyes and he leaned forward, elbows on his knees and body taut with excitement as he rested his chin on folded hands. "Kids are the greatest things God ever put on this planet, and to think he took the biggest mistake of my life and turned it into this . . ." He shook his head, throat convulsing with a hard swallow. He shot Steven a sideways glance. "I'll tell you what, you have my word—I'm going to do right by Glory."

"I know that, Walsh," Steven said. His gaze met Joe's. "But what about Maggie?"

A harsh chuckle erupted from his throat. "Yeah, like Maggie would ever consider me when she's in love with you."

"I think you're wrong."

Joe flashed him a sharp look. "Why?" His tone was terse . . . and yet held a thread of hope.

"Because Maggie's in love with her little girl and wants to be a mom more than anything in this world. Which is why she was willing to go so far as to trick me and close her eyes to the hurt she might cause her sister. She was in denial, Joe, a woman so desperate to become a mom to her daughter, she was willing to do almost anything."

The edge of Joe's mouth tipped up. "Including marrying me, I suppose?" A grin hovered. "You saying a gal would have to be desperate to marry me, O'Connor?"

Steven grinned. "Pretty much."

Joe's laughter rang out into the frigid night, clouds of warm air swirling into the heavens above. Steven smiled. *Like my prayers . . .*

"Well, heaven knows I won't find the woman I love in a more vulnerable position." He chuckled again, eyes in a squint. "You really think she'd consider marrying a clown like me?"

371

Steven slid him a sideways glance. "She'd be crazy not to, Joe. You already have a foundation of friendship and you like each other."

A grin split Joe's face. "Well, I do anyway . . ."

"She will too, Joe, in time. But you're gonna have to woo her, lure her into falling in love with you."

Joe cocked his head. "Yeah? And how do I do that, O'Connor, since you're the all-fire expert when it comes to Maggie Kennedy?"

Sinking back in the swing, Steven folded his arms, studying Joe with a pensive smile. "A proper courtship, dates alone, dates with her and Glory, and all aboveboard, with you in control."

"In control?" His grunt echoed in the stillness of morning. "It's one thing to be friends with Maggie, but for me to date her? Not sure it's possible to be in control in that scenario."

"You have no choice," Steven said with a weary sigh. "Your future, Glory's, and Maggie's depend on it." He scratched the edge of his brow. "Maggie's as tempting as that apple in the Garden of Eden, Joe. You want to taste it, you want to bite it, you want to swallow it whole, but if you do, I'm telling you right now, it will be the fall of man."

"What do you mean?" Ridges popped in Joe's face.

"I mean if you start dating Maggie, she's going to do her best to tempt you in every way possible, because underneath that beautiful body is a very insecure woman who needs to know the man in her life finds her attractive. The more you turn her away, the harder she'll try, which is why we had so many problems staying out of trouble." He sighed, his smile going flat. "Trust me, I was raised in a devout family, so in the beginning I actually did have the morals to say no, but all it did was make her desperate to get me under her spell, which, regrettably, she did."

"Ha! Maggie—desperate for me? Now that's something I'd like to see." He shook his head. "I don't know, Steven, I don't think I'm strong enough. I've always been over the edge about Maggie anyway. God knows I won't be able to say no to the woman if she starts kissing on me."

"Yeah, you're right, he does."

"Huh?"

Steven angled to face him, arm draped over the swing. "God *does* know exactly how weak we are, Joe, but it doesn't matter 'cause he's strong enough for the both of us."

Joe blinked, eyes in a squint. "Come again?"

"I mean that in order to win Maggie's heart, you're going to need God's help—his strength, his guidance, *and* his confidence." He fixed Joe with a firm gaze. "Ever since I've known you, Joe, you've always acted like second fiddle to me, like you're not as smart as me or as attractive to the girls as you think I am."

"Not think, Steven, *know*."

Steven shook his head. "See? That's what I'm talking about. You have this crazy idea you don't measure up as a man, and the reason I know is because I had it too. When I was a kid, I killed myself trying to please my father, because I never thought I was good enough next to Sean, never felt like I earned Pop's trust like Sean did. And then when I hit college, I flat-out didn't care anymore, and any trust Pop may have had died on the vine." He scrubbed his face with his hand, heaving a weary sigh. "So when I met Annie, I was scared to death I couldn't trust myself to be the kind of man I needed to be—for her. Ironically, it was Annie herself who held the key—living for God instead of yourself."

His hand dropped to the back of the swing once again as he stared at Joe through solemn eyes. "You need to turn to him, Joe, pray for him to change your heart and run the show, then pray for him to help you be the man he wants you to be. The man Maggie needs you to be. And the man Glory needs as a father. Because they're too precious to risk doing it our way, a way that left both of us hollow and unhappy. Once you do, I swear to you on my life, you'll never be the same." A slow grin eased across his lips, bordering on cocky. "And when your confidence is in him, he puts his confidence in you, and you mark my words, Walsh—that kind of confidence will draw sweet Maggie Kennedy like flies to honey."

Averting his gaze, Joe stared out into the dark night, Steven's words obviously rolling around in his brain. He finally glanced over. "His confidence, huh?" He huffed out a sigh. "I've never had all that much myself, Steven, so I'm not sure I'd even know what it feels like. I was just content hiding in your shadow, you know? A second fiddle who was never first with anybody except you, the best friend a man ever had."

Steven gripped Joe's shoulder. "That's where you're wrong, my friend. You've always been 'first' with God, you just didn't know it. So give it a shot, Joe, put God first, talk to Maggie, and then go from there. Because whether your future is with her or not, God has a plan that'll make your head spin. And then look out, Walsh, 'cause you're in for the ride of your life."

A sheepish smile crept across Joe's face. "Not on a carousel, I hope. You know how I can't stand those things."

Rising to his feet, Steven rolled a kink from his neck. "Nope, on this ride you won't be going in circles, buddy boy. But the speed at which your life changes for the better?" He grinned, groaning with a stretch of arms high overhead. "Trust me—you're gonna be *real* dizzy."

※

Annie stirred, awakened by a soft giggle floating from Glory's lips as she slept, spooning in her sister's arms.

Correction: her aunt's arms. Annie wondered if she'd ever get used to the shock that Glory was Maggie's daughter instead of her sister. Since Maggie had come home for good three weeks ago, she'd primped and pampered and played with Glory as if she were an oversize doll, taking her everywhere during the day and cuddling all night . . . except for the nights she was out late with Steven, of course. Like tonight.

Pure torture.

Annie sighed and shimmied close to Glory, eyes weighting shut with a heavy malaise that ushered in another lonely night despite the bundle of innocence snoring in her arms. She'd heard Maggie come in after midnight, and the faint click of the front door in the foyer reverberated through her as if it were the slam of her bedroom door, jolting her body despite the cocoon of Glory's warmth. And all because she knew that on the other side, Steven O'Connor was walking away, out of her life, again and again, a serial nightmare that never seemed to end . . .

No! Annie squeezed her eyelids tight, desperate to stem the flow of tears that inevitably swelled, whispering the Scripture from Jeremiah 29:11 that Faith had given her to memorize.

"For I know the thoughts that I think toward you, saith the LORD, thoughts of peace, and not of evil, to give you an expected end."

An expected end.

Tears seeped onto her pillow. Up till three weeks ago, she'd "expected" to fall further in love with Steven O'Connor and marry him, having his children. But not anymore. Her expected end had taken an unexpected turn, and now Steven would marry her sister to make a proper home for their child.

His child.

Glory. The little girl who slept in her arms, Steven's blood and issue. With a quivering hand, Annie touched the wispy curls of Glory's head, her heart breaking that this little girl and her mother would always belong to Steven while Annie never would. With a soft little snort, Glory turned over and scooted away, depriving Annie of the closeness they'd shared.

Just like her daddy.

Stop! She shot up in the bed, hugging her legs to her chest and forehead to her knees, clinging to Faith's words of wisdom to ward off the pain. "I will not feel sorry for myself," she whispered through gritted teeth, "I will praise you in the face of this, God, and I *will* move on with my life. Thank you that you have blessed Glory with parents, Maggie with a husband, and Steven with a wife." The words spilled from her lips in a rush, her mind anxious to say them, confirm them, *feel* them. "Your Word says all things work together for good for those who love you, and I believe that, Lord. Not only for Maggie, Glory, and Steven . . . but for me."

Stillness settled on the room as well as her spirit, and she marveled at the holy silence that prevailed, chasing away the shadows. A tranquility like none she'd ever known, unmarred by the soft breathing of her niece or the distant chime of Aunt Eleanor's grandfather clock, heralding the hour of three. Silver moonbeams spilled across the floor in hazy ribbons of light like the grace of God pouring into her soul, flooding her heart with peace and promise. All at once, tears stung and gratitude swelled in her throat when joy surged like adrenaline, connecting her soul with his. "Oh, Lord, I would be lost without you . . ."

Weeping may endure for a night, Beloved, but joy cometh in the morning.

"Oh yes, Lord," she breathed, that very joy trickling down her cheeks. "Your peace and your will forever . . ." Easing back on the bed, Annie lay there in a wonder, a faint smile on her lips while the steady beat of her heart stole her away to much-needed slumber.

Clink.

Her eyes popped open, and all breath stilled in her chest.

Clink.

She sat up, body trembling and pulse racing.

Ping. Louder this time, thinning her air.

Lengthy pause. *Ping . . . thud.*

Annie vaulted from the bed with a gasp, blood pounding in her ears as she flew to the window. Peering into the shadowed backyard, she saw the silhouette of a man bending to pick up a stone, and she stifled a scream. He rose to his full height while his gaze lifted to her window, and when moonlight revealed his handsome features, her legs nearly buckled beneath her gown.

Steven!

Her fingers shook as she heaved up the sash, the rush of cold air unable to thwart the warmth in her cheeks. "What are you doing here?" she whispered, her tone strained.

He parked hands low on his hips, his smile a glorious gleam of white in the dark. "We need to talk—climb down."

"No," she whispered, shooting a nervous glance at the little girl snoring in her bed. "Glory is sleeping here, and you're engaged to my sister—go away."

The flash of teeth spanned wide as he folded his arms. "Don't make me come up there, Annie, because I will."

"You wouldn't!" Goose bumps popped that had nothing to do with the cold.

Moonlight glinted in his eyes. "Try me, kid—I dare you."

"The trellis won't hold you," she pleaded, her voice hushed with panic. Her heart thumped wildly, faster than Glory's during one of their tickle fests. *Thank you, God, that Maggie's room is on the other side of the house.*

"Then come down."

"No." She worried her lip.

"Fine." Latching his foot at the base of the trellis, he started to climb.

"No!" Her voice was a hiss.

He stopped, head cocked. "You coming down?"

"I c-can't—I'm in my nightgown."

His mouth crooked. "Put on a robe."

"I can't."

He exhaled loudly and continued to rise.

"Stop—I'll get my housecoat." Hurrying to her closet, she wrapped her thick terry robe around her body with a trembling jerk of her sash and donned her slippers before returning to the window, stomach quivering. She stared down where he waited, his face washed in moonlight, and a knot hitched in her throat.

He arched a dark brow. "Anytime, Annie—the sun won't be up for three hours or so."

She chewed on the edge of her lip, fingers fiddling with the tail of her sash. "I . . . can't," she whispered, afraid to go down, afraid to be near him, afraid of what might happen if she did.

He huffed out a sigh. "Why?"

Drawing in a wobbly breath, she sat down on the sill, scrambling for excuses. "I promised I wouldn't climb down that trellis again."

He mumbled under his breath. "Who the devil did you promise that to?"

"You," she said, a smile tickling. "When you walked me home from Ocean Pier, remember?"

"Blast it, Annie, forget the stupid promise! Now climb down before I lose my patience."

Glory snorted in her sleep and Annie jumped, thoughts of Maggie and Glory sobering her considerably. She leaned out the window, a plea in her tone. "Steven, please don't make me. I don't want to come down. You belong to Maggie, and I can't be near you."

"I don't belong to Maggie," he said, his voice low and harsh. "Now either you come down, or I'm coming up. I have something to say, and I don't want to yell it from here." He waited, his jaw as hard as the sill beneath her hand.

She hesitated.

The trellis rattled as he continued to scale.

"Okay—stop!" She slid another anxious look at Glory before dipping one leg over the ledge and then the other, careful to close the window till it was open only an inch. Gnawing on her lip, she slowly picked her way down the latticework, pricking her finger on the way. She hopped from the lowest slat and turned to face him, throat dry as she peered up at his chiseled face. "So, what do you need to tell me?" she whispered, arms clutched tight at her waist. The scent of cloves teased her senses and she took a step back, steeling her tone. "It's cold."

With a swoop of her stomach, he bundled her close before she could speak, stealing her breath when he pressed his mouth to her ear. "I'll keep you warm, you have my word." She opened her mouth to object, and he silenced her with a kiss that made good on his promise. "I love you, Annie Kennedy," he whispered, "and I want to marry you."

Her heart clutched and she shoved him away, tears sparking her eyes. "No! How can you be this cruel when you're going to marry my sis—"

He dazed her with another kiss that blotted out everything but him and the sweet taste of peppermint as his mouth explored hers. "I can't marry your sister," he said, his words warm against her skin while his mouth trailed to her ear. "Because I'm in love with you . . ."

She jerked back. "But Glory—"

"Is *not* my daughter."

The intensity of his voice matched that in his eyes, and her heart slammed to a stop. "What do you mean?" she whispered, barely able to breathe.

He tunneled gentle fingers through her hair to cradle her head while he fondled her mouth with a tender kiss. "I mean, Maggie confessed I'm not Glory's father, so the engagement's off."

"B-but . . . how? W-who . . . ?" The words stuttered from her tongue, as fractured as her thoughts. She wavered on her feet, knees ready to give way.

He swept her up and carried her to a wrought-iron bench on the cobblestone patio, settling her on his lap while he wrapped her inside of his coat. "I broke up with Maggie the summer of sophomore year, and she was angry at me, so she got drunk one night and—"

"Glory . . . ," she whispered, her heart wrenching for all the heartbreak her sister had obviously endured. She pulled away, eyes spanning wide. "Then, who—"

"Joe," he said quietly, softly brushing a strand of hair from her eyes.

Her breathing stilled while a weak gasp wedged in her throat. "Oh, Steven, no . . ."

"Afraid so." He cuddled her close and kissed her head. "That's why I'm so late getting here tonight. I went to Joe's after Maggie confessed, and we had it out. Seems he's been in love with her all along, only he was too ashamed to tell me." He grunted, a trace of irony in his tone. "And all through college, I just thought they were really close friends. And they were . . . until Maggie and I broke up. Then all it took was a bottle of booze and one fateful mistake."

"A mistake that God turned into a blessing," Annie said softly, her heart filling with wonder at how God redeemed the sin of her sister with a gift as precious as Glory.

"In more ways than one."

She sat up on his lap, slippers dangling. "What do you mean?"

He pressed a gentle kiss to the tip of her nose. "You're the reason Maggie confessed."

"Me?" Her voice cracked.

"Yep." He caressed her face. "Because of your love and deep faith in God, Maggie's ready to turn her life around with God's help." His eyes were tender. "Which is exactly how you won me." His voice trailed off as he bent to nuzzle her lips, gently, reverently, melting her heart into a puddle of pudding, along with her bones. "And," he whispered, skyrocketing her pulse when his mouth wandered to the lobe of her ear, "Joe wants to marry her."

"What?" His words jolted her back, the shock of his statement tingling as much as his touch. "He said that?"

He grinned. "Yep. Guess I never told you, but Joe's a sucker for kids. Spends a lot of time with his nieces, nephews, and kids in the neighborhood, but he's always wanted his own."

Annie shook her head, in complete awe of God. A thought struck, and a frown puckered her brow. "But does Maggie want to marry him?"

"Maggie wants to do anything that'll let her be a mom and give Glory a good home."

Her heart twisted, robbing her joy. "But . . . she's in love with you," Annie whispered.

Steven tucked a finger to her chin and slowly grazed her jaw with his thumb, his solemn gaze meeting hers. "Hear me on this, Annie Kennedy—your sister is not in love with me any more than I am with her. We care about each other, yes, and we always will. But we talked it out, and she knows I'm in love with you, and she's okay with that. Maggie and I were in love once, it's true, and we have a history, but both of us were doing this for Glory's sake and nothing more." His eyes flitted to her lips and back, taking on a smoky quality that matched the wayward curve of his smile. He leaned in, his lips a mere breath away. "Now you?" The smile spelled trouble as he slowly slid his mouth against hers. He gently tugged and tasted while his husky chuckle feathered her lip. "Another matter altogether, Baby Doll."

She swallowed hard, a dozen hummingbirds taking flight in her belly. "S-so . . . where do we go from here?" she breathed, pulse throbbing.

"Glad you asked, kid." His smile eased into a grin. "Why don't we go here," he whispered, teasing her with a gentle sway of his lips before taking her with a kiss that tingled all the way to her toes. "And here . . ." He nipped at her earlobe, his mouth tracing from the curve of her neck to the hollow of her throat, nuzzling to unleash a silent moan in her chest.

"S-steven . . . I . . . need to go in . . ." Her whisper was weak, head drifting back to allow him full range.

Eyes closed, she felt his fingers twine with hers. He lifted her hand and skimmed her wrist with his lips, caressing her palm with a lingering kiss. "And finally, Annie Kennedy," he said softly, voice husky with intent, *we go here . . .*"

Her eyes popped wide at the touch of cold to her skin, and she gasped when something hovered on the tip of her finger. Moonlight glittered off the diamond ring he held, blurring into a million halos of light as tears welled in her eyes. "Oh, Steven . . ."

"Say it, Annie," he whispered, the love in his eyes glowing like the diamond in his hand. "Make a liar out of a man who said he wouldn't fall in love with a kid."

A grin tipped her mouth. "I don't know, Agent O'Connor, I distinctly remember you saying no pushy kid still wet behind the ears was going to tell you what to do."

He grinned. "Okay, then," he said with a wink, tossing the ring in the air before slipping it back in his pocket.

"Oh no you don't," she hissed, jerking it back. "Put it on, O'Connor—*now*!"

He chuckled and slid the ring on her finger. "Well, aren't you the pushy little brat," he said with a grin. He paused, shifting her hand to squint at the underside of her finger. A pucker creased in his brow. "Hey, you cut yourself coming down that blasted trellis, Annie." Assessing the blood on the tip of her finger, he bent to gently suck it away, and her stomach pulsed when his heated gaze connected with hers.

She yanked her hand away. "It's fine," she said, her voice a near croak, "but you're going home, Steven O'Connor—right now!"

A slow smile eased across his lips. "You're a bossy little thing, you know that, Kennedy?" Ignoring her protest, he dipped her back on his lap, mouth roaming her throat. A low groan rumbled from his chest when his hand skimmed the curve of her thigh.

"Steven!" Arms flailing, she scrambled up with a hand to his chest, her breathing as heavy as his. "You haven't begun to see 'bossy,' " she said with a vault off his lap. Stepping out of range, she plunked hands on her hips, determined he'd play by her rules, engagement or no. She jabbed a finger toward the street. "I love you, Steven O'Connor, but go . . . home . . . *now*. Or this ring will be back in your pocket like that." She snapped her fingers and hiked her chin with a fold of her arms, biting back a smile at the shock on his face.

Lumbering to his feet, he buttoned his coat with a boyish grin that faded to soft. "Have I told you just how much I love you, kid? 'Cause I do." Mischief twinkled in his eyes. "And don't get your knickers in a knot, Miss Kennedy, because you're not the only one who intends to do this the right way. I may be stubborn and have a one-track mind at times, but I'm not stupid." With a gentle twine of her fingers, he led her to the trellis and nodded up. "Go on up. I'll leave when you're safely inside."

Her sigh billowed into the cool air, the smile on her lips growing along with the love in her heart. "Thank you, Steven," she said softly, lifting on tiptoe to brush her lips against his. "And I love you too—with all of my heart. Good night."

"G'night, Annie," he whispered. "Call you tomorrow."

She wedged her slipper into the first slat and turned, extending her arm to gaze at her hand. "Mmm . . . must be a magical ring," she said with a touch of smirk. She wiggled her brows. "Sure has a lot of power."

"Yes, ma'am, you're the boss," he said with a lazy smile. "For now." He grazed a final kiss to her lips, the dangerous gleam in his eyes causing her stomach to tumble. "But I wouldn't get too used to it, Baby Doll." His chuckle was husky, a warm cloud floating up to caress her face like a kiss. "Because when the vows are said, the power *will* shift." He winked. "And the ring on my hand will trump yours."

Epilogue

or unto us a child is born, unto us a son is given: and the government shall be upon his shoulder: and his name shall be called Wonderful, Counselor, The mighty God, The everlasting Father, The Prince of Peace."

The Prince of Peace.

Annie closed her eyes, the sound of Mr. O'Connor's voice filling her heart with peace and joy like nothing she'd ever known. She snuggled into Steven's embrace on the love seat in the O'Connors' parlor on this Christmas Eve, and he scooped her close. The spicy scent of cloves from his Bay Rum mingled with the smell of pine and cinnamon and popcorn fresh-popped to loop a tree that touched the ceiling. Boughs heavy with colored lights and ornaments glittered and swayed with strands of tinsel, the breeze from the radiator causing the tree to shimmer and shine as if it breathed the same intoxicating air as she. The parlor lights were dimmed, lending an ethereal air to a cozy room where a fire crackled and children sat spellbound on the floor while Steven's father read about the birth of a babe.

Annie's eyelids edged up to scan the room, drinking in a wealth of love and tenderness she hadn't experienced since Christmases long ago when she and Maggie had been small and her parents so very much in love. The bittersweet memory made her miss Maggie and Glory all the more, and she prayed their evening with Aunt Eleanor, Joe, and his mom would be just as special.

Marcy sat on the couch next to her husband, the glow of peace in her face matching that in Annie's heart. Beside them, Faith and Collin cuddled, arms looped around three precious daughters while a brand-new son snoozed over the shoulder of a very proud father. Luke's head rested on the back of a chair by the hearth, his arms encircling Katie and Kit, both snug in his lap. Gabe, Hope, and Henry lay sprawled on the floor next to Teddy and Molly while Mitch and Charity lay in Patrick's new La-Z-Boy with her head on his chest. Butted against Annie and Steven's love seat, Brady cradled Lizzie between his legs, chin resting on her head as she held baby Sara in her arms. A sigh of contentment wisped across Annie's lips when Steven slowly grazed her arm with his thumb, her heart spilling over with gratitude for God's gift of his Son . . . and for Marcy and Patrick who had given her theirs, along with the precious gift of family.

Patrick closed the Bible with a quiet thump, and Gabe and Henry shot up at the very same time, tightly coiled springs exploding with excitement. "Can we open presents now?" Gabe shouted, skinny legs dancing as she hopped up and down, and Annie couldn't help but smile.

"Yeah, can we, please, please?" Henry echoed, for once in sound agreement.

Tongue to teeth, Marcy glanced at the clock. "Not till Sean and Emma come," she said, voice raised to override all groans. "They said seven, and it's only ten minutes past."

"Why are they late, anyway?" Steven asked, absently fondling a strand of Annie's hair before pressing a kiss to her cheek, causing Annie to lean back with a sigh.

"That's what I'd like to know too. Anyone know?" Katie shifted to get comfortable on Luke's lap before zeroing in on her sister with a suspicious lift of her brow. "Charity?"

Charity blinked, obviously caught off guard. "Uh . . . I think they had an appointment."

"On Christmas Eve?" Faith ruffled the dark hair on Brennan's head, an exact replica of his father's. "Who would schedule appointments on Christmas Eve, for goodness' sake?"

"Not sure," Charity said, tongue gliding across her teeth in the same nervous habit as her mother. She attempted to scoot out of the chair. "Eggnog, anyone?"

"Oh no you don't," Katie said, eyes in a squint. "You've got guilt written all over you, so you may as well spill it. Where are they?"

"Charity Katherine Dennehy, do you know what's going on?" Steel edged Marcy's tone.

"Mother, they're fine, I assure you."

"It's not like Sean to be late," Steven said, buffing Annie's arm, as if to ease the hint of tension she'd seldom seen with his family before.

Patrick prodded a pipe cleaner through the stem of his pipe before tapping the bowl in his palm. "If you know something, Charity, you best spit it out, because I won't have your mother worrying herself sick on Christmas Eve."

Unleashing a weary sigh, Charity's eye skimmed the room, mouth pursed as she studied the worried faces of her family. Drawing in a deep breath, she exhaled once again, lips flat. "Okay, all right, already! But nobody here better dare accuse me of not keeping a secret . . ."

Katie leaned forward, and Annie found herself doing the same, awaiting Charity's answer while Katie arched a brow. "So? Where are they?"

Charity's mouth slanted. "If you must know, Sean and Emma are—"

"Here at last! Sorry we're late, everybody. Merry Christmas!" Sean stomped the snow from his feet at the front door, along with Emma, their cheeks ruddy with cold and arms loaded with bags.

Relief seeped from Marcy's lungs in a slow exhale of air. "For heaven's sake, you two, where have you been?" Her eyes flitted to the mantel clock and back as she hurried into the foyer to give Emma a hug. Whirling to do the same with Sean, she stopped, outstretched arms frozen midair. She blinked at a dark woolen blanket draped over his shoulder. "What on earth?" Stepping close, she lifted the edge to peek in and gasped as tears welled in her eyes.

"Merry Christmas, Grandma," Sean said with a broad grin, the glimmer of moisture in his gaze matching that in his mother's. "Unto us a son is given . . ."

Oh, Lord! Marcy's hand quivered to her mouth as pandemonium broke loose, but she barely heard the babble of voices and questions, all laden with laughter and tears. Prying the bundle from her son, her heart soared as she cradled her sleeping grandson in practiced arms that were shaking nonetheless while daughters hugged and hovered over Sean and Emma.

"B-but how? W-when?" she stuttered, peeling the blanket back to stare in awe. She gazed in wonder at the perfect little face before her, a wisp of dark lashes against rose-petal skin.

Emma laughed, a mist of tears in her eyes as she skimmed a finger across her son's silky cheek. "Patrick was born a week ago, and we weren't even sure till this afternoon whether we'd be able to take him home for Christmas."

"P-patrick?" Marcy whispered, throat swelling as she glanced up at her husband who peered over her shoulder, his eyes as soggy as hers.

Hand cupped to Emma's waist, Sean reached to grip his father's shoulder. "Patrick Daniel O'Connor, but we can call him Daniel, Pop, if you think Patrick would be too confusing." His easy grin was in place despite the sheen in his eyes.

Marcy swallowed a sob while Patrick's Adam's apple dipped in an obvious effort to battle his emotions—further evidence of just why she was desperately in love with this man.

He cleared his throat, returning Sean's hold with a tight grip of his own. "Whatever you decide will be an honor," he said, his words a hoarse croak.

"Yes! The O'Connors live on! Good job, Sean." Slapping his brother on the back, Steven draped an arm over Annie's shoulder with a grin. "At least till I'm up to bat."

"Steven!" Annie elbowed him, cheeks as red as the berries in the wreath on the door.

"Hey, Danny Boy," Charity cooed, eyes moist as she peeked up at Emma. "Good thing you got here—they were about to lynch me up if I didn't spill it, and it was close, let me tell ya."

Emma laughed and tucked an arm to Charity's waist. "You're a vault, my friend."

"It wasn't easy," Charity groused, twisting to give Mitch a pointed look when his arms looped her from behind. She grinned at her father. "Dennehy tumbled the lock, but I threatened him with his life if he tipped off Grandpa at work."

"Threatened him with his life?" Faith peered at the baby over Marcy's shoulder before shooting Charity a teasing grin. "I think you accomplished that when he said 'I do.'"

"Excuse me," Gabe said, waving skinny arms toward the parlor like a traffic cop at rush hour. "If you must pass the babies, *please* do it in there—*please*—we have presents to open."

"You're gonna want one of these someday, squirt," Sean said with a tweak of her neck, "after you get married, and then you'll understand what the fuss is about."

"Yikes, I hope not," the little spitfire said with a shudder. "Boys are saps."

Katie grinned. "Yep, felt that way too, at your age, Gabriella Dawn, but the right boy has a way of gumming up the works." She sighed, lifting on tiptoe to give Luke a kiss.

"Okay, okay, let's move this party into the next room before Gabe pops a button," Sean said with a laugh.

"Yip-peeeee!" Gabe took off like a shot, with the rest of the cousins hot on her heels.

Everyone else herded into the parlor while Lizzie gave Baby Patrick to Emma, who fondled his peach fuzz as if she couldn't believe he was real.

A joyous sigh drifted from Marcy's lips as she took her place on the couch next to her husband, eyes misting over this season of gifts, the greatest of which was God's Son and the blessing of family. No matter the age, size, or maturity, they were children, all. *And all* ours—*Patrick's and mine!* Her gaze traveled to where Steven nuzzled Annie on the love seat, and more gratitude bubbled in her heart for this girl who was already like a daughter.

Resting her head on Patrick's shoulder, Marcy wished this evening could go on forever, precious moments in time when her family cleaved together in an unbreakable bond. *Oh, Lord, how many more Christmases will we have together?* Placing a protective hand on Patrick's leg, she pushed melancholy aside to revel in the here and now, when life was as it should be, a joyous celebration of heart and soul.

The circle of love became a circle of gifts opened one by one, where hearts were unwrapped as well as papers and bows.

"Luke, you're next," Gabe shouted, jarring Marcy from a reverie all too sweet.

He rattled a shoe-box-size present next to his ear. "Ah, the new Keds I've been wanting."

"You think so, huh?" Katie said as he ripped off the paper.

"What can I say?" He waved a Keds box in the air, his smile cocky. "I just have a knack for being right." He tore into the tissue paper, his smile fading when he held up a child's baseball glove and turned it over, a pucker in his brow. "Well, I do need a new glove, Sass, but this is for a little kid." He shot Collin a smirk. "Heck, with this, I'll look like McGuire out on the field."

"You wish," Collin said, Baby Brennan straddled across his chest.

Luke deposited a kiss on Katie's nose. "Thanks, Sass, but we'll have to exchange it."

"Why? If the glove fits . . ." Brady's chuckle floated through the air.

"I think we need to keep it," Katie said with a secret smile.

Luke blinked. "Keep it? But why—" The whites of his eyes expanded. A lump bobbled in his throat as he laid a shaky hand to her stomach. "You're not telling me you're . . ."

She nodded, and he devoured her with a groan, unleashing a chorus of cheers.

Marcy jumped to her feet, dizzy with jubilation. *Another grandchild—oh, Lord, it truly is Christmas!* She waded through a sea of grandchildren and paper to join her daughters in showering Katie with hugs. "When is the baby due?" she breathed, thinking of law school.

A grin bloomed on Katie's face. "August sixteenth—three weeks after the bar exam, don't you know."

"That's cutting it awfully close, McGee," Brady called from across the room, his congratulations merging with the chuckles and heckles from the rest of the men.

Luke grinned. "Which is why I'm the only one who can whip Collin in horseshoes," he volleyed, a gleam of pride in his eyes. He cupped Katie's face in his hands. "This is the best gift you could have given me, Sass. And nothing makes me happier than knowing we both get our dream." He tucked the glove under his arm and wadded up the paper, aiming it at Collin. "See, McGuire? Timing is everything, like I always say on the court."

"Ahem . . ." Gabe stood with arms folded, presiding over cousins and trash as if she were queen. She patted a big box wrapped with a large bow. "I believe there's one more gift to open."

"Go for it, Gabe," Sean yelled. "That box is a monster, and I want to know what it is."

"Don't hafta ask me twice," Gabe said with a grin, cocking her head to read the tag. "To Gabe from . . . ," a knot dipped in her throat, "Mom and Pop." Swabbing a hand to her eyes, she proceeded to claw at the box, paper flying in her wake, like a dog digging a hole. Lifting the lid, she bounced up with a squeal. "Holy moley—a million pieces of Dubble Bubble!" she screamed, vaulting into Marcy's arms from halfway across the room.

Marcy laughed, tears stinging as she locked her new daughter in a hug. "Not quite a million but a definite one-year supply." She pressed a kiss to her cheek. "But that's only the wrapping, Gabriella Dawn—the present is deep inside."

Gabe jerked back, eyes wide. "Really?" She jumped up to pounce on the box, practically diving in until she unearthed a carved cherrywood box. Holding it as if it were a priceless treasure, she slowly slumped to the floor with mouth ajar, a look of wonder in her eyes. "A jewelry box," she whispered, one nail-bitten finger tracing the carved initials on the polished lid. "G.D.O. Gabriella Dawn O'Connor . . ." Her voice trailed off, hushed with awe.

"Your father made it for you," Marcy said, throat catching as Patrick squeezed her waist.

Gabe opened it up and fingered red velvet that cushioned a pink vellum envelope. She glanced up at Marcy with a sheen of tears in almond-shaped eyes, and Marcy nodded with tears of her own. "Open it, darling," she whispered.

Setting the box down as if the most fragile of gifts, Gabe unfolded pink vellum paper. Her voice shook as she read the first sheet that Marcy had committed to memory.

Daughter of Our Heart,

God saved the best for last. We give you our love,
our hope, and our prayers . . .
and a name God always meant you to have,
Gabriella Dawn O'Connor.

Love,
Your very proud parents

Gabe's lips trembled when the second sheet—the signed adoption document—fluttered to her lap, and with a choked sob, she shot into Patrick's arms. He pulled her onto his lap and tucked her close while she wept like a baby, eyes moist as Marcy wept along.

"Hey, squirt—we're finally related," Luke said, redness rimming his eyes and Katie's.

"I call dibs on the first sisters' pajama party at my house with all the girl cousins," Faith shouted, prompting a roar of approval from the little girls in the room.

Gabe sat up, her awestruck gaze wandering the room while Marcy handed her a handkerchief. "Wow . . . this means you're my sisters now, doesn't it?" A glint of mischief lit in her eye. "Which means . . . ," she leveled a smirk at Henry, "you have to call me Aunt Gabe."

"Noooooooo . . . ," Henry moaned, burying himself in the sea of trash.

"I think plain ol' Gabe will be just fine, darlin'," Patrick said, tilting her chin. He angled a brow. "Don't you?"

"Uh . . . yes, sir," Gabe said with a shy smile, so out of character that Marcy grinned.

Patrick shook his head and laughed. "Sweet saints, Gabriella Dawn," he bellowed, "if I'd known adoption was going to change you this much, I'd have done it years ago." His gaze shifted to Marcy, thinning into a stern tease. "And don't say one word, Marceline."

She kissed his cheek while Gabe sprang up to join the cousins on the floor. "Not even 'I love you and you're the most amazing man and father on the planet'?"

He grunted, his smile veering into a quirk. "No, darlin', *that* you can say," he whispered, brushing her lips with his own.

"Time for dessert and games?" Gabe tossed a paper wad at Henry while her "sisters" rose to pick up trash.

"After cleanup," Faith said with a chuckle, collecting discarded paper and bows.

Marcy started to rise and Faith nudged her back. "Oh no you don't—you two sit right there while the men pick up trash and we sisters oversee kids and dessert." She waved a hand toward the roomful of people. "Makes me tired just thinking about what you two started, so you need the rest."

"Amen," Patrick said with a chuckle, tucking Marcy close as the room cleared out. His sigh blew warm against her skin. "Faith's right, darlin', just look at what we started."

She wrapped her arms to his waist, moisture blurring the Christmas tree into a haze of brilliant lights. "It's hard to believe, Patrick, isn't it? It doesn't seem so very long ago that you and I were like Steven and Annie, poised to embark on the greatest adventure of our lives." Her blissful sigh matched his. "A wonderful journey from the hand of a wonderful God."

"Indeed," Patrick said with a kiss to her cheek. "I shudder to think of such a journey without him, Marceline. He's been our strength and our peace through many a trial, not to mention a world war, near death, and agonies of the heart only he could heal."

"A threefold cord is not quickly broken," she whispered, thinking of all the times she and Patrick had cleaved to God for their strength over the years. A touch of melancholy stole into her thoughts. "Patrick?"

"Yes, darlin'?"

"It's been such a wonderful year . . ." She swallowed hard, unbidden tears suddenly springing to her eyes. "I . . . almost don't want it to end."

He shifted to face her, still able to flutter her stomach with the look of love in his eyes. "Yes, a wonderful year is over, Marceline, closing another chapter in our lives, *but* . . ." He gave her a lingering kiss, and she tasted all the sweetness of the years when his mouth caressed hers. "We have a family of children who love us, a houseful of grandchildren who need us, and a God who'll never forsake us. All in all . . . ," his mouth trailed to hers, mingling with the salt of her tears, "it's not an end, darlin' . . . ," he whispered, his words warm with promise. "Only a new beginning . . ."

Acknowledgments

To my incredible reader friends—when I count my blessings as an author, YOU are right at the top! It's a privilege and joy to be both your friend and an author you read.

To Erica Hogan, Ashley Roberts, Carol Moncado, Emily Reilly, Kayla Hughes, and Eileen Jo Legat—winners of my contest to have a character named after them in this book—thank you, not only for your boundless enthusiasm and support, but your precious friendship.

To the Seekers—sisters all—when it comes to talent, humor, and support, you ladies rock!

To my agent, Natasha Kern, and my editor, Lonnie Hull Dupont—two of God's many touches in my life—thank you for your faith in me.

To the great team at Revell, thank you for your patience and support—you guys are THE BEST!! Especially Cheryl Van Andel and Dan Thornberg for another great cover and Barb Barnes and Julie Davis, both of whom possess endless patience and a true talent for spit and polish.

To my prayer partners and best friends, Karen, Pat, and Joy—what a touch from God you are in my life!

To my aunt Julie; my mother-in-law, Leona; and my sisters, Dee Dee, Mary, Pat, Rosie, Susie, Ellie, and Katie for your love and prayers; and to my sisters-in-law, Diana, Mary, and Lisa—I am blessed to call you family.

To my daughter, Amy, my son, Matt, and daughter-in-law, Katie—true examples of God doing abundantly, exceedingly more than I ever hoped, thought, or prayed. I love you guys!

To my husband and best friend, Keith—*my* Patrick O'Connor—thank you for giving me my own personal romance novel on which to base Marcy and Patrick's marriage. As Marcy says to Patrick midbook, I would be lost without you.

Julie Lessman is an award-winning author whose tagline of "Passion With a Purpose" underscores her intense passion for both God and romance. American Christian Fiction Writers 2009 Debut Author of the Year and winner of 14 RWA awards, Julie Lessman was voted #1 Romance Author of the year in Family Fiction magazine's 2012 and 2011 Readers Choice Awards, #1 Historical Fiction Author, #3 Author, #4 Novel #3 Series, and Booklist's 2010 Top 10 Inspirational Fiction. Julie resides in Missouri with her husband, daughter, son, daughter-in-law, and granddaughter. You can contact her through her website at www.julielessman.com, where you can also read excerpts from each of her books.

Stay in Touch with

Julie Lessman

Visit **www.JulieLessman.com**

to learn more about Julie, sign up for her
newsletter, and read reviews and interviews.

Connect with her on

 Julie Lessman

 julielessman

"Julie Lessman's passionate prose grabs your heart and doesn't let go!"

—Laura Frantz, author of *Love's Reckoning*

Filled with intense passion and longing, deception and revelation, the Winds of Change series will leave you wanting to read all of them.

Revell
a division of Baker Publishing Group
www.RevellBooks.com

Available Wherever Books Are Sold
Also Available in Ebook Format

"Guaranteed to satisfy the most romantic of hearts."

–Tamera Alexander, bestselling author

Full of passion, romance, rivalry, and betrayal,
the Daughters of Boston series will captivate you
from the first page.

R Revell
a division of Baker Publishing Group
www.RevellBooks.com

Available Wherever Books Are Sold
Also Available in Ebook Format

3 2953 01154897 3